"I can be very amiable, *chérie.* Only if there's a reason do I lose my temper."

"And thus far, Catherine, you've given me probable cause in all instances. You argue, you goad, you oppose. What kind of man was LeClerc that he could not tame you?"

She flinched, her eyes showing the hurt he inflicted. "Now you are who I've come to expect. Heartless and cruel."

Danton tried to apologize—a formality that didn't come easily for him. "Catherine—"

"Non. You answered me. It's only fair you have your turn." She bravely met his gaze, her shoulders squared and proud. "I have seen enough greed to last me a lifetime. I don't want to see yours."

"You are mistaken about me. I'm not a greedy man."

"Monsieur Cristobal, the colors of your flag are quite clear."

"There is more to me than a flag." Suddenly he needed to prove to himself, to Catherine, that he wasn't completely dead inside. "I can be gentle, *chérie,"* Danton murmured. "Let me show you."

Her cheeks flushed with panic. "What are you doing?"

Bringing his face closer, he whispered, "I'm going to kiss you."

Books by Stef Ann Holm

King of the Pirates
Liberty Rose
Seasons of Gold

Published by POCKET BOOKS

King of the Pirates

Stef Ann Holm

POCKET BOOKS

New York   London   Toronto   Sydney   Tokyo   Singapore

This book is a work of fiction. Names, characters, places, and
incidents either are products of the author's imagination or are used
fictitiously. Any resemblance to actual events or locales or persons,
living or dead, is entirely coincidental.

An *Original* Publication of POCKET BOOKS

POCKET BOOKS, a division of Simon & Schuster Inc.
1230 Avenue of the Americas, New York, NY 10020

ISBN: 0-671-79733-6

First Pocket Books printing January 1994

10 9 8 7 6 5 4 3 2 1

POCKET and colophon are registered trademarks of
Simon & Schuster Inc.

Cover art by Lina Levy

Printed in the U.S.A.

For my daughters:
Whitney Linnea
and
Kayla Rose

A child's imagination is a
literary treasure chest

Chapter

1

September 1719
Tamatave, Madagascar

"F-Five thousand pieces o' eight . . . my friend," the Englishman's badly decayed teeth gritted as he struggled to hold up the thick, gold-fringed edge of a fine red carpet, "and it's . . . y-yours?"

"A cursed king's ransom!" Danton Cristobal narrowed his eyes critically. His right hand slipped over the hilt of the ruby-encrusted cutlass resting low on his waist.

The scraggy rug seller abruptly let the tapestry fall to the earth, sending up a light cloud of terra-cotta dust. He cringed at Danton's exhibition and skulked backward into his vendor's booth. His behind hit a heap of plundered goods. "Th-This is a king's c-carpet, Danton. Ye may not be the King of Spain . . . b-but ye be the King of the P-Pirates."

"A nefarious title put upon me by the variety of royal navies that plague my ocean. Do I look like a cutthroat to you, Henry?" No sooner asked, Danton swiped a long river of hair over his shoulder. His brows darted to a deep frown as he put on a fierce face.

Danton deliberately took a short step out of the tarpaulin stall's shade. The hot sun poured over him and he felt the rays warm his ears and the gold cross that dangled from a hole in his lobe. White light reflected off the brace of pistols, dagger handle, and curving blade in his belt.

"N-No, Danton," Henry sputtered. His thin mustache

twitched. "Ye look like the nobleman ye are. Refined and polished and gracious. Most gracious. A truly generous—"

"You're braying like an ass, Henry. Shut up."

Henry's gaunt face blanched as he swallowed the remainder of his praises.

Danton knelt and ran his hand across the exquisite rug, embedding his fingertips into the gules silk pile. Hatred wound around his muscles and crept into his bones. The veins atop his hand became noticeably prominent.

Staring at the elaborate pattern, his gaze burned into the tapestry's center and the royal emblem of Spain's King Philip. Weft azure, sable, and vert had been used to weave the age-old coat of arms. Pure threads of silver and gold framed the figure. A deep cinnabar dye encompassed the heraldry which nearly filled out the ten-by-ten-foot space. Danton recognized the artisan's work as Persian.

Very lavish.

Vulgarly expensive.

Anger almost choked him when he thought of the man who was meant to possess the carpet before it had been sacked on the high sea. An all-consuming knot of loathing fueled his vengeance. He would foil the king the only way possible; he'd take from the sovereign as King Philip had taken from him. King Philip would not tread his feet on this carpet. It would not adorn his halls, nor his chambers, nor the base of his throne. The prize would belong to Danton Luis Cristobal, formerly the Marquis de Seville and now the King of the Pirates.

Jittery, Henry shuffled his wares on a high table at his side. His pewter cuff button tinkled against an open tin of thimbles. "F-Four thousand p-pieces o' eight, Danton? Or if ye be light o' that coin," he rushed on, clumsily spilling a stack of tobacco boxes, "ducats, francs, doubloons, or guineas. Whatever your man has in his coffer."

Danton casually glanced at his companions, Antonio and Eduardo. Loaded with weapons, both men were built like cannons and just as explosive. Antonio had a strongbox perched on his shoulder; Eduardo's brawny arms crossed over his bare, sun-glazed chest—a silent sentry to guard Danton's back. Eduardo's wolfish gaze scanned the crowded market.

Danton stood. "One hundred twenty francs—the value of the sailor's life you undoubtedly took to get this."

"It-It weren't me, Danton, who killed him. Trevor Tate run him through before he s-sunk the Spanish galleon. We drew lots on who was to get the carpet. It belongs to me fair."

"Wrong, Henry. It belongs to me."

Danton nodded to Antonio, who lifted the hinges of the strongbox and counted out the correct coinage. Henry's sad eyes stared at the scant silver. Without a word, he opened his fist and accepted the highly discounted price.

Danton gave his men orders in Spanish to roll the carpet and follow him.

The tight press of the *Zoma*'s canopies barely gave Danton room to go around the open-air stands. Haggling voices peppered the sultry, late afternoon air. For all the sparks in their tones, the disputes were conducted in a fluid blend of Malagasy and French, which Danton found pleasing to the ear.

Both African and Indonesian, the people of Madagascar lived by some customs Danton thought morbid; others made perfect sense. They'd named their marketplace *Zoma*, the Malagasy word for Friday, simply because Friday had been the busiest market day.

As Danton walked, slivers of sunlight sliced through canvas cracks. The intensity of the heat shafts ripened fruits, filling the air with a sweet-rotten fragrance of mangoes, litchi, and strawberries.

Pausing, he selected a green apple from a local woman clad in rainbow colors and draped in a flowing white *lamba*. Her dark brown face was creased like an old parchment by a thousand fine wrinkles. She gave him a smile, more gum than tooth, as he motioned for Antonio to pay her—quite well.

Taking a bite out of the apple, he continued on, savoring the flavor of the fleshy meat. His black silk shirt absorbed the heat and seemed to sear his back. Its collarless neck marked his throat in a plunging vee of string lacings which he'd left loose and untied.

He informally appraised the profusion of goods around him. Most of the stalls belonged to the Malagasy tribes, but many had been infiltrated by pirate brokers. Brigand sea wolves had blown onto Madagascar's coastlines and turned the island into a hotbed of stolen commodities. The worst of the lot, bloodthirsty buccaneers, made Tamatave home and had installed booths of their own where pilfered goods exchanged hands.

Danton surveyed the wares. Beeswax and fat combs dripping of honey attracted insects. Zebu-horn spoons and magic amulets caught his attention, but he was not swayed by their promise of luck. He had no use for pots of indigo and resins, columbus root and dragon's blood. Green bozaka grass bowls contained ginger root, peppercorns, and manioc root. The gnarled limbs of black charcoal were priced far too high.

Seeing nothing else of value, Danton left the crowd behind and headed for the quay and his three-masted square rigger, *La Furia*. He finished his apple and threw the core into the ruins of a fallen mud house, then paused to examine the half-dozen sloops, man-of-wars, snow rigs, and frigates floating in the ocean.

A Dutch flute slowly drifted into the harbor. Danton was reminded of a crippled white moth. Her sagging sails were her wings, fighting to hold onto the wind with topsail and jib. Danton had seen the ship earlier this morning, about an hour off Île Ste. Marie's Sorcerers Point. The round-sterned and broad-bottomed *De Gids* had ridden the sea in an unbalanced manner, as if she were taking in water on her port side.

The flute received a hearty welcome from a band of pirates on the narrow wharf. They easily captured the berthing ropes, twisting them into bowlines to drop onto the pier's bollards. Danton knew the men to be merciless, and the assistance they offered bore the marks of great deception. Their scarlet, scarf-covered heads lowered in anticipation as they secured the gangplank; their broadsword blades icily winked. As the plank came into place, they clambered aboard and stormed their prey like an army of red ants.

The quarterdecks and upper decks were quickly overrun, the crew taken by surprise. Startled, the Dutch looked on helplessly as the pirates lifted their swords and pistols against them. They fought back in vain. Unaccustomed to such ruthless combat, their blood spilled.

The ruffians slipped into the ship's bowels and returned with coopered barrels. They hurled the casks over the sides. A few landed in the water, bobbing before sinking; others crashed onto the wooden deck. Staves shattered and split apart, scattering clouds of white flour and gritty salt. Kegs labeled Beer, Wine, and Rum were handled with more care, heaved in a line of efficiency to a waiting man and ox cart on the dock.

Danton felt no mercy for *De Gids* as a worn portmanteau hit the beach and burst open. Life on the sea was rough, and those who couldn't weather the storm didn't belong. The craft was obviously ill-tended from the looks of her many coats of tar and resin doctoring the hull together. The devil take her if her captain didn't give a damn.

Leaving the carnage behind, Danton headed for the second anchorage, where *La Furia* was docked. He blotted out the sounds of curdling wails. He thought of the return trip home, beyond Johanna Island and Mehila to the surrounding Comoros Islands. Perhaps during the journey he would meet up with his enemy, Sadi, and finally be able to kill the Turk.

An agonizing plea pierced through Danton's head and he clenched his teeth against the pitiful sound. *Madre de Dios!* He could never get used to death cries.

Then a chilling scream of utter despair cut through the tropical sky, seemingly tearing open the cottony clouds above Danton. No longer able to remain impassive, his head shot up and he drank in every detail of the flute from bow to stern. On the half deck the last survivor, the captain, fell.

"Jesu," he said softly under his breath, thinking the tone had been so feminine that . . . Damn the man for being such a woman in the end.

Then the terrorized scream came again and Danton knew the sound hadn't come from the dying captain.

A young woman appeared at the top of the landing board, her wealth of golden-blond hair tumbling to her waist. She was not alone. She protectively cradled a little girl next to her bosom. Why had she been on a ship not meant for passengers? By appearances, she could have been the captain's mistress, although the presence of a child baffled him.

Her escape was blocked by the pirate in charge of the belly wash. His leering face didn't make her reconsider and turn back.

Defiantly she refused to be intimidated. She took the ramp, half sliding, half running down the steep grade with bent knees. Once at its base, the thief jumped in front of her. His hand snaked out and grabbed hold of her arm just as a large, iron-banded trunk soared over the prow. On impact, the chest ruptured with a thunderous bang. Silver and gold pieces showered and pattered over the wharf like metal rain.

"Lor'!" he roared, eyes wide with greed. He abruptly let her go and scrambled for the money.

The woman darted across the pier. She scanned the beach for what he assumed would be a safe direction.

Danton swore he wouldn't get involved. He'd already failed the one woman and child that had mattered to him. He suffered the intense guilt of that failure each day of his life.

So he told himself to keep walking, to forget he ever saw her in her brown linen dress which seemed to have been ravaged by the jungle and whose fabric had been often mended with odd-shaped patches.

He wasn't a savior.

Cursing, he strode toward his ship. The heels of his thigh-high boots hit the sand in hard falls. Dammit, he lived his life by the Malagasy saying: "Be like a chameleon. Keep one eye on the past and one eye on the future." That didn't leave a lot of room for his present—let alone anyone else's.

The woman would only mean trouble. Even if he did go after her and the girl, he couldn't get them out of Tamatave without being seen by the dogs raiding the *De Gids*.

And he was in no mood to start a bloody battle over a woman whose flowing hair caught the sun like a new doubloon.

Then he heard the child's sobbing voice: *"Maman, I want you!"*

Danton turned around.

Tiny arms clung to her mother's neck; she dangled a doll

from one of her fists. The woman pressed a quick kiss on the girl's flushed cheek before taking off toward the market.

The little girl's call penetrated the hard walls of his heart and he heard a voice from his past.

Papá, I want you!

Danton squeezed his eyes closed and saw in reflection his three-year-old son visiting him in a darkened chamber, a slum of a prison, and himself behind bars. The boy had to be forcefully taken by his wife, Elena, when the guards told her she must leave.

Papá, I want you! Esteban had wept.

Danton forced the memories out of his head, willing himself not to hear his son's mournful cry. He didn't want to relive his private hell.

When he opened his eyes, the woman and child were gone, enveloped by the white-squared roofs of the marketplace.

There's no place to hide, Catherine thought. Winded, she had to rest, had to pause before she collapsed under the paltry shade the canopies offered.

A host of curious people stared at her disheveled appearance. She'd thought to blend into the throng of vendors, but had made a horrible mistake.

Heads turned upon her intrusion. The natives' large, luminous eyes warily observed her. Brown-skinned and fine-boned faces watched, waiting for her to move on. The raffish white men, sabers glinting at their sashed waists, gaped with unbridled desire.

Her lungs hurt from exhaustion. Blood raced through her body, pounding loudly in her ears. Her arms were on fire from waning strength, and keeping a grip on her daughter turned into a complete labor. Madeleine cried and wriggled to stay held. Catherine hoisted her daughter's thighs over her skirt gathers, trying to subdue Madeleine's frets with a soothing tone.

"Be still, *mon chou.*"

The overpowering smells of the market choked Catherine. The reek of spoiling fish, bananas, tomatoes, and other fruits she couldn't name, clogged the cramped aisles.

Catherine took a blind step backward. The sole of her shoe hit a knobby stick.

A goat bleated in anguish, startling her. The animal rested by her ankle, its devilish yellow eyes bulged in annoyance. The surprise of seeing the goat so near made Catherine stumble into a high table. She braced her hand against the top so she wouldn't fall with Madeleine. Her fingers landed on wiry ropes. Looking down, her palm was covering lengths of braided, human hair.

"Oh, mon Dieu," she whispered, yanking her hand back as if she'd been burned.

"Don't ye like me trinkets?" the pirate behind the counter asked in English, then laughed. Bulky and filthy, he wore a full, curling black beard and a satin tricorne. His mauve damask coat hung over his shoulders in wrinkles, with wine stains on the lapels.

Stunned, she could only stare.

"A good luck charm for ye, wench?" He opened a wooden box covered with colorful seashells. On a bed of shabby velvet were twenty or so small and pointed white objects that resembled monkey teeth. He shook them at her with a lopsided grin.

She shivered.

She had to get out of here.

"What is it, *Maman?"* Madeleine asked, her face buried in Catherine's collar.

"Nothing to be scared of, *mon chou."* She gently put her fingers on Madeleine's neck so she wouldn't look up. "Just some silly teeth."

Fighting to keep her wits, Catherine slowly moved away. Leaving the awful man behind, the noises of the market-place closed in: chickens squawked, geese hissed, and a fatty-humped cow grunted. Funny little black-faced and ring-tailed monkeys chattered at her from cages.

She kept her gaze fastened to the ground as she eased through the aisle. Vanilla pods and cloves scented the stuffy area so pungently, her eyes watered.

Woven canisters of rice obstructed her flight, and she had to lift the hem of her dress to go over them. From the corner of her eye she caught the gleam of precious jewelry: emerald rings, strands of oyster pearls tangled in masses, sapphire waistcoat studs, ruby broaches, turquoise earrings, and gold crucifixes. Fortunes spread out inconsequentially, as if they were nothing more than pastes.

Everything had to be stolen. Stolen by the same type of murderers who'd taken *De Gids*. Violent and heartless. The agonizing pleas for mercy she'd heard from her steerage room had fallen on deaf ears. Just as hers would on these filthy men displaying their riches. She and Madeleine were no more safe here than they were at the ship.

But where to hide?

A woman with a basket of twisted bread on her head blocked Catherine's escape. She squared her shoulders and silently confronted the Malagasy, who, without conflict, moved aside.

Relief flooded her as she left the marketplace. Once in the bright sunlight, Catherine sped eastward toward a string of overlapping rectangle houses in pink, light brown, and pale blue.

Bounced in her mother's arms, Madeleine started to giggle. Catherine counted herself blessed that her daughter had momentarily forgotten her tears.

Pausing for several fatigued breaths, Catherine peered over her shoulder to see if they were being followed. The sun's dazzling rays nearly blinded her; their intensity reflected off the hundreds of opaque canopies. She couldn't be sure, but she thought she saw the outline of a man. Very tall, and bearing down on them. Something twinkled at his hip. A sword? A pistol?

She faced forward, not wasting precious seconds to identify the object.

The thrum of her heartbeat raced with her legs as she came to a series of red soil stairs fit between the pastel dwellings. She dashed up the steps, keeping to the middles, where years of feet and weather had indented them. The narrow alleyway of abodes spoke of poverty. Faded curtains hung out of the glassless windows in tattered tails. Urns, cracked pottery, and rain barrels were crammed on stoops.

A building with a high-peaked thatch roof emerged at Catherine's left. She rounded its walls and flattened her back against the deteriorating plaster.

"What are you doing, *Maman?*" Madeleine loudly asked.

"Shhh," Catherine cautioned in a whisper broken by her shortness of breath. She put a finger to her mouth. "We are playing a game. We have to be very, very quiet. You can't say anything. *Tais toi.*"

Madeleine nodded, her blue eyes serious.

Clutching the child close, Catherine's soaring pulse ticked off the seconds. She listened for footfalls until her head ached from the strain.

In the distance, a drum beat. A fruit fly annoyingly hovered overhead. Hot and humid air clung to her face, damping her lower lashes. Despite the lightweight fabric of her muslin dress, her shift and single petticoat molded to her skin like a damp dishcloth. Misty beads of perspiration formed on her upper lip. She closed her eyes and licked her lips, tasting the salt on her skin.

Just as she felt a flicker of relief, strong fingers cupped her mouth. Her eyes flew open in shock. She had no chance to scream. A sturdy leg flattened the slightness of her skirt; a knee slid up her thigh to rest intimately between her legs.

Pinned to the wall, Catherine tried to see who'd captured her. All she could make out was a black ruffled shirtsleeve. She shuddered at the thought of his horrible face, envisioning a rotten-mouthed and lice-infested madman bent on killing her . . . raping her.

Madeleine screamed and screamed.

Oh, please, not in front of my baby!

Catherine fought to break free while keeping a steady grip on her daughter. She viciously kicked, trying to hit her captor's shin, his leg, but only landed an ineffectual blow to the air. Where was the rest of him? Around the corner?

The man yelled something at her in a language Catherine didn't understand. She thrashed and continued her assault through Madeleine's outburst. Desperate, she bit him.

"Mierda!" he bellowed as she sharply nipped the flesh of his finger. His hand moved away and a pair of angry silver eyes filled her vision. The ebony rings around his irises enhanced the metallic color, making his gaze both terrifying and beautiful.

The man was nothing like she'd imagined. His jaw thrust forward, shadowed by stubble. His skin looked smooth, bronzed by wind and sun. The bridge of his aquiline nose was a little crooked, leaving the impression it may have been broken once.

He didn't look dirty.

No vermin nested in his hair. Dark as midnight, the untied strands framed his face and fell past the breadth of his shoulders.

"Mierda." Clean white teeth flashed as he cursed again. He spoke in a deep and thunderous tone, rattling off words in that strange tongue whose origin she couldn't place.

He may have been less loathsome than she'd imagined, but that didn't change the fact he held her against her will. Unsettled, she demanded in French, "Let us go! Let us go! I don't understand what you are saying!"

"Understand this, *mon maki sauvage,"* he returned in her own language. *"Merde!* Shut the child up if you want to get off Madagascar alive."

Catherine's mouth dropped open. He spoke French! And quite foully.

"Quiet the child," he repeated, his head dipping dangerously near hers. She smelled the ocean on him. And his breath smelled like . . . apples. Not sour, as she'd assumed. "I grow impatient. *Maudit!"*

"Stop swearing at me!" she shouted above Madeleine's screech.

"Then do as I ask!" A silken thread of warning polished his order.

Abruptly, she mollified her daughter. "Madeleine, hush . . . it's all right."

Madeleine's lower lip quivered as she curtailed her hollering. She blinked away her tears, a few stragglers splashing off her lashes.

Why she'd done as he'd asked, Catherine couldn't be sure. Perhaps because he didn't look as lethal to her as she'd expected. He had an air of nobility about him. Despite the gold cross hanging from his ear, and his untamed mane of hair, he could have graced the finest salons of the aristocracy.

His handsome eyes probed hers. "Don't fight me and I won't hurt you."

Unable to speak, she nodded. He slowly brought down his knee in a manner that made her tremble. The sensual way in which he dragged the strength of his thigh down her own left her feeling the heat of a blush stain her cheeks.

No longer able to support her daughter's weight, a tingling numbness in Catherine's arms forced her to set Madeleine on her feet. Though he said he wouldn't harm her, she tightly grasped Madeleine's tiny hand in case he changed his mind. She asked with deceptive calm, "Who are you?"

He stood away from her, and she swept her gaze over the length of him. A dark figure of a man. Tall and proud. Sinewy in places her husband, Georges Claude, had never been.

His fawn breeches indecently molded his narrow hips and lean legs; his elegantly tooled leather boots rode above his knees. The tropical breeze caught his jet shirt and blew the shimmering material about his forearms. Feet apart, arms akimbo, he answered, "I am Danton Luis Cristobal."

Catherine asked the question foremost on her mind. "Why have you followed us?"

His smile lacked humor. "Don't make me reconsider by asking for an answer."

"How did you find us?"

"I spotted you in the *Zoma*. The rest was easy since I know the streets of Tamatave."

She found his confidence disturbing. When she tried to speak, her voice wavered. "What are you going to do now?"

"You ask a lot of questions." Danton frowned, the line of his black brows grim, as if the answer he would give her displeased him. "Take you out of Madagascar."

"Out of Madagascar?" she echoed faintly.

Danton's expression grew hard. "Or would you rather stay with the dogs who attacked your ship?"

"Non!"

"Then you'll come with me. To my ship."

"And take us where?" she asked as fearful images began to build in her mind.

"Where you have no choice but to go, *mon maki sauvage.*"

His second reference to her being his wild lemur confused Catherine. Whatever a lemur was, she didn't want to be a wild one for him or anyone else.

Madeleine's short forefinger reached up and grazed

Danton's dagger handle. "Do you kill big girls, Monsieur Pirate, and eat them?"

Danton seemed more perturbed by her inquisition than perplexed. Visibly unnerved, he retreated a step so she couldn't touch him. "I do not." Then glowering at Catherine, he snapped, "Why would she say such a thing?"

"The men on *De Gids* told her."

"Captain Dekker," Madeleine supplied, wiping her nose with the sleeve of her dress, "said pirates are can'bals."

"Cannonballs?" Danton repeated gruffly.

"Cannibals," Catherine clarified, hoping Danton's offense would be minimum.

"Maudit! I never claimed to be a pirate."

"But you are, aren't you?"

He didn't answer. Appearing indignant, his footsteps kicked up dust as he stomped to the house's corner. "Eduardo! Antonio! *Vienan ustedes aquí!*"

Two men appeared, and Catherine's apprehensions rose. Sleek and brawny, they were the most lethal barbarians she'd ever seen. Between them, they effortlessly held a rolled tapestry on their shoulders.

Danton spoke to the men, and they set the carpet down and unrolled its great length halfway. He brought his gaze to Catherine's. "You and the child get in."

Her misgivings increased twofold when she realized how he meant to take them away. *"Non!* We won't. We'll suffocate."

In one stride he came nose to nose with her. An urgency claimed his silvery eyes, making a cold knot form in her stomach. "You can't stay here. If they find you, they'll use you in ways you could never imagine. And when they're through, you'll be taken up the lagoons to Tananarive and sold into slavery. But not before you're raped by the slave master. In the end, you'll wish you were dead."

She lowered her head, not wanting to hear anymore.

He caught her chin with his callused fingers and brought her head up. She wasn't prepared for his touch, a gesture that came from nowhere and caused her to quake. He demanded her attention, and gaining it, wondered in a low tone, "And what will happen to your daughter then? She's pretty. Young, but—"

"Stop!" She was mortified. "Don't say it! Don't even think such a thing!"

"Then don't let them take you," he ground out through clenched teeth.

Despair consumed her. "How do I know you aren't going to do—to do the same thing to me?"

"You don't," he countered coldly. "Now get in. You won't suffocate. Stay close to one end. Put your daughter in front of you. High. Her face next to yours. I won't have them roll the carpet tight."

"Maman, I don't want to." Tears threatened Madeleine's eyes anew.

Catherine grappled with more uncertainty in this single instant than she had her entire life. Danton Cristobal had set out to scare her, and heartily succeeded. She didn't think—didn't want to believe—he would abuse them. But could she trust him? She doubted he was a scrupulous man, but how desperately she needed the safety he offered!

The decision was hers to make. She'd wanted to make them after Georges Claude's death, hadn't she? He'd always made the decisions and had given her no power to challenge him. Now she was in control of her life, to do with it as she pleased.

But so far she'd failed miserably. She should have waited for the English merchant bark, as her Indian guide, Hadi, had advised before she left India. Her impatience had thrown her daughter into danger.

Madeleine. Madeleine was all that mattered.

Catherine knew she had no choice but to accept Danton's aid.

"Come, *cher enfant."* She hid her foreboding well. "We will play another game." Leading Madeleine to the carpet, she tried to smile. "Remember the time *Papa* and I gave you a ride in the picnic cloth? You laid in the middle and we each held an end and swung you."

"Oui, Maman. I remember."

"And you laughed as we carried you. Remember?"

Madeleine nodded while Catherine stiffly laid down and stretched out her arms.

"Come, then. Bring Nanette."

Madeleine studied her doll and its uneven tufts of black hair.

"We will pretend that we are being swung by big"—Catherine glanced at Eduardo and Antonio—"elephants. They have us by their trunks, and we will have great fun. Come to *Maman,* Madeleine. *Viens."*

Pouting, the child acquiesced and fell into her mother's arms. She pressed her cheek to Catherine's and squeezed her eyes closed.

Danton approached them and dropped to one knee. In quiet French he asked, "What is your name?"

"Catherine LeClerc." She swallowed the reservations that gathered in her throat. "And Madeleine."

"Don't make a sound, Catherine LeClerc, and you won't get hurt."

Then her world spun and she and Madeleine were plunged into a tunnel of darkness.

Chapter

2

"Who are you, Danton Luis Cristobal?" Catherine took in the crystal chandelier suspended from the rafters of a great cabin. "This is not an ordinary captain's quarters, monsieur." She quickly scanned the gilt mirrors, long lyrebacked divan, and upholstered red satin chairs, waiting for his reply.

"And what do 'ordinary captain's quarters' look like?" Danton stood in the doorway, his ample shoulders filling the narrow frame. He crossed one knee in front of the other and leaned into the jamb.

Catherine tucked Madeleine under her arm, drawing the child close on the rescue carpet they shared. But her daughter didn't need to be comforted. She stared, mouth sagging open, at the lavish furniture. Catherine supposed she should allow Madeleine this breach of manners, knowing her daughter had never seen such surroundings.

Her little girl had been courageous during their frightening journey. Antonio and Eduardo were amazingly gentle as they'd shouldered them onto the ship. Catherine had been able to mark their progress out of the marketplace. The distant calls of bartering, the salt-laden smell of the ocean; then the creak of a wharf, the snap of sails, and finally, orders shouted by Danton. They'd been carried down a flight of steps, their escape ending in this enormous room. A shockingly elegant sight, spacious enough to accommodate the rug's full size.

"I've only been privy to one captain's cabin, Monsieur Cristobal," Catherine explained at length. Then asked, "Or am I to call you *capitaine?*"

"Cristobal is fine."

"Very well, Monsieur Cristobal." She opted to use his surname because he wasn't a captain in the respectable sense. "The other cabin was sedate and dingy compared to yours."

"Then," Danton said as he pushed away from the door, "you haven't played in the seas long enough to see its finer side."

"Who lives here, *Maman?*" Madeleine's eyes shone as she scrambled to her feet. "A king and queen?" She bounded for the bed, whose size was well over that of the cramped cabin Catherine and Madeleine had shared on *De Gids*.

Catherine started to stand. Danton came to her side and extended his hand to assist her. She noticed, for the first time, the tiny white scars on both the palm and the top of his hand. A thick silence fell between them as she studied the markings, wondering how he'd come to have such wounds. His deep tan seemed to heighten the paleness of the jagged cuts.

Danton lowered his arm, stalking away without a backward glance. Catherine berated herself for offending him by her delay. She hadn't meant to stare. And she hadn't been horrified by the blemishes either; oddly, she'd found herself wanting to say something reassuring to him.

Rising on her own, Catherine turned and found Danton leaning over a desk. Cut in the wall behind him was a round window. A brilliant sunset spilled through the opening, making an arc above his head. His hair seemed to be threaded with bronze highlights. Again she was struck by the feral beauty of the man.

Ignoring her, Danton centered his energies on a map. He picked up a pointed instrument and maneuvered the utensil to make a perfect curve. She had the feeling he didn't really need to be plotting his chart. She sensed he was a man who demanded perfection; meticulous and precise. One such as

17

he would have already done this and not left anything to chance.

"Maman," Madeleine called, breaking into Catherine's thoughts. "Come feel how soft the mattress is. The blankets even smell good."

Turning her attention to her daughter, Catherine covered her cheeks in abashed horror. Madeleine was sprawled on Danton's herringbone-patterned coverlet. "Madeleine!" She crossed the cabin floor. "Get off of Monsieur Cristobal's bed right now."

Madeleine's bottom bounced across the downy tester. She landed at the pedestal bed's edge and dangled her legs over the high side. Dimples accented her smile as she patted a pillow at the headboard.

"Madeleine," Catherine warned tightly.

To Catherine, the bed seemed to be turned around. When occupied, feet rested where logically a person's head should have been. The footboard met with the five stern panels of glass at the cabin's end.

The reason why Danton had organized this particular piece of furniture in such a strange manner piqued her curiosity.

Quietly she looked up.

Danton's steady gaze bore into hers, stripping her emotions raw. She felt vulnerable and weak, having left nearly all of her courage in Madagascar. His eyes told her everything; she was not wanted here, her questions would not be answered.

She broke free of his pinning stare.

"Are you a king, Monsieur Pirate?" Madeleine jumped down and gathered Nanette lovingly in her arms. She brought the doll to her cheek and began to suck her thumb.

Catherine vowed she would not let Danton intimidate her as she awaited his reply to Madeleine's question.

"A purse of gold buys any man a crown." His mouth curved into a smile. Distant humor softened his rugged face. Catherine caught herself boldly staring as he reflected on something, but he kept the thoughts to himself. Then suddenly he snapped out of his recollections, his hard expression returning. "You can sleep here while we're sailing." Rolling up his chart, he tucked the cylinder under his arm. He started for the exit, then stopped. "I'll have some food brought to you. There's water in the pitcher."

Catherine bent and picked up Madeleine. "Thank you, that's kind, but I really must know where we're—"

"What I say is the law on this ship," he said, blotting out her inquiry. "Remember that and we'll all get along until I figure out what to do with you."

The biting remark left Catherine speechless as she watched him quit the cabin.

"He's a mean pirate, *Maman*," Madeleine said, talking around her thumb.

Catherine's eyes remained on the firmly closed door as tension lingered in the air. "I don't think there are nice pirates, *mon chou.*"

"He didn't say if he was a king."

Catherine met Madeleine's crystal-blue eyes. *"Non.* He didn't." She couldn't help kissing the top of the girl's nose.

A short time later, Catherine lay on the covers of the bed with Madeleine in the crook of her arm. As her daughter had declared, the bedclothes smelled good. Like vanilla and wind; sweet and clean.

"Do you think *Papa* is winking at us, *Maman?*" Madeleine's tiny whisper sounded fragile.

Through the tall, rectangular windows, Catherine gazed at the sprinkling of stars awakening to night. Just shy of four years old, her daughter's imagination and perception amazed her.

"Oui. I think your *papa* is out there." She breathed in the unique scent of her child. "That one there." She pointed through the cabin's unlit interior to a bright star. "That one is your *papa.* See how he shines? He would have been very proud of you today, Madeleine."

"And you too." Madeleine grew quiet a moment, then asked, "Are there cobras in Paris, France, *Maman?*"

"Non," Catherine answered softly.

She hated that Madeleine had to know about cobras. Madeleine had begun to accept her father's death surprisingly well. She had cried and asked for her *papa* for several days after his burial, but as the Indian sunsets passed, her calls had lessened. She'd started to grasp, but perhaps not understand, that her father wouldn't be with her anymore.

"I like this bed, *Maman*. We can look out at the ocean."

"I like it too." Catherine sighed. "Are you sleepy yet?"

Madeleine shook her head. She popped her thumb from her mouth, her brows rising to serious curves as she turned to her mother. "We have to ask Monsieur Pirate what that fruit was."

Catherine smiled while stroking Madeleine's silky hair. They'd been brought bowls of spicy rice, cool water, and a type of orange fruit. The cut pieces of fleshy meat had been full of juice and quite delicious.

"Do you have to use the convenience, Madeleine?"

"Oui, Maman."

After exploring all the likely places, they finally found the necessary pot in a rosewood cabinet. Catherine lifted a deceptively pretty lid.

Madeleine clapped. "He *is* a king, *Maman!* He has a throne for his pot!"

Catherine couldn't help laughing at her daughter's observation. "Hurry along, it's time for you to get some sleep."

Once again the two huddled in the bed to watch the sky. They softly talked of the day's events, said a prayer for Captain Dekker and the others from *De Gids,* and soon after, Madeleine's eyes closed.

Catherine didn't move, wanting to make sure her daughter slept peacefully before she got up. Her thoughts drifted. As much as she'd wanted to leave India and adventure behind, she would miss Hadi. He had been Georges Claude's guide, a friend and playmate for Madeleine. There had been many times when Hadi had quietly looked the other way on her husband's illicit business dealings. Recalling the incidents made Catherine's face hot with shame.

During this last winter, she'd fallen out of love with her husband. Four years in India and, prior to that, two years in the hardwood forests of Africa's Ivory Coast, had drained the strength she needed to keep their vows alive. They'd coexisted as strangers. When the monsoons came, she'd let Georges Claude slip away and they'd lived together in name only. He hadn't fought for her love. He'd freed her— emotionally and physically.

But for Madeleine's sake, Catherine had held onto the

illusion of happiness. Until seven weeks ago, when she hadn't had to pretend anymore. Georges Claude LeClerc had been killed by the venomous bite of a cobra.

Now, at age twenty-four, she didn't have a man dictating to her. Control was something she could use, not have used against her. Despite the bitter years, the one good thing had been Madeleine. Because of her daughter, she'd not change what she'd done with her life thus far.

After a quarter of an hour Catherine's arm began to fall asleep and she slid it from under Madeleine's neck. Inching to her feet, she slipped her shoes on and tread quietly to the portal. She hesitated, then turned the knob and entered the passage.

Dimness greeted her in the tight corridor. Lit only by a single candle lantern, the hazy light rocked with the ship's motion. Feeling her way along, Catherine's toe touched the steps and she gripped a railing as she climbed.

A deep coat of midnight-blue washed over the smoothly sanded deck. In contrast to *De Gids,* Danton's square rigger was immaculate. The decks were cleared of a roundhouse and waist-high bulwarks could be removed for cannon barrels. Ropes were piled in neat efficiency; no kegs or water casks cluttered the upper deck.

Despite the late hour, men kept watch on the fo'c'sle, covered the quarter deck, stood on the half deck and roved the main deck.

Though they saw her, they did not approach. She almost wished they would so she could ask them where she could find Monsieur Cristobal, instead of her having to search for him herself.

"Bonsoir, woman." A masculine voice came from behind Catherine. The words had been spoken in fluid French, but the accent was not from France.

Catherine spun around. Tall and brown, a man stood not three feet from her. Cut-off trousers fringed his well-molded calves and a sleeveless white tunic draped his chest.

"You are *la femme brave* the *capitaine* told us about." A woven hat kept his face in shadow. "I am Rainiaro, the quartermaster for *La Furia."* He moved the straw brim back on his brown curls. Catherine recognized his features as

21

those of the Malagasy. The moonlight caught and reflected off an object at his hat's braided band strap—a carved alligator whose eyes were diamonds.

"C-Catherine LeClerc." Her reply faltered, having never seen the likes of such a man in her life. In India the natives' dark faces had been beautiful and kind, but famine and poor crops had made the men thin and supple. Rainiaro was something all together different. His limbs were hard with muscle.

"Do not be afraid of me, woman. I am no one to be feared. The *capitaine* is the one who is the King of the Pirates who works his power like a god. I am just a *mpanandro*—an astrologer, who reads the celestial bodies for life's meanings and accepts what is thrown my way."

"You speak French," was all she could manage, her wits deserting her as she thought of Danton Cristobal and his imposing throne of high piracy.

He tipped his head back and roared with laughter. His white smile was brilliant against his coffee-colored skin. "I speak French, Spanish, the language of Madagascar, a bit of Arabic, and a little Turkish. Though not anything too useful—I only know how to curse and insult a man about his figs."

"Figs?"

"They're a nasty fruit, woman." A grimace shook him. "Full of tiny seeds."

She regarded him with a sidelong glance.

"Where is your *enfant?*" Rainiaro rifled through his baggy shirt pocket. He took out a rolled banana leaf and brought it to his lips.

"She's asleep."

Spreading his bare feet to steady himself, he rapidly struck two pieces of flint together until they sparked and burned the tip of his green cheroot. "It's good for her to rest," he exhaled. An acrid odor scented the balmy air. "The *capitaine* travels long."

"Are we going far?" The thought of leaving the well-traveled shipping lanes distressed her.

"Outside the Comoros Islands—upwind from Madagascar." Shrugging, Rainiaro jammed his fingers into his waistband. "The *capitaine* never sails a straight course."

"Where is Monsieur Cristobal?"

"Up there." Rainiaro gestured to the main shroud.

She craned her neck. Below the main topsail midway on the riggings, Danton balanced with an easy grace on the ratlines, unaware that she and Rainiaro stood below him. He'd discarded his billowing black shirt and high boots. Stripped to near nakedness, his sleek torso was painted in night hues. Seeing him thus, the mentally rehearsed speech she'd planned to recite to him was forgotten.

Danton's sturdy legs steadied him enough to leave his hands free. He dangled effortlessly, suspended like a spider in a web as he scanned the heavenly horizon with a spyglass.

Catherine could feel the masculine strength that made him so self-confident. Where Georges Claude's confidence came from his vast knowledge of art history, Danton's came from his physical build. Defined by lean planes and taut swells, he necessitated respect. She was sure he could—and did—crush his opponents with his fist.

She'd never encountered so many men who were hardened with muscles since meeting him and his crew. The vigor of pirating apparently put tone in the places reputable men wore flab.

One look at Danton Cristobal and she could see that to anger him would be foolish.

But to accept her fate would mean surrender. And she'd already conceded what seemed like a lifetime.

Catherine shifted her attention back to Rainiaro. "Is there a threat of the pi . . ." She trailed her thought, unsure how Rainiaro would react to her reference, for surely the entire company of *La Furia* were pirates. She licked her lips and started again. "A threat of the heathens from Tamatave following us?"

"Not likely. Antonio and Eduardo hid you well, woman." Rainiaro took a pull of his banana leaf, letting the smoke curl out his nostrils. "No. The *capitaine* is searching for a man to kill."

Catherine's heartbeat tripped.

"The *capitaine* usually chooses less final punishments for his enemies—insects to feast on their wounds, sewing up their lips with a sail needle, or perhaps keelhauling." From his smile, she wasn't sure if he was serious. "But the

23

Turk —the Turk he's been after for several years. I know he will kill this one."

Catherine felt dizzy; her stomach pitched with the sway of the ship.

"You've been strong, woman—*la femme brave.*" Rainiaro braced her elbow. "Don't lose your faith now. The *capitaine* will not harm you and the girl."

"I should go." Waves seemed to be crashing in her head, and suddenly she didn't want to talk to Danton Cristobal. "I need to be with Madeleine in case she wakes up."

"You there! On the upper deck!" Danton's shout swooped down on her, raising the fine hairs on the nape of her neck. "Catherine LeClerc, I did not give you permission to come above."

She caught herself trembling, just as she had the first time he'd touched her. But unlike before, he didn't have her in his iron grasp. She found quick thinking came easier when there was distance between them. She erased the horrid tale Rainiaro had told her, wondering if he'd been sent to scare her into obedience.

Steadying her ragged breathing, she recovered enough to face Danton.

She stood her ground. "Nor did you tell me to stay below, monsieur."

Rainiaro chuckled. "I can see you will be safe without me, woman. I'll see you tomorrow."

Catherine's gaze remained on Danton, sensing his impatience with her. She did not hear the quartermaster leave.

Meshing her fingers together, Catherine rocked back on her low heels. She lifted her chin a notch, but said nothing further.

Neither did Danton, or if he did, his voice was lost in the snap of sails.

She clenched her hands until her nails entered her skin. She could swear he assessed her with cold, hooded eyes. She felt his attack through every pore, until her heart tremored so wildly she could stand the terrible tension no longer.

Deciding to approach him with caution, she asked loudly so he could hear her, "What are you doing up there?"

Her question made him incline his head and say with indifference, "There are ghosts in my sea."

She scanned the measureless dark space. "I can't see any."

"You aren't peering through my glass." The breeze whipped his long hair, tumbling the lengths over his brow. "Come up and I'll show you what my demons look like."

"You mock me, Monsieur Cristobal." The same wind caught her skirts and flattened them to her legs. "You know I'd never climb up those ropes."

"No. I suppose not." Bringing his spyglass to his eye, he stared at the ocean, slighting her for the second time that evening.

Catherine did not like to be put off. "Where exactly are we going?"

"What were you doing on *De Gids?*" he shot back, his gaze fastened on the unfathomable skyline.

His blunt question landed heavily on her shoulders. She'd had enough trouble admitting her hasty mistake to herself. Confessing her irresponsibility to Danton would be humiliating. "I don't think the reason I would give you would have any bearing on our situation."

"I need to know what kind of woman you are."

She watched his mouth move, uncertain she'd heard him correctly through the noise of crackling canvas. "What kind?"

Danton brought his search to the west. "Were you his mistress?"

"His mistress?" Her composure wavered along with the sails.

"The captain who said I was a cannibal." He lowered his glass to the tight outline of his thigh and stared at her, waiting for her reply.

"Captain Dekker's mistress." The statement wasn't a fact, but an utterance of shock. She rallied quickly. "I think not, Monsieur Cristobal. I was widowed nearly two months ago."

"In a day you could become someone's mistress. In an hour, in a weak minute. Under an expert touch," he said with all the silkiness of a fine bolt of cloth, "you could succumb in an instant."

"But I did not!" Frustration tore at her. "I fail to see how this is relevant to my asking you where we are going." She put her hands on her hips, addressing him as if he were a child in sore need of a scolding. "Climb down from there so we can discuss this matter without yelling."

Catherine's request fell on deaf ears as Danton shifted his precarious position. If she weren't able to see the hemp ladder lines between his bare legs, she'd swear he dangled in the air with no support of any kind.

"What sort of woman would bring her child on board a flute clearly not seaworthy? You do not strike me as stupid, Catherine LeClerc. Tell me why."

She found his interrogation and refusal to leave the mast annoying and she decided not to respond.

"Why, Catherine?" he asked sternly and with no empathy. "Why did you endanger your child? What could you have been thinking of? Definitely not her welfare. Where was it you needed to go so badly?"

"Paris," she blurted, his goading trampling her better judgment. "And I *was* thinking of her welfare; I'd never intentionally bring harm to my daughter. I needed to get home, and the flute was the first ship available to me. I didn't want to wait for something more sound. I thought *De Gids* could make the journey. Why would Captain Dekker sail her if she weren't seaworthy? But I was mistaken. *Oui,* I was careless." She knew she was being impudent, but she needed something to undermine the degradation he'd put on her.

"Oui, vois êtes."

His tone did not demean or badger her further, as she'd expected. He simply reaffirmed her admission.

She didn't know whether to laugh or cry. She felt as if she'd been struck and was still reeling from the blow.

The noisy ripple of topsails and the wind-induced clang of the ship's bell intruded as he mumbled, "Paris is a rotten city."

Disbelief made her shake her head. "Is it not enough for you to ridicule me? Now you must insult my country as well?" She crossed her arms. "Apparently your parents thought France redeeming enough. Why else would they have given you a French Christian name?" she argued, wanting to put some of his puzzling pieces together for a change. "Why is your surname Spanish, as is the title of this ship? Are you French or Spanish? Or both?"

"I support no country," he replied. "The sea bears my devotion."

"But you were born to a country, monsieur. You were not born unto the sea."

"Perhaps I should have been. . . ." His voice died away on a resentful note and he put the spyglass to his eye again.

Her eyes leveled on his chest and the faded scars that flawed this part of him as well. The healed lines trailed over the compact rise of his breasts to rest above his heart. Maybe the cuts had sunk inside him, deep into his spirit, and wounded him where the pain could not be seen.

But he suffered just the same.

For the briefest of seconds she gave him her pity, then thought better of that. He'd spit her compassionate words at her feet.

He may not have been born to the sea, but neither had he been born a pirate. He had the look of an aristocrat. Even half clad, he dressed himself in nobility. She saw it in the way his nostrils flared with agitation, the intolerant clench of his jaw, the crooked set of his nose.

As the soft glimmer of stars hit him, bathing his flesh in shadow and light where muscle began and ended, she found herself caught up in his forbidden allure. Even without weapons balanced at his hips, he projected strength and virility; dangerously attractive.

To look at him was a purely sensual experience.

She hadn't thought of any other men in this way. None of the guides she and Georges Claude had encountered, or the tradesmen and marketeers, had kindled this kind of response in her. They had been her husband's acquaintances, and she'd not looked beyond that for anything more—even after she'd resigned herself from her marriage.

"I am of mixed blood." Danton's succinct answer had been so long in coming, it took Catherine a moment to fix on what he was talking about. "My mother was French and my father was Spanish." He swung to the larboard, engrossed with the unseen.

From his use of the past tense, Catherine assumed his parents were deceased. Despite their obvious differences, it appeared she and Danton Cristobal both shared the loss of their families.

Perhaps he could be appealed to.

Catherine spoke with quiet determination. "I need to know where we are going. I cannot help but be concerned, since we seem to be traveling north when I need to go south."

"We are sailing to my island. Isle of the Lost Souls."

Isle of the Lost Souls? She'd thought he'd take her to a convenient port where she could book passage on another ship.

She managed to curb her knot of panic, choosing her next words very carefully. "It isn't necessary for you to bring us to your island, monsieur. I'm sure you have your . . . your priorities . . . and a woman and child would only serve as a disruption. As much as I appreciate your help, I can't go with you."

His subtle laughter floated down to her, snuffing her argument to smoke. "You have no choice."

Catherine would not let him see her fear. A thousand thoughts bombarded her, getting off his square rigger before she lost her bearings being foremost. She couldn't allow him to take her farther away from France.

"We're off the eastern coast of Africa, are we not?" She grappled for a quick solution. "You could take me to any harbor on the seaboard and—"

"No."

"Why not?" She wanted to shake him.

"Politics."

"Politics?" she echoed. "I don't understand."

"Go to bed, Catherine."

"You can't dismiss me without an explanation!"

His back to her, he yelled, "I can do whatever I like."

Catherine took a deep breath to calm herself. She would not be maligned by this man. He had no right to control her destination. She would not give up what she had so recently gained: Power to do what she felt best. Perhaps if she knew where his island was located . . . perhaps if there was a visible shoreline on the way . . . *Dieu,* she knew she was grasping, but there was the possibility she could signal someone for help.

"Where is your island on the map, Monsieur Cristobal?"

At last he lowered his looking device, the wind tugging at

his hair. His eyes bore into her, yet she had the strange feeling he didn't really see her at all. A chill twisted around her frantically beating heart, numbing her from head to toe. He whispered hoarsely, *"Au bout du monde.* Now go to bed, Catherine. Go before I have Rainiaro carry you away."

She didn't doubt him. He would use force on her. She felt a wretchedness of mind she'd never felt before. Being on her own meant she had to face harsh realities. She'd get nowhere with him tonight. Tomorrow she'd try again.

Catherine turned away from Danton, sensing his penetrating gaze on her. Painful tingles shot up her legs with each retreating step; she'd nearly been paralyzed from his reply.

Au bout du monde. . . . At the end of the earth.

Chapter

3

*D*anton watched a white mass piled on the sunny horizon. The clouds detached themselves from the sea, and the tips of high mountain peaks, small and remote, stippled the edge of the sky like tiny inlets. In spite of outward appearances, there was only one body of land.

His island.

A moderate circumference of tropical and arid regions ringed by a velvet-blue ocean. Colonies of coral rose from the water, creating spiny necklaces; deceptive jewels that were more treacherous than beautiful.

From his high lookout on the main topmast shroud, Danton let his gaze drift to Catherine LeClerc. She stood at the teak railing with her daughter in her arms, warily studying the reefs *La Furia* had entered.

Judging by the animated expression on the little girl's face, she asked her mother questions. Questions he could not hear from his vantage point. A captivating smile dimpled her pink cheeks as she pointed to a school of vivid fish, then a flock of egrets soaring toward the coast.

Observing her easy pleasure made him think of Esteban. He'd once given his son a tour of *La Estrella del Cabo,* the brigantine he'd sailed for King Philip. The boy's bright brown eyes had taken everything in, running across the timbers and up the quarterdeck stairs to pretend he manned the rudder. Esteban had waved to him, grinning and saying he would be a great naval captain one day like his *papá*.

Danton pulled in a slow, deliberate breath. Raw grief constricted his chest as something clicked in his mind.

He'd never brought a child on *La Furia*.

Nor a woman.

Until now.

Their skirts were out of place amid sailcloth trousers. The woman and girl didn't fit in with the crew, who despite being deathly loyal to their captain, gazed at Catherine with more than idle curiosity. The lingering stares didn't sit well with Danton, for reasons he didn't care to analyze.

He didn't have that kind of inane logic.

His had been sunk to hell when he'd heard Catherine's scream while on board *De Gids*. And even worse, the crying girl's call for her mother. Though every instinct he possessed had warned him against getting involved, he simply could not have left them on Madagascar. No matter how much he'd wanted to.

Looking back, he knew he'd made the only decision he could have. That his actions held traces of honor came as a surprise to him; he'd thought his reverence had shriveled long ago.

But he wouldn't wait for ethics to hit him again. He had to contend with the woman and child now, not when a conscious-minded mood struck him. Though an easy solution hadn't sailed into his mind either.

As a warm mist sluiced the dawn, Catherine had come above deck hand in hand with her daughter to stand by the balustrade. Fatigue softened Catherine's shoulders and she'd stretched with discretion, first her legs and then her arms. The stout cotton of her dress had pulled across her back's slender width and defined the feminine curve of her buttocks, an image that disturbed his forced indifference. She wore no underskirts that he could tell; if she did, the petticoat had to be as thin as gauze.

She would be considered a tall woman by most men, the top of her head leaving only several inches space to the average portal. But compared to his own height, he found her size agreeable. Too much so.

After she'd left him last night, he'd found his concentration on Sadi thin like a drying river. Instead of focusing on the Turk, his thoughts had turned to Catherine. He eventually had to give up his vigil and go below.

What little sleep he'd had in Rainiaro's hammock had been fleeting and left him feeling unrested. He'd risen early, climbed the riggings, and vowed to keep his attention where it belonged.

But once Catherine had appeared, he wasn't able to heed his own advice. Cloaked in the haze, she'd looked delicate and in need of his protection.

She hadn't seen him, focusing instead on the spray of water as the prow cut through the Indian Ocean. She'd tied a ribbon at the end of her fat braid and a sadness passed over her features.

That defenseless look cut him to the bone.

A cold sweat broke out on his forehead and the ratlines in his hands became damp and rough.

He fought against making the inevitable comparisons between Elena and Catherine. They were completely different in both appearance and mannerism. But in so many ways, his current situation paralleled his past. He was once again responsible for a woman and child.

The first woman he'd committed to helping in four years.

He caught himself dredging up his former way of life. He'd had prestige, esteem, and social standing. Yet with all those qualities, not to mention the finest sailors in the king's navy, he hadn't succeeded in keeping Elena and Esteban safe. He'd botched his duties when he'd been a respectable man. As a seafaring bandit with nothing more than a motley group of devoted outcasts, how could he hope to accomplish what he hadn't before?

Devotion only spread so thick.

"*Capitaine!* Starboard or port? Give me a direction!" Rainiaro's shout broke through to Danton. The quartermaster had taken over for the helmsman, controlling the tiller with an expert hand under Danton's supposed guidance.

"To the port! To the port, *maudit!*" Danton's irritation was directed to himself.

Catherine swung her head upward and spotted him just as *La Furia*'s hull bumped and lightly scraped the razorlike fans in the shallow waters. She gripped hold of the railing with her free hand and braced herself.

Danton coupled his legs through the halyards and gritted his teeth as the mast creaked. *Mierda.* The ship protested as the men on the yardarms frantically furled the topsails, securing them in bundles with buntlines to slow the ship.

Rainiaro spun the wheel to the left, then to the right to straighten the rudder.

"The flag." Danton climbed higher, not acknowledging Catherine's stare, but feeling every inch of it searing his back. "Bring her down and raise the colors."

A Malagasy, thick with muscle and bare from the waist up, lowered the modest banner of three silver chevrons on a red background. In its place he attached another flag to the poop staff and raised the emblem of a skull and crossbones. A white dagger took up the bottom third of the rectangle.

Danton watched the Isle of the Lost Souls come alive. No longer did the formations look like separate pieces of land. The points grew, climbing and coming together. A distinctive line of green and brown became visible on a writhing border of white where the surf splintered the shore.

A dozen canoes glided through the water as dark-skinned oarsmen gained ground on the rigger. Danton raised his hand in greeting, speaking Malagasy to the party of natives who'd come to welcome *La Furia* home.

He flexed the muscles in his back and shoulders, then expanded his lungs with deep gasps. His mind prepared for the impact, the surge of blue all around him and the feeling of weightlessness. Clearing his head, he focused on the reefs, knowing a single miscalculation could land him in the claws of coral. He braved the danger, finding perverse pleasure in the challenge.

Sucking in a great breath, he dove into the ocean.

Catherine hadn't expected Danton to leap through the air in a beautiful arc. Her eyes froze on his long, lean form. His image awed her and filled her with a peculiar discord that seemed to send everything inside her jumping around. As his fingertips hit the crystal water, his entry made no splash. Gentle rings marked the surface where he'd touched the ocean. His disappearance left her heart pounding from surprise.

Madeleine clapped.

"Oh, *Maman!*" The child giggled, hanging onto Nanette by the hem of the dolly's dress. "Look at Monsieur Pirate!"

Catherine searched the wavelets, waiting for Danton to surface. The anger she'd felt toward him quickly yielded to apprehension. No one could hold their breath for such a duration. Panic engulfed her and she was just about to warn Rainiaro when Danton emerged. With a flick of his head he shook the water from his hair.

He let out an exhilarated whoop that reached Catherine's ears. Her upset abated to swift envy. She didn't know how to swim. She'd asked Georges Claude to teach her, but he'd refused, saying it wasn't necessary for a woman to learn. Now that she was on her own, she intended to tutor herself. At least to learn to float in water that wasn't deep.

The dugouts quickly reached Danton. Grabbing the side of the one nearest to him, he hoisted himself up and inside. The three natives went to unusual extremes to touch him, to pat his back, to clasp his hands, to welcome him home.

"Bring her in, Rainiaro!" Danton wrapped his fingers around an oar and dug the tip into the water. The craft began to turn around, and the others followed his lead.

As Danton and his entourage navigated a course directly for the beach, Rainiaro steered *La Furia* toward a wharf that jetted from the longest point of the island.

Activity on the rigger quickened as anchor lines were secured and the plank engaged. The men filed in ranks of efficient order and unloaded the booty hand over hand in a neat line all the way to the beach.

With all the work to be done, Catherine and Madeleine were forgotten.

Catherine set her daughter on her feet and held her hand. "We'll go look for Monsieur Cristobal and ask him about our arrangements."

She took the gangway onto the pier. Goods were left on the beach, systematically arranged and sorted through by apparent size and value. Already the items stretched longer than the ship from which they'd come.

Gazing into the distance, Catherine viewed the ocher hills

dusted with yellow-green. Settled on a low mountain was a solitary pink dwelling framed by groves of palms. The house's walls reached far and wide, testimony to the vastness of the interior.

Without warning, colorfully dressed Malagasy women descended upon Catherine and Madeleine. Foreign voices exuded welcome and amazement. Curious white smiles abounded. Subtle hands stroked Catherine's hair as if it were threads of gold. Her dress, worn and much-mended, was the object of delight. Brown fingers smoothed over the seams and joyful choruses sounded.

Catherine didn't know what to make of this bizarre commotion. Holding onto Madeleine's hand, both she and her daughter were examined and glorified.

"Have you never seen a white woman before?" Catherine asked in French.

The sarong-clad women tittered behind hands without giving a clue if they understood her. A child approached and held out a bouquet of periwinkles for Madeleine.

Madeleine took the flowers and smelled them. The women laughed.

Catherine brought Madeleine closer. *"Blanc."* She raised her sleeve and smoothed her skin to show its whiteness. *"Blanc."*

"Oui!" the Malagasy cried. *"Vazaha!"*

Vazaha? Catherine shook her head, disturbed and troubled that she couldn't communicate with the islanders. "I don't understand."

"Vazaha!"

"Oui," she tentatively agreed. *"Vazaha.* Thank you for the flowers. We must be on our way now. Good-bye." Then to get her message across, she waved and bid Madeleine to do likewise.

"Those ladies were nice, *Maman,"* Madeleine commented while walking and admiring the pink periwinkles. "I liked that girl who gave me these."

Catherine's shoes sunk into the soft sand as she awkwardly trudged along, practically pulling Madeleine behind her. The child gawked at this and that, not paying attention to where she was going.

Catherine came upon Antonio and Eduardo taking the

infamous red carpet toward the pink house. She ran after them.

"S'il vous plaît, where can I find Monsieur Cristobal? I must speak with him."

Bewildered, the brawny pair stared at her.

"Capitaine?" she said too loudly, as if by yelling they'd understand her French. She mimed with her hand a great height—or as tall as she could raise her hand on tiptoes—to indicate Danton's striking size. "Danton Luis Cristobal?" She put a question to the name, hoping to convey something.

Eduardo nodded. *"Capitán."* Then he pointed midway down the beach.

The pirate captain stood in the midst of three opened crates, conversing with Rainiaro.

"Merci." Catherine set off to single him out.

Madeleine tucked her dolly under her arm and adjusted her hold on the flowers. "Where are we going, *Maman?"*

"To have a talk with Monsieur Cristobal."

"Do we have to leave here?"

"Oui, we do."

"I like this island. There's lots of pretty things here," Madeleine said as they walked past an open chest. Inside were candlesticks, religious statues, chalices, and patens—the silver plates used for communion.

"Of course those things are pretty, *mon petit chou chou.* But they're stolen. Do you remember what *Maman* said about taking things that aren't yours?"

"It's not nice to do that."

"Not at all."

"Did Monsieur Pirate steal all these pretties?"

"I'm afraid so." Catherine sidestepped a pile of inlaid fowling pieces and damascened pistols. "So you see, that is why we can't stay here. Monsieur Cristobal is a thief."

"But he saved us, *Maman."*

Catherine sighed. "Our misfortune that he had to."

"What does that mean?"

"Never mind."

They fast approached Danton, who'd begun to take out bales of damask, striped and raw silks. Rainiaro assessed bolts of uniform cloth and pieces of velvet.

Danton didn't seem to notice her bearing down on him. He was engrossed with the task of counting his spoils. His hair wet and his damp skin glistening, he'd strapped on a red sash and his cutlass, but remained without his boots and shirt. It seemed rather odd for him to be armed on his own island. Perhaps he felt more comfortable with a weapon. Did that mean they were under the threat of attack? If so, her resolve to make arrangements for leaving as soon as possible became all the more important.

Catherine tightly gripped Madeleine's hand and stopped just short of the first crate. "Monsieur Cristobal, I need a word—"

"Have the bolts of sheer linen and bales of laces put in the cellars," Danton instructed Rainiaro, paying no attention to her interruption.

"I'll see that it's done, *Capitaine.*"

Danton stalked away before she could stop him.

"Monsieur Cristobal," Catherine called, "I must—"

"The spices go in the larder." Danton briefly paused to see to another pirate's wares, then off he went again.

Catherine trailed along.

He came to a line of chests with open lids, and several Spaniards awaiting orders. "The trinkets—the porcelain, ivory, and such can go into the caves to settle up with the crew."

"*Sí, Capitán.*"

"Monsieur! Wait." Catherine scooped Madeleine in her arms so she could run after him.

Danton's long legs afforded him a faster pace. Catherine tripped behind, her efforts made harder with her daughter in her arms.

"Where's he going, *Maman?*"

"In the wrong direction!" Catherine spoke in a voice clipped with agitation. "Monsieur! Please slow down. I must talk with you!"

Danton pointed to a pair of gleaming brass cannons on wooden dollies and the Malagasy men yanking them up the shore with pieces of hemp. "Those can be stored with the other gunnery."

"*Monsieur!*" Catherine lost all patience.

He abruptly turned, and she nearly collided with him. Breathless, she faltered and fought for composure.

"And the woman," Danton said to Rainiaro, who had caught up with them, "can go into the old cook's house." Then he turned and she was dismissed.

On his final rejection, her tolerance shortened like an ignited fuse. She exploded. "I will not! Not until I've had a word with you, Monsieur Cristobal. I am not one of your prizes," she said to his naked back, "that you can stuff here and there."

All activity halted. The muscles across Danton's shoulders tensed. He turned to face her.

"I've already explained the situation to you." His hand brushed the hilt of his sword. "Can't you see there are tallies to be taken? What is it you want?"

Now that she had his attention—and everyone else's—she was overcome with self-consciousness. With all the fortitude she could muster, she lowered her tone. "I wanted a civil word with you."

"Speak."

She gasped. "I'm not a dog either, monsieur. Can we not partake in a courteous conversation about this matter of my going to Paris? I—" Her next words stuck in her throat, and she screamed as he came at her, snatched her arm and glared into her eyes.

"Take the child, Rainiaro," he ground out.

"M-Madeleine stays with me," Catherine managed, trying to ignore his deathly strength. He could crush her like a bug.

"We're going to talk. That's what you wanted, isn't it?"

"But Madeleine—"

"I shall look after her, woman," Rainiaro assured, reaching for her daughter.

"It's all right, *Maman*. I like the chocolate-colored man."

Biting her lower lip with indecision, Catherine finally said, "Madeleine, be a good girl."

"I will. I'm always a good girl because I like . . ."

Catherine couldn't hear any more, for Danton forced her to walk with him. Indignant, she winced. "You're hurting me. Why must you always be so brutal?"

"You've never seen me brutal." He loosened his hold on her.

"Why are *you* angry?" She caught up her skirts in one hand so she wouldn't trip on them. "It's *me* who should be angry. I've had my life taken from me."

Danton advanced to a half hogshead filled with wood curls. He reached inside, seized a bottle of French brandy by its neck and tilted it downward. "And mine has been turned upside down from the minute I took you on board my ship."

"I didn't ask you to."

"I should have left you on Madagascar. If I didn't have any morals, I would have." He let her go and, without warning, drew his cutlass.

Catherine recoiled as he wielded his honed blade. "You could forget your morals and take me back! You needn't kill me!"

The sound of breaking glass sharpened the air as he nipped the cork and sliced off the bottle's top. Brandy immediately poured onto the sand and he righted the bottle to stop the flow. "I don't kill women unless they're ugly."

Choking on the scare he'd given her, she called him the first thing that popped into her head. *"Cochon!"*

"Pig?" He peaked one brow, then took a drink of the fine amber liquor, careful not to let the rough edge touch his lips. "Not very original, *linda.*"

After slipping his weapon into its scabbard, he tugged on her sleeve. "Keep walking."

Danton took a narrow path up a slope. The hilly trail wove around beds of pastel impatiens, yellow orchids with long tubes, ferns, and vibrant moss. Colorful birds cried from the tops of screw pines.

The pink house came into view. Up close the majesty and grace of the residence hit Catherine full force. Flat stones had been paved to the entryway where columns were covered by vines. A spectrum of nature's color filled this secluded world, putting an artist's palette to shame.

Danton opened the door. "This way," he ordered, releasing her as they entered.

The house seemed to flow in one continuous space. Every wall curved, feeding a spirit of openness. Every window, every doorway, acted as a frame for some particular view, whether that be the vista of rugged coastline or the luxuriant tropical vegetation.

The main living area opened to the cooling breezes, sheltered by palm thatch and palm trunks.

The assortment of decor showed Danton's true nature; a gatherer of prizes from a variety of countries.

Catherine absently traced the edge of a linear candle holder.

Danton set his liquor bottle on a table. "I once allowed a Greek captain to anchor his sloop on my island for careening. Grateful I didn't kill him, he allowed me to choose whatever I wanted from his hold. The pair are Byzantine."

"They're lovely."

"They're priceless."

"Of course," she remarked bitterly. "Your home is very interesting."

"Come into the study."

Catherine followed him into a shady gallery where the exterior walls were framed by mural-painted silk. Small treasures had been strategically placed throughout; ivory elephants, French sculpture and watercolors. A collection of gold and silver betel nut boxes sat on a wedgelike shelf. And numerous books on Turkey, Arabia, and Islamic culture. Danton rounded his desk—a converted Chinese altar table, and took a seat in a wicker chair whose back fanned wide. "You wanted to talk. Then talk, Catherine LeClerc."

She stared at a large Sung urn filled with rolled maps and wondered if one of the charts represented France and a route to sail there. "I think we should discuss the arrangement for my sailing to Paris."

He brought one bare calf up and crossed it over his leg. That he was comfortable with his near nakedness unnerved Catherine. She, on the other hand, felt herself blush every time she looked at any part of him not covered. At this particular moment she couldn't help noticing how large his feet were. "What is so important in Paris? A lover?"

Catherine inwardly cringed. "No. I need to resume my old life. To see civilization."

He said nothing, his astute gaze drinking in the patches on

her clothes, the outdated style of her dress. She felt pitifully destitute when he looked at her. "Where have you been?"

"India. Before that, Africa."

"Why?"

Catherine didn't want to have to explain about Georges Claude. She didn't owe Danton Cristobal answers as to why things had turned out the way they had. "Does it matter?"

"Perhaps not. Perhaps yes." Danton knit his fingers together and absently rubbed at his jaw with his thumbs.

"Please, monsieur, don't play games with me. Take me to a civilized harbor where my daughter and I can be put aboard a decent ship."

His subsequent silence served as a battleground. She would not surrender without a fight. She would reason with him, even if her pleas were peppered with desperation. "Is it money you're after? If so, I have nothing of value. Everything I owned was in a portmanteau on *De Gids*. As soon as I get to Paris, I'm going to gain employment. I could repay—"

"Save your money." His demeanor took on a haughty arrogance. "Whatever you could hope to earn in a lifetime is sitting on my beach tenfold." Leaning back into his chair, he steepled his fingertips over his chest. "I'm a rich man, *linda*, and I would gladly take you and the girl to wherever it is you want to go."

A cry of relief broke from her lips. *"Merci!"*

"But I cannot."

Catherine's hopes were destroyed, and she struggled to keep the hysteria from her voice. "Why not?"

"I'm a wanted man by many governments. If I sailed *La Furia* into the well-traveled sea lanes, it would be suicide. The lives of my men are my responsibility. I won't have them gunned down because you need to get to Paris. Believe me, I don't want to deny you, but right now I have no alternative."

"Then what am I to do in the meantime?" she asked, frustration consuming her.

"You wait until I can think of a solution. Until then, consider yourself marooned."

I'm digging for treasure, Monsieur Pirate." Madeleine sat on her haunches with a kitchen spoon in her hand. The hem of her yellow calico dress was bunched above her bare knees.

"You won't find any here," Danton countered sharply, his shortness with Madeleine provoked after nearly squashing her under his heel. The shadows created by palmetto fronds had concealed her as he'd rounded the palm's trunk. His mind had been on his accounts, not the playing spot of a pint-sized girl.

"Yes I will." She scooped sand and dumped the soil into a fishing basket. "I'm looking for a big treasure chest." She stuck her face into the shallow hole and pawed through the depression with her fingers.

Danton frowned. "Who told you there was treasure buried on my island?"

Madeleine sniffed and wiped her nose with the back of her dirty hand, the spoon still in her grasp. "Captain Dekker. He said all pirates bury their treasures." She lowered her voice to a whisper. "And do you know what I'm going to find?"

Danton grunted.

"A ruby necklace," she said softly. "A big one. And pearls. Maybe a wedding ring. A gold one. And lots of francs for *Maman* because we don't have any money."

The bluntness of the child's statement jarred Danton. "What happened to your money?"

Madeleine shrugged. "I don't know. Ask my *maman.*"

Danton hadn't spoken to Catherine in a week and suspected she was sulking. On more than one occasion, he'd spied her on the beach, walking its jagged length, staring out at the sea and searching for salvation. He could have told her no ship dared enter his harbor without facing retribution.

His irritation with her had not cooled. Each time he recalled her calling him out in front of the crew, his blood boiled. If one of his sailors had dared talk to him as she had, the man would have been hung from the yardarms.

Seven days had passed and he hadn't been able to come up with a dispatching port safe for both Catherine and her daughter and those on board *La Furia.* Thus far, he'd discarded a dozen harbors in the vicinity as unsuitable. He'd have to continue poring over his maps and take his search farther in order to find the right city. And quickly. His pirating life had enough complexities without having to deal with a distraught mother and winsome child.

"Are you mad, Monsieur Pirate?" Madeleine broke into Danton's thoughts. "You look like you're going to bite me."

"I only bite ugly little girls," he said rhetorically.

Without intending to, Danton caused her to grin. "You're teasing."

Her dimples wrenched his gut. He made himself believe the spasm came because he wasn't used to having children around, though his island had plenty to spare. Many of his crew had Malagasy wives. Lusty as his men were, most had no less than six children. But the isle tykes kept their distance, fearing the mighty Danton Cristobal—King of the Pirates.

At times he chuckled over their rebuff; and other times, he felt lonely and empty, wanting nothing more than to hear their innocent voices.

"Maman said we're going to Paris, France, but I can't tell you how." In low tones she advised, "It's a secret."

Danton shrugged off her remark as nothing more than childish prattle and wishful thinking.

Madeleine jabbed at the beach with the spoon's handle,

unearthing an opaline shell. "Look! A treasure. I could make a necklace out of this seashell. With some ribbon. Then I would wear it to my birthday party. Did you know I'm going to be four?" She held up her hand and splayed her fingers. "I was going to have my party on the ship, but everyone got killed. Can you give me a party?"

"What?" Danton had been listening with half an ear. The girl was a chatterbox.

"Do you like parties, Monsieur Pirate?"

Danton hadn't been to a party in years. The last time he'd heard the notes of a clavichord, Elena had been in his arms. The ball had been on the eve of his commission to sail to Calcutta for King Philip. *Mierda,* that illustrious night seemed eons ago.

"Will you?" Madeleine chimed.

"Will I what?"

"Give me a party."

Uncomfortable, Danton put her off. "We'll see."

Madeleine smiled. "That means you will. If you say 'I'll think about it,' you won't. I know, because *Maman* says 'We'll see' for *oui* and 'I'll think about it' for *non.'*"

The anxious look on her face doomed him. His only saving grace would be that he wouldn't be around when her birthday came.

"Where is your mother?"

"In the cottage saying mean things about you—some swear words I heard my *papa* say." Madeleine's eyes widened. "She sent me outside and said I wasn't allowed to say bad words. Only *Maman* can. And *Papa* could too."

So Catherine LeClerc could swear. No doubt she was calling him much worse than a pig.

Hunkering down, Danton regarded the girl on her own level. He could smell the perfume that only a child wore: sunshine and purity; the earth and windblown traces of tallow soap.

His own privilege to nurture and parent had been stolen from him. Literally ripped from his arms. Shuddering, he shut out the painful memories, wanting to forget. But by the same token, he feared as the years went on, he would not be able to remember Esteban's face.

"Tell me about your *papa,* puppet."

"My *papa* is in Heaven with my *grandpère* and *grandmère.* And my *oncles.* And Captain Dekker." She frowned. "Do you like snakes? I don't."

Madeleine's abrupt topic change threw him. "I don't particularly like snakes, no."

"A cobra killed my *papa.*" Her lower lip quivered, then stiffened. "Do you have any snakes here?"

He stored the tidbit about her father away, thinking the death of a loved one, no matter how, must be just as devastating for a child. He promised himself not to tread so harshly on the girl in the future. "The snakes on my island are harmless." The impulse to brush Madeleine's hair from her brow took hold of him from nowhere. He forced his confused emotions to order.

"Do you have any black bears and jackals?"

"I have pet lemurs."

"What's a lemur?"

Danton stood and put his hand on his hip. "Nuisances that, more often than not, wake me up in the middle of the night with their jabbering."

"What does a lemur look like?"

Danton thought of Pousse-Pousse. The lemur reminded him of a tan and brown bear with a long tail. Razana's large and round green-gold eyes reflected spirits past. Playful, yet wise beyond human imagination, Dokobe was Danton's favorite. There was no way to describe them; each animal had its own unique and individual traits, though they were the same breed.

After a spell he answered, "They are beautiful beasts. Like monkeys, only better."

"Can I see one?"

Madeleine's persistence rattled him. "We'll see." He inadvertently promised the girl by using Catherine's vague answer. He started to walk away.

"Where are you going?" she called after him.

"To see your mother."

"She doesn't like pirates."

Danton laughed richly. "And I thought it was me."

He left Madeleine sitting in the shade and went to find

Catherine. The short length of discreet trail he followed emerged at his courtyard and was within calling distance of the cottage.

The cook house hadn't served its purpose in quite some time. Not since Danton had constructed an open kitchen for Tanala off the main house. The aged Malagasy woman had been with him for three years, faithfully devoted. She was an excellent cook who could make rice taste pleasing.

The earthen dwelling, with its shaggy thatch cap for a roof and walls of sun-dried red soil and cattle dung, had remained dormant, but habitable. Recently Danton had begun to store his reserve ammunition in the empty larder, as well as in the worn grain bins and the cellar.

As he neared the house, the trumpet-shaped blossoms of jacarandas sprinkled the grounds like violet snow. He went to knock on the door just as it opened.

Catherine inhaled and put her hand to her breast. He noted her face had tanned considerably since her arrival; the honey color brought out the blond of her hair. She was a good-looking woman. Beyond pretty. Beautiful. Slender and moderately tall, she would fit neatly in his arms if he ever desired to put her there. And to his chagrin, he thought about doing that now.

Not waiting for an invitation, he stepped inside the cool interior. "Where are you going?" he asked offhandedly, his eyes adjusting to the room's veiled light.

"To check on Madeleine." She spun around under the doorway, clearly vexed by his intrusion. "You didn't tell me I had to stay put."

"You can go where you like," he commented dryly, amusing himself with the way she'd furnished the room. Hanging on a metal arm in the hearth that had once been used for kettles was a branch of vanilla orchids. A half-dozen canisters of gunpowder had been arranged in a pyramid under the window, the child's doll sitting on the single can at the top. The open cupboards housed her wardrobe—clothes folded with neat precision. Agitated for her calling him out on his beach, he hadn't readily told her he'd had her portmanteau retrieved before sailing out of Madagascar. He'd waited until the end of her first day on his island, then sent Rainiaro to deliver her trunk.

"Your daughter is just outside, digging for treasure," he said at length.

"I know." Catherine left the door ajar and skirted him. Meshing her fingers together, she pressed them into the flat folds of her drab skirt. "What are you doing here?"

Danton studied her. Pristine and starched, she met his stare. Defiance etched a cold path in her blue-gray eyes; rebellion stained her cheeks. "I've come to talk to you." He picked up one of Catherine's shoes from its spot on the sideboard. She'd mended a tiny hole in the striped serge, her limited sewing kit not yet put away.

"An interesting idea, since just this morning that was my very intention."

Danton glanced up. She stood so primly, he thought she'd snap her spine. Attired in another mended frock, her child's words echoed through his head. *We don't have any money.* What sort of husband had LeClerc been?

"I was told by Antonio you couldn't be disturbed."

"I was working."

"*Oui.* You are always conveniently working, Monsieur Cristobal. I've come twice before and received the same welcome—which was none at all."

"I'm here now."

"Shall I get hopeful?" Snatching the shoe from him, Catherine put it back on the counter. She dropped her spools into the basket and jammed down the woven top. "Does your presence imply you're ready to be more sympathetic to my plight? I'm not trying to be difficult, but I really must get off your island."

Though she tried to hide her anxiety, once again her voice was laced with despair. Her plea shook her shoulders and she fidgeted with her toiletry articles next to the dry sink. He couldn't fathom what was so important about that stinking city, Paris. What had happened to make her leave in the first place?

He had a lot of questions, but her answers would only serve to involve them further. He didn't need the ropes of compassion about his neck; he'd only hang himself.

Her all-fired hurry to get to France puzzled him—a riddle he'd still not figured the solution to. Despite knowing how dangerous knowledge could be, he asked quietly, "How long has it been since you were in Paris?"

She organized her brush and comb, tooth powder and a cracked looking glass. "Six years."

"I was there five years ago."

His statement garnered her attention. She met his gaze. Plainly she wanted to ask him why, but held back.

Danton left the counter, locked his hands behind his backside and walked the old kitchen's circumference. Her portmanteau rested in the corner, the lid up. A sea of snowy undergarments were visible. "I trust you were happy to see your clothing."

"Thank you," she replied. *"Oui,* I was quite surprised when Rainiaro gave me my belongings. He said you'd had them recovered before we left Madagascar. How did you know?"

"The trunk practically landed on my feet." He crouched down and fingered coarse white cotton, then lifted up a plain petticoat for inspection. "I didn't think your Dutch captain and his crew outfitted themselves in such a manner, and could only deduce the luggage was yours."

She snatched the intimate article from him. "Please, don't touch that." Stuffing the underpinning into her case, she slammed the lid.

Straightening, Danton watched as she nervously wet her lips. Her mouth was not overly wide, but full enough to kindle his interest.

"You said you were in Paris, monsieur," she prompted, pulling him from his thoughts.

He distanced himself from her. "During my commission in the Spanish Royal Navy."

"You were in the navy?"

"Does that surprise you?" he asked.

"Well, frankly, yes."

"How do you think I learned to commandeer a ship?"

"I don't know. Maybe it's inborn to all pirates."

He smiled, but without humor. *"Chérie,* I was not born a privateer."

Catherine ignored his barb. "Tell me about Paris."

"Since you persist," he said dryly, "I will tell you my impressions. An enormous populace overran the streets.

The rich and poor were knit together by the threads of velvet coats and the unraveling empty pockets of beggars." Danton wove his tale with ribbons of color, yet with black and white truth. "The smell of garbage and fine perfumes clashed in the soot-filled sky."

"I don't believe you."

He paid her skepticism no heed. "Narrow boulevards were nearly impassible from the convergence of chaises, wagons, coaches, chariots, and sedans. The drunks that slept on the cobbles were lucky not to be trodden under. In short, Paris is a slum for the impoverished, a paradise for the affluent."

He read the skepticism in her eyes. "That's not the Paris I remember, Monsieur Cristobal."

"You'd be much better off in a country devoted to its people."

"I don't wish to discuss politics with you," Catherine protested. "I'd much rather know why you've come to see me. If you've a desire to goad me, I'd advise you not to. I'm in a foul temper."

"Ah, yes. Swearing."

Her brows arched.

"I was informed by your daughter that you were on your high ropes."

Catherine ground out, "I am. What do you have to say for yourself?" She took the doll from the gunpowder keg and set the bedraggled thing on a cot by her side. One by one she disbanded the triangle of kegs and hefted each canister into a low-lying cupboard. "Hopefully you've brought me good news. Living in a gunnery is not a suitable environment for Madeleine. I don't like endangering my daughter."

"She won't be harmed. She couldn't blow up the house unless you left a flint about and she knew how to strike it."

"You'll excuse me if I'm not consoled by your reasoning. Obviously you've never had a child, monsieur."

Danton felt as if his heart had caught in his ribs. He held his raw sorrow in check, not revealing the deep wounds her words had inflicted. His stomach gnawed on emptiness; a war of conflict raged within him. He would have liked to inform her he did know a thing or two about children, but that was a secret part of his past known only to a select few.

He tried to separate himself from his sense of loss and the desire to strangle her for tormenting him. For lack of a better place to put his hands, he grabbed a caned chair and yanked it from under the table. Straddling the seat, he braced his arms on the ladder back. "I sent Rainiaro to Tamatave three days ago in my schooner, *Negro España.*"

"Why then," she gasped, "didn't you have him take us along? We could have waited until an appropriate captain pulled into port. I would have gone wherever he was sailing and made arrangements from there."

"A possibility, one of which I'm glad I decided against."

"Pray, why?"

"After Rainiaro left the Madagascar coastline, he sailed around Île Ste. Marie. Once the *Negro*'s colors were spotted, she was fired on by an English naval cutter. A hit to the galley did her damage, but not enough to sink her. A chase ensued. Rainiaro's expert navigational abilities and the excellence of the schooner allowed him to get away."

"Rainiaro could have turned *me* over to the English!"

Danton's feet thumped on the floorboards as he drew in his knees. "And have my quartermaster risk being captured? I think not. The waters are becoming overrun with dog-watch fleets, and most certainly so are the decent ports. I won't jeopardize my crew by sailing into a harbor where they'll face certain death. I told you that already."

"You're being extremely trying, monsieur," she said with quiet emphasis. "I'm trying to understand why you're doing this to me, but I don't understand anything at all. Especially your islanders."

"What do you mean?" He trifled with the trinkets on the tabletop. A variety of seashells and rocks; next to them, a dried and lifeless comet moth whose long, yellow-tailed wings were marked with pretend eyes. "Has anyone treated you unkindly?"

"No, but the women keep calling me *vazaha*. I agree with them, only to silence their ridiculous chant."

He reserved his smile. "They call you 'foreigner.' And that is what you are to them."

"But to me," she whispered, "it is they who are the foreigners." She turned away from him, the end of her thick braid swishing above her hips. He couldn't help wondering how long it had been since he'd undone a woman's braid . . . seen hair this golden color spread out on his pillow.

Unbidden, the image of Catherine lying next to him with her glorious hair sifting through his fingers took hold of him. He couldn't afford thoughts like this; the price would cost him his concentration—an asset a wanderer of the sea could not do without.

Abruptly standing, Danton shoved the chair under the table. "I will release you when the time is right," he said curtly. "Not a day sooner. There may be a way to get you out through Madagascar, but it's doubtful. With this latest incident, even Diego Suarez and Fort Dauphin are ill choices." He headed toward the door. "In the meantime, I want you to stay inside tomorrow."

Following him, she queried, "Whatever for?"

"I'll be away, and I'd feel better knowing where you are."

"Where are you going?"

"To a neighboring island for tar." The lie came to Danton easily. Isle of the Lost Souls could outfit him with whatever he needed for his ships. In actuality, he would be chasing a Spanish *flotas*. Rainiaro had gleaned information while in Tamatave of a *flotas, Manuela,* so heavily loaded with textiles, muskets, and ivory, seawater washed over her gunwales. She'd mapped a course from Porto Belo around Cape Horn to Lisbon. Danton intended to intercept her in the Mozambique Channel.

"Stay put," he insisted, stepping out into the sunlight. Confronting her at the doorway, he cautioned, "I don't want you getting into any trouble. The natives on my island are friendly, but misunderstood by a *vazaha*, I can't vouch for their behavior."

She put one hand on the jamb and looked past him toward her daughter. *"Oui,* I shall consider your request, monsieur, with as much sensitivity as you are considering mine."

The square rigger's timbers shuddered with every wave she cut through. Dark and damp, and smelling of bilge water, this compartment of *La Furia* proved to be less of a haven than Catherine had thought. She never would have done anything this drastic if she hadn't been so desperate.

The outlook for her release, which Danton had painted, looked bleak at best. If there was a chance to find someone who could take her, she had to try.

Even if her approach meant being a stowaway.

"Do we still have to whisper, *Maman?*" Madeleine sat beside her, a warm comfort to lean against in their dreary world of uncertainty.

"I suppose not, *mon chou*. No one can hear us with the ship under way."

"I wish we could light a lantern. I don't like the dark."

"Nor I." Catherine squinted, gazing across the darkness to the single, mist-covered porthole. Eerie trickles of moisture bounced off the oakum walls, emphasizing the unknown. She didn't know if or how populated the island Danton intended to sail to would be, but she had to take the chance there would be someone to help her—if not there, out at sea. "I'm sorry, Madeleine, but this was the only way."

An hour before dawn, Catherine and Madeleine had boarded the rigger undetected while the sailors slept. Looking for a safe hiding place, Catherine moved deep into *La Furia*'s chambers, wanting to be as far from the upper decks as possible. The rotten odor of sulfur had permeated this lower area and she'd almost turned back. But she decided they would be all right in this cramped cabin whose interior had been cloaked in black. Surely none of the crew or Danton Cristobal would expose themselves to such vile air. Whatever the source, its horrid smell would be a deterrent.

Catherine realized her misjudgment too late to fix her error.

Now with the sun high in the sky and vague light seeping through the filmy round glass, she was able to see exactly where they were.

Weights of powder, crates, racks of muskets, kegs, pikes, boarding axes, square bottles filled with gunpowder, and cannonballs shared their company. She had brought them to the one place she'd longed to be free of: a magazine with enough firepower to sink a fleet of ships.

"It smells in here, *Maman*. I don't like it."

Catherine had positioned them as far from the crockery jars—the origin of the foul odor—as possible. Apparently some kind of odd firing power; she didn't know what it was, only that the stench had been strong enough to bring out her handkerchief. Breathing through the linen, she watched Madeleine put Nanette to her face and bury her nose in the dolly's dress.

"How will we know when Monsieur Pirate gets to the other island, *Maman?*" Madeleine's question was muffled.

"When Monsieur Cristobal slows down."

"How can we tell?"

"The ship will stop."

"I wish it would stop now." Her voice quivered. "I'm hungry."

Catherine felt for the knapsack at her side. Her portmanteau had been too heavy for her to carry, much less conceal in the event she'd been caught. She'd taken one of her petticoats and stitched the hem together, gathering the top where the waist ribbon had been. Inside, she'd packed the barest of necessities: a dress each for herself and Madeleine, toiletry goods, and leftover portions of food.

Given the short notice, Catherine hadn't been able to horde much. Mainly last night's supper. Since she and Madeleine dined alone in the cook's cottage, there'd been no one to see that she barely touched her meal. Instead she put her spiced and herbed crayfish into a linen, as well as the boiled yams and beef-nutmeg biscuits Rainiaro had called *achica*.

After morning had streaked the sky and *La Furia* had covered a fair distance, they'd eaten the cold crayfish and drank water from a gourd.

Fingering for the foodstuffs, Catherine brought out the *achica*. "Have a biscuit, Madeleine."

"I don't like these very much. They're not sweet."

"Then have some yam too." She fished out the wrapped cloth and gave a small yam to her daughter.

Madeleine took a bite. "Remember that time when we were in the Him'laya mountains and *Papa* was with us and we ate chocolate?"

Catherine's thoughts grew distant. "I remember." Georges Claude had met up with a hunter from England. He'd been titled, a duke from Bristol traveling with an extensive assembly of noblemen. They were on a trophy expedition, boasting they would fill their great halls with tiger heads and elephant tusks.

The duke traveled in comfort, inviting the LeClercs to dine with him. On folding tea tables they'd been served the most elegant meal Catherine had ever eaten; ironically, the backdrop for such a refined repast had been the wild jungle. Madeleine had just turned two years old, and apparently the treat of chocolate candy had wedged itself in her mind.

Once dinner had broken up, and long after Madeleine had been put to sleep, Georges Claude took Catherine into their tent. He'd been drunk, while she'd had more than her share of claret and was feeling the sensual affects of the liquor. She'd tried to forget they had problems, and to salvage the fraying ends of their marriage.

He'd made love to her with an urgency that hadn't claimed him in years, but as in times past, she felt the same distancing of body and mind radiating from Georges Claude. She tried to reach for him, for the undefinable need that always began, but left her disheartened and empty when their intimacy was over.

Come morning, Catherine realized the marriage had run its course and she could no longer pretend otherwise. She asked her husband if they could return to France to raise Madeleine in civilization. Once again he'd refused to leave India, and life went on as it always had. With Georges Claude in charge. He still had adventure in his blood, and he gave her no choice but to obey him.

She was his wife.

After that night, he never touched her again.

"Oui, Madeleine, I remember." Catherine swallowed her sadness. Looking back was difficult. Would she ever have someone to comfort her? To hold her and kiss her as if she were the most important thing in his life? Could she trust herself to love, or had her chance passed her by?

Madeleine finished her snack with a drink of water, then laid her head in her mother's lap. "Are you scared, *Maman?"*

Absently stroking her daughter's fine hair, Catherine said, "A little," as Madeleine yawned. "There's nothing wrong with being afraid."

"I'm not afraid when you're with me."

"That's right, *mon petit chou chou,* you have nothing to be afraid of when I am with you."

"You'll never," Madeleine yawned again, "leave me, will you?"

"Never." Catherine felt Madeleine's muscles slacken, then she heard the measured breaths of her daughter's sleep.

Catherine was left alone with her thoughts. She closed her eyes and tried to remember the Paris she knew. She pictured the wrought iron around her childhood home; the woman who sold cheese in *Les Halles;* cathedral bells in Notre Dame as they chimed.

Danton Cristobal was wrong. Paris was beautiful.

Danton . . . the mere name made her think about him in ways she had no business doing. He was an enigma. A former member of the Spanish Royal Navy who had turned to piracy. Why? She imagined that whatever the reasons were, he had entered into his new world with a passion and vengeance. From what she'd seen, he did not take or do things lightly.

She wondered what it would be like to be loved by a man such as he. She sensed when he loved, he would love deeply; absolutely. Any involvement with him would be filled with inner excitement, but also perilous. Because a pirate only had love for one thing:

Treasure.

And she already knew what a cold second a woman came to that.

The motion of the ship made her drowsy. Her thoughts drifted to the familiar manner in which Danton had caressed her petticoats. He had made her extremely conscious of their threadbare state. No man, not even her husband, had taken the liberty of examining her underclothing. Why had she felt an unwelcome quickening when he'd done so? Since his visit yesterday, she'd been preoccupied with picturing his arresting face. She quickly dismissed any obvious reasoning for her behavior. She didn't want to know.

Sleep disconnected her musings. She let exhaustion take her and dozed.

Catherine sensed a bright light waving in front of her face. She lifted her tired lids, blinded by the glow of a lantern.

"Blame me," a squeaky English voice heralded. "If it ain't the cap'n's lady and her lit'le one lurking in the hold!"

Disoriented, Catherine sat up and tried to shake the shadowed dreams from her mind. *Mon Dieu,* they'd been found. Had she not been aware of the ship stopping?

Her throat rough with sleep, Catherine rushed, "Don't tell on us. Please."

The lad raised his lamp. His hair glowed russet from the flame's cast. His expression was marked with indecision and freckles that were scattered across his face like sand. The vibrant red of his hair may have caught her stare, but his canvas shirt kept her eyes fastened on him. Knotted just below his shoulder, the left sleeve hung empty.

"'Fraid I can't promise you that, lady. Cap'n sent me down here to spark the lamps in the light room. Most o' the crew'll come to take up their muskets."

"Muskets?" Catherine was fully awake now and sat up, careful not to wake Madeleine. "Is there trouble?"

"Not yet, lady." The boy hooked the lamp's wire handle over a nail in the rafter. "But we've entered the Moz'mbique Channel, and that's where she'll be. Not to worry, Cap'n'll find her."

"Find who?"

The boy gave her a bewildered gaze, as if she should have known the answer. "Why the Spanish *flotas* Cap'n plans on sinkin' for her royal treasure."

Shock flew through Catherine. Danton Cristobal had lied to her. He'd said nothing about an attack. He purposefully led her astray.

Her plans for escape were now mapped out on a bloody collision course with a Spanish ship. She'd put Madeleine in danger. She didn't know who to be mad at more—herself or Danton.

"Why're ye sittin' down here in the magazine, lady?" The youth scratched behind his ear. "Cap'n's cabin is a far sight better then the stench o' rotten eggs."

"Monsieur Cristobal didn't want me on board." She wondered if she could trust the boy. Thus far, he hadn't shouted out any warnings. She banked on that fact and pressed on with her story. "I need to get to Paris, and your captain has been less than enthusiastic about my going there. I thought if we went to the other island, I could get help. But it would seem I'll need to rely on the captain just as much as I did in Tamatave."

"I heard about that. Cap'n didn't have me aboard the day he smuggled you and the tyke out o' Madagascar. Left me at the island to pour grenades." He snorted. "Treats me like a babe sometimes, he does. Don't much care for that, but Cap'n's been good to me otherwise."

"You're not Spanish."

"Nay. A Londoner I be. Pardon me manners, lady. Name's James Every, formerly of Her Majesty's Navy, now taken up the sweet trade."

Madeleine stirred in her sleep and pressed Nanette to her cheek. She slipped her thumb in her mouth, and Catherine cradled her near. "I'm Catherine."

"I know." James sobered. "Cap'n'll be sendin' the crew, and I can't hide you. He'll think I had a part in it."

"I don't want you to get in trouble."

"Neither do I." James shrugged as if weighing his options. "Only way is to come on up with me. Cap'n ain't a coldhearted devil. He'll treat you fair."

"I'd like to share your opinion, but I highly doubt I'll be given a warm welcome."

"We'll just have to see." He blew out the lantern, but the gun room didn't darken as Catherine expected. "Best bring the lit'le one."

Resigned, she gathered Madeleine in her arms without waking her and tried to stand. Her legs had cramped, and if it hadn't been for the quick support offered by James, she would have fallen. *"Merci,"* she whispered.

"That means thanks." Half smiling, he led the way out. "Cap'n tries to teach us a little French now and then. You speak English well."

Catherine stepped around the grid of cannonballs strapped into racks by heavy leather bands as she followed James into the next chamber.

A window had been cut in the wall between the magazine and light room. Swaying before the glass pane was a big brass lantern housing a dozen burning candles; thus the reason the magazine hadn't grown dark when James put out the light. Hot splatters of wax stuck to the soles of Catherine's shoes.

The narrow passage upward loomed ahead. Knots of dread hitched Catherine's breath. She couldn't discount what lay ahead of her. Danton would be furious, as she'd expected. But she'd been preparing herself for his tirade with the thought in mind that she'd merely imposed herself on his pleasure ride—not a ride to sunder a galleon.

This brought an entirely different argument to light, and she had little or no time to prepare her defense.

Climbing a few steps, the air cleared and Catherine gratefully gulped drafts into her lungs. The taste of the sea, salty and clean, stayed with her.

James ascended two decks before reaching the level that housed Danton's lavish cabin. The boy stopped and turned. "Perhaps you should put the lit'le one in the cap'n's bed." Hesitancy lightened his tone. "I wouldn't want . . . that is . . ."

"You wouldn't want Monsieur Cristobal's yell to wake her?"

James held onto a sorry grin. "He may become a bit loud, aye."

Catherine allowed James to open the portal. Crossing to the bed, she laid Madeleine on the counterpane, easing her daughter from her arms. She pressed a loving kiss to her child's temple, then reluctantly left.

Outside, the world seemed brighter, and Catherine had to shield her gaze from the sun. Clouds dragged across the sky, tattered by wind. Several crew members crossed the path James led her on and they stared wide-eyed at her presence.

"This way, lady." James went around a pair of men loading guns. "I seen him on the fo'c'sle deck. Best you get things over with."

Catherine pulled her courage and determination together and made them hold fast like a rock inside of her. No matter what happened, she couldn't show Danton her fear.

She caught sight of him by the foremast. He cut a cool figure in his white shirt and breeches. A saffron bandanna covered his hair, emphasizing the golden cross in his ear.

He didn't see her. He held onto his infernal spyglass,

looking due west. Across his right shoulder hung a brace of pistols in leather slings. A powder flask dangled at his waist on a belt.

His string of curses reached her ears. *"Mierda,* she should be here." Scanning the vast sea, he scowled. He pivoted and took his search north, then dead east to the exact spot where she stood with James Every.

Danton stiffened; his square jaw visibly tensed. Slowly he lowered the glass.

Nervous as a caged cat, Catherine pretended not to understand his meaning. "I am here."

His expression changed from disbelief to stony rage. *She would not tremble . . . she would not tremble.*

A tense silence enveloped them as the crew halted their maneuvers to gape.

Though not unduly hot, she felt flushed and faint.

"Catherine, you have defied me." His tone, low and tightly reined, prickled her flesh. "Any member of my crew would be flogged for less."

She waited, her silence inviting him to persecute her.

Her challenge goaded him, and he came at her in a fury. "What punishment, *mon maki sauvage,* shall I see carried out on you?"

Chapter

5

*W*hatever you like." Catherine refused to take a step back, though her knees were ready to buckle.

Jumping from the forecastle, Danton suggested, "Perhaps a bowline knot under your chin and a dance upon nothing."

"If you wish." A buzzing whirled in her head, yet she held onto her fragile control.

"Or a run on the gauntlet." Reaching her, he wrapped his steely fingers around her forearm and jerked her toward him. He whispered harshly, "Cat-o'-nine strokes, keelhauling, or dying in your shoes would rightly serve."

Quaking, she kept her eyes straight ahead. She felt as if his hand had closed around her throat instead of her arm. "Whatever punishment you plan, monsieur, I suggest you do so quickly. I don't intend to be in the line of fire if you meet your Spanish ship."

Danton's eyes darkened and he spared James a fleeting glance. "You're mistaken, *linda,*" he growled. "I will find the *Manuela,* and when I'm finished with her, there'll be nothing left to sail."

Horrified, Catherine turned her head. He'd inclined his face inches from hers, his forehead practically grazing her brows. Riveting eyes probed into her very soul. The savage inner fire in his gaze trampled any danger she'd faced in her past to insignificance. To be trapped in this man's claws was a fate far worse than anything she could imagine.

Danton Cristobal knew how to extract blood with mere words.

"*Manuela* to the starboard!" Rainiaro's call nest-high on the main topmast turned all heads to a ship close on the horizon.

Danton threw Catherine at James. The abrupt release left her reeling. "Find the child, James, and take them to my cabin."

"The tyke's already there, Cap'n."

"Antonio!" Danton charged the ladder to the f'c'sle. "*Vien usted aquí!*"

The giant appeared under the scrolled overhang and looked upward. "*Sí, Capitán?*"

They exchanged words in Castilian, then Antonio caught a key ring Danton tossed to him.

"Looks like we been ordered locked in, lady," James said under his breath. "Come quiet like."

"I don't care if you endanger me," she cried, "but don't put my child's life in jeopardy!" She tried to run but found herself trapped between Antonio and James. Each took hold under her arms and dragged her away. She thrashed her legs and lost the dignity she'd so tried to hold on to. "You lied to me, Danton Cristobal!" Her words became viperish. "You don't deserve to captain a ship!"

"You and so many others," he rallied, "have made that very same observation. And yet, *chérie*, I'm still standing at the helm."

"*Cochon!*"

His dark laughter taunted her all the way below. She felt a wretched defeat. Danton Cristobal was merciless and cruel with a black heart to match his black flag.

Antonio threw open the door. The crash woke Madeleine, who sat up in bed and began to cry. Seeing her mother restrained, she bolted from the mattress and clung to Catherine's waist.

"*Maman! Maman!*" Great sobs shook her. "Let my *maman* go!" She shoved Antonio's shin. He grunted his annoyance, then released Catherine.

Catherine dropped to her knees and took her daughter in

her arms. "There, *mon petit chou chou*, it's all right. I'm not hurt."

The portal slammed closed; the lock clicked.

James blushed the color of his hair. "I'm sorry, lady."

Catherine stood with Madeleine in tow. She fought the nausea rising in her stomach; the overwhelming desire to be finished with this nightmare churned inside her. "I couldn't expect you to help me, James." She sat on the edge of the bed and soothed the child's tears.

Crossing to the desk, James hesitated, then ensconced himself in the captain's chair. Catherine watched him put his hand on the desktop, then in his lap, as if touching anything personally belonging to Danton was forbidden. He shifted positions on the cushion, obviously ill at ease with Madeleine's hysterics. Abruptly, he patted his shirt pocket. "Would the tyke like a piece o' peppermint candy?"

Madeleine raised her head from Catherine's breast. "Candy?" she sniffed.

"Aye, tyke." James brought out a half stick of solid white. "I have it 'round for seasickness—not that I'm ever bothered by fits o' the belly, mind you. Just in case anyone takes the plague."

Madeleine wiggled to be free. Tentatively, she walked to James. He held out the candy with his only arm, and she snatched the offering. *"M-Merci."* Her voice wavered from spent tears. She ran back to her mother and cuddled on her lap to eat her treat. "Where's your arm?"

"Madeleine," Catherine admonished.

"It's a'right, lady. I'd rather someone ask than stare and wonder."

"What's your name?" Madeleine asked, licking the peppermint.

"James Every. I'll not harm you."

"Will he, *Maman?*"

"He won't," Catherine reassured, her eyes trained on James.

La Furia had slowed considerably. With the stern windows thrown open, she could hear snatches of the crew's conversation on the upper deck. If she screamed, would her voice carry to the Spanish ship when they sailed near? The risk was worth the reward if someone would hear her. She could plead to be taken aboard the *flotas*.

She set Madeleine on the bed, got up and walked quickly to the stern.

James flew from the chair, reading her thoughts with precision. "Lady, don't do it. I know what you're thinkin'. I don't want to have to gag you. But I will. It's me life, and I value what's left of me years."

She whirled. "I have to make our presence known! He's keeping me against my will, James!"

He shook his head sadly. "I have to see to it you stay out o' trouble. I'll gag you, lady. I swear." Lowering his voice, he implored, "Don't make me. The lit'le one's been upset enough."

From above, a bell clanged. Then suddenly *La Furia* veered at a sharp angle.

The change in direction threw Catherine off balance and she stumbled into James. He caught her by the shoulder, butting her into his chest. With an awkward hold, he steadied her.

James threw his gaze heavenward, then brought his right hand to his side. "Blame me. He's turnin' the floggin' ship 'round."

"What does that mean? Is it a trap?"

"Nothin' o' the kind. Cap'n's runnin'!"

The winded stretch of sails and scurried footfall above gave Catherine cause to think James was telling the truth. She couldn't believe Danton would actually heed her appeal not to put Madeleine in harm. "Why is he doing this?"

"I can't figure." James went to the windows and looked out. "Only thing that makes sense is Cap'n doesn't want to fight with a woman and child aboard."

"I don't believe that," she said. "He doesn't listen to me. He's a thief, just like—" She stopped herself from saying Georges Claude's name for Madeleine's sake. "Like someone else I knew, only Danton Cristobal's worse. He kills people to get what he wants."

"Never for personal gain, lady, and only if he has to." James's thin defense didn't influence her opinion.

A thunderous shot detonated, and Madeleine clapped her

hands over her ears. Catherine dashed to comfort her. "I'm here. There's no need to worry."

"Fireworks, *Maman!*"

"Lor'! The *Manuela's* firin'—" James tripped on his implicating word. "It's shootin' fireworks, and we ain't even declared a bat—er, ain't even declared our intentions!"

A cannonball landed so close to the hull, water sprayed through the aftercastle windows. James bounced across the high bedstead and closed the leaded panes.

Rebounding, he shouted, "Behind the desk everyone!"

Catherine's heart leapt as she scooped Madeleine into her arms and raced for cover. "If I had known this was what he planned on doing, I never would have come," she declared softly, stating her feelings aloud.

Huddled in the tight space between hewn wall and desk, Catherine juggled Madeleine on her crossed legs. The girl's sticky fist held fast to her peppermint. Madeleine puckered her lips, her cheek full of the candy she'd taken a bite out of. "Is this another game, *Maman?*"

"If it is, *mon chou,* I find no amusement in it."

James tried to act gallant. "Now I'll tell you—"

Boom!

"—tell you," he ignored the blast, "how I lost me arm."

Madeleine nodded, as if in all the excitement, she'd forgotten he hadn't answered her.

"I was a cannon runner for Her Majesty's Royal Navy. The cap'n o' our ship—Nivel Spears—I still remember his name . . . I'll never forget it." His eyes grew distant, then clear. "Anyway, he was a sadistic bas—"

Catherine shook her head and frowned.

"—blighter." James shrugged his apology. "He kenneled us on the decks like hounds. Made to sleep with the bloomin' fog as our blankets. He'd punish the mates by makin' them swallow cockroaches and jammin' their mouths full o' hot iron bolts. They gagged on their blood—"

"Really," Catherine chided. "I don't think—"

Bang!

"*Mon Dieu,*" she softly pleaded.

James continued in a loud timbre. "Me life was hell, lady. A pit o' fire and damnation. I had to check the cannons, make sure they was loaded and the fuses long enough for the lighters. One day I was checkin' the wick and a flyin' spark lit her without me knowin'. Next thing happened, the cannon backfired and I got me arm blown off. Only thing saved me life was the cylinder. I was thrown into the hot metal. It burned me and cauterized—"

Boom!

"I'm sorry for your loss." Catherine's nerves were splitting like weak threads. "You spin a very colorful tale, but I can't hear of any more violence!"

"I ain't got no more violence to tell you."

"Did they have to put a bandage on your arm?" Madeleine asked, crunching the peppermint.

"What was left of it, aye. For near a month."

The groaning pitch and sway of the ship intruded upon the cabin. Catherine strained to hear the calls of those on deck, or the shouts of their pursuers. Nothing. The volley of shots died in a watery grave.

Madeleine finished her candy and wiped her fingers on her bodice. James brought his knees to his chest.

There was no need to talk. Catherine knew where they were going. She felt *La Furia* sailing a course northward. *North.* Not south, nor east or west. North to Isle of the Lost Souls. To *his* home. To *his* life of adventure and risk.

He'd won. How could she bear the sight of him without breaking down and begging him to let her go?

Catherine's misery was so acute, it bordered on physical pain. Her energies had been wasted. She felt bereft, and grieved for the freedom he'd snatched from her.

Defeated, she bowed her head. She wasn't up to coping with any more upsets.

"Look, *Maman.*"

Catherine raised her chin.

"Look at me." Madeleine pulled the cuff of her sleeve over her wrist and fingers. "I don't have a hand! A cannon shot it off."

Danton let two days pass since his aborted mission to plunder the *Manuela.* Forty-eight hours, and he hadn't seen Catherine except when she'd disembarked *La Furia* under the escort of James Every. He hadn't wanted to talk to her, afraid he might strangle her for her foolish daring. Even now he felt the constraints of his anger as he recalled the insubordinate look she'd given him on the beach when he'd stopped her.

"From now on," he'd advised, "there will be a guard posted at the cottage whenever one of my ships leave the island, so this stupid incident will not be repeated."

"If you'd told me what you intended on doing, I never would have hidden on your ship." She eyed him critically. "You deceived me, and because of that I put Madeleine in danger. I cannot forgive myself—or you. Please don't make me turn to such measures again," she said. "Surely there must be a way off this isle you haven't thought of."

He should have throttled her, and recognized his strong discipline in not doing so; instead, despite the temper she'd put him in, he couldn't keep from studying her. She exuded loveliness, not only through her physical attributes, but through her maternal devotion to her child. Such a steadfast constancy gained his respect, and for that reason alone he denied her.

"No, Catherine," he flatly refused. "Today you witnessed how hostile the sea can be. Just as you cannot forgive yourself for putting your daughter in jeopardy, I cannot live with a decision that would bring you harm. You will have to leave the matter to my judgment."

Unshed tears glimmered in her eyes, and her voice broke with deep emotion. "You will not," she spoke each word slowly and clearly as if they pained her, "control me."

"Au contraire, chérie." With an indifference that had taken years to build, he closed himself off to her desperate appeal and thought only of her welfare. "If ever a woman tested *my* control, Catherine, it is you."

She hadn't demanded to see him since, and he could only speculate she'd been busy plotting a way to launch him into eternity. By all accounts, he should be thinking of the same destination for her.

She'd ruined his attack. She'd lost him a horde of Spanish riches and sent his sails awry. Never before had he fled from an opposing ship, but because of Catherine's plea to keep her daughter safe, he'd done the unthinkable.

He'd turned the rudder to keep them both out of harm's way.

Jesu, had he lost his mind? Or was she driving him insane?

With a short sigh, Danton willed his thoughts to change direction, not wanting to analyze his decision or mental soundness. Open to the cooling breezes, he stood underneath the conical patio off his bedchamber. He gazed at the dusk-darkening inlet below. Remnants of sun harpooned the clouds, highlighting the coral-encrusted shallows. He brought a cobalt glass of flip to his lips and rolled the sweetened spiced rum over his tongue.

How well he knew those jagged reefs. They haunted his dreams.

Four and a half years ago his only hope had been to brave them with his naval crew and swim for the safety of the shores the coral protected.

His hands and feet cut and bleeding, the broad sunlight burning his face, he'd awakened to this other life. He hadn't known what impact their marooning would have on him until a year later. He and his men had beaten their stony adversary. After a month, they were rescued by a band of pirates who'd recently lost their captain. Disorganized and searching for a new leader, the freebooters agreed to take Danton and his men to Madagascar without harm. From there they gained the help of a Spanish galleon and sailed into Spain to report to King Philip that his fortune had been lost. Stolen by a mad Turk named Yousef Ahmed Sadi Ahram.

There had been no leniency from King Philip for Danton. The majority of the goods pilfered could have been replaced. What could not were thirteen diamonds hallmarked for their unique colors and considerable carats.

The largest was pear-shaped; sixteen carats of flawless clarity full of fire and brilliance worth a hundred fortunes. The remaining stones had been of varying cuts and carats from ten to twelve—all distinguishable by their color: five red, bursting with rosy sparkle; four near colorless canary; and three blue, containing bundles of inclusions that made the stones look like cat's eyes. The loss of the gems had sent Philip into a madman's frenzy. For their unplanned part,

Danton's men had been flogged, fined, and expelled from the navy.

Danton had been stripped of his title, Marquis de Seville. His holdings had been confiscated, his wife and son cast into the streets to bear his shame publicly.

Agony ripped through him, carrying the burden of his outrage as he remembered the past.

Anger and torment had become his sovereign.

The once-heralded Captain Danton Luis Cristobal had then been awarded his final medal: iron shackles.

An involuntary shudder claimed Danton when he thought of the prison's dark and clammy hole. Lice crunched underfoot like shells on a garden path. The stench and odor of prison damp had crept into his skin, and no amount of washing could rid him of the smell for months afterward.

He'd served part of his sentence before Queen Elizabeth, who'd been rumored to have taken over Philip's duties due to his melancholia from the death of his first wife, decided to overrule her husband and have Danton banished from Spain for ten years to pay for his crimes. But not before the Angel of Death had its day of revenge. The mercy shown himself and his crew turned to poison. He'd been helpless to save his wife and son from poverty's cold fingers.

The price he'd paid to live had scarred him. Constant reminders that choices were permanent.

Death was permanent.

He'd served four years of his exile, with six years remaining. Even after his sentence ended, he would not return to his homeland. Spain no longer meant anything to him. He'd become a renegade without a country. He sailed in search of Sadi, the man who'd been at the helm of his fall from grace.

And when he found the Turk, he meant to kill him.

Walking to the edge of the paving stones, Danton gazed far into the sea's horizon. His eyes traveled the length of the black beach. A lone fisherman poled homeward, easily balanced in his canoe. Danton took in the forests of ebony and rosewood clothing the distant hills. He breathed the heavy air scented with ylang-ylang and lemon grass.

All this was his.

His island. His castle. His people.

No longer a marquis, he'd taken the throne of King.

Rainiaro had once told him, that every man had to go through hell to reach his paradise. Such was the case, he'd given his due.

By choice, he'd isolated himself from every facet of his former self. He wanted no woman to confuse his priorities, no child to breathe nurturing spirit into him. He'd had his chance, and lost his bid for happiness. He was destined to be alone, never again to revel in the loving embrace of a wife or cherish the eager dimples of a son.

Why, then, had he begun to question his fate?

From the moment he'd taken Catherine and Madeleine LeClerc's welfare into his own hands, he'd plunged into dangerous waters. As their days on his island continued, he grew preoccupied by their presence. They triggered memories of his family in ways that differed from mourning. He found his current life sorely lacking warmth and love.

His thoughts of Catherine went beyond her soft beauty and his fantasies of touching her hair . . . kissing her. She had a confidence that drew him to her in ways he'd not been pulled in many years. He'd begun to doubt the permanence of his being alone, and that he'd never find a woman who could fill the vacancy Elena had left in his life.

And as for Catherine's daughter . . .

Long suppressed desires of parenthood surfaced when he was in Madeleine's company—which he'd avoided unless the girl came upon him unawares. The day on the beach when she'd been playing in the sand had left him so unsettled, he hadn't recognized himself.

She was only a child . . . a beautiful child whose simple talk fractured his complex heart.

He needed to disentangle himself from Catherine and Madeleine before his resolve weakened and he forfeited his private war.

Albeit Catherine proved herself a worthy opponent in their battle of wills.

She set his temper on fire. She tested him, pushed him and drove him to the limits of his self-control. To his thorough annoyance, it was her temerity that drew him to her. She stood up for what she believed in, and that demanded great courage.

Danton smiled wryly.

He'd been wrong about Catherine LeClerc. She didn't need his protection. She was as strong as the fabric that clothed her. Mended in more places than not, but still holding together.

In as much as he could define her attributes, she was also a puzzlement to him.

This morning he'd found an ink drawing on his doorstep beneath a rock. He'd lifted the parchment to study the picture clearly executed by Madeleine. She'd sketched her impression of a girl—a long-maned, oval figure with big slippered feet standing next to a blob of black ink. Written below in neatly penned French was: *Happy Birthday Madeleine*. After a minute's examination, Danton assessed the splotch to be a tart of some kind with three candles.

Did Catherine intentionally set out to run him through with her knife of guilt by leaving her daughter's picture of a party? Did she mean to woo him to feel sorry for a child destined to have her birthday in the company of brigands?

He should desert his principles entirely, deposit Catherine LeClerc in any port and leave her to chance. Not an hour ago he'd discarded five more harbors because of insufficient information or because quays were too tight to make hasty retreats from. He should sail her back to Madagascar and let her independence see her all the way to France. He—

A woman's scream rendered the night's stillness.

Swift to react, Danton threw his glass goblet onto the pavers and bolted down the hillside.

The cry had come from the span of beach below, obstructed by thick palmetto and ferns. Leaves slapped at his cheeks as he brushed through the thorny vines of berries. He felt the pricks of scratches on his forearms where his sleeves had been pushed back.

Throaty and desperate, the scream came again. Danton sensed the woman in peril was not a Malagasy. No. This tone he knew. The pitch had bristled him often enough. Who on Isle of the Lost Souls *dared* harm her? He'd thought he knew his men; he trusted them not to be forceful in their sexual appetites.

Panic came to him in a hot rush and his mind burned with tumultuous images. He felt suffocated by the memory of his past, as if he were racing down failure's path once again. His heart thumped madly as he dodged a pollarded tree, hopping over its dense head of new growth. He swore that whoever was causing her distress would pay. Dearly.

Jumping onto the sand, he ran a short stretch before catching sight of her. Standing alone, she made no move, no effort to flee from whatever demon had accosted her. Tiny pieces of driftwood and dry branches lay scattered around her.

Danton neared and had gotten no more than ten paces when, shaking, she pointed into the brush. He came to an abrupt stop, his heart jumping in his chest. Deep-seated habit made him reach for the cutlass at his hip. The brass guard protecting his hand, he stalked his unknown prey in the overgrowth.

Shifakh! Shifakh! came the animal sounds.

Several pairs of glowing eyes blinked from the shrubs. Looking like monkeys, but with faces resembling bears, three lemurs descended on Danton in leaps.

Graceful in the air and awkward on the ground, they fell over themselves. Pousse-Pousse circled his leg, her creamcolored tail curling up his thigh; Razana, chocolate cap of hair on his head shimmering, noisily chattered; and Dokobe clambered up Danton's calf, midriff, and back to take a place on his shoulder.

The blameworthy creatures competed for his attention as he faced Catherine. "Is this what you were afraid of? Ferocious beasts of the jungle?" He couldn't quell his chuckle of amusement.

Fright clearly shone in her eyes. "They attacked me!" she insisted. "They nipped at my hands and tried to climb up my skirts!"

"Rascals." Danton sparked his words with mild reproach. "I've taught them to go *under* skirts—all but Pousse-Pousse, who's a female, and I couldn't expect her to be interested in that."

"Make all the jokes you want, monsieur, but not at my expense." Her voice wavered between fear and anger. "What are they? A type of monkey-cat?"

Danton stroked his fingertips through Dokobe's tan fur. "These miscreants are called lemurs."

"Lemurs? You've been calling me a wild lemur. I don't resemble one of these in the least."

Peering into Pousse-Pousse's face with her black nose and brown ear markings, Danton couldn't resist smiling. "No, but you did bite me."

"Out of self-defense! Let me assure you, I'm not in the habit of such attacks," she said. "Shouldn't they be in the jungle?"

"Their parents were killed by a fossa, and they would have died if I hadn't taken them out of the *tsingy* forest. They're my pets. They must have thought you brought them food."

"All I have to offer is troubled solitude."

He put her sarcasm aside and mockingly tipped his wrist before sheathing his sword. "Good form, *chérie*. Or shall I say, *touché?*"

"En garde would be more appropriate, since our conversations are plagued with strife."

"Ah, Catherine." He sighed her name while walking toward her, appreciating the soft curve of her cheek and wanting to rest his palm against her warm skin. "Has someone been teaching you to fence?"

"You, monsieur." Her defiant stance didn't falter as he approached. "Your tongue is sharper than any sword."

His laughter was dry. "Full of wit you are tonight."

The beams of a rising moon bathed Catherine in silver light. She'd left her thick hair unplaited, and the wind gently ruffled the pale curls. He gave her clothing—simple and clean—little regard, while the figure beneath earned his undivided attention. She had fine hips, a narrow waist, and breasts rounding out to the right proportions. Her smooth skin matched the shade of pale oak; elegant and just as rich.

Madre de Dios . . . she looked ethereal in the dim light.

He'd been so caught up in ridding himself of her, he'd ignored the jewel that had fallen into his lap. He hadn't counted on Catherine to carry the allure of an emerald he yearned to have.

She frowned at his lengthy perusal.

"What were you doing on my beach?" He spoke with cool authority, tamping the rush of heat to his loins.

72

"Walking." Her voice betrayed her; he detected nervousness.

"Walking?" He plucked Dokobe from his shoulder to cradle the lemur in his arms and scratch its belly. "What are the twigs for?"

"Madeleine," she replied quickly, without looking at the branches strewn on the beach. "Madeleine likes to pretend they're swords."

"Swordplay."

"She's very impressionable, Monsieur Cristobal. I fear she's already been taken in by your men. Rainiaro's teaching her to tie ropes. Antonio and Eduardo give her rides upon their shoulders. And James allows her to mimic his loss of an arm." She knit her fingers together, a mannerism he was coming to recognize as a sign of preparing her thoughts. "I needed a walk to sort out my dilemma. The only thing peaceful about your island is this ocean, and now even that small tranquility has been taken from me."

Danton slid his gaze downward to the glittering drops of water on her bare feet and calves. She'd put a knot in the hem of her dress to keep the fabric from getting wet while she strolled in the sea foam. Always so starched and in control, the image of her abandoning her propriety quickened his pulse. His blood raced like quicksilver through him, discomfiting his rock-solid willpower.

"Have you eaten a banana?" He masked his inner turmoil with deceptive calm, dissuading himself from thinking of her as anything but an encumbrance.

She shook her head.

"A stalk of bamboo?"

Clearly nonplussed, she rebuked, "Why would I eat bamboo?"

"To save your life if need be. They're high in water."

"I shall remember that, monsieur. As for a banana, *non,* I did not eat one with my supper."

"Coconut?"

"No."

"They must have smelled food of some kind on you. Flower blossoms?" Danton bent to massage Razana's head.

"They've not been on the menu," she countered.

"Then you must be wearing a very appetizing fragrance." Just as wary of his emotions around this female as his lemurs, Danton held back rather than try to discern whether she'd perfumed herself. "Your scream confused them and sent them running for cover."

"And you to my rescue." Catherine's smile did not indicate gratitude. "But who will save me from *you?*"

Danton let his gaze linger on her and speculated that very problem. She didn't miss his obvious inspection and lifted her chin a notch. Her passionate challenge was hard to resist, and he lazily appraised the soft rise and fall of her breasts as she fought to contain her outrage. He felt himself grow heavy and warm, aware that if he'd had a moment's doubt about one of his crew ravishing her, that doubt came back to him two times over. He wasn't a man to rape, but he did desire her. He couldn't deny it. Rather than try, he fairly snorted, "Just before you interrupted my evening, I'd been thinking I *should* abandon you to your own resources. However, *chérie,* if you cannot confront a lemur one-third your size, it is doubtful you could manage the animals in Tamatave."

"How I manage my affairs shouldn't have to be your concern."

"Dokobe, down." The lemur crawled across the length of Danton's arm and did a belly flop into the sand. "I'm afraid you are wrong, Catherine. What happens on Isle of the Lost Souls," he nudged the lemur pushing on his knee, "Pousse-Pousse, go sit—is my concern. I am the law here." Danton bent and shucked one boot and stocking free. "Razana, wait with your companions. Stay."

The three lemurs sat on their haunches, tails raised and hands poised together as if begging.

Balancing himself on one leg, Danton slipped his left foot from his remaining boot.

Eyeing him with distrust, Catherine inclined her head. "What are you doing?"

He went for the nearest coconut tree. Grabbing hold with hands and feet, he scaled the gray trunk. "I'm going to rid myself of a nuisance."

"Shall I be lucky enough to consider I'm the source?" she called up to him.

"Jesu, woman, you are full of raillery tonight. What *did* you have for your meal? Perhaps you've unknowingly imbibed the pages of Molière." Glancing down, his gaze fell on her. She watched him, prolonging the moment and trapping him midway to his goal. He sensed they shared the same chaos over their entrancement, and from the tilt of her head, maybe a hint of fascination as well. Was it possible she saw something good in him?

He quickly rejected the notion. The devil hang, a mutual attraction would be hazardous for both of them. She wouldn't stay with him any more than he wanted her to.

Shaking free of their eye contact, Danton climbed up a frond's mid-rib to reach the coconuts. He nearly laughed aloud. There was nothing redeeming about him at all; she must have imagined a flicker of warm light in his heart, for surely his lamp had grown cold and died long ago. He wielded his cutlass and slashed off a cluster of the nuts. They landed on the beach, one-two-three, with muffled thuds.

Pousse-Pousse, Razana and Dokobe assailed the fruits with delight, their tails twitching.

Danton fixed his weapon and made an effortless decline. Nearing the trunk's base, he sprang into the air, much as his lemurs, and landed in front of Catherine. She took a quick hop backward.

She stared at him long enough for the surf to run upon the shore. Her extended silence made him think she wanted to say something but didn't dare, which was strange for her since she always spoke her mind.

He arched his brows upward, wordlessly urging her to utter whatever she wanted. His hide had the strength of leather; he could survive her verbal stabs.

Taking his cue, she spoke up. "You've an affinity with heights, do you not, Monsieur Cristobal?"

The absurdity of her question unbalanced him. He'd expected her to rail for her freedom, to call him a pig or better. Instead, her evaluation of his person had been a petty observation.

Danton leaned toward her, finding satisfaction in the way her eyes widened with caution. This close, she did smell like flowers, but not a scent he could name. "How came you by this conclusion?"

Her pearly teeth caught her lower lip. "You place yourself precariously on top of the world. You've this fixation to be high, whether the source be the mast of your ship or a coconut tree." Swallowing, she added, "From the looks of you, I'd say you should be more careful."

Unaware until now, Danton noticed the thin lines of dried blood on his arms. "These, *linda,* are products of my perilous journey to rescue you from savages." He felt the razor-fine cuts on his jaw and cheekbones. "I broke a very valuable cobalt goblet on my way."

"You cannot blame me for the damage," she said. "And you've not answered my question."

"The ludicrous one about heights?"

She nodded.

"The reason I climbed the coconut tree should be quite apparent—to feed my lemurs." He indulged her with an answer that he thought ridiculous to even expound upon. "And the motivation for my climbing the shroud of my rigger is to look for enemies. I'd much rather sink them than have them sink me, so my being there has its advantages. Anything else you'd like to know?"

"Yes."

The way her swift response came to him, Danton immediately regretted his invitation. He didn't want to hear what other quirks of his she'd picked up on.

Catherine plunged ahead without any reservation. "Why is the bed on your ship backward? Why do you call your island such a sorrowful name? How did your parents meet? And who is this Turk you intend to kill?"

He felt a muscle pulling at the corner of his mouth. Frowning, he refused to let her know her interrogation rubbed him the wrong way. He'd been fine until she mentioned Sadi. He hid his discomfort well, focusing instead on the fight he'd provoke with Rainiaro for talking too much. "That's all you want to know?"

"For now."

"My bed faces the sea to remind me where I've been. My island was named for the men's spirits that died here. My father was a captain in the Spanish Royal Navy and met my mother while in port at Marseilles; he died in a coaching accident when I was ten, and my mother passed on of natural causes at a young age. And the Turk robbed me of something very precious and I intend to make him suffer." He set his hands on his hips. "That's all you'll hear from me on that subject."

Her expression softened. "I didn't think you'd answer me."

"I can be very amiable, *chérie*. Only if there's a reason do I lose my temper. And thus far, Catherine, you've given me probable cause in all instances. You argue, you goad, you oppose. What kind of man was LeClerc that he could not tame you?"

She flinched, her eyes showing the hurt he'd inflicted. He damned his thoughtlessness as her lashes shadowed her cheekbones. She gazed at hands once again folded at her waist. "Now you are who I've come to expect. Heartless and cruel."

He felt every bit the bastard. He'd trampled on her when she hadn't pushed him. It had been himself he'd wanted to push away. He didn't want her tame; he liked the rebellion in her. That was what attracted him to her, and it scared him. In many ways she was too much like him. She was the first woman since Elena that he'd wanted to know more about than her name and how she'd feel beneath him. There was more to Catherine than that; more than what a physical release would give him. Right now, he couldn't deal with that type of complication.

Danton tried to apologize—a formality that didn't come easily for him. "Catherine—"

"Non. You answered me. It's only fair you have your turn." She bravely met his gaze, her shoulders squared and proud. "My husband was a thief, monsieur. Just as you are. He stole from the natives of Africa and India and sold their sacred treasures in the black markets. He profited from nations, stealing government-owned antiquities. I have seen enough greed to last me a lifetime. I don't want to see yours."

His jaw tightened; he wasn't as immune as he'd thought. "You are mistaken about me. I'm not a greedy man."

"Monsieur Cristobal, the colors of your flag are quite clear."

"There is more to me than a flag." Suddenly he needed to

prove to himself, to Catherine, that he wasn't completely dead inside. He was still human. He felt, he grieved, he had the power to love if he allowed himself. "I can be gentle, *chérie,*" Danton murmured. "Let me show you."

He slipped his fingers around her waist and pulled her to him. His hands reached up into the unbound hair at her nape and he crushed the lustrous curls in his fingers. The lush tresses felt soft as the finest velvet.

Even in the vague darkness, he saw her cheeks flushed with panic. "What are you doing?"

Bringing his face closer, he whispered, "I'm going to kiss you."

Chapter

6

I don't want you to." But Catherine had no chance to withdraw. Danton's lips covered her protest, drowning her plea. Shocked into submission, she pressed her fists against the silk fabric covering his chest.

His kiss sent pools of warm waves rippling through her. The softness of his mouth defied the cold and hard man he presented to the world. Her heart hammered foolishly as his arms held her prisoner. He stroked the sensitive base of her neck, sending tingles of pleasure down her spine. She knew she should break free, and yet . . .

He drugged her senses, and Catherine fought the desire to be close to him. But his invitation claimed her with a fiery sweetness, and she found him difficult to resist. His kiss felt like sunshine and burned brightly within her. It would have been so much better to stay entwined in battle with him, rather than entwined in arms. She couldn't fight him. She had no experience defending herself against this sort of assault—a thorough ravaging of her sensual spirit.

When he kissed her, all her resolve crumbled. Her legs weakened. Her heartbeat echoed in her ears. The strength of Danton's pulse tattooed beneath her fingertips.

His tongue coaxed her lips apart, gently gliding over her teeth. She jolted, but his hands cradled the back of her head to keep her still. He ran the tip of his tongue over the fullness of her lower lip, then teased the inside of her mouth again. Over and over he repeated his erotic dance, until the heady sensations left her mindless.

Unwittingly her fingers relaxed and curled into the billowing drape of his shirtfront. She let him steal her very breath.

Catherine's thoughts spun and she would have fallen were it not for the firm hold he had on her. She trembled. She shivered.

She lost her rationality.

Inching her arms upward, she wound them around Danton's neck. The cords of his shoulders were harder than granite, stronger than any rope. Since she'd first seen him, she'd been intrigued by his reckless air, his glossy hair, his earring.

Now she discovered him. She edged her fingers into the lengthy strands of ebony, appreciating the silky texture. She touched the gold cross dangling from his earlobe, feeling the soft skin where the stud pierced flesh.

She forgot who he was and what he stood for. She might hate herself for her weakness, but she'd gone beyond logic.

Danton's lips brushed hers as he spoke, his tone roughened with huskiness. "Why did you leave your daughter's drawing at my door?"

His jarring question was slow to register through her dizzy haze. Thinking coherently while his hips pressed hers was not easy. "I didn't."

She couldn't figure out why he suddenly dragged his mouth away and stared at her with eyes darker than the night. Slight hesitation calmed his features, as if he believed her. But as the brittle silence gathered force between them, his apparent suspicions won. His gaze flashed dubious lightning. "Don't deny what you did, *chérie*. You gained the desired effect from me. I felt sorry she would spend her birthday here."

"Birthday?" The word drowned Catherine's thudding heart. *What was he talking about?* Her erratic breathing began to subside. Reality set in. She gazed at the man whose arms supported her, whose legs merged with hers. With a wretched moan she realized the truth. A truth that should have relieved her, but did not.

They were strangers again.

"Oui," he challenged, his embrace leaving her chilled. "In your own writing you penned: 'Happy Birthday Madeleine.'"

"I did," she returned, wrenching free of him and taking a step backward. "I did write Happy Birthday. She's always asking me to spell things out, but I assure you, I did not leave the picture for you. If you found it, it was only because Madeleine wanted you to have her drawing."

Danton cursed in Spanish, then said, *"Pourquoi?"* Why?

"She likes you. She wants a party, monsieur." She punctuated the formal address with animosity. He'd thrown their kiss into an obscure shadow, acting as if the intimacy between them had never happened. She hated him for that; she hated herself even more for feeling rejected. "I promised her she would have one on *De Gids,* and we both know that's not possible anymore."

"Unpromise her."

She would have liked to hit him for that remark; to punch him in the belly, to kick his shin, to blacken his eyes. She was not a violent woman by any means, but he brought out the worst in her. He was such a presumptuous blackguard. He had no idea what it was like to have a child. To be the only one left to care for, to promise, to make a little girl's fancy come true. She had only herself to fall back on, and she'd already reneged on one party due to circumstances beyond her control; she'd not fail Madeleine again. "I will not," she said evenly. "Five days hence, no matter where we are, my daughter and I will celebrate her fourth birthday. I don't care if there is not a single attendant. I don't care if you like it or not. I don't care if we are adrift on a sinking raft in the Indian Ocean. She is a child. An innocent. Remember that when you are making her suffer."

Danton's wind-bronzed face darkened. Catherine thought he'd strike her. Truly, she cringed over his retribution. She took two quick steps away from him, snapping one of her twigs underfoot.

"Suffer?" His voice remained surprisingly calm; placid. Dangerously composed. "You have no idea the meaning of the word. Your daughter does not suffer here. She plays upon the beach, digging for buried treasure. She draws. She sings. She talks to herself. She enlightens me with her childish way of thinking."

"Then let her go!" Catherine caught herself imploring him again, and she didn't care. "Let us both go before—"

"Before you try something idiotic again?"

Catherine grimaced. Thus far he'd not mentioned a single aspect of her attempted escape, and now she was afraid she'd baited his wrath. She would not cower; she would not falter under the accusatory glare he gave her. "I did what I thought best. How was I to know you were going out raiding?"

"You should have stayed put like I told you." Danton tossed one unruly length of long hair over his shoulder. "You're running, Catherine LeClerc, and I don't think it's to France. You're running from your dead husband."

"You know nothing—"

"I know enough. You don't talk about him unless provoked. That doesn't sound to me as if you loved the man."

"How dare you!" she gasped.

"I dare because I'm right." His arrogance would have put a shine to dull brass. "You keep your most deplorable memories stored behind a mental lock and key—as do I. You may think you can control the past, keep the demons safely tucked away, but you cannot." His expression grew distant and sad. "Your mind's eye will unlock itself and give you a glimpse of what you're running from. You cannot hide from your past, *chérie.* Believe me, I've tried. And each time I have, I've died a little. I die a little each day."

The tone in which he spoke raised the hairs on her nape. How could he have guessed her memories of Georges Claude made her tremble? She'd dreaded the dense jungles of India, the wild animals of Africa, the bloodthirsty men her husband had dealt with, and the government officials who had always been a day behind Georges Claude. She'd wanted to run from the adventure, the daring, the endless days in hiding with her baby. But her pleas had fallen on deaf ears.

Without the risk, Georges Claude said, he was nothing. Many times since her husband's death she'd awaken from a cold, dewy sleep, thinking she'd never get home. The dreams served to strengthen her resolve, and returning to Paris had become an obsession. In France she would be at peace.

She had to break free of Danton Cristobal. If she stayed here, she was in danger of succumbing to him. Tonight had proved just how much trouble she really was in. She'd been swept away as sure as the tide. She needed to be on safer ground.

The incessant buzz of nocturnal insects brought her to the present. She licked her dry lips. "I have to go. I've left Madeleine far too long. If she wakes and I'm not there, she'll cry."

Catherine turned without a backward look and headed for the embankment.

"Catherine," Danton's voice chased her, "you may run from the devil himself if you so choose. But don't run from yourself. Accept your fate."

She kept walking, scattered leaves evening-cool under her bare feet. She didn't understand what he meant.

She didn't want to.

Madeleine squealed with delight, letting the foamy wavelets chase her up the barren beach. The noon sun browned her smooth skin, putting rosy color on her cheeks and the bridge of her button nose. A pink ribbon kept her hair out of her eyes, the strands at her forehead bleached blond. She wore her shift and nothing more, the wet cotton turned sheer.

She ran toward the edge of the ocean's wet sand again, laid down on her tummy and waited for the waves to strike her. She laughed as the sea splashed over her legs to spray her bottom.

"Maman! I'm pretending I'm a turtle!"

Catherine looked up from her pile of dry wood and smiled. "That's very good, *mon chou.* You're a wonderful turtle. Don't go in the water. Stay on the sand."

"Oui, Maman."

Catherine went back to arranging driftwood, glad the water occupied Madeleine. She didn't want her daughter asking questions. How could she explain the guilt tugging at her? She knew going against Danton's wishes was wrong, but getting involved with him would be more of a mistake.

A week ago Catherine had established this spot as their point of rescue. The evening the lemurs had startled her, she'd been collecting twigs and had been afraid Danton would press her for a detailed explanation; but he'd seemed appeased with her evasive answer. Every day she'd gather timbers along the walk here, tie them with strips of sheeting, and add them to her mound. She'd only missed one day—the day Rainiaro apparently sailed somewhere in the recently repaired *Negro España,* for there had been the promised guard posted at her door and she hadn't been able to go outside.

But now she had enough to make a hearty bonfire when the necessary moment came. She would light her signal fire when a ship neared the island. Of course there was the problem of getting to this spot and seeing the ship before it passed by. She'd hoped to gain access to Danton's spyglass.

That could prove to be a problem, and she'd been trying to think up a solution all morning. Short of stealing, she hadn't contrived an easy answer. To borrow the spyglass without Danton's knowing would be wisest. All she would have to do was sneak into his home. A dangerous feat with his watchdogs Antonio and Eduardo, but necessary. Then she would be ready. Even if she didn't know exactly the right way to set the fire, the smoke alone would be white flag enough.

At last they would be free.

They would be saved.

"Now I'm a fish, *Maman!*"

"Hmm." Catherine glanced at her daughter, who frolicked near the shallows. "Remember, don't go in, *mon chou.*"

"I won't."

The ocean looked inviting. The motionless air left little relief, and sweat dampened Catherine's brow. No doubt her face was smudged like her arms. Although the water looked cool, she had no time to douse herself. Frolicking was out of the question for her.

Catherine had assembled her pieces of twigs and dried

timbers on the easternmost shores of Isle of the Lost Souls. The arid beach was predominantly white and gray, with little green, bordered from behind by hundred-foot limestone peaks. Red water flowed from a river's mouth. Catherine couldn't find where the source came from at this distance. Maybe from a hidden crevice. The crimson water unnerved her. It was as if the island poured its lifeblood into the sea from some deep laceration.

The towering spikes behind her were called *tsingy*, that much she knew. Rainiaro had told her, mentioning this span of the island in polite conversation—one she'd manipulated. She felt bad about tricking him, gleaning information that in the end would deliver her; but she'd had no other route to take. She'd needed to know of a place that no one visited, a place that couldn't be stumbled on by Danton or one of the islanders.

This parched portion of the isle was perfect. Secluded. Untouched. The walk hadn't been too tiring, just under an hour from her cottage. Madeleine had enjoyed spotting the tiny chameleons and tortoises with diamonds of yellow and black on their backs, which slowly trekked over the sand. Thorn-studded trees reminding Catherine of cactus grew in the hard, orange clay. Water-gorged baobab rose in vertical splendor, looking like upside-down trees, their roots where branches should have been.

A heron flew overhead, then disappeared into the brown brambles. Even plain and dull, this part of Danton's island held a special appeal. A beautifully unique place unlike any she'd ever seen.

Checking on Madeleine with a quick glance, Catherine saw her daughter at a safe distance from the water, digging in the sand with her hands.

Satisfied she'd done the best that she could with her signal of distress, Catherine stood back, hands on her waist. The pile of wood didn't seem high as it should be—about six feet in circumference and two feet tall. She wondered if this would be enough. Shrugging, she accepted the mound as ready and decided to add more to it while she counted off the days.

"Madeleine, let me help you rinse and dry off. We must get back before we're missed."

"Who would miss us?" Dripping and coated with sand from head to toe, Madeleine skipped to her mother.

"Your friends, *naturellement.*" Catherine smoothly marched Madeleine back toward the water and made her stand ankle deep to splash away the dirt.

"I miss Hadi." Madeleine didn't do a very good job rinsing. She bent her knees to look for shells.

"Me too." Trying not to get her shoes wet, Catherine finished the job as best she could and collected Madeleine's dress, shoes, and stockings. They began the lengthy walk to the cottage. "But you have other friends now. Rainiaro, James, Antonio and Eduardo."

"And Monsieur Pirate," Madeleine added soberly. "He's my friend."

"Yes, he is," Catherine agreed. It would have been unfair of her to discredit Danton in her daughter's eyes.

"When we leave here, I won't have any friends again." Madeleine kicked up the dusty trail with her bare and now muddy toes as water dribbled off her undergarment's hem. "Will there be friends for me in Paris, France, *Maman?* Every time I make friends, you make us go away."

An abrupt invasion of reprehension descended heavily on Catherine's shoulders. She hadn't realized how much Madeleine had come to accept the pirates as her playmates. The idea wasn't right. A child Madeleine's age should have children to play with; a brother or sister. Her stomach fluttered. The notion came without preamble, and Catherine felt the emptiness in her womb. For her there would be no more babies.

"There will be friends in Paris for you."

"But not my *grandpère* and my *grandmère* and my *oncles* you told me about." Madeleine plucked a waxy leaf off a bush and squeezed the moisture out.

"Non. They're with *Papa.*"

"Why does everybody have to be with *Papa* and Jesus?"

Catherine's heart cried. "I'm not, *mon chou.* I'll always be with you."

Dropping her keepsake, Madeleine smiled and grasped Catherine's hand. "I like you, *Maman.*"

"I like you too."

They returned to the old cook's house unnoticed, since

today they hadn't had a guard on their doorstep. Other than the stalwart pirate who made sure Catherine didn't leave the cottage on sporadic days—days when a ship left Isle of the Lost Souls—both she and Madeleine had been ignored by the islanders. Even ignored by Danton.

Since the night he'd saved her from his lemurs, he hadn't sought her out. Which was for the best. She couldn't afford any romantic delusions. Surely her preoccupation with Danton was nothing more than curiosity. She'd never kissed a marauding rover of the seas before.

Actually, she'd never kissed any man on the mouth besides Georges Claude.

Danton's kiss had been far different from her husband's. Georges Claude had a set routine when lovemaking entered into the night, and he'd made sure she learned his system. First a chaste kiss, second a moment's fondle, and third her nightgown raised. Their sessions of marital coupling had all been the same. An obligation and a duty without complacency.

Nothing less was accepted from her and nothing more was given from him.

In her brief liaison with Danton, she'd discovered she knew nothing at all. He had been unpredictable, uninhibited, and quite expert in what he was doing, without making her feel lacking or inexperienced. How could she use the methodical system she'd known, when her very bones were melting from the heat? That he'd been able to inflame her with a mere kiss was frightening. And thrilling.

Yes, it was just as well she hadn't seen him since.

She planned on spending the remainder of the day with her daughter in quiet play. Then this evening she would unveil her surprise for Madeleine.

That decided, she undressed Madeleine, wiped her off and buttoned her in a fresh dress. She plaited her damp hair into a braid that hung between her shoulder blades, then tied a ribbon on the end. Catherine removed her own soiled clothing, washed up, and slipped on the rose cambric dress she considered to be her best.

Catherine was brushing her hair when a knock intruded upon the room and Madeleine ran to open the door.

"*Bonjour*, Monsieur Pirate!"

Catherine's spirits sank.

"Bonjour, Mademoiselle LeClerc. How are you today?" His deep voice took hold of the tiny space, humming through Catherine and sapping her will. Why couldn't the pitch of his speech have been high and nasally instead of velvet-timbred?

"I went swimming at the beach where *Maman—*"

Blinking, Catherine reacted quickly. "Madeleine, why don't you let Monsieur Cristobal in?" That was not exactly what she wanted, but the invitation prevented Madeleine from saying more.

Madeleine stood aside. Danton remained in the doorway, dwarfing the opening with his inordinate height. His hair dipped over his brow and across his shoulders as he looked down at Madeleine. A white shirt draped his muscular torso, while tan breeches molded the narrow and muscular outline of his hips and thighs. Her perusal lingered indecently, then she jerked her stare away, only to meet his frown of refusal. "I can't," he said.

Madeleine sulked. "Why not?"

"I have someplace important to go. I want you to come with me." He caught hold of Catherine with his eyes, his gaze hotly skimming her mouth as his lips had the other night. The expression on his chiseled face spoke more distinctly than words. He was reliving their kiss. She felt herself blush, and loathed herself for doing so. At least when he finally did say something, his cool authority broke a little. "Your mother can come too."

Madeleine twirled around, the tail of her braid swishing across the side of her neck. "Can we go with him, *Maman?"*

Discord welled in Catherine. Danton's presence made it difficult for her to think. She searched her mind for the right words to deny him, but all that came out was, "Not today."

Danton drew himself together quite nicely, standing straight and tall. Very tall. Very handsome. "For once, Catherine," his long fingers drummed on the door molding, "be reasonable. Say yes."

His mandate piqued her. She was on the verge of telling him she was always reasonable, or at least tried to be, but one look at Madeleine's expectant smile and she decided to quash her debate. The prospect of spending the afternoon with him was tempting. Her determination fled as well as all common sense when she replied, "All right. We'll join you."

Madeleine dashed outside before Catherine could take her hand.

Catherine sidestepped Danton, who remained a part of the doorway. Despite her best effort, she bumped into his forearm. Her every nerve ending focused on him, and she resisted the urge to look at his face; she kept on walking. She didn't have a chance to discredit her response and make excuses why she always felt so out of sorts near him, for once past the door, her gasp of surprise took over.

Beneath the lavender swash of jacaranda trees, Antonio and Eduardo held onto the poles of an open sedan chair. The gold enamel shone like fire under the sunlight; tufted in red leather, the padded seat beckoned.

"Who is that for?"

Danton answered her question by ordering the two men to kneel.

"For our journey." His matter-of-fact tone left her momentarily speechless.

Recovering, she asked, "And where will you sit?" Surely the colossal Spaniards were strong, but Danton was a strong man himself. The three of them would be too much for Antonio and Eduardo to handle.

"I have Santo."

Then she saw the snowy white Arabian horse several yards away. Catherine had not seen horses on the island, and didn't think Danton kept them. Like his imposing house and the worldly possessions inside, this animal was flawless.

Unable to break her admiration of the horse, she headed toward the chair.

Danton came to her side and held out his hand to help her. She didn't dare touch him. Politely disregarding his offer, she grabbed the side, put one foot on the floor and hopped in.

She did so feeling his watchful eyes on her.

She helped Madeleine aboard, then Eduardo and Antonio lifted the sedan in one smooth motion. She'd never ridden in this type of chair before, though they'd been prominent in India. The height made her giddy, but pleasantly so. She felt like a bird.

Danton's horse had no reins or saddle, yet he mounted him with a fluid grace by grabbing hold of the trimmed mane. Danton's finely tailored tan boots hugged the stallion's ribs as he gave the command to the Spaniards to move ahead.

The ride in the chair was steady and balanced. She settled in for the duration, glad she'd given her consent.

Madeleine giggled with delight. "It's just like we're on an elephant, *Maman!* Way up in the sky!"

They plunged on into the dense forest, shaded by hardwood trees. Catherine had not yet discovered this section of Danton's island. The chitter of birds came from every tree. Screeching gray parrots fluttered from limb to limb; ringtailed lemurs sailed in the air, calling to one another with shrill notes.

Giant tamarind trees and grassy meadows filled out the terrain, a far cry from the stark beach she and Madeleine had visited earlier.

Shafts of sunlight pierced the leafy canopy to show off butterflies and insects Catherine wasn't able to define.

Danton reined closer, and she couldn't help smiling at him. Smiling at the grandeur surrounding them. The India she knew had not been so lush, so sweet-smelling. "This is very pretty, monsieur."

"It only gets better."

And he was right.

Groves of clove trees with golden-green leaves scented the warm air. The pungent flowers were white, their leaves frosted pink at the tips. The smell reminded Catherine of spiced sweet biscuits fresh from the oven.

The trail grew narrow and overgrown. Danton steered his horse in front of them. Telling herself to place her gaze elsewhere was a wasted directive. The masculine shape of his buttocks and thighs in his breeches distracted her.

She seemed destined for her indifference to be tested. And to her utter chagrin, each time she came out the loser.

"Flowers, *Maman!* A great pool of them!" Madeleine leaned precariously close to the edge of the seat, and Catherine quickly snagged her daughter's sleeve. "Sit still, Madeleine. You'll fall over and hurt yourself."

Her daughter scoffed at her scolding and gazed at the crater filled with impatiens running riot in a clearing.

Danton led them right through.

Wading in the four-foot-high wildflowers was like cresting a red and pink tide. Right at this moment Catherine found herself enchanted by Danton's island and couldn't imagine anyplace more beautiful.

Numerous short and violent rivers leapt from mountains, foaming and hurling themselves in spectacular waterfalls over cliff faces. The crystal curtains plunged into lava rock basins.

Danton held his hand up, and Antonio and Eduardo stopped. From his seat on Santo's back, Danton turned and questioned Madeleine. "Have you ever seen bats?"

"I don't know." She looked at her mother. "Have I *Maman?*"

"No."

"Don't be afraid. Watch this and sit very still." Danton's mouth inched into a ghost of a smile. He checked his horse, holding the Arabian still with his knees. Then he clapped his hands under a tree. Hundreds of roosting bats swept toward the sun with an explosive slapping of beaten air.

"Fruit bats," he yelled above the riotous noise.

Madeleine pressed her face on Catherine's shoulder, but kept watch on the flock as it soared.

The huge bats looked like flying foxes to Catherine. Their russet fur glinted, large black eyes sparkling, and the sun outlined every finger bone in the translucent parchment of their wings. They made her shiver as she recalled what Georges Claude had once told her.

Bats got caught in hair.

She snatched the loose curtain of her hair and wove a hasty braid she prayed would stay put by sheer will long enough to leave the bats far behind.

They proceeded, much to her relief.

Madeleine lifted her head and turned her attention to the left and right, sweeping in all the newness. "I love this forest, *Maman*. It's the most beautiful forest I ever saw."

"I like it too." And she truly did.

Ten minutes later they came upon a small village of sorts.

A house loomed in a tiny clearing which bordered a lagoon. Built of split slates from a thorny bark tree, its peaked roof was thatched with bunchgrass. Yellow cosmos bloomed everywhere—around the split railing stabling a herd of zebu cows—growing up against the house and spilling down the trail that they now crossed.

The rustic door opened. Rainiaro appeared with a banana leaf cheroot clamped between his lips. He hailed Danton in Malagasy. Catherine was surprised to see the quartermaster here; she hadn't envisioned Rainiaro living amongst such subtle beauty. She'd expected him to reside with the other privateers in the huts that faced the beach.

"Ah, *la femme brave.*" He left his porch and walked to meet them. He crushed his smoke under his bare heel. He wore a formal type of dress, a burgundy silk cloth with gold threads that wrapped about his waist; his coffee-brown chest remained naked but for the adornment of a ceramic necklace bearing a pair of glazed black dolphins. "And she brought her *enfant. Bienvenue, mes belles amies. Bienvenue.*"

Antonio and Eduardo set the sedan chair's legs into club moss and Madeleine jumped clear.

"Hello, Rainiaro." She embraced his knees, and he bent to lift her into his arms.

Touching the tip of her nose with his finger, he asked, "Do you remember what I told you about a hug, *enfant?*"

Madeleine's blue eyes grew thoughtful. *"Vola—"*

"Volo," he corrected.

"Volo." She bit her lip and raised her brows as if she weren't quite sure. *"Volo mihitsy."*

"Bon, mademoiselle!" Rainiaro squeezed and tickled her. Her joyous giggle merged with the bark of a dog.

Conflicting emotions pulled at Catherine. While amazed by her daughter's accomplishment, she was also saddened that her papa had not been the man to tutor her. Georges Claude may have been excessive and a wastrel, but he had been the only father Madeleine had. Her parenting stretched so far, and her views were always of a feminine mind. Perhaps when they reached Paris and after they settled, she would think about marrying again.

Though Rainiaro had been nothing but kind and favorable, he was still a pirating quartermaster who took to the seas in savage contests. Madeleine needed a father figure. Someone respectable. A butcher, a tailor, a clock maker, or even a dustman or metal gilder.

Any man who earned his living honestly.

If only Danton Cristobal . . . *No!* What was she thinking? He would surely laugh at such a union, and she would never allow herself to be caught in the same trap as before. She could not easily forget what the lure of riches did to a marriage.

Catherine disembarked with a shake of her head, ridding herself of such whimsical thoughts about Danton. Instead she put aside her prejudice toward the quartermaster. She'd not tread on Rainiaro's toes, castigating him for something she disapproved of. Madeleine doted on him so much, she negotiated with her sterner self and compromised by accepting his flaws. "What is this about a hug, Madeleine? What did you say?"

"I said a hug is worth its weight in gold. That's M'gasy language."

"Oh, how very smart of you."

"I know lots of things," she proclaimed proudly.

"Oui, you do."

Danton swung his leg over Santo's neck and jumped to the ground. Without his cutlass and pistols, his calabash and spyglass, he seemed ordinary. More like a man who did not make his living pillaging. And more stunningly virile than Catherine wanted to admit. Rather than look at him, she put forth an exaggerated effort to study the orchids and ferns and the cosmos.

"We've come to see Reniàla." Danton headed toward Rainiaro.

"She will be glad. She's not seen the *vazahas,* though she's heard much about them."

That word again, Catherine thought. *Foreigners.* At least she was gleaning a little of the Malagasy speech herself.

"Come inside." Rainiaro took the single step up to his planked porch. The entire house front was in cool shade, sheltered by the boughs of rosewood trees.

"How come you're almost nude, Rainiaro?"

"Madeleine!"

Her daughter shrugged without chagrin. "But he is, *Maman*. Why?"

Rainiaro's baritone laughter rumbled from his bare chest. "Have you never seen a *papa*-man without his shirt on, *enfant?*"

"Hadi always wore his tunic. Sometimes my *papa* didn't wear his, but he didn't have a necklace like yours."

"This necklace," he held up the pendant, "brings me luck. I wear it on special days. My *lambahoany* too. That is my skirt."

"Boys don't wear skirts."

"They don't?" Rainiaro's face lit with mock surprise. *"Sacre bleu!* I'll take mine off."

Catherine gasped as Madeleine touched her fingers. "It's okay, *Maman*. He can't take his skirt off. That would be too embarrassing. He would have to show us his—"

"Madeleine!" Catherine's heartbeat leapt into double time and she felt herself flame from the roots of her hair to her heels. "Madeleine," she repeated with strained calm. "You needn't tell us what we already know."

Her daughter had the good grace to appear sorry, staring at the tips of her scuffed shoes.

Then came laughter that was deep and resonant.

Catherine's chin shot up. She saw Danton butted against the railing, one leg indolently before the other. She couldn't recall ever hearing him laugh. The tone was rich and pleasant and brought an unconscious smile to her lips. She couldn't believe she allowed him his amusement over the . . . well, *that* word.

"Really," she chided under her breath without much steam, trying not to give into her own fit of laughter. "Really, you shouldn't let her know you thought her funny." Catherine turned away so Madeleine couldn't see her smile.

Rainiaro maintained the sense of propriety she and Danton seemed to be lacking. "Mademoiselle Madeleine, the men in my tribe always wear skirts. It is our custom."

Catherine sobered with a sniff. "And a very beautiful skirt it is. I apologize for my lack of control. It was quite unlike me."

"Then it would seem both you and the *capitaine* are out of character." Rainiaro slid apart a curtain of netting beyond

94

the doorway. "Coincidence or providence? We should consult the *ombiasy*." Then he entered the house, motioning them to follow.

Madeleine chased after Rainiaro, leaving Danton and Catherine behind on the porch.

Danton pushed away from the railing, his visage dark, deliberate and dangerous. She could see no humor in his silver-gray eyes, no spark of light or happiness. His eyes were fathomless and unreadable. "Rainiaro should be gagged. He's no expert on my character." Danton's mouth pulled into a sour grin. "I do laugh . . . when the mood strikes me."

She didn't want him to be this way. Why, she couldn't explain. Oddly, she'd so appreciated his laugh, she couldn't accept this cold and distant soul. She tried to bring him back with a smile. "And what is an *ombiasy?*"

Danton swept the sheer curtain aside to allow her entrance. She brushed past him, very close. Close enough to feel the soft texture of his shirt. Close enough to smell the lingering traces of his soap. He caught her with a stare and she stilled. Unable to move or think clearly, she stood there waiting for him to say something. To do something.

She felt him everywhere on her without him even touching her.

He must have read the jumbled thoughts in her eyes, for he broke away without further pause. "An *ombiasy* is the village wise man. He tells fortunes."

That was that. Danton had closed himself off, and she should have been happy with the turn of events. But his laugh had touched her heart, Catherine thought as she went inside, and she wanted to hear it again.

There was a small room at the front that opened to a large living space. Mats covered the floor and two chairs stood at one end of the rectangular house, for the foreigners to sit on. Catherine quickly deduced this as Madeleine occupied one while Rainiaro sat cross-legged on a woven mat.

"La femme brave has arrived. And the *capitaine."* Rainiaro addressed a sari-clad woman who busily pressed flowers. Without interrupting her labors, she snatched a glimpse of Catherine, and Catherine noted her eyes were clouded, but attentive and wise. Wrinkles creased her flesh, skin that was dark as bitter chocolate. The old woman,

perhaps eighty by Catherine's guess, apparently saw enough; she once again gave her flowers her full attention. Her nimble and bony fingers worked a stone roller over a yellow-orange cosmos.

She spoke in Malagasy to Danton.

He answered back with smoothness, and she nodded her head. Her wiry hair had been sculpted into braids. She motioned for Madeleine to come closer, and she pointed to her bozaka basket of flowers. She gestured for Madeleine to pick a few and lay them on her wooden board.

Quietly her daughter did. Then the woman flattened them with her roller.

"Her name is Reniàla," Danton told Catherine from where they sat. "In Malagasy that's Mother of the Forest. She's ancient, but she's keen. She's making wallpaper. I thought Madeleine might like to watch her."

Confused over his gesture of goodwill, Catherine merely nodded. Why had Danton done this for her daughter? He left her torn with conflicting emotions. He'd shown her he had compassion, and in the process stoked the gently growing fire of fascination she'd begun to feel for him.

Madeleine was encouraged to pick more cosmos from the basket. Then Reniàla worked with the fibers of a shrub, encrusting the papyruslike material with the cosmos, grasses, and leaves. When she had a strip finished, she held it up to the light from an open window. The transparent runner was finer than any paper Catherine had ever seen.

The woman grinned, her top teeth missing. *"Mom mini ina."*

"What did she say?" Madeleine wanted to know, asking no one in particular.

"Life is sweet," Danton translated.

The three of them stayed with Rainiaro and Reniàla for over two hours. Catherine left her chair and ended up sitting on the floor with Madeleine to have a better spot in which to watch the Malagasy woman work. They ate supper with her; steamed rice with bits of chilies and spices and peppercorned fish seasoned with coriander; oranges and papayas—the fruit she'd ended up asking Rainiaro, not Danton, about, that had been served to them on *La Furia*.

When the meal was over, Danton and Rainiaro thanked

Reniàla then led Catherine and Madeleine outside. Dusk descended, and someone had lit a bevy of torches along a walk where vanilla plants wrapped around tree trunks in clinging embraces.

"Where are we going, Rainiaro?" Madeleine skipped alongside of him. "This is fun. I like that lady. I like those flowers. She gave me one. See?" She held up a yellow cosmos, drooping and in need of water.

"We are going to a surprise, *enfant.*"

Catherine wondered what he was talking about. The hour had grown late, and her own surprise for Madeleine may well have to wait until morning now. She'd made plans to honor Madeleine's—Catherine stopped short, nearly tripping on her shock.

There, at a narrow table fashioned with paper lanterns, sat Danton's crew. A ragtag group of Spanish and Malagasy pirates respectfully unarmed. Hats had been removed; hair had been washed and combed and slicked.

Seeing Madeleine, they stood at once, a shuffle of buckle-booted feet, large and heavy. "'Appee Birfday, Maddee." Off key, their broken English stumbled in unison.

Catherine immediately looked to Danton. He remained passive and nonchalant, saying simply, "They were the best I could do."

Chapter 7

"Where the blasted hell is my spyglass?" Danton shouted to a study empty of company save his own. He sat behind his Chinese altar rummaging through the countless charts and ledgers of neutral harbors. The instrument had been in the top left corner of his desk two days ago, amidst his miniature Tunisian studded chest, silver and crystal Louis XIV brandy decanter, his sixteenth century *blanc de chine* figurine, and his aepyornis—elephant bird—egg over a foot tall and without a single crack to the shell.

In his irritation he slid the egg aside to search beneath a pile of papers. The oval wobbled perilously in its ebony stand. With both hands Danton clamped his fingers firmly over the egg to save it from disaster.

"*Mierda . . .*" he muttered, a wave of panic whisking the blood through his veins. The aepyornis egg was a mystery, laid by a bird Danton had no clue as to its looks. No one could find one. To Danton's way of thinking, that put more value on the egg than any single one of his belongings.

He rose and put the elephant bird egg on a safe ledge with his betel nut boxes. Rounding his desk, he crouched down and inspected the tile floor underneath. He found a quill whose tip had splintered, a glob of sealing wax, and a fragment of orange coral, which he picked up.

No spyglass.

Returning to his chair, he tossed the wave-smoothed coral onto a mound of tallies, then steepled his fingers together.

He needn't question how the coral made its way into his study. He also needn't ponder why several of his accounting papers had stick figures drawn on the back. Nor reflect why a length of blue hair ribbon was tied onto the iron ring of this chamber's door. Or puzzle over the sticky residues of candy on his German globe.

No, the answer to these worldly wonders was simple: Madeleine.

The girl had invaded his life. Invaded his domain. Invaded his daily routine. Ever since her party a week ago, she'd stuck to him like a sea urchin. And she was indeed an urchin. Incorrigible, distracting, and a chatterbox. She could drone on and on and he hadn't the foggiest clue as to what she was prattling about. He'd catch snippets of verse. She talked about wedding gowns a lot; and someone named Nanette; and did he like rice? She did.

The little hoyden . . . but so cute it pained him to gaze at her for an overlong period.

She'd venture into his study in the morning and end up staying all day. She'd get into the house past his stalwart watchmen, Eduardo and Antonio. He snorted, having long since figured that mystery out. The traitorous bodyguards let her in. They adored the *niña preciosa* and made fools of themselves over her. One would carry her on his shoulders, the other would sail her into the air. Her peals of laughter rang through his halls. Then she'd appear in his doorway, her hair mussed and her stockings sagging at her ankles, or barefoot, with a stick of peppermint in her slight fingers. He suspected she gained her candy from James Every. He'd have to take a strop to that boy for aiding a nuisance.

A chime tolled from his gold-filigreed clock. Inside the glass dome a naked, bejeweled siren revolved to strike her tiny mallet onto the bell eleven times.

Madeleine hadn't come yet. Why not? Maybe her mother had at last put the bridle on her. He'd come to the grim conclusion Catherine had propelled the child toward him as retribution for him not taking her to Paris. She plotted to unbalance him. Little did Catherine LeClerc know, a man less in the head could not steer his rigger!

His mind filled with reflective thoughts. Catherine had been astonished the night of Madeleine's birthday, as he'd wanted her to be. After getting over her initial wide-eyed response at seeing his crew spit-polished, she'd given him a gracious and awarding smile. A smile that had had the strangest effect on him. He caught himself wanting to kiss her again. To explore her mouth. To mold her soft curves into him.

As the evening lengthened, he'd watched the different expressions playing over her face. Happiness. Delight. A self-conscious shyness when she caught him looking at her.

Washed in torchlight, she'd resembled an angel. Her blond curls fell to her waist; wispy fringes framed her delicate face. She'd tanned further. He thought the natural color enchanting, bringing out a light blanket of freckles on the bridge of her nose.

Catherine had sat next to him for the celebration. Madeleine sat at the table's end. Reniàla made her a coronet of gay cosmos which the little girl promptly displayed on her sun-brown hair. Danton had given Tanala instructions to make a cake and bring it to Rainiaro's lodging earlier in the day. His cook didn't know much about cakes, but had concocted confections: orange biscuits, sweet potato pudding, fried banana pancakes, and coconut candy.

Catherine had been pensive most of the ride home with Madeleine asleep on her lap, a guide from Rainiaro's village lighting the way. He'd kept Santo in sync with Eduardo and Antonio and caught her sparing glances at him, as if she weren't quite certain what to make of the evening—or him. He took pleasure in knowing he'd thrown her off kilter. He liked to see the light of confusion in her eyes, because he felt every bit as confused in his heart. He was becoming enamored with her, and reasoned he could endure the war between them a little longer as a test for his feelings.

But he had to assume Catherine's patience had obviously reached an end with this, her newest attack: a chattering forty-inch pistol named Madeleine LeClerc, who was bound to fire on him in any moment.

Danton tattooed his fingertips on the desk's scroll edge. He'd so come to expect Madeleine that he couldn't work.

Every noise, every creak and groan that echoed through the hallways, distracted him.

Abruptly he ceased his tapping.

Maybe the little girl was ill. He stood, then sat down. She couldn't be ill. She was the picture of perfect health. Pink cheeks, full in the flesh, and with a mouth of strong white teeth.

But Esteban had also carried those traits.

Danton thumped his elbows on the table and pressed the heels of his hands over his eyes, unwilling to think of his son as anything but a vigorous three-year-old. He'd not been with him when he died; no one had been except his mother and those who begged in the streets of Madrid. From his family physician, who'd remained loyal even though Danton had not a single centavo to pay him, Danton had learned his son had succumbed to pauper's disease. A week later Elena had suffered the same death. Jesu. Why couldn't he have saved them?

Because he'd been rotting in jail.

And now fate delivered him another blow, one so strong that just thinking about the child waned his strength. *Dios,* could he save *himself* from Madeleine LeClerc? She troubled him, she brightened him. Each day, her cheerful face melted his cold mask of pretense. Each day, she brought sunshine into his heart. He felt himself diluting, weakening, growing soft around the edges.

Mierda.

He'd not been on a raid since his bungled attempt on the Spanish *flotas.* This was not like him. Not at all. He'd spent two weeks poring over maps, arcing latitudes and longitudes, meridians and parallels; making grids; studying the African coastline for a place to deposit the LeClercs without getting himself and his crew blown out of the water.

Just this morning, out of desperation, he'd found an agreeable port to deposit them in. But he was reluctant to take them there. He felt responsible for them now, and decisions concerning their welfare could not be made lightly.

He'd been mildly relieved when Rainiaro had informed him several hours ago, a Turkish East Indiaman was rumored to be in his waters. Danton dared not chase Sadi—not when he still had Catherine and the girl on his island. But by the same token, if the ship indeed belonged to the Turk, he had to pursue it. He couldn't sit behind his fences, so to speak, waiting for something to happen, and stare out at sea—which now, dammit, he could not even do since his bloody spyglass was missing!

With a groan he slowly raised his head.

The sight in the doorway paralyzed him, crucified him. A knot of horror twisted inside him. Madeleine had arrived, her fingers, bodice, cheeks, chin, and lips caked with dried blood.

Madre de Dios!

Danton bolted from the chair. He scooped her into his arms and crushed her to him. "Where are you cut?"

She didn't answer. *Merde,* she'd fainted.

Frantic, he held her at arm's length and jiggled her. Her blue eyes danced in his vision. She made a vibrating sound from her throat. "Don't-t-t-t shak-k-k-k-e me-e-e-e."

"Dios, puppet, I'm sorry!" He felt like an incompetent. "How did you get cut?" She had the smell of sweet and sour on her; blood. It was the blood. A new wave of panic practically knocked him over. "Where are you cut?"

"I don't have a hurt, Monsieur Pirate."

"Of course you're hurt!" he yelled. "You're covered in blood!"

She screwed up her face and gazed down at her dress. "That's not blood. That's berries."

"Berries?" His own blood was beginning to simmer, to fester, to boil. He was about to explode. *"Berries?!"*

"The ones that grow by your big tree." She pursed her reddened lips. "I was eating them and I fell into the bush. *Maman* will be mad at me. I was crying. I got lost from Rainiaro and went to the cottage, but *Maman* wasn't there to hold me. So I stopped crying. I came to see you so you could hold me."

Danton slammed his hands on his head and stood. *"Hijo de la perra!"*

"What's that you said, Monsieur Pirate?"

"Bad words. Foul words. Cussing words!" He trudged to his liquor shelf, grabbed a bottle of Spanish port and popped the cork. Not bothering with a glass, he took a stiff pull right from the mouth.

A tap peppered his thigh. He glowered at Madeleine. *She* who *dared* to peck him with a *berry-stained* finger.

"You don't like me, do you?"

He hadn't the sanity to lie. "At this moment, no."

"Will you like me when I'm five?" She held up all her fingers, plus a thumb.

"You won't be here when you're five."

"I know. *Maman's* got your spyglass right now and she's going to find us a ship to sail us to Paris, France."

"My spyglass?" he railed. "She's got *my* spyglass!"

"*Oui*. I took it for her."

"*You?*" Danton's knuckles whitened on the bottle's circumference. "You stole my spyglass?"

"My *maman* asked me to." Madeleine's lower lip began to protrude.

"Why?" Danton asked with a forced calm, seeing that he was on the verge of giving her a fit of weeps.

"I told you. To look for a ship to take us to Paris, France."

"Where is your *maman* now, puppet?" he ground through teeth clenched so tight his jaw ached.

"She's prob'ly at the desert beach. *Oui,* that's where she is. She told Rainiaro to watch me, but he got lost when I was eating berries." Madeleine scratched the berry juice on her wrists. "She took the flint and striker with her. I asked her why, and she told me to hush up. She always takes them with her. Every day. To the stick pile."

A picture began to form in Danton's head. A flint and striker made a flame. A spyglass sought a ship. A warning fire could bring that ship to his island. A ship that could be freebooters, filibusters or military.

Catherine LeClerc had just condemned him.

"Antonio! Eduardo!" Furious, Danton slammed the port back onto the shelf. The bottom didn't catch the ledge. The bottle plummeted to the tiles and shattered. Wine splattered his boots and the wide hems of his nankeen pantaloons.

Madeleine stared at the mess on the floor. "You're mad. You want me to cheer you up? I can fly like a bat. Watch this, Monsieur Pirate."

He purposefully neglected her, but she persisted.

"Watch this. Watch this."

Grunting, he gave her his faint attention as she hopped in a circle and flapped her arms. "I'm not really flying, I'm jumping. I'm just pretending I'm flying. Do I look like a bat?" She gave him a wide grin that pulled in her dimples; a faint pink tinted her teeth. Her blue eyes twinkled like the sea catching the afternoon sun.

Madeleine stopped a hand's width away from him and yanked on the bottom of his leather jerkin. "Do I look like a bat, *monsieur?*"

She'd done it. She'd wounded him with her eyes, her smile. The tangle of nerves in his belly would never unravel without ripping his guts out. He felt the pain, the smothering, the death of his being.

Danton broke away from her, freeing the gentle tug on his clothing. He had to conquer his inner turmoil, he had to fight to keep himself in one piece.

"Antonio! Eduardo!" He restlessly paced the room. When he could bear her eyes on him not a second longer, the two Spaniards entered. "Stay with this child and don't let her out of your sight. I want all the men put on the alert. Sound the alarm. There may be trouble sailing toward us."

"Sí, Capitán," they replied in unison.

Danton bolted from the study, stopping in his bedchamber to buckle on his belt and slip the leather strap that carried his narrow-bladed dagger over his shoulder. He sought his two inlaid miquelet pistols and tucked them into his waistband. Without a wasted step he quit his home, entered the corral and mounted Santo.

He chased the wind, galloping over manioc and succulents until a clear stretch of coastline loomed ahead. The sun, reflected from the dazzling sand, beat in his eyes until his head buzzed.

The desert beach.

There could only be one place on his island that would fit such a description.

The northeastern shores.

Danton's spyglass was heavier than Catherine had imagined, and the enhancement not as clear. The brass piece weighed down her hand and fatigued her arm muscles. She peeped through the opening to see a sphere of sky and ocean. She'd been looking at this fuzzy circle of blue and bottle-green for three hours without a single sighting.

She'd been optimistic the first day, and then equally the second. This, her third day of searching the waters without success, exhausted her confidence. A steady throb established itself in her brain.

Isle of the Lost Souls must be too remote for her ever to be located. Release would only come when Danton was ready to provide the service.

The night of Madeleine's party, she'd been willing to concede to Danton's wishes and let him handle matters as he saw fit. He'd gained her respect by showing her what a generous and compassionate host he could be.

But what happened three days ago changed her outlook.

She'd found Madeleine in the cottage, sitting on the floor with a loose plank lifted, digging in a storage box of some kind. She'd gone to her daughter's side and felt ill upon seeing the *toys* Madeleine had found:

A case of pistols.

Thankfully, they hadn't been loaded. Madeleine knew better, of course, but the impulse to touch and play with the shiny silver guns had been too much for her to resist. If the weapons had been full of powder, she could have been hurt. She could have accidentally discharged one and . . . it was too horrible to think about.

Danton could give Madeleine all the lovely birthdays in the world and it wouldn't have made up for the petrifying incident. She'd spent the rest of the day prying all the floorboards up and searching for hidden ammunition. She'd uncovered nothing further. There had only been the one box. She put the case high on a shelf in the cupboard, way out of Madeleine's reach.

She didn't tell Danton what had happened. Maybe she should have. He'd not intentionally harmed Madeleine, and she was sure he would have been just as upset as she had been. But she couldn't run the risk of something like that happening again.

The next time, her daughter might not be so lucky.

So, she reinforced within herself the conviction that a bonfire was necessary if she wanted to protect Madeleine.

Foiling Danton this way did not please her, and her decision did not rest easy in her heart. But he'd given her no choice.

Danton would soon miss his spyglass, if he'd not already. She'd felt terrible asking Madeleine to take it for her. She would, of course, feign not knowing about its disappearance. He would, most likely, not believe her.

She resigned herself to returning to the cottage, certain Rainiaro would wonder what had taken her so long. She'd misled him, told him that she needed to exercise her frustrations, and had asked if he could keep watch over Madeleine while she took a lengthy walk along the beach.

Today was the first day she hadn't taken Madeleine with her. Her daughter was tiring of the daily walk, and since she hadn't readily found a ship, she hated to keep dragging Madeleine along for no good reason.

About to draw the spyglass away from her eye, a glint on the horizon made her blink. Her lashes connected with the lens and she squeezed her eyelids to clear her gaze. When she next looked, the glint had an outline.

Joy caught in her heart.

The silhouette could be a patch of sail, a line of mast.

"Closer," she mouthed. "Closer . . ."

Her eyes grew dry and gritty from the strain and the glare. She squinted and focused on the skyline. Tears gathered. They were the culmination of hope and fear.

A ship.

She'd spotted a ship!

Should she run get Madeleine first? Would the time it took to collect her daughter be too much? The vessel might well be gone by then. She hesitated, her pulse thrumming.

What to do?

She quickly concluded she hadn't really thought things out at all. To get Madeleine might jeopardize her chances; but to let the ship go by . . .

Catherine tossed the spyglass onto the sand and quickly turned to her hill of driftwood. She picked up the striker and flint and hit them together several times. Tears rolled down her cheeks, not from triumph, but from uncertainty. *Was this the right thing to do?* Tiny sparks flew into the tinder, and as she blew on the embers, breathing life into her crusade, it strongly occurred to her—what if the ship she beckoned held one of Danton's enemies? This Turk? Or even worse yet, the authorities? Whatever she wanted, she did not want Danton imprisoned.

Guilt riddled her and she felt the nauseating shudder of regret. She stopped trying to expand the fire. She looked to the horizon and saw nothing. Nothing without the glass. Biting her lip, she swiftly began to cover the burning twigs with sand. Now that the moment had come, she couldn't do it.

The potential of sacrificing Danton and his crew wasn't worth the price of her freedom. She would have to think of another way.

She stood and ran toward the flat shore. The water, reflecting the sun, blinded her. Shading her eyes from the glare, she tried to determine if the ship neared without her signal. Long moments went by, then something behind her snapped and she turned her head.

Flames erupted from the timbers and she dashed to try and extinguish them. The glowing particles had multiplied and spread. Newborn, the fire hungrily consumed the fuel. Waves of hot air lashed out at Catherine. Afraid, she jumped, the heat so intense it nearly scorched her.

She'd thought she put it out!

Smoke started to curl in choking ribbons of gray. She moved a safe distance away and stared at what she'd done. A glimmer of brass lay on the beach several feet from the burning driftwood.

Danton's spyglass.

Picking up her skirts and bunching the fabric in her fists, she raced to retrieve the nautical instrument.

The breeze had shifted. The orange blaze undulated, drooping, then snapping upward, like rice stalks in a field when the wind blew through the paddy. Catherine kneeled and stretched her fingers, the joints seemingly cracking from the effort. Her face felt baked, her eyelashes felt singed. So close. But not close enough.

She rose, defeated, and stumbled back on her heels a good few paces.

"Please . . . oh, what have I done?"

She brought both hands over her brows, tunneling her vision, trying to sharpen a portrait of a ship. The uneven beats of her heart hammered at her temples. Behind her the roaring cry of fire intruded on her perception. She couldn't think. And then . . .

Columns of masts, the wide spread of sails, three pennants and a dark flag.

She saw a frigate clearly now. It charted a direct course toward her. The captain had seen her signal fire. She dared not take a breath to discern which country the ship sailed for. She had to warn Danton. Tears trickled down her cheeks and she wiped them with the back of her dirty hand.

I have to warn Danton.

Catherine sprinted for the trail. Before she gathered her momentum, her knees locked. A rush of dizziness collided with the frantic pounding of her heartbeat. She swayed, panic rioting inside her.

Danton Cristobal bore down on her astride his powerful Arabian.

Chapter

8

The thundering hooves kicked up a fine spray of sand as Danton galloped toward the bonfire, his speed causing his black hair to flow behind him. He looked every bit the demon pirate in his brown jerkin with gold-studded leather crossing the rippling planes of his chest. His eyes, flashing and vivid, resembled the glowing embers that leaped toward the sky. He held her still with his damning gaze, then from deep within his throat he bellowed, "Catherine!"

She started, her limbs melted and she panicked. With a quick turn she ran in the opposite direction. Her feet sank into the soft grains of earth, slowing her down. She headed for the wet sand's level surface; once there, she flew. She hadn't a thought as to where she'd go. Unlike Madagascar's marketplace, there were no hiding places to be had. The beach was sparse and open, with only a handful of shrubs and the ominous rubble of limestone that had broken off the *tsingy*.

Gasping, Catherine couldn't hear Danton chasing her. She wouldn't squander costly seconds to look over her shoulder and measure the distance between them. Her entire being focused on the great drafts of air she drew into her lungs.

"Catherine!"

The sound of her name shot through her, and she jerked

her head to the left, nearly bumping into the shoulder of Danton's horse. He dismounted and boxed her in between himself and the sea. She had no choice but to veer toward the water. The stark beach offered nothing to stem the nervous march of Indian Ocean waves that broke on the uncompromisingly straight shore. Tepid water swirled above her shoes, around her ankles; her hem became sodden and dragged her into the pull of the waves.

A force of strength wrapped around her waist. She felt herself being jerked back, connecting with Danton's thigh. He brought his knee up to trip her, pushing her into his leg and groin.

"Let me go!" she screamed. Her ribs ached from sharp pain. He held her too tight, constricting, punishing.

A wave crested, then tumbled to white foam. The current captured Catherine's hindered legs and began to pull her under. Together she and Danton fell, the clear saltwater stirring and churning across their shoulders.

Catherine sputtered. Danton cursed. He stood and hauled her up to the shore, his steady grip on her midriff torture. He threw her to the sand and collapsed on top of her. The handles of his pistols cut into her pelvis and she winced. His legs pinned hers; his unyielding chest crushed the protest on her lips.

"Catherine, you test me like no other." His breath was hot against her ear. Salted drops cascaded off a shock of hair at his forehead to splash on her nose. He stared into her eyes and she shivered. "Were you a man, I'd kill you."

"I didn't mean to do it," she said in a choked voice. "You have to believe me."

"But you are *not* a man, *chérie.*" He pressed himself into her softness. Even with her skirts dense and wet, she felt the heat of his masculinity, the dangerous mold of his firearms. A quickening took hold of her stomach. He was a virile man who always got his way. She'd unwittingly defied him— again. Surely this time she would be made to suffer the consequences.

He rolled off her and, with agility, rose to his feet. The radiant sunlight behind him, he appeared paganlike. "Get up."

Very seriously, Catherine considered running. She could

give him chase again and prolong his wrath. How desperately she wanted to feel the wind on her cheeks!

She took a deep breath. Even she knew there was no point in thinking to elude him here. He'd proven he was faster and stronger than she.

"Get up, Catherine." Danton's even tone brooked no argument as he extended his arm—a gesture she'd once hesitated too long in accepting.

In the distance an explosion erupted. Within seconds water spouted at the frigate's broadside, barely missing her hull. Apparently a warning shot by Danton's crew had been launched.

"If you value your life, Catherine, *get up.*"

Catherine did not vacillate this time. She fit her hand in Danton's. He closed his fingers around hers. His hold encompassed more than her fingers; her whole consciousness focused on him. In one forward motion he had her on her feet.

"We can't stay here. You see, *mon petit maki sauvage,* you've beckoned the wrong ship for help."

"I'm sorry! I tried to put the fire out."

"A fire which *you* started." He pulled her along, and she had no choice but to go. He did not give options.

The driftwood continued to burn and charge the air with smoke and flame. Danton released her at a safe distance and walked toward the inferno. Catherine watched in horror as he retrieved his spyglass without concern of being burned. Dauntless, he turned his back on the fiery tower. Not even the shifting winds put him ill at ease.

He roughly took her hand and kept moving. "I have no desire to be shot at."

Sand clung to the folds of Catherine's dress, making her skirts settle between her legs. It was hard to walk this way; even harder to keep up with Danton, who set the pace of a jackal.

"Why can't you listen to me?" Her plea was heartfelt. "I told you that this was a mistake . . . I'm sorry."

"Tell that to my men."

Another cannon shot rang out. This one came from the frigate. Despite herself, Catherine cringed and picked her feet up faster.

"Do you realize what you've done?"

Frightened out of her wits, she cried, "Yes! And I'm sorry!"

"Sorry is not enough," Danton said, his voice cool and exact, "for at the helm of that frigate stands the perverted cutthroat, Trevor Tate."

"Who is Trevor Tate?" She swallowed hard. "Your enemy?"

Danton halted, and she nearly collided with his back. He shoved the spyglass at her. "Mine and many others. Look for yourself." She brought the lens to her eye and focused on the gliding craft as it slowly cut through the sea. "The flag. Describe what you see."

A cooperative wind made the standard easy to read. A single silver chalice stood out on a black background. "It's a goblet. What country is that?"

"No country," Danton stated, taking the apparatus from her. "No country would have him. He's the worst kind of sea wolf. The cup is Tate's little grotesque joke. After he captures his enemies, he kills them and drinks their blood out of a silver chalice."

Catherine felt the blood in her own face drain. "I . . . don't know what to say."

A volley far up the beach reported. *Boom!* one. *Boom!* two. *Boom!* three. Danton's pirates clearly had no intention of letting Trevor Tate and his men get a league closer to Isle of the Lost Souls.

Suddenly Catherine knew where the shots were coming from. The inlet where Danton kept *La Furia.* "Madeleine." The vision of her daughter being caught in a cross fire sent her into a frenzy. "I must go to Madeleine!"

She took a step away, but he grabbed hold of her upper arm. "Traveling on an open beach without trees for cover could be suicide. I won't risk your life."

"But you would risk yours were I not with you." She made the mistake of looking down at his hand. His scarred hand. Fingers that had been cut so badly at one time, they were covered with hairline wounds that had healed to white; a subtle contrast against the olive-bronze of his skin.

His gaze followed hers to his disfigurement. "My life is not my own."

"Nor is mine. I have Madeleine, and I've done a terrible thing. I won't do another and not be with her."

The exchange of cannonballs continued in the background as each refused to give in to their condemnations. Then, with a sudden shift in maneuvers, the frigate began firing its iron rounds at Catherine and Danton.

"Mierda! Tate has just figured out it's me he's got in his glass." He crouched and, with a wordless gesture, advised Catherine do the same. "Run, Catherine, and don't stop until we reach my horse."

She did exactly as he asked. They raced toward the Arabian, who'd nervously stayed upwind from the fire. Tail high and nostrils flared, Santo came when Danton called to him.

Danton braced Catherine's arms to drive her upward and onto the animal's back as if she were weightless. She sat sideways, one knee up, the other leg dangling over the rounded belly of the animal. Danton grabbed hold of Santo's mane and hoisted himself behind her just as a series of fresh cannon fire stormed down on them.

Terror weakened her limbs and numbed her senses. If it weren't for Danton's protection, she might well have fallen off the horse. He wrapped his arm around her waist and leaned forward, nudging his knees and heels into his stallion.

As they sped across the beach, the ineffective shots of too-far-off muskets railed over the sea and the potentially dangerous explosions of cannonballs erupted.

The force of the breeze stung her eyes, creating moisture; tears of despair.

"Trevor Tate never knew where I took my boots off!" Danton yelled against the wind. "Now I've lost an important edge." His commentary fell hard on her. "My island is well-protected, but there are those who would encroach upon it just for the sport of trading gunpowder."

How could she make him see her apology? It was useless to try again now . . . he didn't believe her.

The jungle loomed ahead. A blessing of thick and concealing green. Once they entered into the palmetto, palms, and vines, they were no longer targets.

It had taken Catherine less than an hour to walk to the

beach; on Danton's horse they were back to the main inlet in just over fifteen minutes.

Out of the smoke-filled sky came a startling color, fiery gold and sizzling red. At least twenty-five cannons had been put into position on the stretch of beach where Danton sorted his booty. In a systematic way the pirates set off the smooth-bore metal tubes down the lines, giving the first of the string an opportunity to reload from the muzzle. To catch the recoil, the cannons had been placed on slight tracks and roped behind.

Danton's three lemurs screeched from high on palm fronds. When their master appeared, they sailed through the sky and bounded after Santo.

Catherine coughed, putting her hand over her nose to mask the horrible scent of powder and flame. The air was gray and filled with the acrid smart of smoke. She'd never witnessed such an intense trade of gunfire. Danton's crew would hate her now. Hate her for getting them involved in a hellish battle. She felt blades of shame slice through her heart.

Danton pulled Santo to a halt and quickly dismounted, landing sure on his feet. Without hesitation he yanked Catherine from the horse's back and practically threw her on the ground.

"Go to my house. You'll find Madeleine there."

Then he left her. She saw the strain play across his face as he turned, the forced way in which he ran to captain his men.

Helpless to do anything to aid him, she ran up the winding trail to the pink residence and flung the door open. Her heels rang out over the tiles in the entry.

"Madeleine!" Urgently she checked each room in her path until she heard her daughter's call.

"In here, *Maman!* In here!"

Catherine knew the direction to Danton's study and followed the plastered walls until she reached the iron-studded door that had been slid closed. With a shove she pushed it along its runner. Inside the chamber, Madeleine sat at Danton's desk with Tanala in one of the extra chairs.

She ran to her baby.

"*Maman.*" Madeleine's smile held traces of a desperate

attempt not to cry. "I was a good girl. Eduardo pointed to the chair and put his hand on his dagger. I knew he meant I had to stay here with Tanala or he'd kill me."

Catherine listened with her pulse in her ears as she enfolded her child in her arms, knowing Eduardo would never kill Madeleine." She pressed her lips to a smooth cheek, kissing the trail of her child's sweet tears.

"I was a good girl, *Maman,*" she sobbed. "I didn't go anywhere."

"Oui, mon petit chou chou. You are a very good girl."

The cook, Tanala, began speaking in rapid Malagasy, making hand gestures that Catherine couldn't decipher.

Madeleine said, "She wants us to stay here. There are fireworks outside and I didn't even go to see."

"I'm so proud of you." Catherine wiped Madeleine's tears with her fingertips, smiling bravely so as not to further upset her.

Tanala slumped back in her seat and took a burning pipe from the edge of Danton's desk. She bit on the stem, her teeth clicking. *"Lefona!"* she spat, and inhaled the aromatic tobacco. *"Lefona ala!"*

"What happened to you, *Maman?*"

Catherine glanced at her damp and soiled dress. "I fell in the ocean." She tried to laugh as the shots raged on outside. Now that she'd seen Madeleine was safe, she knew she had to go and see if she could help Danton and his men. To try and make amends for what she'd done. "I'm very cold, Madeleine. I would like to change my dress. I want you to stay here with Tanala."

"But I want to come with you!"

Catherine hugged her, breathing in the scent that was uniquely Madeleine's. "I will be right back. You won't have time to miss me." Putting the child an arm's length away, she said, "I want you to draw me a picture of the fireworks. Remember when we saw them in Calcutta?"

Her little girl nodded. "I remember."

"Use Danton's pen, and here is some paper." Catherine picked up the first sheet her fingers found, not caring what document she'd taken. She flipped the page over to give Madeleine a clean area.

"I always use Monsieur Pirate's things, but I think he doesn't like me to."

"It's all right. I asked him."

Madeleine shrugged and pursed her tiny lips. "Hurry, *Maman.*" She took the quill in her hand and carefully dipped the tip into the inkwell.

Catherine rose and headed swiftly out the door. She quit the house and skidded down the footpath that led to the beach. Once there, she searched for Danton. Amid the haze and ash, she could not find him.

Rainiaro came toward her. His alligator-banded hat was tilted at a combative angle on his head. He looked worn, his gaping shirt showing the glistening sheen of perspiration on his toffee chest.

"Brave woman, this is no time to prove yourself," he admonished. "Get back to the house."

"I can't. I have to know if he's safe."

Rainiaro's face grew curious, then he frowned. "We are all unharmed. The *capitaine's* firing power is persuading Tate to turn around."

Though Trevor Tate and his men were barbarians, the thought of her being responsible for their deaths made her shiver. "Do you think Trevor Tate will heed Danton's warning?"

"No captain wants to lose his ship when he can avoid doing so." And as Rainiaro spoke the words, the artillery from Trevor's frigate ceased and died. The wide-sailed craft veered and began steering a northeasterly course away from Isle of the Lost Souls.

"Danton could have sunk her." Catherine's tone grew hoarse. "And yet he didn't. He's not like . . ." She shook her head. "I don't understand him."

"No, woman, you do not," Rainiaro said softly through the stilted calm. "Danton would never leave men shipless with no choice but to swim for shore."

"Why?"

"There's coral out there that can flay a man alive if he has to swim over the reefs. Can cut his hands and shred the boots off his feet."

Catherine stiffened in shock. In her mind she saw a hand in hers with long and lean fingers the color of sunburnt grass, rich and brown. Despite the jagged scars, the hand was beautifully large and powerful. An image of Danton in the coral formed, fighting the sea's hazards. Then blood. Hands and feet cut and hurting. Her heart swelled with empathy.

Her voice sounded tired and battered to her own ears as she quietly asked, "What happened to him, Rainiaro?"

The Malagasy frowned. "That is for him to tell you, woman, not me. But if you look closely, you will see that Antonio and Eduardo and half of Danton's men are scarred in the same way."

At that moment Danton took purposeful strides up the beach to where she stood with Rainiaro. Dokobe, Razana, and Pousse-Pousse pounced and ran after him, still high-strung and noisy from all the commotion.

Soot dusted Danton's face and left creases at the corners of his eyes. The residue of black powder covered his arms and hands, and flying sparks had eaten tiny holes in the fabric of his breeches. The need to comfort him, to reach out to him and tell him how sorry she was, actually made her tremble. But the lines of his features were etched in stone, his eyes dark and cold and distant.

He pointed an accusing finger at her. "You jeopardized my crew, my island, my lemurs, and your child's welfare." He kept his stern pace, marching right on past her. She could do nothing but watch him retreat. "Prepare yourself and your daughter for travel. Tomorrow I'm sailing you to Zanzibar."

Chapter

9

*W*hat did the owner say?" Catherine asked hesitantly.

Danton glowered at her as he took a seat opposite her at the table. She didn't seem as enthusiastic as she should have been about being in a Zanzibar coffeehouse. Her eyes showed her wariness, and had her well-shaped mouth been hidden beneath the length of black *huibui,* he would not have seen her frown. The cloth had been meant to shroud her face, but it had slipped past her nose. He'd thought the Arabs primitive for covering their women from head to toe, but the lusty stares Catherine had attracted made him rethink his disapproval of the crude practice.

He did not want her on display.

Bringing his boots under the hard bench, Danton said flatly, "He told me to read the *kadhi ya chakula* and advised he didn't control the moon that dictates Zanzibar's tides." His voice bore the evidence of his discontentment, brought on by both the proprietor's smugness and Catherine's careless exhibition of her femininity.

"A *kad*—what?" Catherine struggled to repeat.

Danton's gaze fell on her lips trying to repeat his Arabic words. He should not have looked at her as the other men did. He should have held onto the anger that had been with him since leaving Isle of the Lost Souls. But his fury had started to dissipate the closer they'd sailed to the coastline, and he hadn't let her know that. His concerns turned to a far more serious matter—in his haste, was he doing the right thing by bringing Catherine and her child to Zanzibar? The port appeared to be in inferior condition, with a corruption that hadn't been here during his last visit.

"A food chart," he explained shortly, gesturing to the bill of fare nailed on the wall.

Catherine's eyes widened as she studied the fluid symbols marked with dots and curves. Her face betrayed her emotions; she did not disguise her reservations about the foreign city. "I can't read that."

"It's written in Arabic."

"I assumed so. . . ." She looked around the establishment worriedly. He debated whisking her out of the building and putting an end to this ridiculous pursuit of hers to get to Paris. Had she not infuriated him to extremes, they would not even be sitting here.

He'd not spoken to Catherine since Trevor Tate had besieged his shores with cannon shot. After telling her to pack, he'd gone directly to his study to chart his course. Already rankled, he'd become more so upon finding Madeleine and his cook armed with quill and paper, playing a drawing game on the back of his Zanzibar map. He'd shooed them out, giving Tanala instructions to take the chatterbox to the cottage. He'd taken up his compass and ruler, trying to focus on his work. But with each arc, each scratch of ink and line of westward travel, his mind had inevitably wandered to Catherine.

He grudgingly admitted he had not listened to her on the beach because he could not bear to hear her lie. She had not accidently started the fire. A flame did not come out of nowhere. It pained him to think that she thought so little of him to deceive him. He'd wanted her to . . . what? Care for him? Love him?

No one could love him for the man he was, and she'd proved it.

Sunrise the next morning, she'd boarded his square rigger with a strained smile lacking all malice. Her eyes had been apologetic and she'd said very little. Daughter in tow and her portmanteau at her feet, she'd listened as he'd laid down the law.

He'd ordered her to stay away from him on *La Furia.*

She had.

He'd decreed she keep the girl out of his hair while they sailed.

She had.

He'd demanded she remain below decks, going topside only at dawn and dusk.

She had.

From his perch on the main shroud he had watched her on these select outings, hand in hand with the child. Catherine would pick the little girl up and cuddle her in her arms, and the two of them would stand at the railing and watch the ocean glide by. Spindrift glistened in unbound hair, flowing blond and baby-fine brown, as mother and daughter shared a private moment. Danton's belly had clenched as if he'd been stabbed in the vitals; the picture before him was innocent and uninhibited, and he wished to God he could have been a part of it. To be whole once again. To have a family.

But he'd not confess this to anyone, not even Rainiaro. He could barely suffer his confession in conscience alone. The need weakened him, sapped him of his purpose. He'd barked at his crew and ate his meals in isolation. His mission to relieve himself of Catherine had come back to haunt him. Despite the trouble she and the child caused, he wasn't sure he wanted to let them go, nor was he sure Catherine wanted to leave on the terms she was, but pride kept him from hearing her explanation.

Instead of frittering his energies away on something he couldn't change, he'd held fast to his spyglass and scanned the waters for Sadi's East Indiaman, *Korujus,* plotting the ultimate revenge on the Turk. Sadi was all that mattered. Killing the man was what he lived for.

When the jade and sapphire fringes of coral reefs and a jutting triangle of dazzling white coast came into view, Danton felt a weight lifted off his shoulders. He'd tried to convince himself he would be better off free of her in Zanzibar, so he could get back to more important affairs; neglected activities such as pillaging His Majesty's galleons.

Catherine had kept her part of the bargain. Not an ounce

of disobedience, not a fraction of trouble. He would keep his word and deliver her to the proper craft.

When she'd asked him if she could accompany him into the town, at first he'd flat-out refused. The Zanzibarians were Swahili, of African descent, warm and friendly; the Muslim sultans and *seyyids* were not so permissive. He'd been on the island once before, six years ago, when he'd sailed for the navy to gain ivory and cloves for King Philip. He knew what these Arabs were like.

Catherine's tranquil acceptance of his decision had made him abruptly change his mind. Why exactly, he'd refused to pinpoint. He hadn't wanted to domineer her by placing her on restriction, dammit.

Seeing her so acquiescent, he'd found himself inexplicably dissatisfied. He'd rethought the situation and gruffly told her there were two conditions on which she could accompany him. One, she leave Madeleine in Rainiaro's care for the girl's own safety, and two, she wear the *buibui* he sent Antonio ahead to purchase.

Catherine had agreed to both conditions, though the latter had slipped—literally—away from her.

Danton leaned forward and picked up the end of the dark cotton cloth. "Cover yourself, Catherine." He brought the fabric across her cheeks. His fingertips brushed her silky skin.

She started under his touch, blushing and taking the *buibui* from him to anchor the hem behind her ear. Only the almond-shaped outlines of her eyes showed. An even more sensual picture than her whole face.

Coming to the coffeehouse had not been a good idea. He definitely did not want to stay and chance becoming involved in a fight over her. And from the cautious look that had been on her face, she was eager to depart.

Danton flicked aside some bread crumbs that the previous patrons had left on the table. "I'll tell the owner what we want and we'll take the food with us."

The eyes blinking at him above the black curtain were relieved.

Fifteen minutes later, carrying a braided-grass poke of foodstuffs, Danton led Catherine into the congested streets of Zanzibar. Antonio and Eduardo, who had stood cross-armed at each side of the doorway, fell into step behind them.

The town had no appointed shipping office site since exporting consisted of independent merchants or countries who sailed without representation in Zanzibar. He'd come across the seaport city's map in his Sung vase, and after a lengthy study of its geography and political history, determined the site harmless enough to suit both his and Catherine's needs. Not to mention that he knew his way around.

The port traffic moved daily with the tides; slots that opened upon departures were soon filled by new arrivals. The outgoing activities were not monitored, logged, or duly noted by the Arab officials who governed the island. Because of that disorder, *La Furia* was safe to attach block and tackle and drop her anchor here.

This system of lax ignorance may have served the Zanzibarians, but Danton needed to know where the ships were going if he were to secure one for Catherine.

Reluctantly, but because it was necessary, he headed toward the Bwawani lodgings, hoping Bedr would still be there. He'd met Bedr bin Khalifa while looking to acquire ivory six years ago. The Arab had known precisely where to purchase the best tusks and for a reduced price—but with a tidy allowance for himself. In honor of their transaction, Bedr had opened the doors of his lodging to Danton and his former crew, supplying women, drink, and a turn at the pipe. Bedr dealt hashish and surrounded himself with an unsavory lot, but the self-proclaimed sultan always knew when someone sneezed against the wind.

As much as Danton didn't favor bringing Catherine to Bedr's, if a bark was scheduled to sail for France, or any other European port, the sultan would be more likely to know about it than any merchant in the harbor.

The street Danton chose to travel was crooked and meandering, so narrow that in places wheel hubs had left impressions in the sides of the three- and four-story-tall sandstone buildings. Winding lanes were woven with dazzling sunshine and deep shadow, which highlighted beautifully carved Arab doors, their heavy panels, frames, and lintels richly decorated with patterns of lotus and chain motifs.

"Are we lost?" Catherine's voice wavered with distress.

Danton looked briefly across the length of his shoulder. She lagged, then made up the difference by quickening her short steps to keep up with his broader strides. Eyes alert and assessing, she appeared nervous; fearful and distrusting of Zanzibar Town's cultured main street.

"Chérie, you cannot get lost in Zanzibar. You will always end up in the same place you start. Finding where you want to be can be a problem. But I remember where Bedr lives."

"You know where we're going?" Her veil dipped below her nose and she readjusted her *buibui*—again.

"Don't doubt me, Catherine," was all he said as he stepped around a woven mat laden with polished brassware. "I know someone powerful enough to get you to Paris." In succession they passed hardwood tables touting incense, dried shark, dates, and water-damaged silk and muslin.

A throng of Zanzibarians pressed upon them, and the heavy odor of too many people in too small a space became ripe and thick. Music from gourds and wind pieces floated amid the crowd. The marketplace brimmed with suntanned, bewhiskered men clad in sandals, turbans, and long-skirted *kanzus.* Women were not allowed to purchase or sell.

The bickering male voices around them rose and fell in heated octaves as Arabs and Swahilis bartered and sold their wares. Hilts and ornamented silver sheaths of wickedly curved J-shaped daggers protruded from waist sashes.

Danton recalled touring this confined area with Bedr when a dispute between two rival vendors broke out. The argument had ended with a dirk's point stuck in a belly and a pool of blood soaking the ground.

Without a word Danton snatched hold of Catherine's hand. She curled her fingers securely around his, giving him a fleeting glance of thanks that tugged at him. The familiar weight of the miquelet pistol in his waistband lent him a sense of power. He vowed to protect her at any cost.

Danton followed the avenue to an affluent section of town. Gaily tiled mosques and soaring minarets were prominent on these lesser traveled roads. The holy themes and real gold inlay were a stark contrast to the marketplace.

In this congested maze of dwellings, a red-blossomed rain tree spanned a wide-branched circle nearly a block wide. The sixty-foot-tall top resembled a mushroom, stretching to the white-balconied Bwawani lodgings wedged next to the limbs.

"We're here." Danton left Catherine's side and ordered Antonio and Eduardo to check the narrow alley running behind the house. The two returned in short time, and Danton told the Spaniards to post themselves in strategic locations by the thick walls; one on the south side and the other on the north.

"Are you expecting trouble?" Lines of apprehension creased Catherine's forehead.

"In my trade,"—he picked up the knocker and banged it on the carved wooden door—"trouble needs no cause, only a stupid man's instigation."

Sunlight gilded off the door's brass bosses as Catherine waited for it to open. She felt as if a hard lump had lodged in her throat, and she fought against crying. What was the matter with her? She'd asked for this moment. She'd wanted her freedom. And yet . . . now that deliverance was beyond the door, she was scared to death to walk away from Danton. He'd been her protector of sorts, and she'd grown accustomed to him telling her what to do. But none of that should have made a difference. She'd craved her independence; she should have embraced her impending freedom with open arms.

Why, then, was she terrified to meet her future?

At length the door swung inward. A squat man whose facial hair had been rinsed in henna stood at the threshold. He wore a black, potlike hat on his head. He looked ill-kept, his wiry facial hair in sore need of a trimming. Danton spoke to him in a guttural tongue.

Catherine tried to revitalize her resolve, but could barely maintain her conciliatory smile directed at the servant; then she realized he couldn't see her mouth under her scarf.

Without delay she and Danton were shown into a long hallway and ushered up three flights of intricate, iron-railed stairs to the rooftop. The open space had been decorated with potted palms, baskets of flowers, and short-footed tables.

A turbaned and bearded man lay sprawled on a bright red divan smoking a funny kind of pipe. There was a long, thin hose attached to a bottle, and as he puffed, water bubbled. He took a deep pull from the stem, holding in the smoke for a few seconds before slowly exhaling.

Seeing Danton, he rose, grinning from ear to ear. He was clad in fine silk and cotton garments resembling a nightshirt. He wore many gold jewels: rings and bangles and bracelets. Catherine knew this had to be Bedr. The man who could help her get to Paris.

Butterflies swarmed in her stomach. He didn't look influential.

To her dismay, Bedr and Danton began speaking in Arabic, and she was unable to understand a word.

It was a long, frustrating moment before Bedr addressed her in English. "I am Sultan Bedr bin Khalifa. You may call me *seyyid,* as the captain does. And I will call you Cat." Bedr gave her a salacious perusal that chilled her; she shivered. "He tells me you are French, but can speak English. We will talk English. Come." He motioned to a pallet of satin throw pillows.

Danton nodded in agreement, and Catherine followed him. The rain tree's diamond-shaped leaflets wept on a corner of the patio, but the fragrance was very pleasing.

"You are hungry," Bedr stated, and lifted a bell that lay on the table beside his water pipe. "Let me feed you."

Danton offered the sultan his foodstuffs. "I brought cakes—"

"You insult me, Captain." Bedr grabbed the poke from Danton's hand and flung it over the roof.

Catherine choked on her surprise.

"By the smell," Bedr snorted, "that was not fit for my goats. You will eat my food. Sit. Sit."

The sultan sat cross-legged and gestured for Catherine and Danton to do the same. They did.

The tinkling clapper of the bell rang out as Bedr called for his servants. In short order a harem of women clad in diaphanous gowns came bearing food trays. Their anklets sang metallic tunes and their eyes, limned with kohl, cast furtive glances at Danton.

The inviting stares upset Catherine. She'd been far too

aware of his hand in hers as they'd crossed the marketplace. She had placed too much importance on the intimate gesture. And she'd been far too uneasy with the crowds. Were her apprehensions a prelude to the choking metropolis of Paris? She'd been in the wilderness too long. First Africa, then India. And of late she'd accustomed herself to the serenity of Isle of the Lost Souls. She would have to adjust to a bustling society. She would not smoothly blend into it, as she'd assumed.

"You may have one." The sultan gave Danton a wicked smile. "Or all five if you desire."

It took Catherine a heartbeat to discern exactly what Bedr meant. He spoke of the women. Of the women pleasing Danton if he so chose. After her initial embarrassment, Bedr's shameless invitation galled her.

"No, *seyyid.*"

Torn by her bewildering emotions, Catherine pointedly looked away from Danton. She was glad for his refusal; glad that he didn't find the servants to his liking. The idea of him kissing one of them as he had kissed her brought an agonizing picture to mind. Strange and disquieting thoughts began to race through her head. She tried to attribute her tumult to nerves, but knew it was more than that.

She wanted him to find *her* desirable.

"That was your answer the last time, Captain." Bedr plucked a date from a porcelain bowl at his knee. "You were being faithful to a wife. Do you still have her? Or has Cat taken her place?"

Catherine was barely able to control her gasp of surprise. *Wife?* She had envisioned Danton's past with many things, but a wife had not been on her list. He's married. Married . . . married . . . married. Where was his wife? Had she been one of the comely Malagasy women on his island, and he preferred to keep her in private? Married . . . and he'd kissed her. Married . . . and she'd fantasized about him kissing her still. Married . . . till death do you part. Married . . .

Catherine felt dizzy.

"No, *seyyid.* I no longer have a wife."

Her mouth dry, the statement came as no comfort to her. It didn't change the fact that he'd never mentioned a wife to her. Not that he owed her . . . but she had told him she'd been married. Catherine gazed at Danton. She wanted to put all the pieces together, but he would not meet her eyes.

Bedr clapped his bejeweled fingers, sending the women away; they giggled and vied for Danton's attention as they departed. "Since you no longer have a wife, Captain, you can indulge in my sweetmeats without a toothache to plague your conscience." He gave Danton no chance to decline again, or even change his mind and accept, for Bedr plunged on, his next words directed at Catherine. "You may remove your *purdah,* Cat. I am not so backward that I find offense in a woman's face. I would like to see yours."

Danton did gaze at her now, and Catherine thought she saw disapproval. Still reeling from the shock, she slowly let the black cloth slip down.

"Lovely. Very lovely." Bedr's glassy brown eyes assessed her features. "You are from Paris?"

"Oui."

"And you want to return there?"

"Very much." But her mistakes in making that a reality could not be ignored: first, her faith in *De Gids;* second, her secretly boarding *La Furia;* and third, her fire had been no better than a loaded gun. Would trusting the sultan be her fourth misjudgment?

"We will discuss Paris after we eat."

Catherine wasn't sure she could eat. Any hunger she'd had before had dissipated. This Bedr, this garish man who smelled of burning weeds, how could he make it possible for her to get home? He seemed impudent and cocky, too full of himself to cater to anyone's whims but his own. She didn't like him. She didn't like the way he licked his lips when he looked at her, as if she were some morsel for him to nibble on.

"You are out of uniform, Captain. Are you still in the Spanish navy?"

"I am my own man, *seyyid.*"

Bedr threw his wrapped head back and heartily laughed, as if he were delighted to the curled tips of his sandals. His dull teeth contrasted with the honey color of his lips. "You have turned to piracy!"

The muscles in Danton's neck tightened.

"I know many buccaneers, Captain. Though my Swahili friends call you *panyas*—rats—I like men who take what they want. A very lucrative business, piracy." He sopped a piece of chicken curry with a wedge of bread and waved the hand that held his food. "Eat. Eat."

Catherine looked at the plate before her. She had no utensil. Watching Danton, she saw he ate as Bedr—only with his right hand.

She did so as well, forcing herself not to shiver as the meat's juice ran down her arm when she brought the bite to her mouth.

"You like my food, Cat." It was not a question, but more a statement that Catherine could not politely contradict. She nodded and ate a slice of mango. "It is good," Bedr prodded. "Eat. My pawpaws come from the forest and are sweet as sugarcane." Bedr pointed to an entrée that looked too messy to eat with fingers. "That is *bokoboko*. It is good as well."

The sultan relished his meal, smacking his lips and wiping his fingers on a large cloth. "Now this business of Paris, Captain. How soon do you need to go?"

"She," Danton clarified, looking pointedly at Catherine. His gaze melted her to the core, and she felt her guilt increase twofold. "She wants to leave as soon as possible. There is a child involved. The ship must be legal."

"Today, legality is a problem. Tomorrow, it may not be. That is the way of Zanzibar, Captain. In three days time I can get her aboard a Persian sloop to the Cape. But once at the Hope, she would be on her own to find connections. As you know, ships do not sail from Zanzibar Town to Paris. She will have to take many ships, or perhaps if she can wait a week, there is word that an English cutter will arrive for purchasing on her way to London."

"A week . . ." Catherine repeated despondently.

"A week is too long." Danton pushed his plate aside and swilled the Turkish coffee in his cup. The scent of ginger, cinnamon, and cardamom lingered in the air.

Bedr gaped at Catherine. "Why you want to rid yourself of this flower, Captain, I do not know. She is ripe for the plucking."

Danton's fingers curled tightly around the cup's handle,

but he did not defend her against the sultan's blatant remark. "A week is too long," he repeated. "I can't wait."

Catherine rigidly held her tears in check. If he meant to torture her with his words, he'd succeeded. She wanted to shake him, to make him listen to her and understand.

She'd done exactly what he'd said on *La Furia,* and tried to apologize to him a dozen times. But he would not forgive her. And so she would leave him on this wilting note, taking her misery home. A place that meant nothing, knowing she'd failed him.

On the way to Zanzibar she'd caught him watching her and Madeleine, glaring at her as if he wanted to hurt her. And yet there were moments when she'd thought he wanted to hold her in his arms again, and that lent her hope. But as they neared their destination, she knew how futile that thought was, and his words now confirmed his desperation to be rid of her.

"If you cannot wait, then I cannot help you, Captain. These are the only options. Perhaps tomorrow things will change. The tides are always changing." Bedr finished his banana and tossed the peel onto his empty plate.

The man who'd opened the door to them earlier came onto the patio with his palms pressed together. He bowed to Bedr, then stooped to speak with the sultan in a discreet voice. Bedr nodded while frowning; then the servant bent at the waist and left.

The sultan came to his feet. "If you will excuse me, Captain. There is a matter I must see to." He gave Catherine an appraising stare, lingering over her breasts and the curve of her throat. "You will stay until I come back, Cat. I will help you. Yes."

Then he left.

Danton rose in a jerky motion and flung the remainder of his Turkish coffee over the rooftop. He poured himself a glass of clear liquid which seemed too syrupy to be water.

The tension between them lay heavy. His persistent anger was evident on his face and in the forced tightness of his walk. Catherine sensed he was still piqued about Bedr mentioning his wife. The wife he no longer had. She wanted to ask him about her, but suppressed her curiosity. He would tell her to leave him alone and mind her own affairs.

But she so wanted to know about the woman that had once been in his heart.

Instead Catherine made a weak inquiry. "What's that you're drinking?"

"Rice wine," he said tersely. "I'd offer you some, but it would make you sick."

"I can drink liquor."

"Now's not the time to prove it to me."

Catherine abandoned her plate and stood. Walking to the pillared white railing, she looked out at the city's harbor. "Of course it's not," she stiffly agreed.

The fluted, stiff fronds of palms caught the trade winds and made rustling noises. The scent of the rain tree wafted in the air. In the water, fishing boats tilted drunkenly on their sides. The old wooden Arab sailing ships Danton had called dhows teetered precariously, their lateen sails in triangular shapes. She saw *La Furia,* but at this distance could only make out thimble-sized figures on the deck.

She missed Madeleine very much and wished she was with her daughter. Turning, she faced Danton, who'd drawn up to her side, but anything she had to say died on her lips. All she needed to know was in his eyes. Eyes that were normally unfathomable were now crystal clear.

"I won't leave you with him for three days only to have you packed off to Cape Town. It's still Africa, *chérie,* not your beloved Paris."

Despite her own qualms, she tried to smooth things over. "You can stay with me and Madeleine while we wait for another ship. He's your friend—"

"Friends kill friends over women, and you, *linda,* are a prize worthy enough for a man to risk his life." Danton gripped the banister with one hand. "Now I have to wonder if he will attempt to slay me."

"He wouldn't . . . kill you."

"Who knows what Bedr will do." Danton swallowed the remainder of his drink. The breeze ruffled his ebony hair, sending a shock into his eyes. He shoved the wayward strands from his vision. "I never should have brought you to the Bwawani."

His statement intensified her doubts and made her wonder why he changed his mind. She thought he wanted her out of his life. His change in direction served to kindle her uncertainty about fitting into France and her apprehension about her own independence. She'd done such a poor job at making decisions so far, she wanted to weep in frustration.

Nothing seemed to be going right. Even Zanzibar had proven not to be an easy answer. But the sultan said he'd help. How so? By killing Danton so he could have her?

"Is there any other person you know?"

"I could know the whole of Zanzibar and it wouldn't make a difference. I can't dictate when a captain sails his ship." Danton's face darkened. *"Maudit!* And I can't stay in the harbor for a week. Even Zanzibar Town has had its share of raids from the authorities. Not so frequent, but there is a chance I could be hanged here."

Whatever Catherine wanted, she did not want Danton's death. "Then go. Leave us here. Take your ship and your men to safety. All I ask is that you find a suitable inn where we can wait and—"

"No."

A long pause separated the distance between them. Quietly and without caution, she asked, "What would your wife have done if she wanted to go home?"

Danton's nostrils flared. "My wife would have obeyed me."

Catherine felt the hot moisture of tears trickling down her cheeks. Of course. Just as she had had to obey Georges Claude. Couldn't Danton understand how wrong that was? That in time obedience crushed one's soul?

"I don't want to fight with you, Danton." The sounds of the harbor drifted upward; the brisk calls of fishermen and traders. Catherine took in a shaky breath. "What are we going to do?"

Danton lifted his head. "I'll wait a day or two and see what I can find out." Scanning the crowded bay, he said, "So many ships. One of them has to be decent enough to take care of you."

"And if you can't find one?"

"Then you'll have to come back home with me," he kept his gaze on the tangle of riggings, sails, and hulls, "until other arrangements can be—" He stopped short. His eyes narrowed to slits and his hands on the railing became a death hold.

Catherine stared at the ships, wondering what Danton had seen. She saw nothing out of order. "What is it?"

"Jesu." His voice came out low and angry. His knuckles whitened. "It's Sadi. His East Indiaman is in the harbor."

Chapter

10

*D*anton had sent Antonio and Eduardo ahead to warn Rainiaro and the crew. And now he pushed himself to the limit, racing the beats of his heart; he felt the strain ignite a path of fire up his thighs. If he knew such a torment, Catherine's legs had to be begging for respite. Yet he pressed her further, not giving up the killing pace he'd set.

Sadi! his mind screamed as they flew through Zanzibar's twisted streets.

"Run, Catherine!"

Winded and panting from exhaustion, she kept up with him, her slight fingers meshed in his. She made no protests for rest; she didn't cry or hold him back. Her slippered feet sped alongside his boots, kicking up the hem of her skirt and petticoats with her demanding steps. Together they raced over the sandstone walks, pebbled roads, and the powdery earth. Her stamina surprised him, for he'd always thought of her as fragile in body, though strong on opinion. He'd been mistaken.

The crammed marketplace loomed ahead, bursting out of the city, jutted with tents and stalls and populace. Danton had no choice but to head into the crowd if he wanted to reach the harbor straightaway.

Wet from slop, the ground grew slick and muddy. He felt Catherine lurch and she whimpered. He steadied her with an arm around her waist, and for a moment he studied her face to make sure she was able to continue. Dust and sweat lined the corners of her eyes and dampened her lashes. Still, she did not appeal to him to give up.

"Sadi is the Turk," she choked on her gasps, "isn't he?"

Danton mutely nodded.

"Run!" she shouted. "Run before—" A sob caught in her throat. ". . . Madeleine . . ."

Slipping his arm from her middle, he grabbed her hand again and gave her fingers a tight squeeze.

Danton ran, dodging crates of colorful fowl and two-wheeled carts chocked with rice bags. He understood her terror. The same thought had crossed his mind, and he hoped the crew had already seen Sadi's East Indiaman. Should a battle erupt before he reached his rigger, he would be cut off from his men.

And Catherine LeClerc's child.

Danton knocked a stack of baskets out of his way. As wicker toppled, the angry curse of a golden-capped vendor assailed their backs. Cages of green parrots bordered the narrow aisle, their screeches and fluttering wings raising feathers and bringing shouts from disgruntled merchants.

"This way!" He could see the three tall masts of *La Furia*. The beach spread out before him, filthy and smelling of garbage and rotten food. Their footsteps raised flies and insects. The stench permeated the air in a heavy cloud.

Catherine gagged and brought her free hand to her mouth.

"We're almost there!" Danton yelled, balancing over the rough sand and veering around mounds of waste. "Keep going!"

The rickety wharf's planks creaked under Danton's weight as he climbed up the shallow incline. Catherine's low heels tapped against the salted timbers. The few sailors and merchants that milled around got out of Danton's way when he drew his pistol from his sash and pointed the muzzle toward the scorching sun.

His temple throbbing, Danton snagged hold of the plank lines and pulled Catherine behind him toward the deck of his square rigger. Rainiaro met them at the cutaway. The Malagasy was prepared for conflict; he'd tucked a sheathed stiletto in his waist and belted a musket across his shoulder. The rest of the crew worked to clear the decks of unwanted obstructions, hoisting the bulwarks and scurrying into fighting positions.

Rainiaro's dark skin glistened through the opening of his vest. "We've seen Sadi, not far down on the quay, in a Turkish *han* called Hamasa. He's not alone. Three of his men are with him. How shall we take him, *Capitaine?*"

Danton tucked his pistol in his breeches and shoved Catherine at his quartermaster. Rainiaro easily caught her by her elbow as Danton ordered, "Hoist the upper yards and sails."

Rainiaro's brown eyes narrowed critically. *"Capitaine?"*

Shoulders slumped and waist bent in weariness, Catherine took in great gulps of air. Leaning toward Rainiaro, but not using him as a support, she looked into his face. She struggled to regain her breath. "Where . . . where's Madeleine?"

"Below with James," Rainiaro said without delay, then stared hard at his captain, as if he hadn't been certain he'd heard Danton correctly. *"Capitaine?* Your orders?"

"Set the lower sails. Secure the hatches," Danton reaffirmed as Antonio and Eduardo appeared from the hatch that led to the magazine. "Get out of the harbor, Rainiaro. Take *La Furia* down the coast and back to the island."

"Run, Capitaine?"

"Yes, run! You're leaving Zanzibar." Eduardo stalked to Danton, holding a brace of matchlock muskets in a leather sling. Danton took them and tossed the heavy weight over his shoulder. "I'm staying."

"No!" Catherine protested in a rush, straightening her spine. "If we go, you come with us." Her *buibui* left behind at Bedr's, tendrils of her pale blond hair escaped her braid. She looked wild and untamed and spirited; ready to do battle if he'd hand her a firearm. He felt a fierce admiration for her, a strong desire to fold her in his arms and tell her he wanted to stay but had a meeting with Destiny. But he feared she wouldn't understand what it meant to extract revenge. To kill with premeditation and know you'll be damned to hell for putting a man's blood on your hands.

Cathcrinc was too civilized, too sensible, to ever find compassion in what he was about to do.

Danton met her desperate stare, then without any thought for the watchful eyes of his crew, pulled her against him and kissed her. The kiss was not soft, nor lingering, but urgent and filled with fire. She pressed her open lips to his and his last words were smothered on her mouth. "You will be safe, *chérie*. Take care of your daughter. She needs you." He released her and turned to his comrade.

Eduardo handed him several pouches of powder and a calabash, which Danton looped over one of the gun's stock. He made sure he had enough patches and balls, fixing on what he must do and blotting out all else.

"You can't stay alone!" Catherine grabbed his sleeve.

He brought his gaze first to her quaking fist dug into the fabric of his shirt, then to her blue-gray eyes. Her tears had a powerful effect on him. He hadn't thought himself capable of falling prey to a woman's weakness. He could, in this single fragment of his tortured present, forget everything he'd vowed to retaliate against. Scratch off the last four years of searching and denounce his revenge. He could sail out of Zanzibar without Sadi even knowing he'd been here. His life would go on as it had. Be he pirate or man, he'd still be embittered, tormented, and alone, without any integrity.

Four years ago he'd lost his honor on the indigo seas; today, he would regain that honor and dignity as soon as he'd killed Yousef Ahmed Sadi Ahram.

He had to kill the man if he wanted his freedom. If he wanted to start over.

"I can't stay." Danton's words sent a fresh splash of tears over Catherine's cheeks. Had he the indifference he so often claimed, he would brush the tears from her face and feel nothing for having done so. But he could not. Because he did feel for her. Care for her.

With great determination, he pried her fingers from his shirt and forced himself to break free of her immobilizing gaze. "Eduardo and Antonio will come with me."

Rainiaro stepped forward. "But this is half the crew's quarrel as well, *Capitaine*. This is the day they've been waiting for."

"I need them to man the rigger."

"And how will you get back?"

"I will find a way."

"Capitaine," Rainiaro ground out, lowering his voice, "don't make this your private war. You have men to back you. To stand by you."

Danton glanced at Catherine. She stood tall and passionate, daring him to change his mind. He fought the demons in his head and willed himself to turn away from her. "Eduardo. Antonio. *Vamanos.*"

He bid his quartermaster a silent farewell. Rainiaro's ire held fast, but Danton refused to acknowledge his friend's grievances. Nostrils flared, the Malagasy threw the bejeweled hat off his head and slammed his fist on the polished railing. Danton supposed he could allow the man that much. Jesu, he might never see Rainiaro again. . . .

Not until Danton and Antonio and Eduardo took the gangplank to the landing did Danton hear Rainiaro curse and give the command. "Raise sails!" he bellowed. "Secure hatches and weigh the anchor!"

"No . . ." Catherine called softly, so softly Danton barely heard her. "No. Danton you cannot. Come with us. You'll be killed."

Danton inclined his head toward her. "I will return, *chérie.* I've lived too long. I will keep living."

La Furia made ready to sail, and Danton kept walking. He ignored the sounds of the sails as the trade winds punched them open. There was no going back.

Flanked by Antonio and Eduardo, Danton took purposeful strides away from his ship, and Catherine. The pressures of his miquelet pistols and flintlocks weighed down his steps. Reminders of what he was about to do.

The day, four and a half years ago, came back to him with startling clarity, as if it had been yesterday. Half of his crew had been slaughtered, the other half disarmed and herded to the quarterdeck, kept at bay with swords. Tied to the mainmast, Danton had been powerless to defend his hold. They'd taken it all. Five hundred thousand pounds in diamonds and three hundred and seventy-five thousand in silks, porcelains, and other goods meant for King Philip.

When the deed was done, all the riches loaded on board Sadi's East Indiaman, the Turk had ordered every survivor overboard into the sea. Then Sadi disembarked himself, bombarded the *Cabo* with cannon fire, and sent her to the depths of the Indian Ocean.

Marooned in waters plagued with sharks, Danton had felt his hatred consume him. That hatred had given him the strength to swim for the shore that was barely within reach. That hatred had given his compatriots the same necessary strength. But the shore had been guarded by razor-sharp fingers of coral. He'd been cut; his crew had been cut. But they had survived.

Danton had survived for this moment.

He headed for the rows of seaside taverns. The breeze picked up his shirt, ruffling the collar and his cuffs. He could smell the salt in the sultry air and taste the blood of revenge on his tongue.

The rest house Hamasa wasn't far up the quay. The arched, double front doors were emblazoned with lotus motifs and etchings of date trees. Danton swung one of the doors open, then he and his entourage entered.

Inside the *han,* Danton quickly accustomed his eyes to the low light of burning oil lamps; gray curls of smoke rose from the spouts to spiral with the sweet tobacco scent of pipes and grape wines. Glazed brick walls bore colorful silk hangings depicting scenes from the Islamic text.

Heavily bearded men in white robes sat at leather-top tables, drinking and playing *shatrang*. Their distrustful gazes converged on Danton and his Spaniards. Danton didn't recognize any of their faces. Though his encounter with Sadi had been brief and humiliating, Danton felt certain he would know the accursed Turk when he saw him.

Danton kept walking with slow, deliberate steps. The jangling metal of his weapons, and those of his companions, announced their presence with unmistakable intention.

Toward the rear of the Hamasa four men convened at a round table provided with pottery bowls filled with olives, figs, and oranges, as well as arabesque-designed, metalwork pitchers. Foregoing the traditional gowns of their religion, the quartet wore dolmans—Turkish robes, in bold colors:

Turkey red, the greens of India calico, Persian blues, and prohibited gold.

Danton dropped his gaze to the man shrouded in gold cloth, feeling the thumping beats of his heart constricting his throat. The man's pointed, coal-black beard seemed faded by the silver hairs running along his jawline. A strong nose and copper complexion dominated his features. Eyes like black currants stared back at him with cocky arrogance, and Danton fought the power of hatred raging through him, making him want to slit the man's throat and be done with it. But he controlled himself, reminded himself that timing was everything when one set out to kill his enemy. And he had at last found him. *Yousef Ahmed Sadi Ahram*. That same malevolent look had been written across the bastard's countenance when he'd overrun *La Estrella del Cabo*.

Sadi lazily plucked a fig from the bowl and bit into the fruit. His movement brought attention to his necklace. A simple leather string with a moleskin pouch.

"Do I know you?" Sadi asked in Turkish, picking a seed from his teeth with his fingernail.

His moment in time had come. Danton had rehearsed his lines for what seemed like a century. "Do you know Danton Luis Cristobal, Marquis de Seville, a captain in the Royal Navy of King Philip of Spain?"

"No." Sadi appeared bored. His three consorts, burdened with jewel-encrusted daggers and traveling pistols, seemed unalarmed. One went so far as to pluck the string on his *rabab*, which lay on the table.

Danton bridled the anger in his voice. Loathing ran deep within him, pumping and heating his blood. "Do you know the man they call the King of the Pirates?"

"I have heard of him," Sadi replied dryly. "I have yet to pass ships with him, but I'm sure when I do, we will cross swords." The Turk admired his fingernails, his hands bearing numerous gold rings. "Why has Allah sent me a man with so many meaningless questions? Who are you?"

Standing rigid and with his heartbeat buzzing in his ears, Danton said, "I am two men. I am no man I recognize."

Sadi drank his wine, then rumbled in a baritone chuckle, "You speak in riddles. Allah is having his fun with me today."

"And I shall have mine, *Sadi.*" Danton lunged for the table and grabbed the Turk by his caftan's soft-fold collar. Antonio and Eduardo were right behind Danton, guns aimed and cocked.

The other three Turkish pirates drew their weapons, but held their fire when Sadi raised his hand to still them.

"You are having your fun," Sadi pronounced snidely, "but I find no amusement in your folly. How is it you know my name?"

"And how is it you have forgotten mine?" Danton met his opponent's drink-rimmed eyes, incensed beyond fury that Sadi could not recall him. Had the man taken down so many at sea, he could not place the faces or names of his victims?

"I asked you to tell me who you were." Sadi narrowed his eyes and lowered his gaze to Danton's hand clutching his robe. "So I can curse your name when I kill you."

Danton seethed with rage; his breath hitched in his throat. "I am the *former* Marquis de Seville and the *present* King of the Pirates," he hissed between clenched teeth. "But you may not call me either. For it is *your* name that will be cursed when I kill *you.*"

Sadi's cohorts shoved their chairs aside to lean into the table. Still, Sadi stalled their attack with his raised hand and an order. "Do not. Not until he tells me how he knows my name."

Danton released the golden fabric from his fingers and slowly straightened. "You took my title, my wife, my son, and my life. You left me with no honor and no way to regain it."

Sadi didn't make a move.

"La Estrella del Cabo," Danton said, wanting to pick Sadi's memory and make the man work to recall him.

"A ship's name." Sadi sneered, his nostrils flaring. "What of it?"

"One hundred and fifty men. Spaniards. Sailing from India to Spain, caught in the trade winds off Johanna Island in the Indian Ocean."

Sadi's expression remained blank.

Danton slammed his fist on the table and brought his face level with Sadi's. "The twenty-fourth of May in the year 1714. On a cloudless day, and with winds beating the sails of my brigantine, you came upon me and my crew, grappled our decks, and seized—"

"The diamonds." Sadi's eyes glittered like the jewels themselves.

The two simple words from the Turk were proof he'd begun to remember the day he took Danton Cristobal's honor.

Danton continued. "The diamonds worth a half-million English pounds in varying carats. The most valuable were the thirteen diamonds that were the hallmark of the lot. One clear, five rose, four canary, and—"

"Three blue. I remember them well." Sadi slowly rose from his chair. The creases in his dolman rippled like a sheet of spun gold. "I attacked your ship and left you to die in the sea with your sunken ship." He smiled in a way Danton thought bordered on madness. "Apparently you did not perish. So now I must dirty my hands."

"You may try," Danton growled and lunged at him, going for his throat. All thoughts of using the forged steel of his weapons fled his mind. He wanted to crush the air from Sadi's windpipe with his bare hands. He wanted to squeeze the life out of him, breath by breath, so the Turk would know what it was like to feel as if he were suffocating. And then it would be over and Sadi would feel nothing at all, but the crescendo of flames from purgatory coming up to lick the flesh from his bones.

The table between them became a hindrance and Danton tried to kick it out with his boots. Then he felt a fire burst inside him just below his ribs. The searing pain cut through his muscles and he felt a wetness start to spread across his shirt. Without looking down, he knew he'd been stabbed.

Stumbling, Danton fell back, taking the leather string and pouch at Sadi's neck with him. The necklace cord snapped and Danton's fist closed around the small drawstring bag.

Fighting not to double over, Danton screamed to Antonio and Eduardo, "He's mine!" He feared his loyal guards would snatch the Turk's life away from him and cheat him out of his coup de grace. But the two Spaniards had embarked on a fracas of handy strokes with the three Turks, felling one with a pistol shot and pairing for a duel of swords with the remaining two.

Danton struggled with the silver butt of his inlaid miquelet, wondering why Sadi didn't finish him with his firearm. The sadistic Turk stood there softly laughing at him. Danton felt his finely tuned coherency slipping and Sadi becoming harder to keep in focus. His arm trembling, Danton raised his gun and cocked the ring-headed hammer back with his damp palm. He curled his finger around the trigger and fired. The flashing explosion momentarily blinded him and charged his ears in a deafening roar, mingling with that of Sadi's bellows.

And then Danton felt himself being pulled into a tidal wave of darkness. His side blazed with pain. The sticky liquid of his own blood spread down his belly. He smelled the sweet-metal scent of his life pouring out of him.

And then he was caught under the arms by Antonio and Eduardo, dragged out of the *han* and whisked into the narrow back streets of Zanzibar before Sadi could give chase.

Danton's last coherent thought was not of the Turk. The picture that clouded his mind was of Catherine. . . .

Would he ever see her again?

Under a dying sun Catherine watched the mauve, lilac, and saffron clouds drift to high buttresses above her as nightfall approached. The surf kicked up the beach, and at her back the jungle achieved a somber blue-green palette.

In the darkened distance, toward the village, drums beat a regular rat-a-tat, a continuous cadence whose rhythm filled Catherine's head day in and day out. From the trees the mournful shrieks of Danton's lemurs seemed to sing in unison with the native's music.

SEE-fahk! SEE-fahk!

Though the sounds did not match the words Catherine had put to them, the syllables made clear sense. The lemurs were saying:

One month! One month!

One month since Rainiaro piloted the square rigger out of Zanzibar. One month had passed, and Danton Luis Cristobal had not returned to his Isle of the Lost Souls.

He'd now become a lost soul himself. . . .

Each day, Catherine came to wait and hope and pray he'd return. And each day the sun would set and he'd not appear.

Though no one on the island dared say, Catherine sensed they thought their leader had perished. Slain under the evil blade of the Turk, Sadi. And Antonio and Eduardo with him. From the silence Rainiaro maintained, it was apparent he had his own doubts about Danton's mortality, but he would not discuss the subject with her, nor with anyone else. He'd holed himself in Danton's pink house, rumored to be drinking heavy amounts of liquor and even refusing to go to Reniàla when she'd summoned him.

Catherine had tried to approach the quartermaster, but he'd put her off. No one said anything directly to her, but she knew the crew and the islanders blamed her for Danton's disappearance.

If she and Madeleine hadn't been aboard *La Furia,* all of Danton's men would have fought with their captain, and the safety of the ship and its "precious" cargo be damned. If she hadn't coerced Danton into taking her off his island, he never would have sailed to Zanzibar Town to begin with. She and Danton wouldn't have gone to Bedr bin Khalifa for help, nor had to run out on the sultan.

So when the pirates on Isle of the Lost Souls began to glare at her with contempt, Catherine welcomed their accusing stares, for she'd already faulted herself a thousand times over. If . . . if Danton was indeed dead, she may well have killed him herself.

Catherine plucked a leaf from a vanilla plant and twirled the stem between her fingers as she walked the lonely stretch of beach.

She tried hard to convince herself Danton was alive. He breathed and cursed and lived to tell her he would not take her to Paris until he figured out another plan. But on nights like this one, when the drums beat on and on and Dokobe, Razana, and Pousse-Pousse chanted and screeched their complaints, Catherine despaired.

She was alone in her sorrow. Alone in her misgivings and fears. Madeleine was the only one that kept her from being utterly devastated.

Catherine dared not ask Rainiaro for anything. She'd

resigned herself to waiting out the southwest rains on the small, luxuriant island when November had come and the rainy season of monsoons began. To sail anywhere around the Cape in this weather would be unpredictable. Many ships were blown off course into rocky, coastal shores and broken apart. It would be better to wait and travel in March, when the drier monsoons took over. Possibly, as the months lapsed, Rainiaro and the others would forgive her.

Until then Catherine went on with heart-wrenching loneliness. A loneliness of emotion Madeleine could not fill up with her sunny smiles. Her daughter had always been able to round out her days with merriment and amusement. Though she still found Madeleine's daily accomplishments a triumph, something was missing inside her. Something she hadn't known existed until she'd lost it and felt the emptiness.

She had the ability to embrace someone else.

A man other than Georges Claude.

And Danton had been that man.

She sighed and dropped the leaf. The crash of waves broke into the thrum of the tom-toms while the sun sank below the horizon.

She hadn't realized the truth about herself until it had been too late. She'd always thought of Danton as a thief, a renegade. She'd been attracted to him from the start, but his danger made him forbidden. The fact that he was so like Georges Claude, in the illicit life he led, had trodden over her better judgment. She hadn't stopped to look at the man himself. The personality that made him so alluring.

He'd risked all defending her and Madeleine. He'd faced the ribbing scrutiny of his crew for abandoning a raid on the Spanish *flotas*. Despite his gruff exterior, Danton was a gentle, compassionate man. He'd given Madeleine a birthday party. A gesture that even Georges Claude had not considered for his own child. Madeleine's prior three birthdays had been spent without her father, for he'd been off on expeditions.

And though Danton's demeanor often spoke of brooding and discontentment, he could, and did, laugh on occasion. Usually at her expense, but she forgave him that now. She reflected on the way he'd teased her for being afraid of his lemurs. And the humor he'd found in a thought or word Madeleine would say with innocent frankness.

There was the intense side of Danton too, which she missed. The man filled with passion and exuding his strength with ease. He'd taken her into his arms and given her the most consuming of kisses. He'd held her hand in his own with an ardent protection.

Had he shared kisses like that with his wife? The wife he no longer had.

She would never know.

Catherine inhaled slowly, allowing herself to admit she'd begun to fall in love with Danton Cristobal despite his apparent flaws.

She'd been attracted to his raw masculinity, his vigor, his foreboding, and his smile—rare as it had been. They were constantly on her mind. That she had a part in snuffing out those qualities left her weak and heartsick. She barely touched the meals Tanala brought, eating just enough for sustenance.

Walking to the swing recently erected for Madeleine, Catherine sat on the narrow strip of wood. James Every, one of the few to converse with her, had offered to climb the mangrove to tie the ropes. She'd gratefully accepted his help, and Madeleine had had hours of joy on the swing.

Now, as Catherine began to idly push herself back and forth with the tips of her shoes, she scanned the sea. The sunset momentarily splashed the water in volatile color, then the clouds thickened and snuffed out the light. As they had done the last weeks, the rains came at night. A tepid shower that at times grew heavy enough to require the shutters on the cottage be latched.

Catherine welcomed the sudden downpour. She bent her knees and pushed at the ground. The swing gathered momentum. She needed a release. Any release from the guilty ache consuming her. This childhood pastime was at her disposal, and she leaned back and stretched her legs out, then came forward and tucked her feet under. She swung higher and higher, swaying into the balmy night much as a pendulum on a clock.

Rain pelted her face and she closed her eyes against the strikes.

Higher and higher.

Her hair floated behind her, then curtained her face with curls. Her heartbeat increased with the arc of her swing; faster, harder, and stronger. She rigidly held her tears in check.

Higher and higher.

She propelled to an elevation that almost put her parallel with the ground, but she didn't quit her pumping. On and on, to and fro, she sailed through the storm. The rain saturated her dress and hair as she prepared to fly. Fly and leap from the swing as she had done in her youth. In that fragile and fleeting instant when nothing would hold her but the Lord's hands, she would be free of persecution. She would be absolved of her guilt.

Taking in a quick breath and opening her eyes, she braced her mind for her landing. She let go of the rough hemp and soared. Then there was nothing. Nothing above her or below her but endless space. Vast space and forgiveness.

She touched down on her feet without falling, amazed she'd remembered how to jump from a swing. The jolt impaired her vision and her legs quivered, but she managed to remain standing. She'd forgotten the bouts of dizziness she'd suffered as a child when she played on swings. She fought the hysterical laughter that marched up her throat.

Her grief somewhat vented, she decided to return to the cottage. James was minding Madeleine, and it was time to put her daughter to bed.

Her eyesight still fuzzy, she took a drunkenlike step toward the embankment. Faltering and widening her eyes for a clearer view of her surroundings, she balked. An apparition of a man moved toward her. Jerking her head back, she saw his outline, temporarily illuminated by a flash of lightning. Tall and hale, clad in an out-of-date velvet doublet with a debonair flick of lace at his throat and cuff, Danton Luis Cristobal stared down at her.

The shadow of a beard darkened the lower part of his face. Drops of rain clung to his damp forehead where he'd tied a vermilion cravat around his head to keep his long hair out of his eyes. The breeches that molded his hips and unending legs were daffodil satin and plummeted to verdant hose.

Narrow shoes set with emeralds in the seams encased his feet.

Catherine couldn't help the titter of jittery laughter that floated from her throat. The phantom Danton gave her a wry smile.

It was him, and yet it wasn't. The Danton she knew would never wear such . . . such garish and foppish attire. In her desperation, she'd summoned his likeness, put together like a patchwork quilt sewn by the blind.

"Mon Dieu . . ." She felt faint and giddy. "Danton . . . I've conjured you from the dead."

Were I dead, flames would be licking at my heels."
Danton kicked off one shoe, then the other. The vulgar pair
bounced in turn off the polished trunk of a nearby palm. He
had half a mind to shed his pants and rip free the obscene
stockings sticking to his calves.

He caught Catherine watching him, a dumbfounded
expression on her face. She teetered, acting as if she'd
imbibed a pint of sack.

"You're . . . alive."

"I told you, *chérie,* I would return." He stepped from the
rise and headed toward Catherine. She stood still, as if
rooted to the soggy ground.

She looked sodden clean through. The thin cotton of her
mended dress lay against her bosom, revealing the palm-
sized rounds of her breasts. Her neckline's square bodice
sagged, teasing him with a view of her shift and apricot skin,
which appeared paler in the dark night. Hair normally the
color of ripe wheat hung in a drenched mass, sweeping the
top of her hips.

As he approached, she took a stilted step backward, as if
she really didn't believe who she saw. He could attest to the
fact he was very much alive; feeling the nagging pain of his
healing wound and the remnants of heat inside him when
he'd watched her flight from the swing. Her daring leap had

caused his breath to catch. She'd sailed in the air like an angel without the aid of wings.

"When you told me you would return . . . I didn't believe you."

"Maybe now you will trust me."

Catherine's generous lips fell open. Moisture clung to her mouth and she licked the water away. "I wanted to, but when you didn't come back, I thought . . . I hoped, though . . . oh, *mon Dieu.*" With trepidation she stretched out her arm and placed her palm on his arm, as if to test his existence.

"I'm here, Catherine." He couldn't keep the huskiness from his voice. He'd thought of nothing but her these past weeks. Her smile. Her unfailing determination. Her courage and wit.

"You are." Her eyelids closed halfway and her chin tilted upward. He thought she might swoon, until he understood her meaning. Prayer. Her rose-tinted lips moved in silent litany. She arched her back in relief, and the graceful column of her neck seemed to lengthen.

He found a subtle sensuality in her pose.

Swaying into him, she skimmed her cool fingers inside his silk-lined doublet. She grazed his ribs through the thin fabric of his shirt. Heat skittered up the compact ridges of his bones. Her hands explored, gentle and lingering.

He allowed her this freedom of exploring him.

Then she pulled him to her, closing the distance between them and tightening her arms around his midsection. She laid her cheek against the lace cascading down his chest.

A sharp and wild sensation curled through Danton's belly, clutching hold of him. He knew she hadn't meant to be seductive, but he couldn't suppress the hot rush to his loins. The material of her dress was slick under his touch, and he brought his hands down and over the swell of her buttocks, pulling her into him.

Catherine lifted her head and gazed at him in silence. Dewy drops trickled down her forehead, the arch of her cheekbones, and the bridge of her nose; silvery beads jeweled her sandy eyelashes. He caught her face between his hands, his thumbs stroking the hollows of her cheeks, and kissed her sweet mouth. Her lips were like warm velvet, her taste like fine brandy; a heady and potent mix to numb his brain and shut out the world. Weaving his fingers in the thick weight of her hair, he slanted his lips across hers and deepened the kiss.

Her fingers splayed across his shoulders, drawing him closer, until their heartbeats vibrated together. Unleashing his penned desires, he kissed her as though he'd consume her, showering her with starved kisses that broke on her sighs. He nipped her lower lip, catching the fullness between his teeth, then grazing his tongue across the pouting curve. When Catherine met him, he penetrated her mouth, dueling with her, feeling himself grow thicker and restless.

Plump droplets of rain fell, drowning them in a moist heat.

His hands left her face and trailed the graceful lines of her neck. A shudder ran deep within him, unlike anything he'd ever felt before. He'd been hit, hard, with an urge he couldn't curb, couldn't command to subside with a mental reminder that what they were doing would lead to trouble for both of them.

"Danton . . ." Catherine's lips brushed against his as she spoke his name, her voice thick with emotion. "I thought I'd killed you."

"But here I stand, *linda.*" He explored her mouth, kissing its corners, rediscovering the sweetness inside. "How could you think you'd killed me?"

Her arms left the protection of his coat and draped around his neck. Her fingers reached into his hair. His desire for her strengthened as she stroked him, appreciated him. "Because of me, you were on Zanzibar," she said, her tone unsteady and laced with pain.

He danced kisses across her cheek, to her ear, catching the lobe with his teeth. He felt her shiver against him. "I could have been anywhere when I met Sadi."

"But—"

Danton put a finger to her lips. He didn't want to speak of the Turk. His thoughts were only of her. The perfect fit of her in his arms; the soft curves of her breasts melded against the flat plane of his torso; his thighs and the aching length of him pressed against her abdomen.

She kissed his throat, the rough stubble of beard he'd neglected to scrape away with his razor. Her hands cupped the edge of his jaw, her thumbs meeting his mouth.

He knew that if she continued to touch him, caress him and thoroughly arouse him, take him to the brink where he would have no control, he would break his resolve and make love to her on the beach with the rain as their sheet and the sand as their bed. She wouldn't stop him, but he knew she'd regret her actions. Their intimacy would change nothing between them, only add to the tension of their inevitable separation.

She would still want to leave him.

And perhaps on an emotional level bound together with his hypocritical denial, he could let her go.

Catherine's hands worked into the edges of his opened coat, drawing him nearer as she brought her lips to his. Breath rasped through his throat; he wanted her so much, he could visualize her unclothed and clinging to him, her eyes glazed with abandon.

Catherine kissed him, duplicating the artful dance he'd started. Despite the potent urge for fulfillment clawing his gut, he couldn't keep kissing her or let her kiss him. He reminded himself again who they were and what their lives would be like once she returned to France. Although she'd married and borne a child, there was an innocence about her, and he suspected she'd not given herself to anyone but her husband. He couldn't take the risk of her leaving him carrying his child. He'd had his share of encounters with several of the islander women, all of whom knew how to protect themselves, preventing pregnancy with strong herbs and potions. Though he stacked his faith in the ancient remedies, he was not willing to chance producing a child with Catherine.

Danton pinned Catherine's hands behind her back, meshing his fingers in hers and stroking her palms. As he savored the feel of her mouth on his, he released her fingers and broke away from her. Her lips, bruised from kisses, gave him an instant's regret.

"We should get out of the rain," he suggested in a reasonable voice that lacked enthusiasm. His heart hammered so loudly, he swore he heard the beats echo in his ears.

"What happened to you? Where were you?" A smattering of droplets hit her face, and he couldn't tell if she was crying or not. That she would cry over him made him feel wanted, cared for . . . needed.

"In Zanzibar Town."

"All this time?"

"I was recovering from a stab wound." Remembrance of the keenly honed blade that collided with muscle just below his ribs surfaced the dull ache where his skin had been stitched by Antonio.

Panic washing her features, she stared at the wilted red stock knotted around his forehead. "Does your head still hurt?"

"I wasn't stabbed in my head." Danton almost laughed. His brain *should* have been run through. His mind, normally constant and clear, could only fix on her; a distraction he couldn't shake and could barely control.

"But your cravat."

"My hair's grown too long. The cravat was the only thing at my disposal to keep it from my eyes." Lifting the tail of his shirt from his breeches, Danton said, "The knife grazed my side. Here." He pointed to the neat pink scar located a fraction above the placket of buttons on his waistband.

"Oh . . ." she sighed mournfully.

He wasn't prepared for the gentle whisper of her fingertips on him. He jerked out of her way so she couldn't touch him, inflame him, when he was just starting to cool.

"Who stabbed you? Sadi?"

Not really wanting to discuss the events, but knowing she wouldn't let the subject rest, Danton resigned himself to telling her the truth. He didn't like having to say he thought he'd killed a man, but she needed to know what he was capable of doing. "Let's walk out of the rain." He took her by the arm and steered her up the embankment. "Where is your daughter?"

"In the cottage. With James."

As he recuperated, Danton had thought of the chatterbox. During the days that dragged on and on, he'd even wished she'd been there to talk him senseless. He never thought he'd miss the child.

Clouds divided and thinned, making the walkway to the cottage more discernible by moonlight. The rain let up to a drizzle, but the lull was probably intermittent. Danton had come to understand monsoons were unpredictable. They would converge their wind flows and then unleash torrents from stirred up clouds.

"The Turk. Did you kill him?"

"I don't know." And he honestly didn't. "I may have." Memories of the Hamasa and the confrontation he'd had with Sadi rushed back to Danton. "I shot at him, but my mind wasn't working. My aim was off."

"Oh, Danton. All of your pain for uncertainty."

He heard the pity in her voice. He had nothing to be sorry for. If Sadi lived, which in all likelihood he did, the Turk was without an important piece of his wardrobe. The moleskin pouch and what had been inside. No one knew what Danton had found. Not even Antonio and Eduardo. At the time, Danton had grabbed hold of the small leather bag without much thought and felt certain Sadi hadn't noticed. But the man had noticed by now. He would definitely miss what had been tucked in the drawstring purse.

"Don't be sorry for me, *chérie*. I don't care that I was cut. I had my revenge in my own way." But that was a lie. He could never truly be free now that he had the pouch and the possibilities it offered. "I confronted him and reminded him who I was and what he'd done to me."

Catherine slowed. Mist shrouded her, opaque and soft. Even dampened by the rain, he'd never seen anyone more lovely. "What did he do to you, Danton? What could someone do to you to make you want to kill them?"

"Now's not the time for stories. The tales of my past would fill up the night until sunrise." He put his knuckles to her cheek and followed the silken contour down to her chin. "But I will tell you, Catherine. I never thought I'd want to talk about what happened to me over four years ago, but I do. Just not tonight."

She accepted his answer without opposition. "Are Eduardo and Antonio all right?" she asked, resuming her walk. "They're with you?"

"Yes." The two men had killed Sadi's companions in short order, then saved Danton's life by getting him out of the *han*, vaguely aware that the disgruntled occupants had begun shouting and throwing chairs.

"Were you chased?"

"Without men at his side, Sadi didn't come after us. We left Hamasa and ended up at Bedr's."

Her gasp of surprise made him smile in spite of everything. "You said the sultan might kill you because of me."

"Well, not when I offered him the services of Antonio and Eduardo for the duration of my recovery." Danton had counted himself lucky the Arab's plight had hit him when it did. Looking back now, Danton smiled at the irony of Bedr's poor fortune hitting him when he himself needed the sultan's lodgings. "The summons Bedr received when we were on his patio had been from a local merchant."

"I remember."

"Bedr found himself in a business predicament." Danton needn't spell out the merchant in question was Bedr's hashish supplier. "One of Bedr's commodity sellers threatened to cut out his liver and cook it with olive oil unless Bedr paid him the liras he owed him. The sultan did, but not until the merchant put a curse on his home. Fearing his doom, Bedr welcomed the extra security."

"Bedr made arrangements for you to sail home?"

Danton snorted. "No. We rode with Henry Greenspot, a fellow—"

". . . pirate," she finished without hostility.

Danton wasn't amused by the admission. "Henry is a jovial sot when he wants to be. He was accommodating."

"Your clothes." A corner of Catherine's mouth lifted in a slow smile.

"Mine were ruined. These," he swept his gaze down his coat front, "were no doubt lifted from a coxcomb nobleman ready for his crypt a century ago."

"They are rather unsuitable for you."

He winced. Vanity had never been a part of his character, but having Catherine see him clothed in the idiotic attire made him self-conscious.

"Your friend—Henry—can you trust him knowing where you live?"

"Henry knows the merit of my quiet warning." Danton knocked a frond from his path and allowed Catherine to pass him by. "He'll not run at the mouth."

They'd come upon the thatched dwelling, light spilling from between the window curtains.

Catherine clasped her hands together. "Would you like to see Madeleine?"

"No." He didn't want to face the girl. Too many new discoveries had plagued him. He'd thought himself immune to a child's appeal, but had discovered the opposite was true during his convalescence. Small as his island was, he'd see Madeleine soon enough. He formed a hasty excuse. "I've not been to my home yet. I've only talked to Rainiaro and a handful of my crew. I need sleep, *chérie.*"

"Of course."

An awkward lapse of silence loomed between them. Catherine worried her lip and he saw her reluctance.

"What is it, Catherine?"

She drew in her breath softly. "About my going to Paris . . ."

He braced himself for her petition, knowing it would have come sooner or later. She wanted her freedom too much for her to give up.

"I think it best, if you don't mind," she rushed, "that Madeleine and I wait out the monsoons on Isle of the Lost Souls until March. One shipwreck is enough for me, and I'd feel safer knowing that when we traveled, the threat of a storm wouldn't be at every turn." She meshed her fingers together. "We won't be any bother. I'll make sure Madeleine stays out of your way."

Catherine's postponement couldn't have surprised him more. "When did you come to this conclusion?"

"Actually, the day on the beach when—"

"You set the fire."

She nodded, gazing at her fingers and then up at him. "I was going to let it burn, Danton, but I realized I couldn't hurt you and your crew that way, and I put the flames out—or so I thought. It truly was an accident, but brought on by something that happened with Madeleine."

"What?" Concern lifted his brows.

"I—I discovered Madeleine playing with a pistol in the

cook's house. It wasn't loaded. She'd lifted a floor plank and found a case of weapons."

"*Maudit,* Catherine, you should have told me."

"Yes."

"What did you do with the guns?"

"I put them where she couldn't reach them."

He was furious with himself over the mishap. "I'll have you moved into my house."

"That won't be necessary," she quickly replied. "There aren't any more dangers she can uncover. I checked."

Danton inhaled deeply. "It would seem I owe you an apology for the insensitive state of your quarters."

"But you had no time to prepare for my arrival, nor did you want a woman and child here. I understand now that you weren't punishing me by keeping me on your island. You were only doing what you thought best for Madeleine and me." She took a deep breath punctuated with a slow sigh. "You don't know how hard it was for me to admit that."

"I think I do."

"I still would like to take Madeleine to Paris. I just won't be bothering you about the journey until the season changes."

Danton found the prospects very satisfying. Without that argument between them, life could be sweet. Thinking about the days ahead made him smile. "You may stay, Catherine, for as long as you like."

Jacaranda blossoms sifted down on Catherine like violet snow. She sat on a weathered bench beneath the showy tree, slicing lemons to make punch. Mingling with the citrus, the woodsy scent of amaryllis drifted from the thick hedges that isolated the cottage from Danton's courtyard.

"I'm having a party, *Maman.*" Madeleine played with her doll by the coffee bushes that grew wild. She plucked the glossy leaves and used them as plates. She set one cherrylike bean on each leaf. "I'm pretending these are sweet biscuits. Everybody gets to have one and Nanette is wearing the new dress you made her for my birthday present."

Smiling, Catherine wiped the juice from her hands. Her daughter's imagination had become the child's only resource; thankfully, Madeleine could invent and create almost anything from simple ingredients.

Madeleine walked Nanette to a circle of leaves, the flower-patterned dimity dress on the doll swaying with her arm movements. Catherine wished she'd had enough material to make Madeleine a new dress too. But she had no fabric left. The doll's dress had come from one of her old gowns that had been mended too often to take another stitch of repair. In places the cloth had become so thin, she was able to rip it with meager pressure.

"Could I invite Monsieur Pirate to my tea party?"

"No," Catherine responded without delay.

"Why not? I haven't seen him in a year."

Catherine held back her smile. Madeleine still hadn't grasped the difference between a week, month, or a year. They were all the same to a child—an eternity.

"Because Monsieur Cristobal has only been back for a day and he's occupied with other matters."

"I don't have anyone to play with me," Madeleine complained.

"I see Nanette in your arms."

Madeleine pursed her lips and huffed. "She can't talk and she's ugly."

"Madeleine," Catherine scolded, "I thought you loved Nanette."

"I do, but she needs hair. Look." Madeleine shoved the doll at Catherine. "See, *Maman.* Nanette's hair is falling out."

Catherine inspected the dolly. When new, the black hair had been coiffured into a stylish coil with three ringlets on either side of her face. Those original lengths that had been crocheted onto Nanette's head had come loose in spots, lost across two continents. A few clumps remained, but the rough bald spots were painful for a child to accept. "*Oui.* She does need new hair. Let me think of something, will you, *mon chou?*"

"How long will it take you to think?"

Turning back to the lemons, Catherine said, "I'll give it my attention while I finish the punch."

Madeleine was quiet, then frowned. "But I can't wait all the day away."

Catherine laughed.

Dejected for a only a matter of seconds, suddenly Madeleine's face beamed. "I have an idea, *Maman!*"

Before Catherine could ask, Madeleine went into the cook's quarters and returned with Catherine's sewing scissors. "I'm going to cut some of the hairy things off the coc'nuts and we can put them on Nanette's head!" she declared proudly.

Arching her brows, Catherine looked at Madeleine with skepticism and tried to be practical without discouraging her daughter. "I don't think that will work."

"*Oui*, it will," Madeleine insisted. Her child's stubbornness tugged at Catherine's heart. She supposed she should let Madeleine try and fix her doll herself. She could sew some of the fibers on the doll's head, silly as that would look.

"All right, Madeleine. Be careful with the scissors," Catherine advised with concern. She'd begun to teach her daughter the basic elements of sewing, and Madeleine knew the care involved with handling shears. She didn't overly worry about Madeleine harming herself; the blades bordered on being too dull to cut. "Even though you know how to use them, remember the tips. Carry them like *Maman* showed you."

Madeleine put the points down. "Like this."

"*Oui*. You stay where you can hear me call you."

"I will, *Maman*." She chose her steps carefully, making certain she kept the scissors dropped at her side. Ten feet or so away, she stopped at a row of pepper vines bearing clusters of peppercorns and snipped several free.

Catherine resumed her work. What had begun as a venture to gain her dolly hair had quickly become the novelty of using the scissors.

A hum of bees provided music for the lazy afternoon. Everything seemed to smell fresher from the rain the night before. The surrounding earth had dried under the hot sun this morning and the jacaranda trees' fragrance lent a richer perfume.

Catherine had risen early and gone to the lemon grove to pick the fruits. She'd decided to make enough punch for the entire crew, and hoped they would accept her peace offering because Danton had returned. And she'd made a mental note to personally take a pitcher to Antonio and Eduardo. She vowed not to be wary of the foreboding Spaniards any longer. They might stand tall as giraffes, and were flanked with enough muscle for a pride of lions, but they'd made sure Danton had been taken care of on Zanzibar. Their constancy had gained her respect.

The tart spray of zest spattered her hands as Catherine cut into another lemon's peel. She should have asked Tanala for a cutting board, but once she'd started, she hadn't wanted to leave the inviting sunshine.

She wondered if Danton would visit her today. She couldn't expect him to. He had other priorities. But his kiss last night had been a wonderful welcome home, and she sensed it had been more than mutual comfort over his return. They'd shared an intense physical awareness of one another and she'd felt a certain sadness when he'd said he had to go.

Being with him had reminded her of how much she'd missed him. Missed his embrace, his company, and his friendship.

She hadn't had a friend since Hadi, and even then, Hadi had been respectful and reserved. She hadn't been able to talk to him on broader subjects. And she had never kissed him.

That her relationship with Danton Cristobal had built into a quiet friendship came as a surprise to her. She'd never thought she would find the companionship of a pirate desirable. She never thought she'd be looking forward to his appearance.

The last lemon pared, Catherine rinsed the sticky juice off her fingers in a bowl filled with water. "Madeleine?" she called absently. Waiting for the routine reply, Catherine didn't look up. She took the towel from her lap and set it aside. "Madeleine?"

When no response came, Catherine looked up. The spot by the peppercorns was deserted. "Madeleine!"

Nothing.

Catherine stood and visually searched the low brush for the top of Madeleine's brown head. Gazing toward the cottage and then the flower garden, she found no traces of her daughter. Not a patch of pink from her cotton dress, nor a show of golden skin from her bare arms.

"Madeleine!" Her voice held a note of impatience. *"Viens ici!"*

Madeleine didn't come back.

Catherine told herself to remain calm. Panicking would be premature. Madeleine had no doubt wandered, engaged with cutting up the entire island. She was probably quite safe and sound, snipping a hedge somewhere. But even so, when she found her stray daughter, she'd have to give her a sound scolding.

Danton wasn't asleep, but neither was he coherent. He drifted in that place halfway between, where he could hear the trill of the cuckoos that sang from the tops of rosewood trees and feel the sun bake his face. The open veranda off his bedroom had looked too tempting to resist.

Stretched out on his hammock, he rested his forearm on his forehead and dangled one leg over the side of the canvas strip. He pushed himself in a slow sway. The cords bound to the porticos groaned, an even lull to relax him further. How often did he lay around in the middle of the day?

He reasoned his wound had left him lethargic.

Smirking in the haze of his laziness, even he had to laugh at that one. He was sound as he'd ever been. No, the basis for his idleness came from a deep-rooted sense of peace.

He'd decided to give up piracy.

Not that he could ever go back to his former life. His old way of living had died with his wife and son. He could never grace Spanish soil again, unless it was to redeem himself. And he hoped to be able to do just that with the treasure map and the sixteen-carat clear diamond that had been in Sadi's pouch.

Though Danton had never searched for the diamonds Sadi had stolen from him, he'd never heard of them surfacing in the foreign markets either.

Since the diamonds had been from a distinct collection, Danton had assumed the Turk would slowly trade out the jewels and gain his fortune—the fortune he had been made to suffer the loss for. But Sadi had apparently buried them, according to the map he'd found in the pouch, and this original diamond was a reminder of the king's treasure.

If he could find and regain the other twelve diamonds, he could return them to King Philip and ask for a pardon. Now all he had to do was find out which island Sadi had buried them on by the markings on the map. The devil knew, the solution sounded too easy. It was going to take many long hours of study to find the correct location, and even then there was no guarantee that his hunch was right.

But if he did find the diamonds, giving them back would be the end of the long journey that had turned him into a bitter man. He could not resurrect the past. He could not bring his son into his arms, nor make love to his wife. He had to go on.

He had to start living again.

Danton sighed and felt his muscles slacken. The sun's heat poured over him, touching him with a sluggish finger. Unable to fight the listlessness that claimed him, Danton's thoughts floated to darkness.

He wasn't sure how long he slept before he felt a tugging on his scalp and *the presence*. Darting his eyelids open, he stared into a pair of frightened blue eyes. The dilated pupils appeared like jet marbles, round and glassy. Madeleine peered at him with a guilt-ridden face.

He let out an imprudent expletive.

"Don't kill me, Monsieur Pirate," she whispered. "It was an accident." Her chin came to the edge of his hammock and she quickly skipped backward.

"What?" he growled, shaking the sleep from his mind.

"Don't tell my *maman*. Please."

From her tone alone, he knew whatever mischief she'd gotten into was serious. "Madeleine, what have you done?"

Her mouth clamped together like he'd come at her with a spoonful of remedy elixir. She gave him a pair of shears. He frowned at them. "Your mother doesn't let you have scissors, does she?"

The child nodded. "I can have them. I'm just not supposed to hurt myself or cut anything bad."

"Did you hurt yourself?"

She shook her head, and he began to get the picture. "You cut something you shouldn't have."

"Uh-huh."

He sat up and cocked his brow, not sure he wanted to know. Had he really thought he'd missed the chatterbox? "What did you cut, Madeleine?"

She held out a lock of hair. Black. Long. *His.*

Danton's palms began to itch and he couldn't stop the twitch at his jaw. Control. He had to keep control. She was just a child, and children didn't know any better—*did* they? "This was naughty of you, *puppet,*" he ground out, flicking his cropped hair over his left shoulder. The length wouldn't stay. The hunk came tumbling back to rest on his collar.

"You won't tell, will you?" Madeleine gazed at him with a mixture of hope and worry.

"Why did you cut my hair?"

The calmly put question set her a little at ease. "For my dolly, Nanette. Over there." Madeleine spun around and picked up a ragged-looking thing propped next to a pot of orchids. "She's missing hair in places and she looks ugly. I was going to cut some hairy things off a coc'nut, but I couldn't do it. The scissors kept slipping and then I was going to try a different coc'nut, but it was hard and green with no hairy things and I couldn't climb the tree to get more. I even shaked the tree, but the coc'nuts wouldn't come down. So I was playing all over and I walked up here because *Maman* told me you were back and I wanted you to come to my tea party, but she said no." She took a breath to seriously add, "I'm glad you came home and weren't killed by bad men. We thought you were dead and my *maman* was crying lots."

Catherine crying over him? Danton mused.

"When I saw you night-night on this swinging bed, and I saw all the hair you had, I wanted some for Nanette because it matches hers. See?" Madeleine thrust the doll next to his head to prove her point. "It really does match. Can I have some?"

"You already have," he noted dryly. Her bottom lip started to quiver, and he rebounded with, "You may keep what you've cut."

"Are you going to tell my *maman?*"

Danton considered what the consequences would be for the girl if her mother found out. He knew too well Catherine could be very uncompromising. The punishment might fit the crime, but would the punishment serve a purpose? Madeleine would continue to be impish. It was the girl's nature to create upheaval. Why snuff her creative energies? As much as he hated to confess, he rather liked her unpredictability.

"I don't think we should bother your mother about this." She smiled as wide as the Mozambique Channel. "My hair needed a cutting anyway."

Madeleine threw out her arms and struggled to hug him. "I like you!"

Danton stiffened. Madeleine's affection chipped away at his restraint. Before he thought better, he awkwardly brought his hands on the girl's slight back. He had difficulty patting her without too much force. He wasn't used to this; it had been a long time.

"I really, really do like you. I know you're not mean. You're nice."

"Hmm," he grumbled. "You'd better leave the dolly with me. I'll have to find someone who can sew the hair on her."

"Oh, thank you!" She leaned away from him. "Now we'll always be friends and I can live here forever and you can be my papa."

Danton choked and covered the tightness in his throat with a loud cough.

"Won't that be nice, Monsieur Pirate?"

He could barely speak.

"Won't that?"

Her insistence called for an answer, but he couldn't bring himself to give her one. He merely grunted, and she took the sound to mean he agreed.

Mierda, he'd just formed a potentially dangerous alliance, bound together by the spit and paper faith of an impulsive four-year-old.

In the late hours of night, Danton sat at his desk, reposed in his dressing gown. Two tall candles burned brightly from either corner of his desk, giving him enough light to peruse Sadi's map. He'd exhausted himself with the paper that was too small, the ink bleeding in places from either water or grease. No doubt the pig had spilled his food on his

necklace. In a bold scrawl the picture depicted an island—
which could have been one of thousands. North, south, east,
and west had been penned in—not much help, as all the
markings told him was the direction the island faced. A
jagged circle had been drawn inside the isle's small outline,
as if it were an interpretation of a crevice . . . perhaps a
volcano of some kind. In red ink a river ran through the
circle. And then an X at the farthest northwest edge of the
sphere. Not original, but it served the purpose well enough.

Tiring of his mental anguish, Danton stretched his bare
feet out and picked up the needle from his sailor's kit, which
he'd retrieved earlier. With a little spit on his fingers, he
poked a few strands of his hair through the eye. Before he
took up his sewing, he lifted a glass of Madeira at his folded
cuff and took a slow sip.

With a steady hand born from mending scores of canvas
sails, Danton began attaching his hair on Madeleine's doll's
head. He didn't want to question why he'd opted to do the
deed himself. He hastily reasoned he hadn't had a chance to
give the dolly to Tanala, and since he'd found the blasted toy
shoved in an open basket near his desk, he'd decided to use
the doll as a diversion. He could think about the map while
he stitched. Besides, he needed the practice. It had been a
while since he'd sewn anything. Not since he'd made his way
from Spain to Madagascar after his incarceration. He'd
hired on several barks as a sailor and had put in long and
laborious days as a seaman.

The process of putting only several hairs at a time into the
soft, fabric head was tedious work. Danton stilled the needle
and brought his glass to his mouth again for another taste;
then he went back to the slow task at hand.

At the rate he was going, he'd be here all night.

As he sewed, he thought of Esteban. He'd been involved
in his son's life to a certain degree. Sailing had taken him
away for long intervals, but he'd always thought of himself
as a good figure for a son to look up to. Now he'd begun to
question his logic. Reservations swirled inside him. He
hadn't really taken care of his son. He had never fixed
anything of Esteban's that had been broken. There had been
his mother or servants to handle such matters. He hadn't

planned a birthday party for his son; he'd just shown up and held his boy while the staff took care of the details.

Now that he'd turned to piracy and seen the other way of life, he realized his old aristocratic ways had been selfish. He should have been more involved with the nurturing of his child.

Somewhere around one in the morning something dawned on Danton just as his gold clock chimed the hour. The single toll stabbed him with a dose of reality as if he'd pricked his own flesh:

There was more to raising a child than one's devoted presence.

Chapter

12

*I*s she going to throw up?" Danton asked anxiously, as if dealing with that malady would send him retching as well.

"I really do feel like I have to throw up, *Maman.*"

Catherine's stomach bordered on queasiness too. But embarrassment kept her from admitting her nausea in front of Danton. He had taken them to the foothills to watch the natives extract from ylang-ylang flowers the pungent oil used in the making of perfumes. The scent had been pleasant at first, but so strong it soon gave her a headache.

"Will she?" Danton repeated.

"I doubt it. She's only thrown up once," Catherine reassured him. "When she was two years old. We were on camels riding up Mount Jammu. I held her in my lap, but the switchback curves and heat did her in." Catherine dredged that moment from her past with a thin smile. "I never knew camels could be so testy." Annoyed by the mess on his mane, the shaggy beast had turned his head, batted his eyelashes, and tried to nip her knee.

"Jammu?" Danton queried while looking beyond Catherine to check on Madeleine. Catherine followed his line of vision to her daughter. She'd pulled the hem of her dress up to her nose, her petticoats knocking against her ankles and slouched stockings.

"In India," Catherine answered him, but without further elaboration. "Madeleine, put your dress down."

The child did so with a wrinkle of her nose. "But the smell makes me sick."

Catherine wondered if she should suggest they move away, but didn't want to offend Danton. This excursion was his idea.

Sighing, she left the departure open to him, but he said nothing. He suddenly seemed preoccupied by the extraction process. She couldn't help but transfix her gaze on him.

Danton swept his tan fingers through his hair to keep the shorter lengths from dusting his eyes. He'd cut three inches from the ends since his return to the island two weeks ago. His previous style had been wild and rakish, mirroring the persona befitting a privateer. Much as she'd been intrigued by his old rebelliousness, his new, tidier—albeit still with earring—image pleased her as well.

Upon their first meeting, he'd reminded her of a nobleman with a daring edge. Seeing him this way, with his classically handsome features, dressed in a pure white shirt, forest-colored breeches, and black leather boots, she was almost sure he had been born to the aristocracy.

Danton hadn't brought up the subject of his past since he'd conceded wanting to discuss his former life. And she wouldn't ask him; she had no right to pry. Though she longed to hear about his wife. Who had she been? What had happened to her? Each day, her curiosity about Danton grew. Even from small, seemingly insignificant events.

Catherine remembered the afternoon Madeleine had disappeared with her scissors. She'd found her daughter at Danton's home, in his study, playing with his collection of betel nut boxes while Danton put his desk in order. As she'd come upon them, a conspiratorial look had appeared on both of their faces. But when she asked what they had been up to, neither had spoken a word. Amazing for Madeleine, whose idea of a secret meant no secret at all.

Danton had invited them to stay for supper—the first such request since she and Madeleine had arrived on the Isle of the Lost Souls. Catherine had seen no reason to refuse.

That night when she'd put Madeleine to bed, Nanette had been missing. Madeleine never went to sleep without her doll, and Catherine thought her daughter would be frantic over its disappearance. Instead she merely shrugged and said she'd probably left Nanette outside.

The next day, Danton brought Madeleine Nanette with a head of new hair. Black and cropped and sewn with neat stitches. Catherine had asked Danton point-blank why he'd put his hair on the dolly's head. He'd only smiled at her and said that was for him and Madeleine to know.

Much as she approved of Danton's friendship with her daughter, she worried that Madeleine was becoming too attached to him. When they left the island in March, it would be hard on Madeleine to let him go. The child so wanted a father. Georges Claude had not been nearly so attentive toward her. This was a new experience for Madeleine—to have an adult male give her his undivided attention. Not even Hadi had done so.

"I won't throw up, *Maman,* if we walk away from the stink."

Madeleine's suggestion hurtled Catherine out of her musings to deal with her own roiling stomach. "I think that's a good idea." Without waiting for Danton to second the motion, she headed for the shade of a tree. He followed.

The three of them stood beneath the branched overhang of an ebony tree and finished their observations from there.

A dozen women clad in bright fabrics, some with babies in scarflike slings on their backs, worked around the heady ylang-ylang trees. The branches had been cut back to keep their height within reach of the gatherers. The boughs drooped gracefully, clustered with the yellow-green flowers. The women impressed Catherine by balancing flat, woven disks on their heads. As quickly as they plucked the fragrant petals, they methodically tossed them onto their baskets without missing.

A gleaming, potbellied copper still steamed with a powerful scent. Saronged men tipped wire cages filled to the brim with flowers into the distillery. They cascaded down in a bright fall of yellow. The oil began to drip out and fill a small vessel. The pungent sweetness of the concentrated essence made Catherine's eyes tear even at this distance.

Seeing her near to crying, Danton chuckled. "Let's go inside."

Catherine nodded eagerly.

Without hesitation Madeleine snatched hold of Danton's hand. Catherine noticed he didn't balk or try to slip away. Her reservations stopped her from giving Madeleine an encouraging smile.

At a distance from the workings, a house with a step-down roof covered by a shaggy grass cap had been built against the hillside. Walls of sun-dried earthen blocks kept the interior cool. Some of Rainiaro's tribe had come down from the mountain to help with the ylang-ylang. Inside, Reniàla cooked rice on a stove vented by a hole in the ceiling.

The aged Malagasy looked up from her labors with a broad smile. She greeted Danton in her native tongue and motioned for them to sit on the bozaka mats.

Already Catherine's stomach had settled, and the smell of spicy chicken with peppers and garlic kindled her hunger. She took a place by Madeleine, who sat cross-legged on the floor. "I don't feel sick anymore, *Maman,* now that I don't have to smell those stinky flowers."

Danton sat next to Catherine and folded his long legs in a manner that mirrored Madeleine's. His finely tooled boots hugged the strong mold of his shins and muscles of his calves. The green twill of his knee breeches grew tighter under the stress of his position, leaving no margin for her imagination. She could clearly see every ripple and sinewy cord that ran up his thighs and strained the side seam.

"Hungry, *mon petit maki sauvage?*" The underlying sensuality of Danton's words heated her cheeks. He'd caught her staring at him as if she meant to devour him.

"Oui," she murmured. Humiliated, she refused to meet his stare.

Reniàla set bowls in front of them, then seated herself across from Catherine on a homespun mat. As the woman ate, she talked to Danton.

"Aloalo." Then she gestured with her gaunt brown fingers.

"What is she saying?" Catherine asked, taking a sip of spring water.

Danton interpreted. "She said she passed a tomb post and she had a vision."

Catherine had come to understand some of the native faiths of the Merina Group—Elevated People—to which

Reniàla and Rainiaro belonged. They were very religious, believing in totems and sacred burial rituals. And the exhumation of bodies. Catherine didn't deem this a godly practice, but she couldn't refute the ways of a people just because they were different.

Reniàla went on with her story, her hands signaling the sky and the clouds and the birds.

Danton said, "She saw a *do*—snake—and out of its belly came a horde of insects, some flying, some crawling. They feasted on the forest, devouring all the trees and animals."

Reniàla's face became saddened. *"Tsy misy ala."*

"If there is no forest," Danton translated.

"Tsy misy rana."

"Then no more water."

"Tsy misy vary."

"And no more rice."

Catherine knew how important the rice was to the Malagasy. The staple was their mainstay food. They even denoted the time by how many rice cookings things would take to do.

"Monsieur Pirate, you said there weren't bad snakes on your island." Madeleine pressed her spoon into her bowl to scoop out a piece of chicken. "Tell that to Ren'àla and she won't be scared."

Danton addressed the woman, translating Madeleine's words. That he would convey her daughter's message pleased Catherine.

Danton's profile filled her gaze, and she studied the angle of his nose and the fullness of his lips. Would she ever tire of observing him? Then he turned and faced her. "Reniàla also had another vision. About you."

"Me?" Catherine squeaked.

"Zanahary," Reniàla said, looking directly at Catherine.

"The Creator," Danton supplied.

"Zanahary ampongalahy kabary."

"The Creator beat his drum and went into a long oration."

Catherine swallowed as Reniàla continued in her low-slung voice. The words she spoke blended together in chords of musical quality. She became animated and ended with a smile. Her hands reached for Catherine's and she nodded her scarf-covered head.

Reniàla's fingers felt like warm parchment wrapped too tightly around sticks. *"La bon femme,"* she stated in perfect French. Then she stood to clear the bowls and begin rice for the next feasting.

"What did she mean?" Catherine asked.

"She said the Creator came to her and told her you were a good woman. A good woman," he paused, his gray eyes contemplative, "for me."

Catherine sat straighter, fidgeting with the loose ends of grass on her mat. "Oh . . ."

"She said the Creator is never wrong. That you came to the island to save me."

She nervously laughed. "From what?"

"Myself." The intensity of his lowered voice cloaked her and held her still.

"I wish I had some chocolate," Madeleine broke in, shattering the spell between Catherine and Danton. "Do you remember that time when that man gave me some, *Maman?*"

"Oui, I remember." But Catherine's thoughts were not on chocolate or the English duke who'd given Madeleine chocolate in India. Danton held her gaze and she could barely breathe. His eyes looked inside her, drawing out her soul and embracing her. If she was supposed to save him, who would save her from falling completely in love with him?

Madeleine nudged between them and fit her hand into Danton's. "I want to go back to the house now. Can I have an orange sweet biscuit Tanala made, *Maman?*"

The child's question cracked the fragile silence between Catherine and Danton. Without giving Catherine a chance to reply, Danton lifted Madeleine in his arms, then hoisted her on his shoulders. Madeleine squealed with delight as he jostled her; the backs of her skinned knees banged against his chest.

"Did you know I have chocolate?" Danton asked.

"You do!" she screamed. "I want some."

"Madeleine," Catherine warned, standing up. "Ask nice."

"Can I have some, Monsieur Pirate?"

"Yes, Maddie, you may." Danton rose, went to the exit and ducked under the doorway so Madeleine wouldn't hit her head on the frame.

Outside, an increasing breeze shredded the hazy clouds. The puffs tumbled over hills of green so intense under the midday sun, they almost shone blue.

"Monsoon's coming," Danton noted. "We better get back unless you *want* to get caught in the rain." Under the thin surface of his words, she knew precisely what he meant.

Catherine thought of the night when he'd come home. The cool droplets covering them, Danton's mouth on hers; the need to be in his arms and the security she'd felt. If only life could be so simple. She couldn't afford to forget what she wanted, her hopes, her visions for her future and Madeleine's. They didn't belong here. They belonged in France.

She had to keep reminding herself of that or she would never want to go back to civilization.

But later that night, when Madeleine slept soundly on the cot next to hers, Catherine couldn't stop picturing herself in Danton's arms. She kept thinking of Reniàla's prophecy. She had been sent here to save Danton. Right now, she'd have to save herself from him, for all she could do was think about him, desire him. She hadn't felt this strong pull toward a man since she'd first met Georges Claude LeClerc.

Danton Cristobal made her want to uncover the pleasures between a husband and wife—for surely she had missed something in her marriage. That Danton wasn't her husband became a weak argument. She still wanted him, and didn't care that they weren't wed. That thought frightened her, so she'd declined dinner at his home this evening for the first time since that night she'd found Madeleine in his study. She had to keep her distance; she had to remain impersonal. If she didn't, she would be hurt. Terribly.

She didn't know how much longer she could go on with polite talk and hidden innuendoes. It was torture of the worst kind, making her ache and feel empty.

Catherine rolled onto her side and tucked the cotton bedding to her chin. The monsoon ripped open the night with furious gales and intermittent flashes of lightning. She shivered as the wind howled and screamed a whining whistle that rattled the window latches.

The thatch roof above her head rustled each time the wind swirled down on the cottage. Tiny particles of dirt sifted from the rafters; then a few drops of rain snuck through the bound pieces of grass. The plaster walls softened from the moisture, restoring the scent of dung and clay to permeate the single room.

Catherine could abide the rain. She liked the puddles it sired, the deep pools to echo the torrent. It was the sound of the wind that left her cold and afraid. Its fury became so strong at one point, she likened the hum to the drone of a thousand angry bees.

The fat drops beat on the windows in a steady lash and the storm churned the fronds of the palms. Branches of the jacarandas scratched and scraped the glass like claws. Drafts curled around her cot. For all her declarations of independence, she would have gladly disavowed them now if that meant she wouldn't have to be alone. She vacillated between waking Madeleine and taking them to seek refuge in Danton's house and staying put. But she feared he'd think her silly for being afraid.

And then the monsoon grew still.

Catherine sat up in bed clutching the counterpane to her breasts. She listened for the wind, but couldn't hear its call. Just the slow drizzle of rain and the trickle of drops from the eaves.

A roar rumbled in the distance, picking up pitch and speed, and then in an instant it struck the cottage. The straw roof blew away, lifted as if by some invisible giant hand. A gust of wind swooped through the interior and flew around the room, tipping shoes and clothing from shelves and knocking over the vase of orange cosmos Madeleine had put on the table.

"*Maman!*" Madeleine bolted upright in her bed.

Catherine raced from her cot and ran to her daughter's side. "Don't be afraid! Come, *mon chou!* We have to hide!"

She picked up her child, her night rail blowing around her calves. Rain and wind sent sheets of spindrift, raked from the crests of waves, to quickly soak them. Catherine dashed for the old grain bin. The cupboard was large enough for them both to fit into. Catherine went first, then pulled Madeleine in after her. She reached forward and closed the door. The cubicle became pitch-dark.

Madeleine's cries increased. "I want to get out, *Maman!* I want to get out! It's tight and scary, just like monsieur's carpet!"

Catherine cradled her close. "I know, *mon chou,* but we can't. We have to stay out of the wind."

The monsoons Catherine had endured in India were drier and tamer; the rain had fallen lightly, if at all. Even having experienced this kind of tropical storm, she knew if the gales had torn off the roof, they could take a child. She wouldn't jeopardize Madeleine in the hopes of reaching Danton's house for safety. She wondered if he'd heard the destruction.

The minutes ticked by in slow, drawn-out seconds. The rain had started to fall in buckets again and Madeleine could not be consoled. Catherine herself felt the heat of tears filling her eyes, but swallowed them, not allowing herself to be weak.

"Danton will come for us." Catherine assured the child as much as she assured herself.

"I don't ever want to be someplace tight again, *Maman.*"

Catherine cupped Madeleine's cheek and held her tiny face against her breast. "Nor I."

The storm howled, and for a moment Catherine thought she heard her name. And then the call came more clearly.

"Catherine!" Danton's baritone voice bellowed, and relief flooded Catherine's stiff limbs.

"In here!" She hugged Madeleine close. "You see, I knew he would come!"

The bin door came down and they were pelted with water. Danton knelt in front of the opening. His hair dripped rain and the dressing robe he wore clung to his torso. "Catherine, are you all right?"

"Yes."

"Maddie, come here, puppet." Danton held out his arms and the child scrambled for his embrace.

"I'm scared! *Maman* too!"

"*Chérie,* take my hand."

Catherine grasped his wrist and crawled out. Standing in the ruined cottage, she welcomed the strength and comfort Danton offered, burying her face in his soaked collar. She didn't care if she appeared defenseless and terrified.

"We're going to the house. Hold onto my waist, Catherine," he advised, the wind curling the ends of his robe. He wore no shoes, as if the noise had sent him straight from his bed with only a second's pause for his dressing gown.

Danton grasped Madeleine under her arms to carry her; Catherine did as he bade, slipping her right arm around his middle and leaning into him.

Antonio and Eduardo appeared in the doorway with lanterns. Eduardo moved to take Madeleine, but she tucked her face in Danton's shoulder and Danton would not relinquish her. He spoke rapidly to the Spaniards and they began removing the gunpowder and weaponry stores from the demolished room.

Danton used Antonio's lantern to light the path. Soon the imposing pink dwelling appeared, candlelight spilling from the windows.

Danton pushed aside the iron lock on the door. The portal hit the wall on a burst of wind, snuffing the lamp on the entry table. Cursing, he shoved the door in place and strode to the reception room.

Thick candles burned in iron sconces nailed into the walls. Tanala, her kinky hair twisted in a braid, had been sitting in a mohair chair and she rushed forward.

"Madame! Madame!" She wrung her hands.

Danton spoke to her and she quickly left the chamber.

"I told her to heat some water for tea and a bath." Danton threw a mound of pillows aside on the divan, then set Madeleine on the couch. She trembled and didn't want to let go of him. "You will be all right, puppet," he crooned in a voice so gentle Catherine's heart reached out to him. "I will take care of you." He swept a lock of hair from Madeleine's brow, his hand unsteady. "I swear it on my life, and this time nothing will stop me." Then he gazed up at Catherine. "You can't go back to live in the cottage."

The emotions she'd battled before consumed her. In no uncertain words he'd said they would reside with him now.

How could she possibly hope to keep her distance from him when she would be right under his nose?

But the alternatives were few and she hadn't one that made better sense.

In a tone that belied her inner turmoil, Catherine said, "We will stay with you."

Chapter

13

〰️

"Drink this." Danton pressed a crystal tumbler into Catherine's hand. "It's rum and lime." He wasn't sure she'd accept the alcoholic punch. When her trembling fingers grasped the glass, he waited for her to take a drink.

"I thought you said you were having tea brewed."

"Would you rather have that?"

"No." Bringing the rim to her pale lips, she sipped the amber liquid. She didn't shudder or gasp. She took another slow swallow.

Outdoors the monsoon raged on in a battery of torrential rains and wind, while the interior of Danton's home sustained no damage. When he'd built his house with the help of his crew and the islanders, he made sure the structure could withstand the strains of seasonal weather.

"Aren't you going to have any?" she asked, noticing he hadn't poured a glass himself.

"No." He'd partaken while she settled Madeleine in for the night in one of the extra rooms. Then he'd gone to his bedchamber, changed out of his wet robe, and dressed in a fresh shirt, breeches, and a pair of calf-high moccasins he'd purchased on an uneventful trip to the English colonies. Returning to his study, he mentally prepared for Catherine to meet him, hoping she'd come back, as he'd requested when she left. He hadn't stopped to consider whether she would be too tired and worn-out for a discussion. His own nerves had teetered precariously on a precipice of undulating emotion.

He'd come to care for Catherine more than was good for him. For them.

When he'd heard the splintering crash, he'd jumped from his bed, where only minutes before he'd yielded to a sleep stormy as the night. His foremost thought had been saving Catherine and Madeleine. He'd been a man possessed, running through the house and flying out the door without shoes and barely a stitch to cover him. He would not fail them as he had Elena and Esteban.

After he'd reentered his study in dry clothes, he gulped a thimble of rum to collect his thoughts, going over what he would say to her and how he would say what he intended. His fear for Catherine and Madeleine's safety had brought the past rushing back. His brain needed no heavy interference from liquor when he told her about his wife and son.

And then she'd stood in the doorway wearing a peacock-blue banyan—his own—and he lost his sequence of thought. He felt a surge of pride rise up inside him and affect his every muscle, but mostly his heart. An instrument he'd often written off as useless—save to keep him alive, pumping his blood, sustaining his hate. Yet now he felt a quiet stirring, an animation . . . a sense of honor that she would grace his company.

She'd come toward him.

She'd tied his silk dressing robe at her waist. The light-weight fabric clung to the high rounds of her breasts and defined the feminine curve of her hips. Her feet remained bare, peeking from the hem when she'd entered into the room. The ends of her golden hair seemed darker from the slight dampness still in the curls. And the locks had a pillow-rumpled, disheveled appearance. He envisioned her curled next to her daughter, speaking in soft tones of reassurance until the girl fell asleep. He'd often imagined what she would look like next to him, on his bed, her head on his pillow. . . .

The steadily beating rain on the rooftop pulled Danton to the present. In an effort to conceal the evidence of his want for Catherine, he clutched his hands together and let them rest at his groin. A bad mistake. The gesture captured her gaze and rooted it to the spot he'd wanted to draw attention away from. He heard himself asking in a strained voice, "Does the rum warm you, Catherine?" He rounded his desk to stand behind the fanned chair.

She nodded and allowed herself another taste. Licking the rum from her lips—a display that added to his discomfort—she said, "At the sultan's I told you that I drank spirits. You doubted me."

"I doubt you no more."

Catherine took another marginal sip, as if she feared consuming too much too soon. "I don't drink often, though. It makes me . . ." She trailed her sentence. From the faint pink glow on her cheeks, he guessed the unspoken. Alcohol made her feel passionate, lighting her blood on fire. Overindulgence had that same effect on him.

Danton could barely curb the full-blown desire that had risen in him. He needed to say what he had to and not think of anything else. Not think of the teasing slash of skin at her throat or the beautiful length of her legs beneath his banyan.

"Catherine, sit down," he ordered hoarsely.

She eyed him under her lashes with a mixture of caution and curiosity, as if she thought, from the gruff tone of his voice, he were about to give her a dressing down. In the end she relented and chose one of the two seats in front of his desk. He then reclined in his wicker chair.

"What is it, Danton?" She'd dressed herself in a cloak of aloofness, visibly working at being calm. "If you're worried about us staying here, perhaps we shouldn't."

He frowned, more than a little bothered she would think of herself as an imposition. "I'm thinking nothing of the kind. I want to tell you about my past."

The blue in her eyes lightened. "Your wife."

"Yes." Danton picked up a quill from the several strewn across his desk and began to set them to order in his writing box.

Catherine stared at him, waiting.

Damn him, he was stalling. Why had he suddenly grown fearful she'd reject him after she knew the truth?

Before he could change his mind, Danton rushed head-
long into his story. "I entered into the Spanish Royal Navy
eleven years ago. I sailed extensively the first three years of
my service—the British West Indies, the Caribbean, Cape
Horn, the English colonies, and the Ivory Coast. On one of
my return trips home, I met Elena Cervantes at a quiet party
for a retiring admiral. She had no immediate family, only an
aged uncle, Juan, whom she took care of. He'd sailed under
the admiral. I thought Elena incredibly beautiful. She was
sweet and shy. I began courting her, and a month later
proposed marriage."

He was relieved that Catherine made no move to stop
him. He couldn't gloss over his feelings for Elena to spare
her. It wouldn't be fair to Elena's memory.

Danton settled the stopper on his inkwell. "Her Tío Juan
died shortly after our wedding ceremony." He had felt solely
responsible for Elena after Tío Juan's death, making things
all the harder on him when he'd been imprisoned; there had
been no one for him to turn to for help. "There was a lot of
speculation as to why we married. There were no titles in her
family history and I was a marquis."

Catherine studied him, but she could read nothing in her
expression other than her smile of conviction. "I knew you
were a nobleman. Your face shows it."

His laugh lacked the appropriate humor. "There are many
definitions of noble, *chérie*. Now I am infamous for my
exploits, not my title."

"But you were born a marquis. You can't wish your title
away."

"No. Nevertheless, I have been cheated out of using it."
Danton fought the urge to pour himself a drink for fortitude. He hadn't realized how difficult this would be. Only a
select few knew the intimate details of his past, and those
few were men. He felt a bonding and loyalty with them, even
a masculine love, but nothing like what he felt for Catherine
LeClerc. He hadn't wanted to thoroughly examine the
reasons why he wished her to know about his banishment
and his son, but now it became a little clearer.

He'd begun to fall in love with Catherine. When it had all
happened, he couldn't be sure. He wasn't immune to her
charms, to her appearance and her strong love for her child.

That was what had lured him to her. Those attributes made him feel alive inside.

"Go on, Danton." Her soft voice coaxed him, drawing him out of his reflections.

"I married Elena because I loved her." Danton watched Catherine straighten her shoulders and try to camouflage a glimmer in her eyes by looking down on her lap. Did she actually resent his loving someone else? Why . . . could she be falling in love with him? He didn't mean to wound her, but he had to be truthful. "I didn't care that Elena brought nothing to the marriage, and there was no one to object. I was the only living son in line for the title. We were married several months when Elena became pregnant. I asked for duties that kept me closer to Spain. I made short trips to England and France."

"Is that how you know about my homeland?" Her tone held a degree of curtness. "Why you think it a slum for the impoverished and a paradise for the affluent?"

"That was my opinion, Catherine."

"I suppose parts of Spain would leave me feeling the very same way," she defended.

"I am sure they would." He couldn't deny her her view, for in all fairness, she was right. Spain had its share of political divisions. Nothing seemed fair to everyone. That was why he'd adjusted to his island so well. All men here were equals, sharing the wealth, sailing together and living together as brothers. But he couldn't make Catherine understand this without knowing more about him. "Elena gave birth to my son, Esteban." He felt his voice grow thick, his throat ache.

Catherine put her fingers to her lips, as if suddenly recalling a hidden detail. The rain battered the silence between them. Her eyes clouded with remorse, and at last she said, "I once told you you didn't know what it was like to have a child. How that must have hurt you, Danton. I'm sorry. Very sorry."

Her apology meant more to him than a pardon from the lunatic king himself. "You had no way of knowing." Danton wanted to take her into his arms and soothe away her regret. But he couldn't. Not if he wanted to keep a clear head. Instead he shoved a pile of accounting books to the side of his desk, regrouping his thoughts. "Three years after my son's birth, I was commissioned to sail to Calcutta. I was to transport a million English pounds worth of diamonds and goods belonging to King Philip—gifts from the retiring viceroy of Spain. Knowing the great value of my cargo, I asked to be outfitted with a naval sloop for its superior speed, rather than my brigantine, *La Estrella del Cabo*."

"What does the name mean?"

"The Star of the Cape." Danton absently looked toward the closed window. Out in the sea, several miles from shore, the *Cabo* lay buried in her watery grave. "I was denied the snow rig and set sail in the brig. She was a good ship, but not a fast runner when loaded down. I'd heard of the dangers of pirates in these waters and made sure my men were alert." He inhaled, gathering his recollections. "We had no problem securing the cargo in Calcutta, and within a week we were on our way home. The *Cabo*'s sails caught the trade winds and we drifted farther west than I would have liked. Just outside Johanna Island, we spotted an East Indiaman bearing English colors."

Catherine drank her rum, the glass nearly empty now. She set the tumbler on his desk without asking for more. "When I was in Surat, we saw several East Indiamans. They're very big and imposing."

"Yes. Bigger than a brig and able to carry far more cannons."

She fidgeted with the tie to the banyan, weaving the end through her fingers. "Sadi's ship—the one in Zanzibar—that was an East Indiaman, wasn't it?"

"It was."

Her expression implied she was beginning to put the pieces together. If not with an absolute understanding, at least with a certain connection.

"The Indiaman caught up to us in the Comoros. Wary, I gave the orders to raise flags. We flew the pennant of Spain just as their English banner came down and Sadi's colors went up. Black with a center skull and bones. I knew then I'd made a terrible mistake."

"But you couldn't have known!"

Danton didn't need her to defend him. He knew in his

heart he'd made a grave error in waiting for the Indiaman to show her colors without having his men ready to break speed. That error that cost him his life without spilling his blood. "I should have had more sense."

"What happened?"

"We were overrun. I only had twenty-one cannons and thirty-four muskets to share amid a crew of one hundred and thirty. My guess would be there had been two hundred raging Turks on Sadi's decks, all fully armed with swords and pistols. We were slaughtered. I lost half my men in the first five minutes. Why Sadi didn't kill me, I don't know." Then, louder, he added, "Possibly because he thought me insane. I still fought, though my sword was broken midway down the hilt. I refused to abandon my ship."

"I can imagine you would fight until the end, Danton."

"A lot of good it did me. I was tied to the mainmast while the remaining members of my crew were taken to the quarterdeck. We all watched as the fortune left our hold for the Turk's." The bitter remembrance was hard for Danton to swallow. "When we'd been lightened of our load, we were pushed overboard. The *Cabo*'s hull was shot to hell, sunk while we struggled with our lives."

"Antonio and Eduardo. They were with you."

"Yes. After Sadi sailed on, I had to make a choice for my crew and myself. Float in the water and wait for the sharks to eat us or swim for the shores we could see in the distance."

"And you swam."

"Through the coral that blocked our way."

"The scars." Her gaze caressed his hands, then roved to his chest. Tears glistened in her soft eyes, and he wanted to put her fears to rest. He didn't regret the scars. They'd come to symbolize a part of his life he couldn't change. They reminded him of who he was and why he'd turned to piracy. On those days when he thought he was fooling himself, that he wasn't any more of a privateer than Rainiaro, he would look down at his hands and remember what made him so. "We made it to the sand. Here, actually."

"Isle of the Lost Souls?" Her look became one of astonishment.

He couldn't help smiling with irony. "Yes. I live on the very island I was doomed to die next to."

"No wonder you call it what you do. I'd always thought the name morbid, but now it has a sad purpose." She finished her rum, her cheeks becoming dusky and flushed. "How did you get off the island?"

"We were here six months before a crippled square rigger sailed into the inlet. She was manned by Malagasy pirates."

Catherine's brows rose in question.

"Good pirates," Danton smiled, "if I may use the term loosely. Rainiaro had been on that ship, trying his hand at piracy after his rice crops failed. Mind you, he's an efficient quartermaster, but the natives are better fishermen and farmers than thieves on the high seas."

"I hadn't imagined Rainiaro as a lifelong pirate," she offered.

Danton stretched out his legs. "The rigger had just lost her pirate captain—killed in a skirmish. The short-handed crew had been scouring the coastlines of islands for a place to patch their damaged ship before sailing onto Madagascar."

"It was a pirate haven then too?"

"This happened over four years ago, *chérie*. Madagascar has been used for many, many years to elude authority in the sweet trade."

"Did these pirates and Rainiaro help you?"

"They did. We helped them first by repairing their ship's hull with the island's resources. Actually, in our time here, my men and I found the island to be a natural wonder. We didn't lack for game or water, and the weather was pleasant enough. Once we had the square rigger seaworthy again, we all took her into Madagascar. During the journey, I was voted their new captain."

"Voted?"

"Pirates," he said, "do things very fairly. A captain is voted on by the majority. I won, no contest."

"But you didn't want to be a pirate, did you?"

"No. I wanted to return to Spain. To see Elena and Esteban. To tell King Philip what had happened."

"And you did?"

"Yes. I refused my 'appointment' and wished the pirates well as a handful of my men and I boarded a Portuguese man-of-war bound for ports near Spain. Some of my crew stayed on in Madagascar, fearing the repercussions for their part in losing the diamonds and goods. I couldn't deny them their right to choose their lives. They'd all been through hell."

"Antonio and Eduardo?"

"They stayed behind." Danton had actually felt relieved that they had. He'd known before he left Spain for India that King Philip had been rumored to be suffering mental distress over the death of his first wife. Knowing the amount of riches involved that had been purloined, the king could have lashed out at all the crew rather than their captain, placing blame where it shouldn't have gone. Little did Danton know, the repercussions wouldn't come close to fitting the crime, and he'd lose his entire identity. But given the chance to do over again, he would have gone back to Spain. Never could he have deserted Elena and his son.

"Once you returned, didn't you explain to the king what had happened?"

"I did. But he saw things the way he wanted to." Danton rose from his chair, unable to sit while he continued. "I was imprisoned immediately for misconduct, not even allowed a moment with my wife and child."

"But you'd asked for a different ship!" Catherine cried. "You did what you thought best."

"But it wasn't good enough." Danton went to the window and stared out into the darkness. "Esteban had had another birthday in my absence and was coming into another one. He would have been . . ."

". . . four," she finished for him softly.

"I spent a month in jail in conditions so foul I won't subject you to a description. I repeatedly asked to see Elena and Esteban, and was denied. I was finally granted permission by Queen Elizabeth. She'd begun to take over some of the lesser duties of the throne for His Highness, who was becoming more and more unfit to rule."

"He had to be unfit to rule," Catherine said. "Why would he put you in jail?"

Danton gripped the windowsill. "To punish me. To make me suffer for losing diamonds that can never be replaced. But nothing could have made me suffer more than seeing my wife and son come to me in rags and coughing with sickness. They'd been thrown into the streets, locked from my home. My title had been stripped, my holdings confiscated. I had no more wealth and honor than a rat living in the gutter."

"Danton," her voice was clouded with tears, "I'm so sorry."

He continued, knowing that he couldn't stop now or he'd never tell her the rest. "I wanted to take Elena into my arms, but the bars prevented me. I wanted to reach for my son—the son I could hardly recognize, and sit him on my lap. Damn him!" Danton cursed so suddenly he heard Catherine gasp. "Damn that bastard Sadi for taking all that I held dear." Danton's eyes stung with unshed tears and he blinked them back. "The guard came to take them away. Jesu," he whispered. "I can still hear Esteban calling, 'Papá, I want you! Papá, I want you.'"

Catherine left her chair and came to him, embracing him from behind. He felt the warmth of her cheek pressed against his back. He couldn't stop the convulsions that racked his chest. He began to cry. Cry for the son he'd lost and would never hold. Cry for the wife he'd loved with every breath in his being.

"Oh . . . Danton." She gently squeezed him, splaying her fingers across his chest.

Danton fought for control, gulping back the tears that had shamed him. He'd never cried before. Maybe he should have. Maybe then it wouldn't be so hard to stop now. He pulled in a shaky breath and willed himself to get hold of his sorrow. "A month later, they died from exposure and starvation. The queen let out of jail for their burial. The last time I was with them was to watch their wooden caskets being lowered into the ground. The final chapter to my life. The death of the Marquis de Seville," he exhaled with a shudder.

Danton turned away from the windowpane to see the anguish on Catherine's face as she slipped into his arms. "I feel so stupid," she said. Tears ran down her cheeks and dampened the open collar of his shirt. "Why didn't you tell me sooner? Why did you give Madeleine a party, knowing that your own son would have been four?"

"I can't look back on my own misery and make life miserable for others. Madeleine deserved a party. I gave her one."

"And so much more!"

Danton didn't want Catherine's gratitude; he didn't know what to do with compliments—especially ones that were spoken on a whim to soothe his suffering.

He turned to look out the window once again. Instead of seeing the storm that ravaged his patio and the beach beyond, he saw his reflection, Catherine next to him.

Like a pair, a couple.

Both sharing his grief.

He licked the salt from his lips and took in a deep, cleansing breath. He hadn't set out to vent his heartache in front of Catherine so that they could despair together. He wasn't a man to wear his emotions on his shirtsleeve. And besides, she had her own problems—one of which was getting to Paris. And he would help her go when the time came. Despite Reniàla's vision, Catherine could do nothing to save him from who he'd become.

He had to save himself.

The key was in the map he'd found in Sadi's moleskin pouch—the jewel safely stowed away in a hidden receptacle of his globe. He'd gone over the crude map so many times now, the edges had begun to curl and grow thin. All he had to do was solve the puzzle and he'd be free.

"Danton . . . are you all right?" Catherine asked.

He snapped from his thoughts and gazed at his likeness in the glass. His nostrils had flared and his breath left mist on the panes. He hadn't made up his mind whether or not to tell her about Sadi's pouch, but there were several things he'd left unsaid. "I wasn't put to death because of Queen Elizabeth. She overruled her husband and declared I be banished instead. I've served four years in exile and am eligible to return in six. But I have no desire to go back to Spain. My country is here. On my island. I am as happy as I can be."

"But not as happy as you deserve to be." She didn't break away from him, and her warmth seeped through the thin fabric covering his arm. He could feel her pulse in her wrist as she touched his shoulder. "Why did you come back to this island?"

"It seemed the only logical thing to do," Danton said without hesitation. "With no money in my purse, it took me months to reach Madagascar hiring on as a sailor for various captains. Once I arrived, I collected Antonio and Eduardo and the few remaining members of my original crew, as well as the band of Malagasy pirates who'd yet to find themselves a captain."

"You became captain again and returned to your island of lost souls."

"Not so lost. Rainiaro was here."

"He hadn't been on Madagascar?"

"In our absence, he and the members of his tribe took up residency here. He found the climate and terrain better suited for the Merina Group. Once we arrived, he welcomed us, knowing his people would be protected from feudal invasion as long as the waters were guarded by privateers. He ended up taking up a sword with us after all."

"You corrupted him." Her easy tone tried to lighten the mood.

"I didn't bend his arm, Catherine."

Danton left the window and the security of Catherine's embrace. He needn't feel the strength she offered. He had his own legs to stand on, his own mind to dictate the outcome of his search; the search that had ended on Zanzibar and began in the Bwawani lodgings when he'd discovered the map while he recuperated.

"It all makes sense now," she said, "why you plunder Spanish ships. I can't say I blame you."

"What better way to get back at the king?" Danton phrased in question, knowing full well the answer. "That bastard Philip stole everything that I ever treasured. I take back what I can."

She was silent for a long pause, then, "You've found Sadi. Has your revenge truly been satisfied?"

"Would you believe me if I said yes?"

"No."

"I need never set eyes on Sadi again. The honor I lost will have to come back by my hands, not by the death of a Turk."

He would decipher the map, regain the diamonds, and clear his name by returning the jewels to the Spanish throne. Of course he might not find them, but he'd already used up four years, what would four more be?

"No, *chérie*, I won't be looking for him in my spyglass anymore, but at least now I know which direction to go."

The rain subsided to a tranquil patter, and the clock on Danton's desk struck two. Catherine couldn't believe the hour had grown so late. She really should check on Madeleine and get some rest herself. But the idea of leaving Danton after what he'd just shared with her left her wanting to be with him. She wondered how he would react to her own past. It seemed mundane in comparison. She'd met a man, fallen in love, married him, borne his child and fell out of love with him. That there had been a lifetime in between meant nothing. Danton had lived through far worse.

If he asked, she would tell him about Georges Claude. Just not tonight. Her eyelids felt heavy. The rum she'd drank earlier had worn off entirely. Were it not for the late hour, she would have asked for another glass to help her sleep. Her mind was in turmoil. She'd never known a man to be so courageous and forthright. Could she leave him? Did she want to?

"You should go to bed, Catherine." Danton poured himself an inch of rum and drained the alcohol with one swallow.

She was reluctant to depart. "If you're going to have another, I'll join you."

Danton peeked at her from the edge of the black liquor cabinet's door. "You surprise me, *chérie*. Not many people do."

She slowly walked toward him and took the glass he extended to her. The rum and lime tasted tart and sweet at the same time. The drink went down her throat with ease and instantly mellowed her insides.

"I'm not proud of the fact I've been drunk on several occasions," she admitted.

"Do tell." His brow lifted and a faint smile caught his mouth.

The first one that came to mind was the night in India

when she and Georges Claude had made love for the last time. She'd been brazen and wanton, doing things she'd never dreamed of. The memory brought a hot blush to her cheeks. "I can't recall the details," she said lamely.

"Liar," he countered, and added a dash more rum to his tumbler. "Whatever you did must have been quite indecent. You shock me, Catherine."

She stuck her arm out, glass in hand, feeling slightly guilty for wanting more of the rum.

He easily obliged her.

"If you match me drink for drink, I may see you indecent before the sun rises."

Catherine racked her brain for a witty retort, but could think of nothing except gratifying his premonition. She had only been intimate with her husband. She hadn't found anyone she cared enough for to want to be physically close to him.

She sipped her rum in quiet thought, gazing furtively at Danton. His back was to her as he busied himself at his liquor cabinet.

As she watched the muscles on his back strain the fabric of his shirt, she appreciated the powerful strength of his arms and the lean hardness of his legs. She thought of him filling the vacancy in her life.

In his own way, he was honorable. He hadn't sunk the Spanish *flotas* when he'd discovered her and Madeleine on board *La Furia*.

As for decent, he could be very gracious without even trying.

Kind . . . he'd proved himself patient with Madeleine.

And loving . . . did she mean loving in the sense of romantics, or loving as a lover? She decided she meant both, but he lived up to both expectations. His kisses had confirmed he knew how to please her.

As for being an upstanding citizen, in his island community, he held the highest honor. King.

He might have been appealing in all categories, but there was one facet she'd overlooked, and it had absolutely nothing to do with Danton Cristobal's character. It concerned the way she felt around him. Quite simply: restless.

Restless for his presence.

Restless for his wit and even for his bouts of temperament.

Restless for his kisses . . . and more.

She'd recently begun to wonder how she would feel making love to a man other than her husband. She sensed that anything between herself and Danton would be electrifying. The sensation would be new and untried; something to end all experiences.

Wild.

Wicked.

Wonderful.

And then the obvious hit her with as much bluster as the monsoon: she loved Danton Luis Cristobal.

Mon Dieu . . . what would she do about that?

The punch lightened her mood and slackened the tension in her muscles, but her mind was as clear as it ever was. A ridiculous and thoroughly unladylike notion took hold of her. What *would* he do if *she* kissed *him* for a change?

"Something funny?" Danton asked. "You've the grin of a besotted milkmaid on your face."

Catherine sobered, but she couldn't will away the tingling ache in her breasts and a great longing to be in Danton's arms. "I can think of nothing amusing."

His eyes narrowed suspiciously. "What are you thinking?"

"I don't think you want to know."

One side of Danton's mouth quirked upward. "Are you foxed?"

"Not in the least."

"Well, after my tragic confession, we're both owed a falling into our cups."

"Your disclosure doesn't make me want to find the end of a bottle. I want to . . ." She put her glass down and took a step closer to him. "I want to hold you because I'm sad for you."

"Don't pity me, Catherine." The bite to his tone left her unsure of herself.

"I don't. I—" She bit her lip. For the longest time, she'd felt herself falling. Falling in love. She no longer tried to stop the plummet. It was a wonderful feeling, and she wanted it to touch her everywhere in her being.

Before she lost her nerve, she braced her hands on his shoulders, stood on her tiptoes and kissed the corner of his mouth. Then she met the fullness of his lips with her own. He tasted like warm sunshine. She deepened her kiss, and his arms came around her waist and slid up the glossy fabric of her banyan.

"Catherine, do you know what you're doing?"

"Yes. I'm kissing you."

On those words, he took over the kiss and thoroughly ravaged her mouth. A headiness fogged her mind. She arched her back, pressing her breasts into him, wanting to feel his bare skin next to hers. Underneath her robe she wore nothing. She hadn't intended for this to happen. She'd thought to hear him out and then retire.

But this was far more pleasant than sleeping.

Far more pleasurable.

If only she could get rid of the confining robe . . .

And then the material slipped off one shoulder and Danton's fingers lightly skimmed her naked arm. She shivered with delight.

Danton nuzzled the curve between her neck and shoulder, kissing her there, arousing her with his mouth.

They stumbled backward, Danton's hips hitting the edge of his desk. She braced herself next to him.

"Catherine, you're so beautiful. I've never seen anyone as lovely." Danton nipped her earlobe while he slipped his hand up to cup her breast. His thumb teased her nipple through the silk, the sensation releasing an erotic burst of tingles to the core of her breast.

"*You're* beautiful," she whispered into his hair. Hair smelling of musky rain and lightly of vanilla. "When I first saw you, I knew . . ." She groaned as he untied the sash around her waist and parted the banyan; the coolness of the room on her bare skin was intoxicating. ". . . knew you were a man unlike any I'd ever— Oh!"

He'd brought his mouth to her nipple and had taken it into his mouth. The heat of his tongue worked over her, leaving her legs weak. If he hadn't supported her, she would have fallen.

Her fingers curled into the thickness of his black hair, to keep his head close to her breast. She wanted to savor what he was doing, make it last and enjoy the moment. She had never known these feelings, and she wanted to explore them until dawn.

Danton opened his legs and she moved in between them, feeling the length of his arousal through his breeches. And then he dragged his fingertips along the curve of her hip and down her thigh; he ended at her womanhood. For the longest time he slowly ran his thumb back and forth over her, in a small circular motion. The gentle and artful massage sent spirals of pleasure through her. She'd never experienced anything remotely like it.

Catherine shivered when his finger slipped inside her, stroking, stimulating. At first she was shocked, then her every nerve ending focused on what he was doing to her; his mouth suckling her breast, his thumb still moving over the center of her woman's core. The heated tension inside her began to build and soar, heading toward a crescendo of ultimate intensity. She reached for it; she wanted to know it. To hold dear what he was giving her and cherish this moment forever.

She felt the borders of a release, feeling as if she'd been imprisoned by her own desires and Danton was setting her free. She wanted to share this pleasure with him, but she was too lost to stop him.

And then her every muscle went taunt; she shuddered and her legs felt numb and weak. She gasped and clung to Danton, letting the flow of sensations consume her.

When he lifted his head, she pressed a breathless kiss on his mouth. "I didn't know," she whispered against his lips. "I didn't know . . ."

He tenderly kissed her. "Then I'm glad I showed you."

She pressed her cheek to his chest, listening to his heartbeat thrumming against her ear. She breathed in the scent of him; a sea-breezed masculine smell that filled her senses. She wanted more than just her own gratification; she wanted to share herself with him.

Catherine gathered the courage to try and free the laces of his shirt, to remove the garment. His skin felt hot under her knuckles. "I want to touch you too," she said as she pulled on one of the lacings from an eyelet hole.

"Jesu . . ." he moaned thickly, stopping her.

Danton's oath caught her off guard and panic raced through her. Had she done something wrong? She stilled. "What is it?"

"Mierda." Danton curled his fingers around her wrists and held her arms away from him. His breath came in uneven gasps and a sheen of perspiration dampened his forehead. He appeared to be in a great amount of pain.

"Mierda," he repeated, struggling to keep her arms up and away from him.

She tried not to be frightened by the anguished look in his smoldering gray eyes.

"Don't," was all he said.

Catherine trembled, the exposed parts of her figure growing suddenly cold and uncomfortably on display. But she didn't make a move to cover herself. "Are you all right?" she managed in a voice stronger than she felt.

"No," he replied hoarsely. "I'm not. But at least I gave you pleasure."

Catherine felt confused; embarrassed. "I don't understand."

"I confess—God save me from yet another one—I want you beyond reason." Danton gentled his hold on her wrists and eased her arms to her sides. "But I won't risk getting you with child." His fingers pressed into her tender skin, seemingly cutting her pulse points. "There are ways to prevent your conceiving—none of which I'm convinced strongly enough will guarantee you won't. I'm not willing to take the chance. I don't want another child. The son I loved is lost to me. I cannot bear losing another."

In the face of her humiliation, she couldn't speak the words that would denounce his worries:

She couldn't have any more children.

Catherine wiggled out of Danton's hold and closed the folds of her robe with quaking hands. She would not show him the deep hurt she felt. "I don't know what to say."

"Neither do I. I do want you, Catherine. More than you'll ever know."

The tick-tock of his fancy glass-domed clock mixed with her frantic heartbeat. "I don't know if I should thank you or hit you."

He said nothing, and she found it increasingly harder to face him. Before she lost her composure altogether, she quit the study without a backward glance.

Chapter

14

Maman, what are we going to wear today if all our dresses are wet?"

Catherine lay in a massive four-poster bed with her daughter's head tucked under her chin. The white canopy drapings lent an airy atmosphere to a room that resembled a slice of the jungle. Jade, vine-patterned paper covered the walls to provide a vital backdrop for the furnishings. Elements in rich mahogany—a cylinder desk and tufted velvet armchairs—contrasted with the pristine quality of the canopy bed.

"I don't know." Catherine wondered if their belongings could be salvaged after the monsoon. The last she'd seen, clothing and shoes had been whipped through the cottage, out and over the edges of the feeble walls. If she could find what remained, she could launder the garments and they would be salvageable. Until then what, indeed, would they wear?

"I have to use the convenience, *Maman.*"

Catherine let Madeleine wiggle out of her arms and bound over the side of the bed.

Catherine put her hands behind her head and stared at the cross pieces of dark wood that made up the canopy. She didn't want to face Danton in the natural *or* dressed. That she had no clothing only meant she could delay the meeting a little longer.

Her embarrassment came back to her with haunting clarity. She had been too bold. How stupid could she have been? She believed him when he said he didn't want any more children. But his reason hadn't made her feel any better, only worse, because she couldn't have any more babies.

The sun splashed its rays across the floor in a long triangle through the windowpanes.

She needed to get up and brush her hair, and then she'd feel presentable. But that brought her back to the dilemma. She had nothing to wear, but her night rail, and that had been ruined in the monsoon. There was Danton's banyan, but that was hardly appropriate morning attire. She hadn't even a clean shift or stockings.

And what of Madeleine? Her daughter had gone to sleep in one of Danton's lace-cuffed white shirts.

Catherine had slept fitfully, imagining she heard Danton in the room; she'd awake, sit upright and look at the shadows. She'd detected nothing. Then she would lie back down, tuck the coverings up to her chin and try to doze again. But the sheets, the linen shirt Madeleine wore, and the silk of her banyan, all smelled faintly of ylang-ylang and vanilla and the wind that had blown through them on the clothesline. The distinctive scent that was Danton's.

"Maman! Look what I found!"

Catherine sat up and peered over the foot of the bed. Madeleine stood in the doorway to an adjoining chamber.

"Madeleine," Catherine said, slipping her feet over the bed's edge, "you shouldn't have gone in there. That's not our room."

"But look what's inside! The things in it are for *us!* I know it." She ran to Catherine and grabbed hold of her hand. "Come on, *Maman!* Let me show you! You won't believe what's in there!"

Catherine allowed Madeleine to pull her along. The floor felt cool beneath her bare feet, but not chilling. From the heat shafts crossing the runners of carpeting, she could tell the day would be a warm one.

As soon as Madeleine neared the open door, she made

Catherine promise to close her eyes. "It will be much better if you can see them like a surprise, *Maman*. All right?"

Catherine humored her daughter and closed her eyes. "Very well, *mon petit chou chou.*" She put her hand on the wall to use as a bearing as she walked into the second room. "May I open my eyes now?"

"Non. Not yet. I want you to be right here when you"— Madeleine tugged on her hand to take her from the support of the wall moldings—"when you open them. Now, *Maman!* Look!"

Standing in the middle of the floor, Catherine opened her eyes and her mouth dropped open. She turned around in a slow circle. Articles of clothing lay strewn everywhere. Quilted petticoats adorned the throw rugs in front of a mock mantel and hearth; across a bedstead, full-skirted gowns were piled high in a rainbow of colors from pastels to vivid dyes; low-heeled, high-heeled, jewel-heeled, and infant leather kids sat in neat rows on top of a secretary desk. An array of childrens' attire—both girls and boys—had been carefully laid out on a small settee: formal coats with wide cuffs, trousers and vests, miniature ladies' gowns, aprons, camisoles and caps. A tin box on the footstool boasted a tangle of jewelry.

"Can you believe it, *Maman?*"

Catherine could not.

This was not ordinary stuff.

It was expensive. Opulent.

Besides finished garments, there were bolts of cloth and bales of embellishments.

Silks. Brocades. Satins. Velvets. Taffeta. Laces. Flouncing. Gold trimming. Silver braid. Ruching.

"I like this one for you." Madeleine lifted a yellow satin ball gown embroidered with delicate flowers of silken threads. "And see. Matching slippers." She bent to pick up a pair of satin slippers with golden diamond roses decorating the wide tongue. She brought them to her nose. "They smell like sweet biscuits and a dresser drawer."

Catherine took the shoes and smelled them. Allspice and cedar. She handed the pair back to Madeleine. The garments and yards of cloth must have been stored in chests to give them their pungent fragrance.

"I think you should wear the yellow one now," Madeleine proclaimed, then ran excitedly to the settee, hopping over the heap of delicately ribboned chemises and laced corsets in her way. She carefully sorted through the dresses, selecting a violet damask linen with matching cap. "I'm going to wear this one. Do you think it will fit me?" She held the dress up to her shoulders and twirled.

Catherine said nothing. She had ceased to wonder where all the beautiful gowns had come from. Since Danton had no wife and child on his island, nor a fashionable dressmaker's shop, there was only one possible answer as to how Monsieur Pirate had procured his bountiful gifts:

They were stolen.

All of them.

From lords and ladies, perhaps kings and queens. The affluent who'd paid fortunes for their wardrobes, only to have them pillaged at sea. How could she possibly garb herself and her child in purloined goods?

Gazing down at the banyan she wore, Catherine realized she had no choice. But she would do so only for this morning, and only in a dress of subtle taste. Nothing elaborate. Nothing rich.

Her first priority after seeing Madeleine to breakfast would be a tour of the cottage to sift through what was left. There had to be something. Anything.

"Can you help me, *Maman?*" Madeleine drew up to Catherine, her arms laden with her chosen dress, camisole, stockings, corresponding shoes, two pearl necklaces, and a broach. "The slippers are too big. Can you fix them?"

Catherine sighed and nodded. "I'll stuff paper in the toes. You can wear the dress for today. But after that, we'll have to give monsieur back his clothing. We can't keep them. We have our own things."

Madeleine looked only slightly dejected, as if she'd worry about giving up the treasures when the time came—if the time came.

An hour later Catherine and Madeleine entered the empty dining hall. Like the rest of Danton's home, this room's most notable influence was Spanish with rich leather-upholstered chairs, an extended rosewood table with matching pedestals displaying gold icons, and gilt-framed paintings depicting scenes in Spain's history.

The sideboard had been spread with a light repast of cakes and marmalade, tea, rice, and *tilapia*—steamed perch, kept warm in a chafing dish.

Tanala came in to serve them, but Catherine's appetite deserted her. Every noise in the household had her lifting her chin to see if Danton was coming. She knew she'd have to confront him sooner or later—she'd hoped much later.

Catherine drank her tea and nibbled on a manioc flour cake while Madeleine consumed a fair amount of the rice and fish, two cakes slathered with orange jam, and a cup of honeyed tea.

They were just finishing their meal when Danton entered the sunny room. Tired lines bracketed his eyes and cut into the sides of his mouth. In fact, he appeared exhausted in his drop-shouldered ivory shirt with its fully gathered sleeves and his brown twilled-cotton breeches.

His presence animated Madeleine, who flew from her chair to embrace his legs. "Oh, Monsieur Pirate! Thank you for the dresses!"

Catherine averted her gaze from his, looking down at the serviette in her lap. She hadn't been able to find a gown of modest proportions and had to accede to a splendid brocade blue with a running pattern of anemones and leaves. The neckline had been cut far lower than anything in her own wardrobe. She'd tried to conceal that fact by cloaking her shoulders with a yard of lace and stuffing the ends into her stomacher. In order to keep the hem from dragging, she'd had to strap on panniers, which then made the hem a little too short. She hadn't worn them since France, and though she'd been used to them once, they now seemed grossly unfamiliar and awkward.

"We won't be keeping them," Catherine said, raising her head. "They won't be necessary."

"But, *Maman*—"

"Hush, Madeleine," Catherine scolded. "I'm sure you meant well in your gesture, monsieur, but we don't need the dresses."

"Make her change her mind, Monsieur Pirate!"

Madeleine cried. "Don't you like this one I picked out?" She spun in a full circle to billow the hem. "How did you know my size?"

Catherine watched him, wondering what he would say. Surely not the truth.

Danton shifted his weight to one foot and gently set Madeleine back on her heels. "I found them."

"Where?" Madeleine stared at him with wide expectation in her blue eyes.

"On a ship."

"The dresses didn't belong to anybody?"

Danton glanced at Catherine. She waited for him to come up with an answer that would be fitting for Madeleine.

"No. They didn't belong to anyone anymore, puppet."

"Imagine that! How lucky we are, *Maman,* that Monsieur Pirate found them for us."

"Oui," Catherine agreed slowly. "Madeleine, why don't you go into the kitchen and find Tanala and ask her for a sweet biscuit?"

"A sweet biscuit?" Madeleine wrinkled her pale eyebrows and put her hands on her hips. "But you said I can never have a sweet biscuit after breakfast. Only after dinner or supper."

"I'm making an exception just for today."

The little girl smiled. "Can I have any kind I want? Not those *achica* ones. I don't like them. I want a sugar biscuit."

"Fine. Whatever Tanala has."

"Good-bye, Monsieur Pirate." Madeleine took his hand and squeezed his fingers. "I like you." Then she scampered off.

Catherine watched her daughter leave.

In the ensuing silence, Catherine remained seated. She was self-conscious enough in the unfamiliar gown.

Knitting her fingers together, she met Danton's stare. "That was a weak story you told her. But I don't want her hearing the details about your exploits."

Danton dropped his hands on the back of a chair at the foot of the table. "The devil knows, I have had my share of unlawful dealings," he said, his knuckles whitening, "but in this case, you're wrong."

Catherine tried to appear interested in her breakfast, but didn't have much luck. The tiny bite of cake she took was dry in her mouth.

"The gowns and children's apparel belonged to a baron and baroness and their two children. Twins—a girl and boy about Madeleine's age."

She said nothing, not sure she wanted to know about the dress she wore.

Danton stepped away from the chair and wandered to the sideboard. His gaze swept over the fare, but he didn't partake. "A year back, Rainiaro and I spotted a frigate, *Iris*, near the Maldives. She drifted, her sails slack and lines dangling. I gave orders for *La Furia* to pull alongside the *Iris*. We grappled her and boarded. The whole of the ship was taken with a fever and ague. No one was able to keep the frigate on course."

Catherine bit the inside of her lip.

"The family had just come from a trip to Bombay and were sailing home to England. I'm uncertain how they came down with their illnesses. By the time we reached them, they were all far gone. We could do nothing to save them."

Suddenly Catherine knew, she'd judged him swiftly and harshly, not giving him the benefit of the doubt.

"They all died within the day. The baron, Pembroke, on his last breath told me to write his family in London and tell them what had happened." Danton left the buffet and walked to the window. His hands clasped behind his back, he gazed through the glass. "Their trunks were brought out from the hold and at Pembroke's request taken into my custody. We gave the family a burial at sea. Then we burned the ship."

Sunlight put a slight russet gleam to his black hair. The gold cross in his ear dangled with his movement as he turned to face her. "So there you have it. Would you have wanted Madeleine to hear the dress she so coveted belonged to a girl who died of a fever?"

"No." Catherine scraped back her chair and stood. The silken layers of her petticoats rustled through the dining room. "I owe you an apology. I was unpleasant. Forgive me, but I didn't get much rest last night."

"Neither did I." Danton's eyes penetrated the cool exterior she was trying so valiantly to illustrate. "It would seem I owe you an—"

"No need." She cut off his disclosure. She didn't want to discuss the prior night's events. She'd made a mistake. She didn't want to make an issue of it. "The dresses are very nice, monsieur, and I appreciate the thought behind them, but we won't be needing them after all. I'm going to the cook's house to collect my belongings." She took a step toward the doorway.

"I've already been there. There's nothing left." His statement stopped her short. "What is, is ruined beyond repair."

She swung around. "But there has to be *something.*"

"Your trunk. Battered and empty."

Catherine's mind clicked to recall what had been in her portmanteau. Her documents of marriage; her wedding ring; a few pieces of inexpensive jewelry; several letters from her papa; the official notification of her papa's and brother's deaths; trinkets from Africa and India. What else? She couldn't remember.

Her throat closed and she mourned the loss of her worldly possessions. "If you'll excuse me . . . I'd like to go see for myself."

"Catherine," Danton's baritone voice washed over her with soothing warmth, "let me come with you."

"No. I'd like to go by myself. If you could ask Tanala to watch Madeleine for me, I won't be gone long."

Danton came to her side and took hold of her arm. She was conscious of the tingling sensation where his strong hand touched her. "You're not alone."

No, but she felt alone. Now, with nothing left of her past to connect herself to, how was she going to keep the pieces of her future together?

"Perhaps not, but I'm not among familiar things either. I'm wearing the dress of a dead woman," she whispered, "whose name may well have been Iris. I'll never know."

Then she fled the room.

Danton sat in the chair behind his paper-strewn desk, intensely perusing Sadi's treasure map and trying to figure out the markings. Adding to the disorganization on his desk were dozens of unrolled diagrams of charted isles and their geographical characteristics. He'd held the unfurled cylinders open with weights—a variety of rocks, nuts, and seashells Madeleine had been collecting of late and giving to him as gifts.

"Jesu," Danton breathed his frustration. There could be thousands of other islands that had not yet been named and charted. Hundreds more island maps to purchase in Tamatave's *Zoma,* and seemingly millions more to sketch himself when he came upon new isles in his journeys.

Danton ran his hands through his hair and leaned back to massage his temples. He pressed the arch of bone behind his brows and brooded at the mess before him. Was he wasting his time trying to decipher the map—drawn by a Turk he considered to be mad? Had his hatred pushed him over the edge? He'd already invested four years in finding Sadi. Now that he'd succeeded, would he invest four more trying to decode the map?

It was a strong possibility that he would waste his life away while the world around him continued to go on. As it had since Elena's and Esteban's deaths. As it had since he'd rescued Catherine on Madagascar.

On that day, his life had changed. He no longer thought for himself and did as he pleased. He felt obligated to see to the safety of a mother and child. In becoming Catherine's benefactor of sorts, he'd pulled himself out of his hole. But finding Sadi had buried him a little. As the week played out, Danton found himself growing ever more distracted by the map and his purpose. He'd withdrawn again. He'd gone back to where he started so many years ago.

The fire of obsession.

And it was consuming him.

Out of respect for Catherine, he'd given her rein of the house and stayed out of her way. They coexisted under the same roof but shared nothing. Meals were taken apart at different intervals, hers in the dining hall, his in his study with an accompanying glass of claret.

Danton felt the rough stubble along his jaw. He hadn't shaved today. An oversight that rarely, if ever, he allowed to happen. He'd slept in yesterday's shirt and breeches, having dozed with his forehead on his arms at his desk. He'd awakened this morning to the cheery songs of Madeleine, who'd intruded upon him with a bouquet of yellow cosmos and pink amaryllis. The stalks still lay at the head of his desk without the vase he'd promised the girl he'd fetch.

Danton took up the bottle of claret and poured the last cup into a glass. He awkwardly arranged the flower stems in the alcohol and hoped for the best. At least he made the effort.

That business remedied, he supposed he should continue with other matters. Namely, his duties to his men. He would have to inform them of his retirement.

Danton frowned. They seemed to be getting along well without him. Rainiaro had reported that in the absence of their voyages in search of Spanish galleons to plunder, half the crew had taken up with native wives and were setting up housekeeping by Rainiaro's village. They bore no resentment over their current domestic situation, and according to Rainiaro, they'd forgiven Catherine for the turn of events in their lives.

By all accounts the crew had plenty to build with. Each had accumulated a share of the booties and were rich in their own rights with textiles, rum, silver and gold, guns and ammunition, and a variety of other treasures; everything from meaningless religious statues and miters to invaluable pewter silverware.

His men would do nicely living out the rest of their lives in comfort if they chose to remain on Isle of the Lost Souls.

On that note Danton began to roll up the charts and put them away in the Sung urn beside the altar. Giving up taking Spain's ships would be easy. He had the most important factor of his new life at his fingertips.

The map that *might* uncover the diamonds.

He should be satisfied. Instead he was agitated and easily provoked. He bordered on being reclusive in his own home. Why? He'd never shut himself up in his house. He'd always taken pride in its design, loving the fact that he could see the sea and mountains from every vantage point.

Mierda, he hadn't even gone outside today to smell the

ocean and wind. The shutters to his study were closed from the prior night's rain, and a squat candle burned low in the Byzantine holder near his wrist.

Danton cocked his ear to listen for the noises that were common to his house.

Nothing.

The house was too quiet for Madeleine to be indoors.

Was Catherine with her?

He lifted the flowers from the claret and took a slow swallow before returning the golden cosmos and rosy amaryllis. He needed a bracer. He felt his face again. He needed to take a razor to his beard. He needed . . . he mused over the possible answers, and one came to mind swift and sharp.

He needed to hear Catherine LeClerc laugh.

On the heels of that revelation, Danton blew out the candle's flame and left his chair. He wouldn't leave Catherine alone anymore. The quiet truce between them was forced on his part, and he was sick of the silence.

But being in her company would be a dangerous temptation. After that night in his study when he'd brought her to satisfaction, he realized how much he wanted to be with her. He hadn't had a woman since Catherine had come to his island.

He'd tried to tell himself he hadn't because he'd been involved with more pressing matters. He'd reconciled himself to the fact he didn't have the time to dally. But then he'd become so high-strung and tense, he knew he had to find release. He'd even gone as far as telling himself any woman would do. He'd gone to the village to seek one of the several women with whom he'd had prior trysts, but found as he'd neared the encampment that he couldn't continue.

His desires weren't for just any woman.

They were for Catherine.

Not only did he crave a physical release, on an emotional level he was dealing with feelings he hadn't contended with for many years. The desire to have a family, a home, a place of stability. He'd even thought of asking Catherine to stay with him, but feared her answer.

Jesu, was he really up to a commitment when his life was still in turmoil?

As Danton quit his study and walked the halls to his

bedchamber, he began to perceive that just as he had been running from his past, so was Catherine. He didn't know much about her husband except what she told him—he'd been a thief. If he knew more about the husband who'd made Catherine unhappy, at least he could convince her he was a different kind of man.

Now all he had to do was find her.

Three quarters of an hour later, bathed and dressed in a scarlet vest and white petticoat trousers, Danton took the overgrown path to the lagoon. The hot sun filtering through the palms felt good on his bare arms and his chest where the vest parted; he wanted his skin to darken and recapture the tropical color he'd gleaned while on his high sea adventures.

A pair of gray and white vorondreos squawked at him from high atop a coconut tree, then swooped away as if they'd heard a threatening noise in the distance. The floral scents of ylang-ylang and periwinkle rose under Danton's footsteps as he walked to the freshwater pool where Tanala had told him he could find Catherine and Madeleine. It seemed the LeClercs had been going to the lagoon every afternoon while he worked in his study.

He heard the delightful shrieks of Madeleine's laughter before he saw her. She shouted loud enough to send every bird from its perch for miles away. And then he heard another kind of scream—a chattering really.

Shshshi-FAK! Shshshi-FAK!

His lemurs.

"Come here Pousse-Pousse!" Madeleine called. "I have a banana for you."

Then splashing.

Danton quickened his pace. He came to the clearing just in time to watch Pousse-Pousse paddle through the water to reach Madeleine, who sat on a rock a couple yards into the glimmering blue pool. The little girl handed Pousse-Pousse a banana and the lemur put it in her mouth and swam back for the shore. Madeleine clapped. He wouldn't have believed that unless he saw for himself. Though his lemurs were not adverse to water, he'd never seen them swim in it. The devil . . .

"Madeleine, I don't want those lemurs in the water with us. They might bite you," Catherine said.

Danton turned his head in the direction of Catherine's voice, to find her behind the rock. She stood just barely able to touch the bottom of the lagoon with her feet. She pinched her nose together with her fingers and attempted to float. She sank and came up with a cough. What was she trying to do?

"Monsieur Pirate!" Madeleine waved to him and kicked her feet. She created small splashes with her bare toes. The camisole and shift she wore were soaked with water. "Are you going to come swimming with us?"

Catherine ducked behind the large rock and peered at him from its edge. Her blue-gray eyes widened with surprise and more than a fair share of embarrassment.

"Is that what you are doing, puppet?" Danton took a step toward the shoreline, and his three lemurs came bounding up to his side, jumping and vying for his attention. He stroked them all on the backs of their heads, then Pousse-Pousse shook the water from her coat and sprayed him with fine droplets. Razana and Dokobe began to play-fight.

"We're not really swimming. We're trying to learn how to. I caught a turtle. See him? In that hat right there."

Danton looked down at his feet to the child's straw hat. It was covered with a corset cover and a woman's stays. The trimming was pink and fancy; ribbons flounced the edge and ran through the eyes.

"Lift up *Maman's* corset and you can see him. He's green."

Danton nudged the stiff satin aside to see a terrapin frantically trying to climb the sides of the hat's crown and escape. "I see him. Why don't you let him go swimming with you now?"

"All right. You can let him go."

Danton picked the palm-sized turtle up and dropped him into the water. He swam a speedy retreat.

"What do you want, monsieur?" Catherine asked him from the protection of the giant rock. Her wet hair fell against the curve of her cheeks, and the long lengths floated around her shoulders. He couldn't see what she was wearing.

"To enjoy your company." Danton shrugged out of his red vest. "I can be of service. I know how to swim."

"You can teach us!" Madeleine exclaimed. *"Maman* doesn't know how."

"I don't want a lesson," Catherine hastily returned. "I'm fine on my own."

Danton balanced on one leg and shucked free first one boot, then the other. "Then I won't teach you. I'll teach Madeleine." He waded into the refreshing water and crossed to the boulder where Madeleine sat. "How did you get out here, puppet?"

"Maman carried me. It's not deep where you are. I can kind of touch the bottom with my feet, but my face goes under a little."

He smiled at the child and heard Catherine making an attempt to move away from behind the rock. "How did you teach my lemurs to come into the water? That's very smart of you, Maddie."

"I just told them to come and get some food and they jumped in." She lifted her shoulders. "I think they like me."

Danton laughed. "I don't doubt that." He reached for the girl under her arms. "Come here and I'll pull you through the water. And Catherine," he added in a low tone, "if you change your mind, I'll pull you too."

"That won't be necessary," came the reply from the other side of the rock.

Danton merely smiled.

"Jump, Catherine." Danton held out his strong arms, but Catherine didn't give in to his request.

"Oui, Maman," Madeleine chimed. "Jump to Monsieur Pirate!"

"I can't." Catherine lost her sense of safety on the mossy surface of the boulder beneath her feet. When she'd been in the pool, the rock didn't seem so lofty; now that she stood on it, she felt as if she were several stories high above the lagoon instead of a few feet. One wrong move and she'd lose her balance and be in the water; most likely in Danton's outstretched arms, whether she wanted to be or not.

To add to her discomfort, she faced him in her underpinnings. Trying to stand straight and put on a brave front when she was in her sodden unmentionables was distracting. She wanted to crouch so he couldn't see her. But he'd made such a to-do about her being afraid to jump into the water, she'd climbed atop the giant rock to satisfy him. Now that she was here, she couldn't go through with the leap.

"Catherine, I'll catch you." The confident tone of Danton's voice didn't assuage Catherine's fears. His generous height allowed him to stand clear in the center of the pool, well beyond the shallow-water boulder, without having to tread water or float. Even if she braced her legs for the impact, she would plunge straight to the bottom. She simply wasn't tall enough to jump in deep water.

Panic weakened Catherine's knees as Danton stared at her. He surveyed her with expectant gray eyes. Then his gaze dropped slowly to the material clinging to her breasts, smoothing over her belly and curving against her hips. She wanted to die from embarrassment.

She'd worn two shifts to swim in, knowing one wouldn't be enough to cover herself if she and Madeleine were detected at the pool. The garment closest to her skin was plain and of a thick muslin. The other, a linen, was more elaborate. Bands of fine lace edged the décolletage, and tiny pink rosebuds, richly embroidered, set off the neckline. Three tiers of lace ruffles made up the elbow sleeves which now drooped over her arms.

Despite the double layers of clothing protecting her modesty, Catherine felt naked. She need not have hidden anything from him. Danton had already explored her body. He'd caressed her breasts, set her aflame with his mouth, and done much more intimate things to her with his hands.

Flustered and now fully out of sorts, she had a good mind to jump so he wouldn't be able to look at her anymore. But just when she thought she had the confidence needed to drop feet first into the unknown, she turned afraid again.

Danton's gaze moved upward. "I swear to you, Catherine, I won't let you drown."

"Jump, *Maman,*" Madeleine said. Catherine turned to her daughter. Madeleine sat in the shallows, a tin pail within reach and a wooden ladle in her hand. "I did."

Catherine's stomach felt as if the bottom had dropped out. Yes, Madeleine had jumped. Right into Danton's arms, and without mishap. Her daughter had liked the daring leap so much, she'd insisted on jumping a half-dozen times more before Danton had challenged her to spring off the boulder herself.

She had.

She'd come up sputtering and choking on the water she'd swallowed, but she'd achieved her goal. Danton had been by her side in an instant and lifted her onto his shoulders for a ride to the shore. Coughing and with tears in her eyes,

Madeleine had pronounced herself a big girl. But she didn't want to jump by herself again.

Catherine inched closer to the boulder's edge. She could see a school of silver fish swimming by. They looked like small white bass, shimmery and sleek. She fought the urge to sit down and call herself a coward. Even her envy over Danton's being able to swim while she could not couldn't convince her to leave the security of the rock. She knew she was being utterly ridiculous. If Danton said he'd catch her, he would. This was her chance to prove she could confront all obstacles and succeed.

"Catherine, I'm not going to ask again." Danton's voice carried up to her. Distracted by her fear, she didn't focus on what he was saying and his next words barely registered. "If you don't want to jump, then——"

Catherine sucked in a great gulp of air, plugged her nose with her thumb and forefinger, squeezed her eyes closed, and fell into the pool, her toes leading the way.

Cool water came up and around her calves and thighs and waist as strong arms captured her. Her head never went below the water's surface, but her splash was enough to drench her hair. She was consciously aware of being crushed next to hard bone as Danton rescued her and held her close. Out of a reflex born from the fear of sinking, she clutched onto him, locking her legs around his thighs.

Catherine's eyelashes flew up and she blinked away the droplets blurring her vision, trying to get her bearings.

"You see, Catherine," Danton murmured into her ear, heightening the rush of her pulse, "I didn't lie to you."

"I never questioned your promise," Catherine said in a breathless gasp. "It was my own worries that made me hesitate." Aghast, she realized the hems of her two chemises had floated up past her hips. She struggled to bring them down and had just down so when she felt herself slipping into the water.

Frantic, her hands gripped the slick planes of Danton's shoulders. He felt warm and virile beneath her palms, his muscles fluid when he moved to shift her more securely in his arms. This new position brought her flush with him. She felt his arousal growing strong, her own desire fanning through her in a wave of hot spirals.

"There are many things I like about you, *chérie,*" Danton said in a silky whisper, "one of which is your frankness." His large hands slid down to cup her buttocks and she froze. "You admit your fears and conquer them."

Not all the time, Catherine thought, fighting the fast-growing fire inside her. At this moment she was afraid of her reaction to him. She wouldn't admit that, not even if her confession would alleviate the apprehension.

She tried to maintain all the prim indifference she could salvage, ignoring the feel of him next to her and the tightness in her breasts. "You can take me to the shore now."

"Do you want to jump to me again?" he teased.

"I've already proven I can do it, so there's no need for a repeat performance." Catherine hated being dependent on him. She hated being at his mercy. He was enjoying himself; he languidly rubbed his thumbs on her thighs. If she knew how to swim, she'd let go of him. She'd unwrap her legs from him and do so quickly. But she didn't have the backbone to risk immersion.

"Don't lose your courage now, *chérie.*" Danton didn't make a move for the beach. "You don't have to get out of the water. I can teach you how to swim."

"I don't want to learn."

"I watched you practice. You have it all wrong. You don't swim with your fingers pinching your nose. Hold your breath in your lungs and water won't go up your nose."

"I'll remember that." Catherine could feel the heat of him next to her. "Right now I want you to put me where I can touch the bottom. I don't want a lesson."

"Maman, you did a good jump!" Madeleine shouted. "Do it again."

"Non, mon chou. Maman is tired."

"Maman," Danton said in a low tone for Catherine's ears only, "is running away from her teacher."

In her mind she knew his statement was true, but aloud she said nothing. Denial was harder when put into words.

Danton carried her to the shallows. His short steps stirred up the pale sand and clouded the pristine water. Fish streaked out of his path like tiny reflective mirrors catching the sun.

He set her down, and Catherine gratefully walked the remaining way on her own.

"Are you coming out too, Monsieur Pirate?" Madeleine dropped a scoop full of sand into her tin.

Danton kept himself waist high in the lagoon, water trickling off his smooth chest. "Give me a minute."

Catherine shot him a glance over her shoulder, knowing exactly what he needed the time for. She met his gaze. His eyes were dark, the pupils large and fathomless. He stared at her with a deep longing that unsettled her. The night he'd fulfilled her, then sent her away, she'd reaffirmed her vow to remain reserved, though cordial, while in his presence. She'd neither be too friendly or too unfriendly.

As it had turned out, they hadn't seen much of each other, so she hadn't put much of her plan to use. Right now was the first opportunity, and she could see she'd have to immerse herself in a wall of neutrality.

It was hard trying to be immune to Danton Cristobal. He was the epitome of masculinity. She couldn't help but be drawn to him despite his flaws. For he too had unfounded fears. She wasn't a virgin with a virgin's innocent mind; she knew there were precautions one could take to prevent conception. If he so feared having another child, he could have done something to ensure that he wouldn't. Instead he'd been the one to run away.

The fine gravel under Catherine's toes felt rough as she went to join her daughter. She knew she could have persuaded Danton that making love with her would not have produced a child. She could have told him she could not get pregnant. But the humiliation had been too much to bear. She didn't want him coming to her because of a guarantee he'd not father a child. She wanted him to come to her because he wanted to be with her.

Madeleine was making a sand house with her tin. She stuck a bright feather in the top of one carefully turned-over bucket of compact sand. "Can I go back in the water, *Maman,* and swim with Monsieur Pirate?"

"No," Catherine shot back shortly. "I don't want you in the pool anymore today."

"Why not?"

"Hush, Madeleine." Catherine picked up the banyan she'd piled on top of her dress, stockings, and shoes. She slipped her arms into the blue folds, then retrieved her corset and cover and put it by her clothing. She couldn't stand to lace herself up in the bone stays again. She tidied Madeleine's dress and plopped the hat next to her tiny shoes.

Catherine hadn't been able to regain any of her clothing, and had to give in to using the baroness's wardrobe. She still didn't approve, but until suitable replacements could be gotten, she and Madeleine would have to wear the finery. Where those replacements would come from, she hadn't a clue.

Above her head, chimes tinkled in the light breeze. Three strings of oyster shells were tied to fishing lines and mounted on three sticks. She'd heard them ring together on the occasions she and Madeleine had visited the lagoon. Someone had attached the chimes to the branch of a mangrove.

"Do you like them?" Danton's voice startled Catherine, and she turned on her heels. He'd come up behind her. Water glistened on his hair and ran down his broad shoulders. Her gaze dropped to his chest and the faded scars that marked him; scars from coral and a scar from Sadi's knife wound. Then she looked lower to the loose trousers he wore. Cinched at the waist, the light canvas material sagged below his naval.

She darted her gaze to his face. "Yes. I like them," she said, referring to the chimes. "Who put them there?"

"I did after I made them."

"You?" She found it oddly intriguing that he would do such a thing.

"Yes." He seemed a bit miffed. "On the days when I'm not scavengering the sea for quarry, I don't like to sit idle. The sounds please me, so on occasion I make chimes."

His sarcasm nettled her. "Do be serious."

"I am."

Catherine glanced at him askance.

Madeleine sighed. "I wish I was big like you, monsieur, so I could reach the chimes and sound them."

"If I lift you, you will be." Danton hoisted the little girl onto his shoulders and she giggled with delight. "Run your fingers through them."

Madeleine did and the lagoon was filled with a natural melody created from the different tones of the shells. "Did you know if you were this tall, Monsieur Pirate, you would bump your head on the trees and say ouch?"

"That thought has never occurred to me."

"You would. Your head would hurt, but I would rub it for you."

"I'm greatly relieved." Danton didn't set Madeleine down. He took the several steps to his discarded boots and vest. He bent his knees and picked up his belongings without faltering. Then he headed down the path toward the house.

After taking up her own and Madeleine's dress and their accompaniments, Catherine brought up the rear.

The lemurs swung from tree branch to tree branch and followed them. Clusters of pale yellow flowers and seed pods from the tamarind above Catherine scattered down onto the path. She stepped over the debris, mindful of her bare feet. Danton, and now Madeleine, overindulged the mischievous lemurs. They treated the trio like human beings rather than wild animals. And in turn the furry barbarians were always up to no good.

A large black beetle scurried across their trail, its thin and spindly legs elevating a waxy body.

Madeleine caught sight of the insect. "Are you afraid of bugs, Monsieur Pirate?"

"No."

"I bet you really are but you won't say for real."

"No, puppet, I can honestly tell you, I have no fear of bugs."

Madeleine sighed. "I don't like snakes."

"Yes, I recall you telling me that."

"I like black bears, though," Madeleine declared. "And I like el'phants and jackals and parrots and goats and dogs and cats and turtles and frogs . . ."

The lazy day's jungle hum was punctuated by Madeleine's one-sided conversation, which took up the rest of the walk back to the house. Her daughter finished her list from the animal kingdom and had moved on to her inventory of favorite edibles as Danton hiked into the courtyard.

". . . and chocolate and rice and sugar biscuits. And I like to eat peppermint and cakes and—"

"Madeleine," Catherine squeaked, "that's enough!"

Catherine felt her nerves spinning out of control like a whirling dervish. Madeleine's rambling had given her the start of a headache. Topping that off, she now had to wonder how and if Danton would fit himself into their lives. Since he'd ended his self-exile, would she see him at dinner?

Apparently that question had been in Madeleine's mind as well. "Are you going to eat with us tonight, Monsieur Pirate?"

After lifting the girl off his shoulders and setting her on the flagstones, Danton tucked his black boots under his arm. The previous good humor etched into his strong profile diminished. At length he said, "We'll see."

Madeleine beamed.

Remaining silent, Catherine didn't share her daughter's optimism.

Danton strode down the whitewashed hallway of his home. Greek artifacts hung on the walls. Gilt plates added light; reredos—ornamental altar screens—and icons lent a solemn brilliance; and a flotilla of old ship paintings added a sense of masculine order.

Thoughts of the Turk's map lingered in Danton's mind as he crossed into the east wing. He'd resumed the tedious work in his study after his swim in the lagoon with Catherine and Madeleine. After two solid hours of examining the Réunion Islands, he needed a recess. He'd intended on going to his bedchamber to change for dinner.

As he passed one of the seldom used galleries, he smelled the rich fragrance of sweet perfume drifting through the corridor on the breeze. He paused at the closed door and sniffed the heady scent seeping from the cracks. *Catherine*. Who else would smell so intoxicating?

Intrigued by what she would be doing in this particular salon, Danton quietly turned the doorknob.

Expecting to see Catherine, he was nonplussed to find Madeleine sitting in the middle of the sparse room singing softly to her doll. The girl had dressed herself up in her mother's linen shift. She'd wound several ropes of pearls around her neck and put a ladies straw hat on her head. Late afternoon sunlight dappled the burnished locks of her hair where it spilled out underneath the short brim. Her rouged lips moved sweetly as she talked to Nanette, making up a tea party game and acting as if she had a visible teapot and cups.

A glimmering reflection of green caught his eye as she moved to reach for a make-believe plate. She wore the emerald-encrusted pumps he'd discarded, and forgotten about, on the beach weeks ago.

Madeleine became aware of him standing in the doorway and looked up.

"Bonjour, Monsieur Pirate." Her animated blue eyes filled with adoration and the brows above lifted in delight. "I'm playing party with Nanette with pretend cakes and I was wishing I had someone to play with me. Will you?"

She waited expectantly for his answer, hope radiating on her lovely face. She didn't mask her feelings with practiced restraint—a trait learned in adulthood to protect the heart. No. Her feelings for him were crystal clear.

Pure and simple: she worshiped him and put her every faith in his buccaneer hide.

He felt a warm heat flow through him when he looked upon her. He'd fought it long and hard, but now he recognized her presence gave him joy.

And then a revelation hit Danton. Magnanimous as being smacked on the head with a Bible.

He loved the child.

"Well? Will you play with me?" she repeated.

A moment passed while he collected his voice, and when he did, his words were scratchy as burlap. "Ah, no. I have things to do."

"Are you going to kill somebody?"

"No," he shot back, his heartbeat skipping over her offhand question.

"I killed a spider. It was crawling on Nanette." She lifted one shoe off her foot and waved the pump at him. "I smashed the spider with the heel."

"Hmm."

"I found these shoes. They don't belong to anyone. I asked everybody in the whole world, and they said no, these shoes weren't theirs. You know what?"

"Hmm?"

She lowered her voice in the clever little tone that belied that the information about to be spilled was strictly privileged. "These green shoes are treasure. And if I keep digging, I'm going to find a ruby necklace."

Too disturbed over the myriad of tender emotions raging through him, Danton couldn't dispute her roughshod claim to riches.

"I wish I had someone to play with me." She sighed wistfully. "Rainiaro is mending nets. James is making cannons. Antonio and Eduardo are polishing guns. And *Maman* is resting." Madeleine's tiny hands drew his attention as she poured air into air to simulate tea being splashed into cups. "I wish I had a sister. Do you think one will come out of my *maman's* tummy?"

"What?" he choked. His thinking stumbled and he grappled for a plausible answer. "Not unless someone puts a baby in your mother's wom—er, tummy."

Madeleine finished with her service and crossed her legs, the other pump sliding off her foot. "Will you?"

Sweat broke out on his temple and he stifled his curse. "No. I won't." He had to get out of the room.

"If you change your mind," she called after him, "make sure you put a sister in my *maman's* tummy. Not a brother."

"Madre de Dios," he said under his breath, taking his steps nearly two at a time.

Four hours after their swim, Catherine and Madeleine sat in the quiet dining hall. Catherine knew it was pointless to wait for Danton. Unlike Madeleine, she knew that promises were not hinged on vague replies. Even straightforward commitments were easily broken, like delicate china. Georges Claude had disillusioned her countless times with his ambiguous answers.

Knowing this, she could accept Danton's absence. But she was angered for her child. She would have to make up an excuse on his behalf.

"Madeleine, it would appear—" But Catherine clipped

her sentence short when she heard a door close within the confines of the house.

"He's coming, *Maman!*" Madeleine shouted gleefully. "And we look so pretty." The long springs of curls at the sides of her face bounced. Catherine had found a pair of curling tongs and painstakingly dressed her daughter's brown locks with hair tapes and decorations of blue ribbon to match her dress.

Catherine tried to remain poised and calm, but the few tendrils she'd curled at her nape tickled her bare neck. She fought bringing her hand up to smooth her tingling skin.

She chided herself for judging Danton so harshly. The rash comparison had been unfair. He wasn't like Georges Claude after all. She'd wanted him to come tonight, but hadn't dared set her heart on his appearance.

Just so, she'd worn a formal gown with him in mind. She reasoned her choice had been to appease Madeleine, who said the daffodil-yellow satin dress was the prettiest frock she'd ever seen. But deep down Catherine had wanted Danton to see her wearing the beautiful gown.

The fit was near perfect, only a touch too tight in the bosom and a few inches too short. Her ankles showed, but the silk stockings on her legs were darned with rose clocks, so the indiscretion was softened by a floral motif.

Now as the moment of reckoning came, she felt absurdly overdressed. Danton would know she was trying to spruce herself up for him. She'd even gone as far as dabbing some narcissus-scented perfume on her wrists and applying a light tinting of red lip rouge on her mouth.

Footfalls over the mosaic flooring in the entryway announced Danton's impending arrival. Catherine sat straighter and checked the bands of dusky rose lace that held her stomacher in place.

The iron-studded door began to slide open and Catherine could hardly breath. It suddenly felt as if Tanala hadn't loosened the laces on her corset enough.

"Evenin' every one," James Every cheerfully greeted from the doorway. "Fine digs this is." He stepped into the room, the heels of his buffed jackboots ringing across the floor. "Cap'n said I was to make meself right at home."

Catherine dropped her eyelashes quickly to hide her disappointment.

"Where is Monsieur Pirate?" Madeleine asked with dismay. Under normal circumstances, her daughter would have been thrilled to see the redheaded youth.

"He had to take care o' some business. Men's work, you know. I ain't obliged to say what it is." James sniffed the spicy aromas wafting from the adjoining kitchen. He walked clear around the master's chair, making a wide arc, as if he were afraid of sitting on the captain's cushion. He selected the first tall chair at the side of the table.

Sitting across from Catherine, James whipped open his bleached serviette with a quick wrist that implied he'd had some training. "Cap'n says you and the tyke been eatin' all by your lonesomes and time's come for you to have some company. Elected me, he did." James brought his finger to his chest with a wide grin on his boyish face. "I ain't never been in the main house afore. Right nice it is."

"But Monsieur Pirate should eat with us too," Madeleine murmured. "I wanted him to come and see how pretty *Maman* is."

James looked at Catherine and dutifully commented. "You look right fanciful, lady." Then he snatched up his fork with his one hand and poised the silver in his fist. "Well, then," he said with a broad smile, "let's put on the feed bag, shall we?"

A half hour later Catherine tried to coax Madeleine out of the armoire in their bedchamber. Having refused her dinner, Madeleine sat in the dining hall staring at Danton's vacant seat. Catherine was so upset, she couldn't eat either. James, too engrossed in the captain's surroundings and the special treatment he was receiving, hadn't noticed anything was wrong.

When Catherine dismissed her daughter from the table, Madeleine fled the room. Catherine excused herself and ran after her. She found Madeleine a moment later. She'd climbed inside the massive piece of rosewood furniture and hid her face in one of the rear corners. Her anguished sobs were muffled by the row of pressed gowns hanging above her.

"Mon petit chou chou," Catherine crooned gently. "Come out for *Maman."* Catherine swept aside the bounty of colorful dresses and rested her knee on the cupboard's base to be closer to her daughter.

"I d-don't want to," Madeleine cried. "I'm going t-to stay in h-here forever."

"You can't live in the closet."

"Oui, I can."

Catherine touched Madeleine's quaking shoulder. Her daughter's curls had begun to droop and had become mussed from the wide skirts rumpling her head. "I know you're disappointed. But Monsieur Cristobal didn't say for certain he would come."

"Oui, he did!" She wailed louder. "He said 'we'll see,' and that means yes. He lied!"

"Oh, *mon chou."* Catherine embraced Madeleine and held her near, trying to calm her tears away.

"It's n-not fair."

"I know. But hiding won't make the hurt go away. Come out now. We'll put on your nightgown and I'll lay down next to you in the bed and tell you stories."

Madeleine allowed herself to be steered out of the armoire, her voice quivering from spent tears. "I—I need a h-handkerchief, *M-Maman."*

Catherine produced a square of linen from atop the desk where a branch of candles had been lit, their flames casting a yellow glow. "Here."

The girl blew her nose and sniffed. "I wish I had a *p-papa."*

"But you do," Catherine said quickly.

"I m-mean a real *papa.* One who's not in heaven."

Catherine had no answer. She couldn't snap her fingers and produce another man to take Georges Claude's place.

Catherine sighed heavily. She didn't know what to say. In times like these, she felt painfully inept. How could she make a four-year-old understand it took more than a figure of a man to make a father?

Unlacing the closures of Madeleine's smock, Catherine said, "Lift your arms."

Madeleine did so and Catherine removed her dainty camisole.

"There's never anyone little to play with me. I want a baby sister," Madeleine lamented as Catherine slid a crisp nightgown over her curls. "Put one in your tummy, *Maman*."

"It's not that simple, Madeleine." Catherine folded down the snowy counterpane and bedclothes and followed Madeleine up the high stead.

Catherine remained in her fancy gown and laid down next to Madeleine, who'd picked up Nanette and brought the dolly to her cheek. Her tiny thumb went into her mouth. Catherine explained, "Just because a *maman* wants a baby in her tummy, doesn't mean she can have one."

Madeleine talked around her thumb. "Monsieur Pirate said someone would have to put one in your tummy for you. I asked him to and he said no."

Catherine swallowed, feeling the flames of the candle as if they were next to her cheek instead of across the room. She could just imagine what Danton thought of all this; he'd probably been rattled like a ring of rusty keys. "Madeleine, I'm happy with you. I don't need any more babies. You're my special girl. I love you."

Madeleine nuzzled Catherine's arm and closed her eyes. "Tell me a story about when you were a little girl."

Catherine searched her mind for a satisfying tale, but her thoughts were far from childhood memories. She was focused instead on finding a certain pirate and giving him the dressing down of his life.

Chapter

16

*H*ow could you?" Catherine's accusatory tone channeled through Danton's nightmares. Then a hard missile smacked the butt of his shoulder and his eyelids flew open.

He vaulted upright in his bed. Some of the rolled maps haphazardly scattered around him fell to the Oriental carpet. "Dammit!" he complained through the lingering haze of his short sleep. His mind was still fogged with the recorded inlets and mountain peaks comprising the Seychelles. He'd been studying the Amirante isles, but none had features to correspond with Sadi's map.

Aided by the softly burning light of the oil lantern hanging from a hook in the framework of his antique Chinese bedstead, Danton found Catherine. She stood by his Chinese table looking ghostly pale in an exquisite yellow gown. It took him a moment to register that she gripped a small object in her hand. "Catherine?"

"*Oui*, Danton, it's me," she answered.

"Jesu, woman, did you throw something at me?"

"I did," she said, her tone cool as springhouse water. "And I'm going to throw something else too." She coiled her arm back and flung what she held at him.

One of the miniature ivories from his mythology collection hit his chest. Poseidon's replica bounced off him and hurtled toward the floor. Danton followed its descent with his gaze. Poseidon landed next to Perseus, who'd lost both the head and sword in his hands. On impact, Poseidon's trident snapped in two. *"Maudit!"* Danton yelled. "What's the matter with you?"

"What's the matter with *you?*" She snatched another Greek deity from the black and gold table at her elbow which displayed his valued treasures.

"Do *not* throw that," he warned, spacing his words evenly. "My God, Catherine, that's Pan. Are you insane?" He bolted off the bed.

"I'm quite sane." She hurled the forest god at him, but missed. He tried to catch the piece in midair but couldn't keep his focus in the poor light, and Pan fell to the floor. Both horns and one goat leg broke off.

"Mierda!" He lunged for her now with dangerous intent. "What's wrong with you?"

"There's nothing wrong with *me!*" She ran away from him, bounding for the caramel leather settee angled in the corner of his bedroom. "Madeleine's heart has been broken as much as these silly little statues of yours."

Since she'd removed herself from the table's vicinity, he stopped his pursuit. "They aren't silly," he ground out, keeping as much of his temper in check as humanly possible, "they're—"

"Priceless."

"Damn right! They *are* priceless, and one of a kind!"

Standing behind the settee's rectangular back, Catherine stared at him with ice-colored eyes. "Madeleine is priceless and she is one of a kind."

He didn't fully grasp what she was getting at. "You don't have to tell me the value of a child." He bent and retrieved the broken pieces of ivory in his palm and stared at the fragments. "My God, Catherine."

Danton gingerly desposited the damaged miniatures on the table and crossed his arms over his chest. The silk of his black burnoose cooled his hot skin and helped him contain his rancor. He'd gone riding this evening in hope of exhausting some of his tension and trying to put a cap on his feelings for Catherine and Madeleine. After he came home, he'd bathed and slipped the hooded cloak on.

"What are you babbling about?" he managed to ask without shouting.

The dry rustle of Catherine's gown charged the brittle air. "If you had any compassion, you would know."

"Don't play games with me," he cautioned, leaning his buttocks into the table's edge.

"I?" Her pale brows shot up. "No, never. I'm always frank with my feelings, am I not?"

"Yes. And at this moment, it would seem you are angry. With me."

"You are so astute." The boldness in her voice lost its effectiveness when she fidgeted with a dark pink ribbon on her stomacher. She inadvertently untied the bow, but made no effort to right it.

Danton had never seen her this agitated before. She was an opinionated and assertive woman, but never destructive. He put her rantings in order and had a strong idea as to their cause, but didn't voice his guess. He'd rather that she herself tell him what was on her mind. "What did I do?"

"What didn't you do?"

"You are playing games, *chérie.*"

"Yes, perhaps I am." She put her hands on the settee's wooden frame. "We shall play a guessing game of questions. I shall go first. What comes after seven o'clock and before eight o'clock?"

"Seven-thirty," he responded tartly.

"True. But what does one usually do this hour of the evening?"

Danton inclined his head slightly. "Isn't it my turn to ask a question?"

"*Oui.* And you just forfeited that question by asking me if you could ask me a question," she explained tightly. "So we now return to my second question. What does one usually do this hour of the day?"

Danton shoved away from the symmetric table. "One eats one's dinner, damn you."

"Oh, don't damn me. You've already damned my daughter."

"I did no such thing."

"Of course you did."

He took a step in her direction and she leaped for the tall

side of his bed. Gripping fast to the pierced carvings, Catherine used the poster panel as a shield. "Catherine, I never promised her I would join you for dinner."

"Not in exact words, but you didn't say no."

"And I didn't say yes," he returned quickly.

Catherine peered at him through one of the lacy pedestal engravings. "In her mind you did."

"You'd better start teaching her the difference between a notion and reality."

"She's had enough reality," Catherine fired at him. "She's lost her father. I never realized how devastating that was for her until tonight."

He could see she was fighting tears now, but he didn't dare comfort her. Her knees weakened and she sat on his bed. She put her face in her hands and asked softly, "Why didn't you come?"

Completely nonplussed, he blurted out his first thought. "Because I'm getting too attached to her. And to you."

He regretted his impulsiveness when she brought her chin up, her blue-gray eyes glistening with unspent tears. "That was the last answer I expected to hear."

Danton inched closer, his gaze holding Catherine's. "Does it upset you?"

"Yes . . . no." Her confusion was evident by the quiver in her voice. "I don't know."

Coming up to the bedstead, Danton stood in front of her. He breathed in, filling his lungs with her scent. He craved her, like a man marooned and dying of thirst. He needed her, needed to drink in her spirit, her warmth, her love. Before he could stop himself, he said, "I could ask you to stay here with me on my island."

"I couldn't, and you know that," she returned quietly. "I would be giving up before trying to make a life of my own."

A seemingly eternal pause lengthened the short distance between them.

Danton thought of her future, bright with hope. His own was still clouded by uncertainty. Would she go on with her life better than he had? He couldn't help asking, "When you return to Paris, will you remarry?"

"I don't know. I had those intentions, but lately . . ." She licked her lips. "I don't know. Will you ever remarry?"

"The prospect is remote." He sat down next to her, and she made no protest. He kept a hand's width of space between them. Resting his elbows on his knees, he said, "You should remarry, Catherine. Madeleine would do well as a big sister."

Catherine made no comment. She stared at the tips of her slippers.

A breeze came in from the open window to stir the sheer curtains, freshening the apartment with the traces of sea and palmetto.

As the air caressed him, Danton was momentarily lost in his own reveries. He had disclaimed his solemn vow not to become entangled with a woman. A woman with a child, no less. But he'd gone against the grain and fallen in love with them both. How could he not help loving Catherine? She was everything he desired in a woman. She was headstrong and intelligent, beautiful and an excellent mother. Left on her own, she'd taken care of her child, not only surviving, but raising a precious, loving replica of herself.

Catherine was everything he ever wanted in a woman and a little more, because she was better. Probably better than LeClerc deserved, and better than any man had a right to expect.

She had been hurt by love. She must have been damaged to the soul by her marriage. She'd thrown the fact in his face often enough that he was just like the man—the thief she'd married. He'd never admitted how much that analogy bothered him. He couldn't help wondering how he really compared to her dead husband.

Danton pressed his fingertips together. "Tell me about LeClerc. Was he your only family?"

Catherine glanced at him with surprise, as if she just now was aware he sat next to her. Then she dropped her gaze back to her shoes. "My mother died from consumption the year before I married Georges Claude. After she was gone, I took charge of the household. I had a brother, Jean, and my *papa*, Armand, to look after. The two of them worked long hours in the glass factory." Her voice was laced with sadness. "To fill the lonely void after my chores were finished, I spent afternoons in a bookstore reading—or reading as much as I could before the proprietor sent me out the door. I met Georges Claude in the bookstore. He'd said he was a scholar of art, and he sounded like he'd been born inside a book, from the educated way he spoke. He didn't care that I came from a simple household and modest background. He had plans. He intended to see the world and discover great antiquities. His claim to fame had awed me. We met every day for six months while he finished out his term at the university."

Danton felt more than a twinge of jealousy when she spoke of the Frenchman. Had his confession about Elena been as painful to Catherine?

"Papa and Jean argued I'd fallen in love with a man who wore his highbrow education on his coat collar—too brash and opinionated. They'd said a schooled man would always make me feel inferior. He had no family, no allegiance to France. And if that weren't enough, he wanted to take me to Africa—to the savages and bug-infested jungles." Catherine glanced at Danton. "Despite their pleas, I wed Georges Claude without their blessing. I bid them au revoir, then sailed to the Gulf of Guinea to begin my marriage."

Danton listened as she told him of her journey to Africa's Ivory Coast. "We weren't in Abidjan a week when I became ill from the change in climate and food. Georges Claude left me at a French post while he went on an expedition. He was gone for three months. My recuperation was slow, and when I did recover, I was beside myself with worry over his welfare." Catherine fingered another bow on her stomacher. "When he returned, I made him promise never to leave me alone again. But of course, he did leave."

Danton wanted to hit something. How could the bastard leave her with no regard? She had more courage and daring than most men.

"We left Africa after a year. Georges Claude said he needed to explore new territories. I think it was because the government was after him." Catherine looked Danton in the eye. "He was a thief, as I told you. He stole official artifacts and more. I watched as he acquired a king's ransom in elephant tusks, ivory, spices, and coffers of jewels. He'd penned a false qualifications document and gained the natives' trust; he took things from their sacred burial grounds. I didn't find this out until last year. Georges

Claude secretly pocketed the finds and sold them in the black market. When I confronted him, he made it sound like he was entitled to them."

Danton drew in a slow breath, his lungs burning. No wonder she despised what he stood for. He'd never denied he was a man who roved the seas pillaging the wealth of another. He suddenly felt disgusted by his own acts and was ashamed for her to see the self-loathing written on his face. He looked away.

"A week before Georges Claude booked our passage to India, a dispatch reached me at the post in Abidjan. Four months old, the letter had been sent by our landlord informing me of my *papa's* and brother's deaths. They'd been killed in a factory accident from an explosion in the glory hole—the open furnace where they spun glass into windowpanes."

"I'm sorry, Catherine."

Tears glistened in her eyes, but she blinked them back. "I begged Georges Claude to take me home to pay my last respects, but he refused. He said there was no point since Armand and Jean had already been buried. Once we arrived in Calcutta, I became ill again, this time because I was carrying Madeleine." She became silently reflective. "The fast-paced traveling we did was hard on me as I progressed. I knew it would be even more difficult with a baby. I asked my husband to reconsider and book us passage for home. Again he refused."

Danton quietly listened as she continued.

"She was born in Calcutta only because I refused to stay in Raipur when my time neared. I had an Indian midwife attend me. She spoke passable English and was able to tell me what to do."

Danton thought of the prominent physician who'd cared for Elena and delivered Esteban. His wife had given birth in the comfort of their marriage bed with several servants to see to her needs.

"When Madeleine was two weeks old, Georges Claude said he was going to explore prospects in the Himalayas. We were leaving Calcutta." Catherine pressed her cheek next to the canopy post and said in a distant voice, "I felt trapped. I had no choice. As we went deeper into India, I lived my life in a shadow for nearly three years. I wasn't able to have an opinion or a voice."

Danton felt the play of a tic at his jaw. The picture she painted filled him with rage.

"And then Georges Claude heard of a venture forming in Bombay to explore the southern coastal regions. He intended on taking us there to be a part of a treasure hunt. We left the interior, but just outside of Surat he was bitten by a cobra. Thankfully, Madeleine didn't see it happen. He was with our guide, Hadi. Georges Claude died almost instantly." Catherine gazed at Danton. "When I was told, I couldn't believe what had happened. I'd wanted to be free of Georges Claude and our marriage for a long time. But I didn't want him dead. He was, after all, Madeleine's father. Flawed as Georges Claude was, he loved his daughter in his own way."

Danton lifted his head and combed his hair back with his fingers. "What did you do next?"

"I went to Surat and boarded the first ship out of the Dutch East India Company's port. My intention was to return to France and start over, even though I had no family there anymore."

"But you didn't get far," he commented with irony. "You met me."

"You saved me, Danton. I should have said thank you before, but foolish pride kept me silent. I wanted to think I would have been all right on my own. But I made a mistake in judgment. Your intervention saved us from a dangerous fate. If you hadn't found me," she shuddered, "there's no telling what would have happened to us on Madagascar."

"You would have survived, Catherine. You are a damnably strong woman."

She smiled wanly. "A woman shouldn't be strong. She should be tolerant and obedient and delicate."

"You don't believe that," he scoffed.

"Georges Claude wanted me to be those things. I'm afraid I wasn't a good student."

"Thank God."

Three golden tendrils curled at her neck, and he felt the impulse to feel the silken coils. But he held still.

Catherine licked her lips. "Georges Claude wasn't the

only one to stifle my independence. My father and brother thought I should be who they wanted me to be. I defied them when I married Georges Claude. Perhaps not the best decision I've ever made, but because of it, I have Madeleine. My only regret is *Papa* and Jean never had the chance to know Madeleine." She absently brushed a wrinkle from her skirt. "Maybe you can understand now why it is so important for me to make my own decisions. I've been denied the right for a long time."

"I understand." But it was his loss that he did. For in doing so, he was rationalizing her resolution. He knew too well the boundaries of empowerment. He did sympathize with her need to be independent, because his own freedom had been challenged and taken. Even though he could return to his homeland in six years, he'd made the inevitable choice to be separated from his country. He'd become his own man. His own master.

Yes, he understood how Catherine felt. He too had known the crushing weight of authority's rock.

"I'm sorry about your figurines." Her apology pulled him out of his thoughts.

Seeing the guilt-ridden flush on her cheeks, he forgave her. "At least you spared Zeus and Hera. Maybe they'll procreate and replace their offspring."

A doubtful smile softened her features. He wanted to cup her face in his hands and kiss her. He'd never seen her more beautiful. She'd done something different with her hair. The subtle and elegant style suited her. He realized she must have gone to great lengths to dress for dinner this evening.

And then he hadn't indulged her with his presence.

Danton watched Catherine as she took a direct and curious look at the unusual bed they sat on. One long side of the bedstead rested against the wall, and rather than having round posters, there were two joining foot-length panels at each corner. The latticework gilt inserts were laced with Chinese patterns and floral impressions. Rather than the customary number of pillows at the bed's head, twenty-five, in various hues of red, took up three of the sides.

"What kind of bed is this?" Catherine queried when she finished her perusal.

"An opium bed."

Her voice rose in surprise. "Really?"

"In China, for a snug price, patrons can enter a den and smoke opium pipes on beds like these." Her luminous eyes widened in astonishment, and he chuckled. "Don't look so shocked, *linda*. They're quite common. I bought this one for the finely detailed craftsmanship, not to smoke opium in."

She studied him with her sweet gaze. "Have you ever considered your sleeping arrangements odd? You sleep backward on your ship and at your home, in a bed once used for smoking poppies."

Now it was his turn to be surprised. "How did you know opium was made from poppies?"

"I'm not as ignorant of the ways of the world as you might think, Danton. I've lived in three countries and have seen the daily rituals going on in all of them. I know more about worldly things than you think."

He observed her with faint amusement, loving the way her smooth skin glowed with pale gold undertones; the way her lashes swept down on her cheekbones when she was heavily into thought. "Such as?" he prodded. "Tell me, Catherine, what worldly things do you know?"

She gave him no hint to prepare him for the nature of her reply. "A sea sponge can prevent conception if it's used properly."

He choked, "My God!"

"Don't be priggish," she chided as if he were her four-year-old daughter rather than a grown man of thirty-three. "Their effectiveness is common knowledge. I'm surprised you didn't know about them."

Danton fought the force of his pulse quickening through him. "I did."

"Then why didn't you ask me to use one?"

He drew his brows together, the fire inside him racing downward. "I can't believe we're having this conversation."

"Why not?" she asked, mindless of the ramifications this type of subject matter had on a man. "You've remarked you like my candor. I'm merely stating a fact and asking you to give me an answer."

"A gentleman—"

She tipped her lovely head to one side and gave him an exaggerated stare.

"All right!" he barked, becoming completely unknit. "So I may not be a gentleman in the *literal* sense. But I do know a gentleman's code of honor, and one would not ask a lady to outfit herself with such a device!"

To his disbelief, Catherine laughed softly. "It would seem you and I share the same false qualities. A *lady* would not find herself in that position."

Danton saw himself floundering in an utter loss of what to say next. Catherine LeClerc was a gem to rival anything in his possession. Jesu, he was going to miss her. He hadn't realized how lonely he'd been before she came into his life. What was he going to do when she was gone?

"Come here, Catherine," he murmured, tenderness infusing his voice. "I want to hold you."

Her eyes shone bright in the scant light of the room. She went to him, and he leaned back on the rows of pillows, bringing her into the curve of his arm. He savored the feel of her. The softness of her breast next to his side. The silkiness of her hair when he pressed his lips to her head. The smoothness of her cheek where he stroked her skin.

She was heaven. Her scent, her touch, and her essence.

"Is holding me enough, Danton?"

Danton rubbed the bare skin at her shoulder. "I think it is." He *was* fulfilled emotionally by her. He'd never felt that way about a woman, not even Elena, whom he'd adored. But he still wanted Catherine. He wanted to be close to her, not only physically, but emotionally. And he knew of only one way to become that close. Could he, should he, risk having another child? He'd fought against the idea for so long, he'd begun to believe himself incapable of loving a child as much as he'd loved Esteban. Now he knew that was not true. He loved Catherine's child. He would love a child they created together. There was no doubting that.

Could they work out a life together? He'd wanted to believe they could. If he could go back to Spain, clear his name and not have every Spanish authority chasing after his shirttails for the King of the Pirate's thievery against that crowned fool Philip, he would feel reasonably assured that anyone in his life would be safe. The question was, would Catherine trust him enough to wait and see if he could clear his name?

Everything rested on Sadi's map. If he couldn't find the diamonds, he had nothing to bargain with. And if he had nothing, he could offer nothing.

When he reflected on his situation, it seemed hopeless. And then he felt Catherine in his arms and swore he would find a way to fix the wrongs in his past.

The lantern's flame above them flickered, stirring shadows on the papered walls. Danton breathed with Catherine, matching the tempo of her heartbeat with his own. He heard her take a soft breath.

"Danton . . ."

"Oui, chérie?"

"Danton . . . I can't have any more children."

Chapter

17

Catherine waited for Danton to say something.

He found her chin with his finger and raised her face to capture her gaze. "Catherine?"

It was hard for her to look into his eyes. "I can't have any more children."

"Why would you say such a thing?"

"My labor was long and painful."

"First labors are long," he insisted, his voice commanding she keep her gaze fixed to his. "And painful for women to endure. You can't use that as any measure to judge by."

"I'm not . . . not entirely. I know I'm not the only woman to have a difficult labor. It's just that I don't think I've fully recovered."

"What do you mean?"

"I nursed Madeleine for over a year, and when I stopped, I didn't regain my . . ." Catherine's cheeks grew warm. ". . . my menses right away. And when I did, they were irregular and few. They're not the way they used to be."

"That shouldn't have anything to do with conceiving."

She tried to break from his stare, but he held her chin and she was forced to endure the speculative silver of his black-limned eyes. "There were times after Madeleine when Georges Claude and I . . ." It was hard for her to explain her exact meaning. "We were together enough to conceive a child. And I didn't."

"Ill timing," he said simply. "You can't be certain."

"I am certain!" The sting of tears blurred her vision and the shame of inadequacy filled her. "A woman knows her body, and I'm telling you, something happened to me after Madeleine. I thank God I was able to have her at all."

"Catherine—" His response hitched in his throat. She knew he felt sorry for her, and she was loathe to hear his sympathy.

"It's all right." She stopped him from saying anything further. "I've reconciled that Madeleine will be my only child. She's enough for me, Danton. Truly." But even as she said the words, she knew her statement was a lie. She had enough love in her heart for a dozen Madeleines.

Danton wound his fingers in hers and kissed her knuckles. He gazed at her through hooded eyes. Her whole being seemed to be filled with waiting. The secret that had kept them apart no longer existed. He knew the truth. What would he do now?

Danton squeezed her fingers and brushed his warm lips over the curve of her hand. "You would have made a fine mother for a son, Catherine." Then he gave her a lingering kiss. She felt transported from her troubled past.

Danton spoke, his lips whispering against hers. "Will you think me a hypocrite if I made love to you now?"

"No," she sighed. "I would be disappointed if you didn't."

He shifted her onto her back and caught her face in his large hands. "Then I'll try not to disappoint you." Pushing her into the softness of the tester, his leg crushed hers; a pleasant weight which made her conscious of his easy strength.

"Remember me, Catherine," Danton murmured. "Remember me when you're gone." Then he kissed her. Deeply and possessively.

She slipped her arms around Danton's shoulders and held him close. She didn't want him to look at her face. If he did, he would see the power he had over her emotions. She loved him and she wanted to stay with him. She was willing to forget everything. Paris and home. Familiarity and stability.

The sensible reasons that made it all the harder losing her heart to this man.

She wanted to fight her desires for him.

But as he kissed her and snatched her rationality with each breath, she submitted to what she could not will away.

She wanted him too.

Danton grazed the corner of her parted lips.

"I will remember you, Danton," she whispered, twining her fingers in his untamed hair. "Always."

The fine texture of his jet dressing gown felt erotic and exotic under her fingertips as she splayed her fingers across his back. His tongue explored her mouth, and Catherine matched his sensual dance, rediscovering him.

She bunched the fabric at his shoulders, clinging to him, her mind filled with sensual images of what he was doing to her, what she wanted him to do to her. She had never felt anything remotely like this. It was an awakening experience that left her reeling.

Danton broke their kiss and reached for the hooks on her stomacher. He tugged on the top closure, then one below. She felt the tiny pulls, and each jerk sent a shiver spiraling through her. One after another he made his way down to the bodice point in her skirt and the ribbon she'd already undone.

The tight cords of muscle on his shoulder rippled under her palm, and as he moved, the hood attached to his cloak tumbled over her hand. In a breathless rasp she asked, "What is this you're wearing?"

"A burnoose." He finished unhooking one side of her bodice and began on the other.

"Burnoose?" As each frail fastener snapped free of its eye, she hitched her breath.

Danton neared the end of the decorative bodice panel. "It's a robe worn by pashas."

Catherine couldn't soften the rise and fall of her bosom. "What is a pasha?"

"A man of high rank, *linda*." And then he stripped away the insert and tossed the wedge of quilted silk to the floor. "No more questions, Catherine," he bade, dipping his head. She felt the tickle of his glossy hair on her collarbone as he kissed the sensitive swell of her breast. Confined in her stays, her bosom was pushed high and full, the nipples restrained by the delicate gossamer of her chemise.

Catherine's hands slid down Danton's arms. She wanted to feel his skin, but the restriction of his robe prevented her from doing so. She hadn't seen any lacing cords at his throat except for one silken frog that had been left undone. The only way he could rid himself of the burnoose was over his head.

She tugged at the material by his waist, but his heavy weight prevented her from freeing him without his cooperation.

"Danton . . . I . . ." She struggled with her words as he made tiny swirls with his tongue across the curve of her breast.

"I said no talking, *chérie*." The vibration of his voice on her naked skin deepened the ache spreading downward to the apex of her thighs.

She wiggled beneath Danton, trying to get him to raise his hips so she could have access to the hem of his garment.

"And no moving," he murmured hoarsely against her. "Not yet." He caught both of her wrists and pinned them over her head. "No moving."

Danton locked his fingers through hers in a grip she could not break. He held her immobile. He bent his head and kissed the peak of her breast, capturing her nipple through the sheer fabric of her shift. The sensation of his teeth lightly nipping her, caressing her, through a veil of fragile linen burst inside her like brilliant sparks of light. She wanted to touch him so badly she trembled.

"Let me go," she pleaded, turning her head from side to side. "I can't . . . I want to touch you."

Danton lifted his hips but didn't release her. Instead he readjusted his position and settled firmly between her legs. His forearms met hers, crushing her still. "You do touch me, Catherine," he said in a low tone. "Every place where we join, you touch me." A stormy gray filled his fathomless eyes. "Can you feel me, *chérie?*"

Through the folds of her gown, she felt the length of him; thick, hard, ready. *"Oui."* Her reply broke on a shaky breath.

Danton inched his face closer to hers. His long hair

cascaded over his brows and touched her forehead. "I may be the one keeping you still, Catherine, but it is you who has the control. You control me with your lush curves, your ripe mouth and the warm place in your woman's center. I want you and I will do what you tell me."

Catherine's pulse soared beyond the boundaries of its limits and she could scarcely contain the raging beats of her heart. "I want you to let me go so I can take your burnoose off."

Without a word he elevated himself to his knees and hovered above her. His powerful legs straddled her. His hands rested on his hips, and his desire made a pronounced ridge in the folds of his robe. Seeing the outline of his proud arousal, she felt no embarrassment or shy discomfort. Only a wanton thrill that sang through her.

Catherine edged to a half-sitting position and began accumulating the yards of material in her fingers, drawing the gathers upward past his flanks. She couldn't suppress a hushed exclamation when she revealed his extended manhood, smooth and full.

When she could go no further without getting up, Danton pushed her hands away and pulled his burnoose over his tousled hair. She slowly laid back down and looked at him. He was all sinew and brawn, chiseled from granite and molded by tight stretches of golden flesh. The light from the lantern glimmered off his cross earring, lending him a wicked air. His black hair fanned around his angular face, wild and untamed.

Catherine dragged the sleeve of her dress down, but Danton's voice stopped her.

"Let me." He gently nudged her aside.

She allowed him to undress her.

He did so with an agonizing slowness. Every touch left her wanting more. Every inch she felt the satin fabric descend across her arm, she uncontrollably arched her back to meet him. When he had the gown past her waist, he urged her to lift her hips so he could glide the wide skirt down her thighs. She heard the scratchy rustle of the yellow satin dusting the floor.

Clad in her underpinnings, she waited for Danton to remove her stockings. He didn't. Instead he eased her onto her side and drew out the bow that held her corset together. As soon as he released her, she felt free, her breasts heavy and warm. He tossed her stays aside and rolled her onto her back again.

Danton caught the lacy edge of her shift in his fists, his knuckles working across her breasts. She strained against him. She felt the coarse hair on his thighs, but he would not kiss her or go further. "Danton . . . please."

In a quick sweep he tore the flimsy chemise down the middle.

Catherine trembled under his searing stare.

"Control, Catherine," he said in a guttural tone that shocked and entranced her. He traced the edges of her swollen breasts. He spent long moments circling, closing in, but not touching her nipples.

When she thought she'd go mad from the pleasure, he rolled each nipple between his thumb and forefinger. He coaxed until she felt full a tightness bordering on torment.

"I have no . . . no control," she panted. "You've taken every shred of it."

Danton's hands lightly glided down her belly and across her hips, to the insides of her thighs. Flushed and shaking, Catherine gave herself to his exploring fingers. He turned her emotions inside and out, stroking her moist center and building the fire in her to the brink of a sweet ache and longing.

She lifted herself to him, waiting for him to take her. Unbidden and unexpected, a thought flashed across her mind. She would never be with another man after Danton.

She couldn't.

Danton exceeded her every expectation. He would demand everything of her. He would take her heart, her breath, her soul, and she would be helpless against his power. There could never be anyone else to fulfill what he would possess.

"Danton . . ." she quietly implored.

He turned away from her for an instant and reached for a pillow. "Lift your hips, *chérie.*"

She did so without question. Danton fit the cool damask of the cushion beneath her bare buttocks. He spread her legs with his knee and touched her with his arousal. Pushing his hips slowly forward, he barely entered her, then withdrew. As if he meant to move that way all night, he came into her again, deeper, but as soon as she arched to meet him, he left her.

This new torment drove her mad. She studied his dark features and saw that he'd lied. He was in control. Very much so. His jaw clenched, showing her a flash of white teeth. His beautiful eyes were hooded and glimmering with passion. A thin sheen of moisture dampened his forehead.

He had control, and she was helpless.

"I'm not a virgin," she gasped under the friction of his languid assault, "you don't need to go slow with—"

"I know what you are . . ." And then Danton plunged the full length of himself into her and she moaned her surprise. She tightened around him, feeling him fit neatly inside her. ". . . and what you are not, Catherine," he said. "I know that a slow death brings a man's past encounters back to mind. While he makes ready to quit this earth, he is left to think of"—Danton moved until he could go no deeper"—that which he enjoyed the most." He covered her mouth and caught her lower lip between his teeth. "I intend to remember you on my dying breath, *chérie*. Now wrap your legs around me."

She did, and at once understood the full meaning of the pillow beneath her. Danton filled her completely. He set a slow rhythm, his hands braced on her hips concentration deepening his expression.

She moved against him, silently urging him to quicken his pace. But he did not relent. He kept on with his lingering movements, taking himself away, then burying himself inside her as far as he could go. The intensity of this torture left her panting and gasping. Her breath clawed in her throat for release and fulfillment—the same she felt that night in his study. She wanted desperately to be at one with him this time, to share the flood of pleasure carrying her on its liquid current.

Danton built his tempo, and she didn't think she could wait for him. Dizzy wavelets consumed her, making her legs around his thighs tingle and weaken. She held on, matching him thrust for thrust, holding onto his shoulders and lifting her hips as high as she could.

"There . . . is . . . no . . . control," he huffed, his hair spilling over his brow. His hands gripped her hips, and as she felt herself being pulled into ecstasy, he tightened his fingers on her and pushed himself so deeply inside her, she shattered.

She welcomed the tide of heat, the tightness and pulsing warmth. Her world spun and her heart thumped erratically.

She felt him shudder, felt his muscles bunch beneath her palms. He groaned, low and taut, and she knew he'd spilled his seed inside her. Seed that would be wasted on a woman like her.

But she didn't want to think about that.

She need only think of the throbbing and tingling running through her every vein. The heat, the warmth, the spinning axis of pleasure.

She held him, cocooned in the aftermath of their love-making. Danton buried his face in her neck and remained within her. She wasn't ready to let him leave; she kept her legs locked around him. She was drowning in the flood tide of relief she'd found for her body . . . her spirit.

In that timeless space, she knew she'd been right. Danton would be the only one she could ever be with. She'd known what it was like to be loved by Georges Claude, where release never went beyond his personal gratification. With Danton . . . she pressed her lips to his cool hair . . . he'd taken every shred of her soul and given her the same in return.

She felt his heartbeat beating against her breasts. Neither said anything for long, quiet minutes.

Danton lifted his head and kissed her cheek. His breath was ragged and hot next to her ear. Pulling back, he stared at her with an odd look of wonder in his smoky eyes. "Don't go. Stay with me for a while."

She nodded, and he kissed the tip of her nose. He shifted, as if he meant to slide off her. "No," Catherine cried. "Don't leave me."

Danton brought his lips on hers. Gently. Lovingly. "If I stay," he murmured, "I'll want more."

"Stay," she said, pushing a lock of black hair behind his ear.

* * *

Danton clasped his hands behind his back and waited for Madeleine to come into his study. She stood in the doorway, her rosebud mouth crestfallen. Tears spiked her lashes and dampened her round cheeks.

"Maman said you wanted to talk to me." She fiercely held onto her dolly as if it would save her from him. All the more to make him feel wretched.

"I do." His uneasiness capsized his belly and he felt like he was on the seas rather than stable land. Apologizing to a pint-sized imp had never been on his list of life's experiences. But he'd commanded enough men to know that stern authority got the job done with the most efficiency and was the key to any situation. He would mastermind the apology to his benefit, be done with it, and she would forget his blunder had ever existed. "Come here, Madeleine, and sit down."

She kept her eyes downcast and shuffled into the room. Quietly she climbed onto one of his chairs and folded her hands in her lap. She refused to look at him.

Merde.

"Madeleine, I called you here to tell you something." He rounded his desk and leaned his hip against the flat surface. "If you knew me well enough, you'd know that what I have to say is not easy for me to admit."

She still would not look his way. The devil and damnation.

"Yesterday when you asked me if I was coming to dinner, I gave you an answer which led you to believe I was."

She resumed her fit of sniffles, and his palms began to sweat.

"It was wrong of me to imply I would be there. I knew that your interpretation of 'we'll see' meant *oui.'"

"Y-You didn't come, a-and *Maman* and I looked so p-pretty for you."

Danton stiffly said, "I know how disappointed you must have been."

Madeleine's tiny chin shot up. "You l-lied to me."

Her accusation pierced his heart. "Not on purpose."

"B-But you didn't c-come."

"A grave error. It will never happen again. From now on

when I tell you something, you can count on it to be my word of honor."

She carefully examined him, picking him apart with her doelike stare. He grimaced under her scrutiny. She wiped her nose with her sleeve and put her doll next to her cheek. "I still like you," she sniffed. "I'll let you be my friend again."

He breathed a tight sigh of relief. "Very good of you to give me another chance."

Madeleine slipped out of the chair, her right knee boasting a fresh scrape. "Don't make me sad again, monsieur. It hurts my feelings."

Danton stifled the jolt that shook him. *"Non, mademoiselle.* I shall make sure I don't make you sad again."

"I have to help Tanala in the kitchen, so I can't play with you now. Maybe I'll come see you later."

"Do that."

"Good-bye, monsieur." Then she left.

In the hollow silence following the child's departure, Danton pondered who exactly had had the authority over the situation.

Catherine hurried to collect the washing—a chore she'd insisted on doing to help in the household—before her clean clothes and the bed linens became wet. Dark clouds had accumulated and the far-off skies showed gray streaks of falling rain.

The wind rumpled her snowy shifts, petticoats, and knit stockings, which were draped over the boxy amaryllis hedges. Dashing down the row and snagging the apparel as she went, Catherine tossed the items into the basket she'd gleaned from Tanala.

A droplet smacked her nose, but Catherine didn't use the energy to wipe it away. She quickly crossed the patch of grassy yard behind the house to the strings of coconut rope James had put up for her. Her dresses and Madeleine's hung over the cords, as well as two rows of bedding. Putting the straw basket at her feet, Catherine began to yank the gowns off the lines.

Another drop hit her head, then one more on her cheek.

The wind stirred her hair and she shook her head to get the curls over her shoulder so she could see what she was doing. The white hem of her morning dress swirled around her bare ankles. She hadn't expected to be out in the monsoon taking in the laundry only a hour after putting it up. Her informal mode of dress befitted a lady's chamber, not the outdoors. She'd been in her bedroom, lying on the bed, trying to rest. She hadn't had much sleep last night.

Catherine recalled with a smile the hours she'd shared in Danton's Chinese bed. He'd been a slow and confident lover, drawing out her sensuality and making her aware of herself in ways she'd never realized.

Just as dawn had ringed the horizon in ribbons of pink and gold, she left Danton to return to her room. She was fearful she'd stayed away from Madeleine too long; she'd checked her daughter several times during the night and found she was sleeping peacefully.

Danton had made Catherine's departure difficult by kissing her each time she moved to the side of the bed. She'd break free of him, but he'd grab her waist again and bring her to him for another kiss. In the end she'd had to make him promise he wouldn't touch her and stay in the bed while she slipped her chemise over her head.

He'd reluctantly agreed to her demand, watching her with a lazy gaze. Her skin heated under his slow appraisal as he followed her movements. The wash of new and untried feelings of desirability and power he gave her frightened her. She could have easily lost her every reasonable thought in his arms if she'd let herself.

She'd had to remind herself who he was and what he did. He'd made no declarations of abandoning his acts of piracy. Finding Sadi hadn't redeemed what Danton Luis Cristobal had lost. He was still the King of the Pirates. As legitimate as he'd portrayed his reasons for retaliation, she feared committing herself to a man capable of being bent on the destruction of another man's life—no matter how much empathy she felt for Danton.

It was growing harder to keep the strength of her argument alive in her mind. She loved him, and that was all that mattered when she was in his arms.

She had padded quietly to the door after having dressed

sufficiently to walk the halls. Her parting image of Danton had been cast in golden lamplight. The broad, muscular play of his shoulders appeared smooth as honey. His ribs were defined ridges of taut flesh, broken by the thin line of dark hair that trailed and intimately curled around him. His nakedness had shown her he wasn't ready for her to leave. He'd given her a drawn-out, suggestive smile, but she'd quickly turned the doorknob and slipped out of the room.

Despite knowing everything about Danton, she couldn't stop wanting him; wanting to feel him next to her, inside her. She'd become an insatiable woman, taking the initiative more than once during the long, blissful night.

Three fat beads of rain landed in brisk succession on Catherine's upturned face as she reached for one of the large muslin sheets.

No time for daydreaming, she chided herself, no matter how much she wanted to relive Danton's kisses. The monsoon would quickly ruin clothes it had taken her hours to wash.

Without warning a hand grabbed her from behind. Strong arms slipped around her midriff. She tried to scream, but fingers clamped over her open mouth and spun her around. As quickly as the hand disappeared, a mouth captured hers.

Danton.

She dropped the linen, heedless of where it fell, to wrap her arms around his neck and pull him closer. She kissed him back with an immediacy to match his own. He slanted his lips over hers, taking quick and demanding kisses from her. Her heartbeat quickly soared to an excited rhythm, and if it weren't for the rain to remind her where she was, she would have fallen down in the grass with him.

"Danton," she breathed against his mouth, stealing a kiss of her own. He didn't stop his ravishment of her mouth, nor cease his hands from sliding down her back to cup her buttocks and push her into him. "Danton," she gasped, "someone will see us."

The linens fluttered around them, giving them shelter. "No one will see us," he kissed the corner of her mouth and tangled his fingers in her unbound hair, "in the laundry."

"They'll—" She arched her back as he kissed the hollow of her throat. "They'll see our feet."

The heavens above opened up, spilling a multitude of droplets that quickly spoiled the remaining clothing on the ropes.

Catherine felt the cooling rain against her warm skin and closed her eyes. Danton's hand reached up to cradle her breast in his palm and tease her nipple. She responded without thought. This was madness. She wanted him. Here. Now. She didn't care about anything else.

Then Danton lifted her into his arms and carried her to the boundaries of his lawn and into the grove of lofty palm and coconut trees fringed with fragrant brush and flowering ylang-ylang. Secluded from anyone's view, he set her in front of a coconut tree and pressed her back into the trunk. With no threat of an audience, he resumed his ardent kisses.

Rain trickled through the canopy of fronds. The droplets were like musical chords when they bounced off full, waxy leaves and hit the mossy ground like natural chimes.

Catherine kissed Danton. Not satisfied with only his mouth, she groped for the fasteners at the side of his breeches.

Danton stroked her breasts, her nipples. He leaned into her, the length of him at her belly. Her hands roved across his back and slipped the shirt hem from his trousers. She slid her fingers underneath the wet fabric and grazed his tight skin, teasing him with a light rasp of her fingernails. He moaned and ground his lips into hers before lifting his head.

There was no time to remove clothing. Clothing that had become a hindrance, a nuisance. Danton lifted her skirts, and she in turn went for the placket of buttons on his breeches. Once the last button was out of its hole, she peeled the side of his trousers open and freed him. Her fingers brushed him, stimulating him further with her touch.

"You're mine, Catherine," he growled, grasping her waist and lifting her off the ground. "Right now, you're with me and you're mine."

And then he came into her, piercing her, consuming her. Catherine hung onto him, her backside feeling the smooth bark of the tree. She wound her legs around Danton's waist as he pushed into her over and over. She was helpless to match the tempo. All she could do was hold on and ride the river of euphoria with him.

She felt the building tension inside her crescendo and release into a hot pool of abandon. And then Danton plunged one last time and shuddered his own release.

He held her still, panting and spent, the tree now supporting them both. Catherine kissed his face: his mouth, his cheek, his eyes, his brows.

Her racing heartbeat met his.

Rain spattered Danton's face and he licked the moisture from his lips. Catherine bent and kissed away the few on his cheek and at the black slash of his brow.

"Jesu, woman . . ." Danton sucked in his breath in a collecting hiss. "I'm behaving like a sailor fresh into port from a year at sea. I've ravished you under a damn coconut tree."

"It's a good thing," she blew a strand of hair from her eyes with a smile, "there weren't any ripe coconuts on the tree or we could have been killed by blows to our heads."

Danton pressed his forehead to hers. "If we keep this up, Catherine, it *will* kill me."

Chapter

18

~~

"Don't spin that," Danton told Madeleine as her hand stretched to rotate his German globe. He sat behind the desk in his study, a legion of charts as his desk mates.

"Why not?" Madeleine eased her short fingers over the rounded top, as if to test the veracity of his warning.

"Because you're hands are sticky," Danton explained.

"Oh . . ." She dragged her sleeve across her mouth. "If I move it with the very tip of my finger . . . ?"

"Your fingers are sticky all the way down." He really didn't care if she got his globe tacky from the residue of candy—she'd already done so on past occasions. His reluctance came from the fact he'd hidden the pouch and diamond inside the sphere. They might rattle lose if she revolved the globe—and knowing Madeleine, she would do so with great gusto.

"If I lick my finger off, can I?" Madeleine asked.

Danton struggled to think up a plausible excuse why she should leave the globe alone. "No. I like to have Spain in my view. It reminds me of my homeland," he lied. The girl would understand the importance behind the word home.

Madeleine left the painted sphere with a sigh. "I don't have a home."

"Yes you do." Danton foraged through the mess on his desk for his compass. "You live with me."

"Not for long. We're going to Paris, France."

Danton grew disturbed, more so with himself. Of late, he was having a difficult time accepting that Catherine was leaving him. "I know. But for now," he said calmly, "you live with me."

"I like living with you," she declared, her blue eyes wide. "But we have to go to Paris, France, to see the Leave."

Danton plucked a map of the Aldabra Islands from his Sung vase. "I think you mean the Louvre."

"*Oui*, that's what I mean," she replied. She made a great show of being bored, rocking on the low heels of her kid shoes and trying to whistle. "There's nothing to play with in here."

"Why don't you go outside and—"

"I don't want to play outside today." She hopped up onto the chair across from him and put her chin in her hand. "There's nothing to do outside. I keep digging and digging and digging and I can't find a ruby necklace."

"You found a pair of shoes."

"Antonio told me those were yours."

"Hmm." The killjoy Spaniard. Danton thought it rather amusing the girl had declared to the whole pirate crew she'd finally found treasure—even if the prize had been a man's pair of emerald shoes.

Madeleine's beautifully curved eyebrows rose. "Do you want them back?"

"Certainly not."

Madeleine plopped both elbows on the table and stared at him with sad eyes.

"Where's your mother?" Danton asked shortly. He'd run into Catherine in the hallway three quarters of an hour ago. He'd spoken a cordial greeting, keeping up the pretext of a cool friendship for Catherine's sake, in case Eduardo or Antonio or any other household member happened to overhear them.

But as soon as Catherine had reached his side and he'd smelled her sweet fragrance, seen the mischief written in her blue-gray eyes, he'd lost his sense of diplomacy. He'd grasped her by the wrist and guided her into the north room. Like a man consumed by his lust, he'd taken her on King

Philip's coat-of-arms red carpet. The Spanish portraits hanging on the walls had been their audience.

Catherine had made no protest. He wasn't entirely convinced of her innocence in the matter. As she'd crossed his path, she'd feigned a light stumble and touched his arm to balance herself. She'd gazed sidelong into his eyes, her full pink lips parted. He'd needed no spoken invitation.

The devil take him, he'd turned into a rutting idiot, having the woman on his mind every waking and sleeping second of his existence. He was on the verge of begging her to stay with him. He couldn't think rationally when she was near, or far for that matter. He'd been in his study for the better part of the morning, and he couldn't concentrate on Sadi's map. Everything he looked at made no sense.

He was loosing his grip because of a woman.

Because of Catherine LeClerc.

He loved her to a fault and he refused to let her go.

Perhaps it was time for him to tell her about Sadi's map. Give her hope that he could find the diamonds and return to civilization without the threat of imprisonment. If he could convince her she wouldn't be throwing her life away on a criminal, maybe she would stay.

Or if she still insisted on Paris, he would go there with her. He could live in the city again, or so he hoped. There was no reason to think that all his days on the sea and the tranquil peace of his island had ruined him from enjoying the comforts of civilization. He could blend in. Or at least try for Catherine's sake.

On the other hand, if he did not decipher the map, he would be hounded by his failure for the rest of his life. He could not ask Catherine to stay with no hope that he could redeem himself. For all he knew, he would waste the rest of his years searching for something that didn't exist. He'd be asking Catherine to spend her life with a renegade. A man still possessed by his past. A king hunted by Spanish law.

His love for Catherine wouldn't be enough if he was hanging from the gallows.

Madeleine's childish voice imposed on his miserable thoughts. "My *maman* went for a walk and wouldn't let me come with her. She said to stay with Eduardo."

Danton grumbled. "Where is Eduardo?" The faithful,

loyal blackguard had begun to fraternize with a certain young, beautiful Malagasy woman rumored to be of a royal bloodline from King Antaimoro.

"He's with a pretty girl." Madeleine lifted her leg and studied her foot. "I think her name is Mia. I saw them by the bushes . . . smooching."

"Mierda," Danton scoffed under his breath.

"That's a cussing word, monsieur. You're not allowed to say bad words in front of me because I might start to say bad words too." She pulled up one of her sagging stockings. "What color stockings are you wearing, Monsieur Pirate?"

"What the deuce does that have to do with anything?"

"Mine are pink."

"And mine are white," he hastily obliged in a tart tone. He was being a bear and he knew the cause. These little, seemingly inconsequential conversations he had with Madeleine were becoming part of a routine. Danton Cristobal never did anything in routine. He did what he wanted, when he wanted. He wasn't quite certain how to handle this new sense of order.

"You want to hear a secret?" Madeleine brought her leg down and grinned.

Danton unrolled the map and held the parchment open with two smooth stones, compliments of Mademoiselle LeClerc. Clearing his throat, he said, "If you insist."

Madeleine giggled, the prelude to some mischief, he was sure. "That night you didn't come to dinner with us—"

Danton hoped to God she wasn't going to bring that back to slap him with.

"—*Maman* had her corset on. When Tanala was lacing her, *Maman* went huh-hah-huh-hah," Madeleine huffed in mime, "and couldn't breathe because it was too tight. She fell down on the bed and Tanala had to loosen *Maman* up or *Maman* said she would be sick."

Danton cleared his throat, not wanting to let the little chatterbox know her story had tickled him. "I see. Well," he grinned, "I'm glad to hear your mother didn't get sick."

"I know some more secrets," Madeleine beamed, "and embarrassing things."

"Not now, Maddie." He feigned concentration on his documents so she wouldn't say anything further.

Madeleine leaned forward and plopped her elbows on the table again. "What's that you're doing, Monsieur Pirate?"

Danton laid Sadi's map next to the one of the Aldabra and said offhandedly, "I'm trying to match an island with the one on this piece of paper."

"Oh." Madeleine scooted off her chair and came around to Danton's side for a better look. Without asking, she climbed onto his lap.

Danton tensed under her feather-light weight, his right hand remaining steadfast at the table's edge.

"I can sit on you because I haven't played outside today. I'm not stinky." She raised her arm and lifted the sleeve cuff of her shirt to his nose. "Smell me."

Danton mildly obliged, sniffing the fresh scent of laundry soap and line-dried linen. And, of course, peppermint. "You smell fine."

As Madeleine wiggled in to get comfortable on his knees, Danton sat stiffly. It had been hard admitting his love for the child. He had an even harder time showing it to her. As always, he thought of Esteban. But this time not with sad reminiscence or the feeling of being cheated. No. In fact, with Madeleine he felt blessed, as if he'd been given a second chance.

Tentatively he put his arm around her waist and held her still. "Madeleine . . ." His voice froze.

"Oui, monsieur?" Turning her head, she smiled up at his face, and his gentle admission turned to mud. He grappled with how to tell her about his feelings toward her, thinking that perhaps she wouldn't understand he could love her like she was his own. But he knew that line of reasoning was a stall tactic. Madeleine LeClerc was very perceptive.

Danton struggled with his awkwardness, deciding not to be too blunt. "Madeleine, I like you very much."

She gave him a smile as wide as his square rigger, as if knowing exactly what he meant. "I like you too." Then she hugged him, clasping her tiny hands around his neck. "But I really love you instead."

Unexpected warmth surged through Danton. He hadn't realized how frightened he was of her rejection. He closed his eyes and rested his cheek on the top of her head, a silly grin on his face. He couldn't seem to stop smiling.

Madeleine was the first to pull away and turn back to the mass of paper on his desk. "Which map are you trying to match?" she asked studiously.

Danton indulged her without prodding. "This one here." He pointed to Sadi's crude treasure map.

"You think it's one of these?" Madeleine inclined her head and poked her face up close to the chart he'd just unrolled.

Danton answered, his voice distant, "I'm hoping it will be."

"It doesn't look like it matches this one." The tip of her nose practically brushed the paper.

"Maybe not to you." Frowning, Danton compared the two maps and saw that Madeleine was right. They didn't look the same. The general outlines were comparable, but not the interiors.

Madeleine picked up Sadi's map and perused the yellow parchment as if she knew how to read the clues. Danton allowed her the luxury, but kept careful watch on her. If she accidentally tore the paper, she would destroy one of the distinguishing lines.

"Puppet," he said gently after a long length, "give me the map back now."

Madeleine's expression grew solemn and she made no move to do as he asked. "I know where this is."

"Of course you do." He moved his hand closer to take the map from her. He knew she merely wanted to help and was making up anything to keep from having to return Sadi's scribbles to him.

"All these spikes are by the desert beach where *Maman* started her big fire and I found a brown turtle." Madeleine nodded with confidence.

"Hmm."

"The brown turtle had diamonds on his back. Not real ones."

"Of course," Danton agreed, stretching for the map again, but Madeleine held it away from his reach.

"*Oui*. And this is the hurting river."

"Hmm." Danton inconsequentially followed her finger as she ran her short nail over a weaving line.

"See. The hurting river in red ink."

Danton narrowed his gaze, his skepticism lowering a notch. "What? What was that, puppet?"

"The river that looks like it has an ouch because the water is red." Madeleine tapped her finger on the map where a stream cut through the crown of spikes—spikes that he had thought were renditions of a volcano or crater.

"I think that's what this looks like."

"Jesu . . . the water that runs out of the *tsingy.*" Danton slipped the map out of Madeleine's fingers. *The hurting river* . . . rock decay that turned red when it hit the current. His heartbeat hammered in his chest as he quickly saw more and more similarities. The peaks and the river running halfway through the jagged circle were indeed familiar. He'd been there before. He'd traversed the needled spikes and forded the red river. He had been through the *tsingy* to the other side. A side where the beach stretched long and clear, broken by fallen sheets of limestone. A beach where a treasure chest could be buried.

"Madre de Dios," he said in a slow sigh. After all of the hours he'd spent poring over maps and charts, the hiding place he wanted was right under his boots.

The diamonds were buried here.

On the Isle of the Lost Souls.

Catherine stared at the remnants of her bonfire on the eastern expanse of beach. The ashes of the charred timbers had been scattered by the monsoons. Blown by the hale winds, the blackened pieces littered the golden sand like bits of obsidian. Looking at what remained, Catherine found it hard to believe that not long ago she'd been so set on leaving Danton, she would have done anything to gain her freedom. And now . . .

She sighed and stared at the rolling blue sea. And now she didn't want to leave.

The ocean's foaming waves thundered up the shore, then dissipated with the gentleness of a bubbling brook. Time washed the sand; time Catherine hadn't thought she had until she'd surrendered to the season of the monsoons. A pact made with the wind and the rain . . . a waiting period until they would subside and she would be able to sail off the island. To follow through with her decision to leave Isle of the Lost Souls.

It had been so important for her to have made the choice to go. She'd begun to realize now a choice need not be etched in stone. She could change her mind. But at what cost? Her pride. She could swallow that if the matter were that simple. She would stay and be content if she knew Madeleine would be safe from negative repercussions. That there was no possibility of the law coming to Danton's island and taking them all. For surely as she and her daughter resided here, they were guilty of Danton's crimes, as they did nothing to prevent him from his raids. However, Danton had not taken to the sea to plunder since she'd thwarted his encounter with the Spanish *flotas*. That did not mean he'd hung up his sword. On the contrary, he'd never declared his intentions to live a legitimate life.

And that was the problem.

Danton Luis Cristobal was still King of the Pirates. Accepting his behavior would not alleviate the gravity of his illegal doings. He still had a thirst for vengeance, and would not rest until he'd paid Sadi back in kind and if he discovered that Sadi were still alive, he would not rest until he'd taken the Turk's life. No matter if that meant splintering his life away while he was in the process.

Catherine walked around the waist-high pile of burnt timbers and skirted its sooty border. She could no longer ignore her feelings for Danton. Since the night they'd first made love, things between them had changed. She'd known the act of intimacy brought two people closer. What they'd shared was as close as two people could get. But the depth of her emotions for him went beyond sexual oneness. Her heart had been touched. Deeply. Completely.

She'd fallen hopelessly in love with him.

He'd given her hope when she had none. She knew that the possibilities of a child were nothing short of nonexistent. But he'd made her feel as if there were a chance. Remote as that chance was, he'd made her feel special. Treasured.

He'd given her life when she was empty. She'd been a mother for so long, she'd forgotten the woman inside. She'd pushed aside her needs and desires, focusing instead on her daughter and the world of a four-year-old. He'd made her see beyond motherhood. He'd held her like a man held a beloved woman. For once, she was the one being cherished.

He'd given her love when she thought she had no room in her heart. And that was the hardest of all for her to accept. Long before Georges Claude had died, she'd poured every emotion she had into rearing her daughter. She'd nurtured, she'd taught, she'd guided and held onto the precious life she'd conceived and brought forth. But in return, she'd forgotten to love herself, to see that she needed to be taken care of sometimes too. Danton showed her in his lovemaking that she was special. That she was worthy of a man's love and devotion.

He'd shown her with his hands and his body the ways he loved her. But he'd never spoken the words. Neither had she. Perhaps they were both too frightened of their impact. The three simple words would mean commitment.

Catherine cupped her fingers over her brows and watched the sun wax the sky in muted tones of gold and blinding white. The sea spanned farther than she could see without the aid of Danton's spyglass. She looked to the east, then south. In a short time she would be a spot on the sea, sailing home to Paris. Her hopes would come true. Her wishes would be fulfilled. She would be reunited with her homeland.

But at what cost?

Maybe if Danton had said he loved her, things would be different. But that vow would be long in coming—if ever. She knew him well enough to see he had too much pride for wasted declarations. She'd made her intentions too clear. He'd known from the start she would leave him. He'd even gone as far as asking her to stay, and she'd refused him.

Catherine fought the turmoil running inside her like the rusty river that flowed into the ocean from the *tsingy* behind her. She was too stubborn. She knew that. She could have—should have—said she'd consider him. Instead she'd turned him down flat, and now she was suffering for her hastiness.

She was so certain she had to be in control of her fate. No one could twist the sands of time against her if she didn't want them to. She had to be in charge. She had to plot her life's chart. But she was quickly coming to terms with the price.

Being alone.

Yes, she had Madeleine and she loved her dearly, but a child wasn't enough. A woman needed to be loved by a man. That love was priceless. A treasure not dug up from the sand in a chest, but a treasure of the heart. Real and gilded. Warm and true. Indispensable.

Loving someone didn't mean she lost command of her life. She was still Catherine LeClerc. She could still think for herself, make decisions for herself. The fact that she wanted to stay had come from her own head and no one else's. She'd not lost any of her control. If anything, she'd gained more. She'd grown stronger by admitting her faults and rectifying what could have been a grave error if she'd left Danton.

Catherine's pulse quickened. Suddenly she knew that she had to tell Danton she loved him. Even if he didn't feel the same way, he needed to know. Whatever demons haunted him, she could help. She would aid him, guide him, stand by his side. She would—

A hand clamped down on her shoulder and Catherine was filled with confusion. Only Danton would touch her so firmly, but this hand felt unfamiliar.

Turning on her heels, she breathed, "Danton?" but the question died on her lips.

Chapter

Chapter

19

Over here, *Capitaine!"* Rainiaro shouted.

Danton heard Rainiaro's urgent tone through the musical backdrop of wind whistling across the *tsingy's* fluted peaks. The sunlight filtering through the merging clouds had all but disappeared, leaving the beach in half darkness. Rain would be falling soon. Danton had ordered torches lit by the handful of crew he'd rounded up to search for Catherine, who hadn't returned to the house when a monsoon hit the island.

Danton raced toward the limestone walls and the river that bled red clay into the sea. His quartermaster stood at the only eastern entrance Danton knew of into the forest ringed by six-hundred-foot cliffs.

"Here, *Capitaine,"* Rainiaro said, looking down at a long, shining object in the sand.

Danton raised the firebrand he held, the burning twist of coconut fibers permeating the swirling air with an acrid smell. The dancing flames caught the gilt handle of a half-buried dagger. Square-cut emeralds gleamed in the wrist guard, lending the wide silver blade rich elegance.

Pulling the knife from the sand, Danton examined the finely honed weapon. Its value was evident, its J-shaped edge distinguishing. The craftsmanship spoke for the knife. The piece was Turkish made. Its location could not have been accidental. The dagger had been placed in a position where it could not go unnoticed; it had been left behind for a reason.

"Yousef Ahmed Sadi Ahram," Danton said, mouthing the Turk's name, his nostrils flaring from the sting of smoke. "He's alive. That bastard is on my island."

Hatred for the Turk rose in Danton tenfold, and a deathly knot of tension wound around his heart. Once he had been willing to spare Sadi's life. This time, the quiet fury inside him would hear no mercy. Sadi had stolen the diamonds that led to the loss of Elena and Esteban; now he'd intentionally stolen a jewel more precious than any diamond. For endangering Catherine, the penalty would be death.

Danton was filled with a rage so powerful, it kept him icily calm. *Sadi is on my island. And for the second time,* he silently added. The Turk had been here before. The day Sadi had left him to die in the sea. Sadi had sailed around to the other side of the island to bury the diamonds, believing that the plundered crew would never reach the shores.

Now it was Danton's turn to muse over irony. Sadi had apparently not known he had come back to the island. If he had, the Turk would have come for the diamonds sooner. Diamonds he evidently kept no watch over. How, then, had Sadi known to find him on Isle of the Lost Souls now? If Sadi hadn't merely returned to look for the buried treasure, then he'd come to find him. But if so, why now?

Only a trusted few knew the whereabouts of the King of the Pirates. Henry Greenspot's navigational skills were marginal at best when he mapped out a course to a well-documented port. Giving directions to an uncharted isle would be a major feat for him. Besides, Henry valued his ale too much to be denied the grog in hell—the precise place he had threatened to send the Englishman if he ran with his mouth.

Then the one-person answer became clear as cut glass to Danton. *Trevor Tate.* Tate had every reason to boast he knew where to find Danton Luis Cristobal. He'd been thwarted by Danton's men, cut down in cross fire and made to withdraw from a battle in front of his crew. *Maudit,* he should have known Tate was not a man to forget.

Lowering his torch to illuminate the surrounding footprints, Danton followed the worn embankment next to the river. The weathered slabs of stone were smooth under the scrape of his boot heels as he passed through a shallow gorge, Rainiaro close behind him.

Almost instantly the crash of the ocean faded away. The warble of bird songs and the drone of night creatures intruded from every crevice of the limestone bluffs. Scrub and thorny plants cast distorted shadows where Danton waved his light.

He sensed Catherine had been here. How he knew, he had no plausible answer. He breathed and he could smell her; he closed his eyes and he could see her; he strained for a sound and he could hear her voice. His every sense focused on her and his mind sang her name: *Catherine*.

Snapping his eyelids up, Danton gazed at a yawning cavern ahead. The dark passage linked into others, a network of channels—seemingly endless miles, accessing the forest. If a man didn't know which passageway to choose, he could become hopelessly lost and vulnerable to the cave dwellers—the gray crocodiles whose luminescent red eyes reflected torchlight when retreat was too late.

Rainiaro drew next to his side. "I'll tell the men to pack up supplies. We'll form a search party and—"

"No." Danton cut off the Malagasy. "I'm going alone. He's taken my Catherine."

Rainiaro's sublime features questioned his captain's orders. "You can't go after Sadi without men. Surely the Turk is armed with the whole or at least half of his crew."

"And I am armed with mine," Danton said briefly, heading out of the ravine and back toward the beach. "The crew will be stronger by lying in wait than getting caught. Which is what I intend to do."

"You cannot—"

"I'm going to get myself captured by Sadi and convince him Catherine means nothing to me. She'll be far safer despising me when I challenge him. I want you to prepare *Negro España* to sail. Set a course for the western shores of the island. I'll draw out exactly where. Wait for me. I can guarantee, if the Turk's not already there, he will be. With Catherine."

"Do you think he'll take her off the isle?"

"No." Danton took long steps full of strength and determination. "What he wants is right here. I have the map to the diamonds, Rainiaro."

"Map, *Capitaine?*"

"Sadi's map." Danton left the *tsingy* and crossed over the wind-ruffled sand. "I took it from him in Zanzibar and just tonight figured out he buried King Philip's diamonds on my island." Danton quickly thought of Madeleine safely at the house with Tanala. He'd make sure she was properly guarded in his absence. He would leave nothing to chance again.

"The Turk buried them here?"

Danton set his mouth in a grim line. "Disgusting humor, is it not? To have the objects of my salvation at my shovel tip and not even know it for four blasted years." He beckoned to his men and they began to walk toward him.

"And now Sadi wants the diamonds, but you have the map telling him where they are buried."

"*Oui.* I have the lunatic's map." Gazing at the walls of the *tsingy*, Danton whispered, "What was to have been the key to my freedom will now free something far more important to me than my life."

The sounds of the forest were deafening; the darkness rang with pandemonium. A string of barking noises exploded, and Catherine would have cupped her hands over her ears to muffle the shrieks if her wrists hadn't been bound.

Yap-yap-yap-yap-yap!

The calls bounced from one tree to another in a furious chorus. Dwarf lemurs swung from their hind feet on branches bearing green fruit the size of cherries. Their shrill screams made Catherine tremble, and even long for the familiar cries of Razana, Pousse-Pousse, and Dokobe.

Catherine sat on a Turkish rug woven with rich pink. Moldering hintsy leaves under the carpet's heavy pile gave the dyed, rose-colored yarn a peculiar smell. Musty and putrid. The dampness of the ground seeped upward onto her backside, moistening the skirt of her cambric dress. A cool mist lingered in the air, sheeting her face with dew.

There had only been one guard assigned to keep watch

over her while the others set up a campsite. She had gone over a dozen ideas and plans of escape, but each one was rejected for the same reason: the journey into the sunken forest had taken hours, and she knew she could never find her way out without becoming lost. Her captors had trekked through a series of rock chambers too similar to note a path back to the beach. In places, trickling streams had taken up the entire cave floor's width. Her shoes and stockings were wet reminders that she'd had no choice but to wade ankle deep in the tepid water.

Catherine worried her lip, holding onto the hope that Danton would come after her as soon as he realized she was missing. She prayed desperately he would keep Madeleine safe. Until then she would have to wait. To try anything rash would prove disastrous. Somehow she knew these men were not opposing pirates bent on robbing Danton of his self-proclaimed title and wealth. They were after something far more valuable—Danton himself. And they were using her to lure him.

The richly costumed band that had abducted her were dark-skinned. Not as brown as the Malagasys, but a burnished red resembling the henna color of Sultan Bedr bin Khalifa's beard. The fifty or more men wore long robes like the Arabs in Zanzibar, and spoke a language entirely foreign to her. They traveled in elegant comfort, evident by the rug she sat on and the panels of Bursa velvet and mosquito netting that had gone up in the camp.

The leader, a man with bushy black eyebrows, deep-set dark eyes, and a pointed beard, had disappeared. It had been his hand on her shoulder, his touch she'd thought might be Danton's. She shivered in remembrance and hoped he would leave her alone. On the beach, she'd tried conversing with him in French and English; even broken Hindustani. He'd repeatedly called her *hanim,* and nudged her ahead of him with the round tip of his long-barreled pistol. He'd paid no attention to her pleas and quickly ordered her wrists tied together with gold cording. Nervous energy made her rush her words in a high-pitched demand to be set free. The man had glared at her and said a word sounding like *kushdili.* Then his heavy brows came down in silent warning—one that she read to mean she'd better be quiet or he'd gag her.

The nearby hiss of a cockroach caused Catherine to stiffen and glance at the bed of decaying leaves at her feet. The fist-sized nocturnal pest raced toward one of the three open tents that had been erected on wooden poles and swathed with drapings of purple watered silk.

The camp had been flooded with lamplight, drawing out every insect within miles. The glass panes on brass lanterns were smothered with moths and winged creatures vying for heat and light.

Men worked around her, but none dared touch her. They gave her coveting glances, and she felt a moment's panic until she realized they were afraid of her. Or more to the point, afraid to go near what apparently was the property of their captain. A cold knot formed in her stomach with the thought.

A shout came from the opposite end of the compound, then another silken canopy rose to meet the pluming trees. A fresh whoop of *yap-yaps!* flushed from the leafy clusters as the lemurs vacated that tree in sailing leaps for another. From aloft in a tamarind tree, a parrot screeched; an owl hooted in the distance.

"Hanim," a baritone voice called to her.

Catherine lifted her gaze. The leader stood above her. He wore a large, wide turban on his jet-black hair. His narrow shoulders were cloaked in a deep blue robe of damask over a cream-colored waistcoat with a standing collar crossing his chest; a finely pleated shirt showing at his throat seemed out of place.

"I don't know what you are saying," she mumbled. "I don't speak your language." The cords at her wrists chafed and she wanted to be rid of them.

He cocked his thumb and pointed at his chest. "Pasha."

Pasha . . . the alien word came flooding back to Catherine. Danton had said his burnoose was a robe meant for pashas—men of high ranking. *Mon Dieu,* who was this man?

Her dark captor aimed a straight finger at her. *"Hanim. Düriye."*

"Non," she repudiated, growing irritated by his constant reference to her as *hanim.* *"Je m'appelle, Catherine."*

"Français."

She asked him a second time, *"Parlez-vous français?"*

He shook his head with a leering grin that prickled the hairs at the nape of her neck.

"What do you want?" she asked in French, regardless, her frustration invading her question.

He did not respond to her voice. Instead he held out his callused hand, palm up, and motioned for her to stand. Her knees had cramped, and without the use of her arms, the task of rising was made more difficult. She managed to get to her feet, stumbled, but took a step away from the pasha's outstretched arm when it looked like he meant to steady her. She felt as if her breath had been cut short.

Her tangled curls fell over her breasts and she tossed them over her shoulders with a rapid shake of her head. The pasha watched her with flashing black eyes which she refused to meet. He inclined his bearded chin, signaling her to follow him. Then he spoke rapidly to the guard who remained at her heels when she walked.

The spongy ground absorbed her footsteps as she allowed the pasha to usher her into the middle tent. Finely woven matting underfoot blocked out the rotting floor. Cushions of burgundy brocade had been placed in the corners and by a low table. Trays with gold fringe held brass plates laden with crusty bread, black and green olives, and several kinds of sliced cheese. Her stomach clenched tight.

Two servants came forward. One bore a silver urn and marble basin, the other carried a folded, gold-embroidered towel over his arm. The first man poured the ewer of oiled water over the pasha's hands, while the other held the basin to collect the soiled liquid. The pasha dried his hands on the offered towel, then motioned for Catherine to repeat his ritual.

Catherine gave him a haughty lift of her chin, defying the churning turmoil inside her. She lengthened her arms to display the cords cutting into her wrists. Rather than immediately assessing her bonds, his gaze lingered at the square neckline of her gown and the scalloped lace insert of her stomacher. His glinting eyes slowly lowered, following the curves of her breasts and the flare of her hips. She refused to be intimidated and stood still for his uninvited examination.

At last the pasha spoke to the guard and the man unsheathed a lethal blade that had been secured in a sash wound several times around his waist. She cringed as the gleaming edge sliced through her bonds, narrowly missing the delicate skin at her inner wrists. Once free, she rubbed the stiffness from her joints and gladly rinsed the dirt from her hands.

The water smelled of mimosa. Quickly drying her hands, she asked in English, "A-Are you a friend of the sultan Bedr?"

"Sofra." Ignoring her query, he gestured to the squat table in the center of the tent. *"Sofra."*

Their communication barrier upset her more than her fear of his sloe-eyed appraisal. "I don't know what *sofra* means. I don't care. I want to know what you want from me. I—I want to know what you plan to do with Danton. Do you know the sultan? Did—Did he send you?" She was yelling at him in French, not caring that he couldn't understand her angry words. "Who are you and what do you want? Let me go!"

The pasha's face darkened to the color of dates. He clapped his hands twice and railed, *"Tais toi!"*

"I won't be quiet!" she snapped, her voice rising an octave from her nerves. "I want—" Catherine sucked in her breath. "Y-You spoke French."

His linear features were impassive as he said in her native language, "When the mood suits me I speak *français.*"

"You knew all along what I was saying!"

"Your bird tongue wears on me. You peck with your barrage of useless chatter, and I found no need to encourage your voice."

A brittle silence grew as Catherine digested his words. He had known what she was asking of him and he had refused to answer her. It told her that any pleas she made to be released would be ignored. Her pulse soared erratically. If Danton didn't come . . . She didn't want to think about that possibility.

Catherine licked her dry lips. "Who are you?"

"I am a pasha." He sunk his knees into a plump cushion and folded his arms across his silky blue robe. "A lord."

"You are not my lord," Catherine denounced, refusing to sit with him. She would not show him she was frightened, and instead resist him with every means she had—physically and verbally. "You're a pirate."

"If I am a pirate, *hanim,* where is my ship?"

"I don't know. Somewhere anchored off Danton's island."

The pasha grew nasty at her mention of Danton's name. "This is not *his* island. The isle is mine. I found it and I gave it to him as his grave. But now I'm taking it back, and what's buried on the beach." The pasha sampled a thin slice of sausage, then said in an absolutely emotionless voice, "First you will serve me my meal, then you will serve me your body."

His comment washed over Catherine in a chilling blanket and she faltered. "I—I will do neither!"

"You will do as I say!"

"Danton will come for me and—"

The pasha rose with a swiftness that took her by surprise. Before she could try and stop him, he'd pinned her arms at her sides. The beetle black of his eyes bore into hers, and despite herself, she couldn't control the tremors that racked her shoulders. "A man who values his woman does not parade her in public. He took you to Zanzibar and you showed your face." The pasha caught a lock of her hair and brought the pale curls over her nose to curtain her mouth. "You did not wear a *yashmak*—your veil—and because of your ignorance, you were talked about."

"You saw me?" she whispered.

"I did not, but word of a Frenchwoman's presence flocked through the city like pigeons after you were gone. They said you were the King of the Pirate's woman. Your skin was white as magnolias and your lips red as pomegranates. Any man who would show his prize does not deserve her. So, Madame Queen, where is your king now to stop me from plucking his pearl?"

Fear wound around Catherine's heartbeat, snagging the rhythm and squeezing her pulse to a desperate pace. A hot, slow sickness spread through her belly as she yanked her hair from the pasha's fingers.

He let her go and she stumbled away from him. Catherine caught her balance, her breath coming in huge gasps.

"There is no disputing who is lord, *düriye.*" The pasha adjusted his turban and combed his pointed beard down with his brown fingertips. Signaling to his servants, he spoke to them and they disappeared. The only one that remained was the guard. He stood in the corner, his gaze leveled straight ahead.

"You will obey me now, *hanim.* You will disrobe."

Catherine choked, her mind in a frenzy. She had to think. He was going to force himself on her, and that would kill her; or he'd kill her when she refused. There had to be a way to buy time. *Think, Catherine!*

"Now, *hanim!*" The pasha settled on his cushion again and crossed his legs. He took great pleasure watching her shiver. She couldn't meet the lust dilating his pupils.

Catherine stalled, knowing there had to be an answer. She would not surrender. She could hardly move, just enough to slip her toes out of one shoe.

"*Dépêchez*—faster!"

She slid off her other shoe, then spoke in a hurry. "I need to be alone for a moment."

"For what?"

"I have to . . ." She lowered her voice to a convincing tone of embarrassment. "I have to relieve myself."

"You will do so later."

She would not let him put her off. "I have to now. If I don't, I may shame myself."

The pasha sized her as if he contemplated the legitimacy of her statement. Narrowing his eyes, he said, "You may have one minute. Ömer will go with you."

She assumed Ömer was the guard. She didn't care if he came with her, as long as she could keep her back to him so he couldn't see what she was doing. "Very well."

The pasha rattled his gibberish at Ömer, and the guard jabbed her with his finger before picking up an extra lamp to guide their way. Catherine slowly moved outside of the tent and into the forest. The moldy decomposition underneath her stockinged feet made her shiver. She headed toward a thicket of bamboo and listened for the stream. She briefly closed her eyes and the sound carried to her. It was like music. She'd heard the babbling as they'd traversed to the campsite, not knowing what a godsend the water would prove to be.

Five feet from the embankment she stopped and glared at Ömer. He grunted to a halt and put his hand on the hilt of his dagger. He could make a big show of his knife all he wanted. She wouldn't run.

Biting down on her lip, she motioned for him to turn his head. He sneered at her, then made a slow quarter turn. He could see her from the corner of his eye, which wouldn't thwart her plan.

Catherine gathered her skirts and crouched at the river's edge. She held her breath as she fingered the ruffle of her petticoat. Firmly grasping the cotton, she coughed and at the same time ripped the delicate material. Clearing her throat loudly, she tore a length off and bunched the fabric in her fist. She spared a glance at Ömer, whose saturnine features were concentrated on what little night sky could be seen through the thick canopy of trees.

Without delay Catherine dipped the white strip of cotton into the clay stream and pushed the weave into the red mud. She brought the cloth up and squeezed the water out. In the meager glow of the lantern, she could see she'd attained the desired result. Hiding the piece of her petticoat in the folds of her skirt, she stood and walked past the guard.

They reached the pasha's tent and Catherine entered through the opening in the netting. Ömer stayed outside. She could see his silhouette through the opaque veil that shrouded the tent. Her captor had partaken of his meal while she had been gone. Bread crumbs spotted his fancy robe and were sprinkled in his silver-threaded beard.

"Undress," he ordered, as if she hadn't left him at all.

A strained sense of strength came to Catherine, and she whispered above the frantic beating of her heart, "As you wish, *my lord.*"

Light came into the pasha's eyes and he smiled with satisfaction.

"But you should know that I am having my menses." She

lifted her hand from the crease in her skirt and showed him her petticoat, her arm trembling. The rusty color of the stream had tainted the cloth the color of blood.

His expression changed from desire to hate as he looked at her with disgust marring his face. "Allah has cursed me with an unclean woman!"

Catherine leveled her shoulders and kept her tears of relief inside her. Her hunch had been true. She'd known the Hindu religion deemed women unclean during their menses, and she'd hoped that the pasha's religious beliefs were parallel to those of the Hindus'. She'd been blessedly right.

"For this female plague upon me, I will haunt your dreams, French Catherine," he vowed, standing and kicking over the table. Empty plates and a goblet fell to the floor, a thick stain of wine spreading across the mat. "Now get out of my sight, *hanim! Destur!* Ömer, get her out!"

Clutching her petticoat to her breast, Catherine slipped her feet into her shoes and fled from the tent. The guard caught and crushed her elbow with his hamlike fist. But she didn't care. She was safe for tonight, and God willing, tomorrow she would be free.

A commotion of high-strung voices awoke Catherine. She bolted upright on her rug, her joints stiff and sore from the hard bed she'd slept on. Ömer had rebound her hands, and she'd had to lie in an awkward position so the cords wouldn't slice into her tender flesh. At some point in the night, he tossed her a large square of yellow silk to ward off the warm moisture thickening the air. He'd rasped *"Bohja,"* then walked to a nearby stool and sat down to smoke a cheroot.

Her fitful rest came in small doses. Through the haze of her light sleep, she'd been aware of the camp noises: the occasional hiss of an insect who'd ventured too close to the cooking coals and been burned, sporadic croaking of frogs at the stream bed, the low laughter of pirates sitting around a fire and drinking.

Bone weary, but wondering what the disturbance was, Catherine shook the hair from her eyes and focused on the gathering of men at the far side of the encampment. Their guns and knives were raised; they'd captured something.

What, she couldn't tell through the wall of their broad backs. Perhaps fresh meat to cook over the braziers whose red-hot coals had glowed all night. No matter the aromas drifting from the spits, she would still refuse to eat.

The pasha flipped open the entrance of his tent and stood under the awning, clearly displeased by the noise. Baggy white trousers fastened below his knees with gold gaiters made his legs look twice the size; he wore polished black boots similar to Danton's. A tunic of sapphire silk encased his shoulders, the fabric shimmering under the muted light of dawn. But it wasn't the opulence of his clothing that caught her eye; a long, gem-adorned broadsword flanked his hip.

He shouted to his men, and all she could make out was the word Allah, and not in a respectful tone.

The group parted in Catherine's view and she wavered, picking herself up on her knees. Walking down the center, with his hands held high above his head, Danton Cristobal bore the indignity of his capture with the poise of a true king. His eyes were narrowed and his wide mouth set in a tight frown. A scratch marred the curve of his cheek. He had no pistols at his waist or braced across his chest in the crisscross of leather belts. His linen shirt had been despoiled by the forest limbs; a tiny tear at his billowing sleeve, and a smudge of green stained his lace collar.

"Danton!" She called out his name in an emotion-filled caress and rose to her feet, finding her equilibrium. For a stroke in time Danton's gaze met hers—too brief for her to read his thoughts. To her surprise and confusion, he showed no reaction. He looked past her directly to the pasha. She took a step forward, wanting to go to him. To have him embrace her and hold her tight. But she was stopped by Ömer, who butted his flintlock into her ribs. "But . . . it's Danton . . ." she whispered, a tingling numbness racing up her spine.

Danton came to a halt in front of the pasha and slowly lowered his arms. An ugly twist caught Danton's face, a hatred so instantaneous, Catherine wouldn't have believed him capable of such vengeance just because she'd been kidnapped. There had been only one man she knew of that could evoke a blinding rage in Danton, and that had been—

"Sadi." Danton ground the Turkish name out as he towered a head's length over the pasha.

A wave of shock hit Catherine. Of course. *Sadi.*

"The King of the Pirates looks like a dirty peddler," Sadi commented in French with a crooked smile, apparently wanting Catherine to understand his smug words.

"How did you find me?" Danton asked.

Sadi gave him an impatient shrug. "Now that I am here, what can it matter? I was surprised to hear you'd returned to the waters of your grave. An interesting notion, pirate king. One which puzzles me. But I have no desire to solve your life's riddles."

"You have riddles enough of your own." Danton's voice held a challenge. "You've been here before. Was the beach as you recall? Or have your markings disappeared?"

"Limestone has fallen in places. I cannot search from memory alone." Sadi took a step toward Danton and shook his head. "The pearl must mean a great deal to you, pirate king. Allah was smiling when he gave her to me."

Danton made no comment, nor did he gaze at Catherine. She felt something was wrong; she watched and listened, trying to understand Danton.

"I would have liked to sail into your harbor, pirate king, knock on your door and demand the map, but I knew my welcome would be honored with rounds of cannon fire."

"So you sailed to the back side of the island and chose the coward's way instead. You took a woman."

Sadi laughed in a low tone. "I knew you would come after her." He drew in his lips thoughtfully. "You came quicker than I'd anticipated. And alone. Quite foolish."

Danton would not glance her way, and Catherine couldn't stay back any longer. She took a step forward. The cold metal of Ömer's pistol seeped through her bodice and dug into her side.

"Who's to say I am alone, Sadi?" Danton asked, his arrogant stance drawing him upward in height, dwarfing the Turk even more.

"You walk with no shadows trailing you." Sadi ran his thumbnail across his teeth. "If you did, you would not be unarmed and escorted into my camp."

The Turk turned to the pirate closest to his shoulder and

gave him a quick order that sent him off into the underbrush with a dozen armed men following.

"All the same, we shall see how alone you are, pirate king. If you have others with you, they will be dealt with." Rubbing the hilt of his sword, Sadi sparked his words, "I want the diamond in the pouch and I want my map, Spaniard!"

Danton put his fingertip on his temple. "The map is in my head now."

"Then I will force it out of your head."

"Try if you like, you bastard, and see how far you'll get." The tone in Danton's voice dropped in volume. "I'm not the fool you once pegged me for. I won't hand over what you want until I get what I want."

"The pearl." Sadi's words were not voiced in question, but rather an obligatory remark.

"No," Danton replied shortly, causing Catherine's heart to skip a beat. "You needn't have taken her at all. It's you I want, Sadi. The chance to fight you to the death for what you have done to me."

Laughter rumbled in Sadi's chest; low at first, then pouring out in a spill of baritone howls. "To *your* death, I think you mean. Allah brings such wit in his fallen Spanish nobleman." Sadi placed his arms akimbo. "You can never have me, pirate king."

"Then you will not have your map."

"Then I will have to kill you sooner than later," Sadi shot back.

"Non!" Catherine cried.

Sadi looked her way, but Danton did not. "The pearl weeps for you, Spaniard. Do you wish to have her watch your death? A slow torture . . . or perhaps I'll shoot you again as you attempted to shoot me in Zanzibar. Your poor marksmanship ruined the *han* owner's table, but I felt my knife meet its mark. Does your flesh still burn, pirate king, where my blade cut into you? Does the pain remind you of me? Or does the pearl release your memory with her luster?"

"I don't care about her," Danton said in a rush, as if he were gasping for a breath.

Catherine flinched at the tone of his voice, but did not believe him. He was acting. He had to be. To protect her.

"I want you," Danton said to Sadi. "Fight me. For the diamonds and the title King of the Pirates."

Sadi chortled. "An interesting proposition from a man with no weapon."

Ignoring the Turk's barbed comment, Danton grinned with inappropriate humor. "You put my life in a box and buried it under sand. Why do you want the diamonds now? After all these years?"

"Because, pirate king, I don't like being shot at! And I want them because *you* want them. You want what they can give you. Your noble respect." Sadi circled Danton with slow, calculating steps, all the while glowering at Danton's back. "I don't need the wealth the diamonds will bring. I never did, but it is such a tempting sum of money they'll fetch," he mused. "Ah, now that no one remembers them, I can sell them anywhere I like. Before, after I'd seen their hallmark colors, I knew I could never rid myself of them even in the black market, so I left them here." Coming around to face Danton, Sadi commented wryly, "I did, however, favor the clear diamond. Such a beautiful stone, is it not? Just like the pearl."

Danton said nothing.

The men who'd been sent into the forest returned, and the one in command gave Sadi a report in Turkish. Sadi pressed his fingertips together and nodded. Then he gazed at Danton. "You indeed are alone, Spaniard."

Catherine wondered if Eduardo and Antonio were near and hiding. They never left their captain's side. She held out the hope that the two men were and they would rescue both herself and Danton. Danton would not have come into the camp unarmed if they were not. What was his strategy?

"Yes, alone," Danton said. Catherine noticed his hands had balled into knots of hard bone and muscle—poised fists ready to fight even with the odds against him.

"You came alone to rescue your woman," Sadi commented caustically.

"I did not come after you because of her." Danton flexed his fingers, the veins atop his hands prominent. "I am here because of you, Sadi. She means nothing to me. She's just a piece of skirt I picked up in Madagascar. I've tired of her. I'm sending her back to France."

Catherine's knees threatened to buckle. A tumble of tumultuous thoughts assailed her. He was lying! It had to be a ploy of some kind. He did not mean what he was saying.

Sadi smiled. "Then if you don't want her, I will keep her."

"Keep her." Danton's slow and deliberate tone sliced through her. It was her love for him that wouldn't accept his words. He couldn't have said anything so cruel unless it was an act to save her.

She would not believe him.

She would not believe him.

"Where is my pouch and diamond?" Sadi's irate shout streaked through Catherine's mind.

"Where is my justice?" Danton's reply registered in a fog. Then their impassioned conversation switched to furious Turkish and she couldn't follow the words.

"I don't believe you, Danton," Catherine whispered, her voice sounding small in her ears. "I don't."

And she would dare him to repeat his words the first chance she got.

Chapter

20

*D*anton had no opportunity to talk to Catherine. Sadi had barked orders to disband the camp. Cook fires had been put out and ribbons of bluish smoke climbed through the sky. Danton had wondered if Rainiaro would be able to see the gray curls at this distance. He figured thirty miles separated the coasts.

Ahead of him, Catherine winced as her foot caught in a bed of twisted roots. Gnarled and mossy root stocks hindered the trail the Turks had chosen to travel. With her hands tied together, Catherine had trouble steadying herself.

Danton curbed his powerful impulse to reach out to her, though his own hands had been tethered. He felt her pain through the limp in her gait as she favored her ankle. The Turkish guard at her side shouted at her to keep moving. He snaked his ringed fingers around her forearm and yanked her forward. Danton's resentment became a scalding fury. The tension in his jaw ground his teeth together.

He wanted to kill Sadi now and be done with it. To get on with his life. His life with Catherine.

His palms ached to cup her face and kiss her trembling mouth. He needed to reassure her and alleviate her fears. But he could not risk hurting Catherine further. Staying away from her and disclaiming her was the only answer.

Acting as if he didn't care for her had been the hardest performance of his life.

He longed to tell her the truth. He loved her beyond anything he could have imagined. But if Sadi knew she was of value to him, she would be valuable to the Turk. He had no doubts Sadi would use her against him to gain what he wanted. Despite the suffering Danton had seen written on Catherine's face when he'd spoken the harsh words, Danton knew this was the only way. He would not endanger his love further. His only consolation was, she seemed unharmed—physically.

The argument he'd had earlier with Sadi lingered in Danton's mind, working him into a rigid temper he held in check. Smugly, the Turk had agreed to spare his life until they reached the beach where Danton could show him the treasure's location. Danton had no intention of doing so; he had his own plans.

Half of Sadi's motley group hacked a clear passage with their cutlasses, the other half brought up the rear, placing Danton and Catherine in the middle.

Danton kept his gaze on Catherine's back, knowing it had been no accident that she'd been placed ahead of him. Sadi meant to torment him, not fully believing his story.

As they progressed deeper into the wooded terrain, he thought of ways to talk with her. None presented themselves. For now, he told himself, silence was best.

A cinnamon-colored fossa resembling a mongoose shimmied up the bark of a thick mangrove, unalarmed by the presence of man. The catlike creature's designs were set on a troop of red-fronted lemurs in a neighboring tree. The fossa's musky scent alerted the lemurs seconds before the animal leaped to the tamarind.

Piercing shrieks were heard through the forest, and the agile lemurs scuttled on thin branches dropping squishy, half-chewed fruit. A blob of orange pulp smacked Catherine's guard on his uncovered head. Incensed, he raised his fowling piece and randomly fired into the tree. Through the puff of acrid smoke, severed twigs and crisp leaves showered the landscape.

The caravan came to an instant halt with shouts of attack.

Men fell into ranks, dropping to the ant-populated jungle floor while half cocking the firing mechanisms of their guns.

Following the frantic actions of the others, Catherine fell to the ground and gathered her knees to her chest. Eyes round with fright, she buried her face in her arms.

Sick with the struggle inside him, Danton held back from telling her she had nothing to fear. Soothing words rose to his lips, but died.

Only the dazed guard and Danton remained standing. The forest resumed its chorus of noise. A goshawk screeched. Geckos and chameleons scurried across the mulch, making crackling noises with their webbed feet.

Danton automatically braced his legs apart when he saw Sadi approaching with an unhinged gleam in his pebbled eyes. The Turk glared first at him, then at the guard whose still-smoking pistol was a telltale sign he'd been the culprit. Sadi spouted an oath so vile that if indeed Allah had ears, he would have sealed his spirit in a mosque, never to be prayed to again.

"Ömer!" Sadi's broadsword remained in the sash around his waist, but he'd freed his blue iron flintlock and aimed the barrel directly at Ömer's heart. "What is the matter with you, ass brain?"

Sadi's Turkish was rapid, and Danton had to concentrate to follow the heavily inflected words.

"The lemur," Ömer whined, his gaze fastened on the gun leveled on his chest. "It threw its fruit at me."

"So you shot at it!"

"The pest made me angry."

"And you've made me angry." Sadi pulled back the hammer on his gun.

Ömer's eyes glazed with horror and sweat beaded across his bushy brows. "S-Sadi, pasha, we are c-cousins," he stuttered. "You were named after our great uncle Yousef Hasan Sadi Bey. You could not harm me. Think of my parents! Your uncle and aunt!"

"Dayi and *teyze,"* Sadi pronounced, his finger curling around the hooked trigger, "would be shamed by your foolish behavior. *Oturtma Allah misafiri."* Then an explosion shook the damp air.

A fast-spreading stain of red blotched Ömer's golden shirt. The guard stared down at the sticky discoloration on his chest, then slumped to the ground with a gurgling sound.

Catherine screamed. Her face paled to the color of fresh cream, a pallor intensified by the dark smudges under her eyes.

Danton felt as if his bones would snap if he didn't go to her, but Sadi's watchful eyes held him motionless. "Do you wish to comfort your mistress, pirate king?" Sadi's lips twisted into a cynical smile. "Does she still warm your blood and feed fire to your loins? Or have you really exhausted your lust for her?"

His pulse hammering at his temples, Danton gritted, "I told you, I've no use for her. It's you I want."

Sadi clucked his tongue. "You're either a liar or stupid. I think perhaps both, Spaniard." Motioning for the pirate closest him to come forward, Sadi stated mildly, "Rasid, see to it the woman keeps her mouth shut. No more screaming. Gag her if you must." Then the Turk pivoted on his heels, trudged to the front of the line, and gave the command to continue.

No one helped Catherine up, and when the rear began to move, Danton was forced to go around her. Their gazes met. He could have reassured her with a softly hidden gaze, he could have mouthed his love for her in English—anything. But the risk was not worth her death.

A mixture of shock and longing were written in her blue-gray eyes. He would not chance alleviating her fears. He could not. And so he walked on, the heavy feeling in his stomach eating away at him, sickening him.

"Up, *kalfa.*" Rasid's belting voice flowed to Danton, but he did not glance behind him. Instead he focused on the pack-laden backs of the men ahead, his vision blurring with hot moisture.

When this was over, he'd never let Catherine out of his arms.

Several hours later the Turkish pirates broke up in a clearing strewn with rocks and rosewood trees. Danton and Catherine were untied and given guarded privacy to take care of nature's needs. The swarthy men passed out circle-shaped sesame cakes and cold *moussaka.* While others enjoyed cool burgundy wine, Danton and Catherine were only given a gourd of warm stream water. Sadi sat in a slice of sunlight and puffed on his *chubouk.*

As Danton watched Sadi, he took perverse satisfaction in knowing the Turk wouldn't be savoring his pipe weeds for much longer. He thought of the scene that would greet the accursed Turk on the beach. Desolate, but deadly. Now all he had to do was deliver Yousef Ahmed Sadi Ahram to the trap.

As the men ground finished cheroots under their heels, Sadi called them to order, rousing Catherine from the short sleep she'd snatched. Danton had been glad to see she was keeping up her strength. Her sorrow and misery held her together—maybe so she could run him through with his own sword. He hoped that to be true. He'd rather have her anger than her defeat. It would fuel her will to survive.

They made camp that evening at sunset, minutes before the sparse light filtering into the *tsingy* forest dissipated to total darkness. Brass lanterns were lit; *kiosks* were pitched on bamboo poles, and food was prepared on charcoal fires in the braziers. The smells of heated olive oil, herbs, rice, and meat seasoned the night. A duo of Turks rolled out Ottoman rose carpets bordered with hunting scenes in blue. They herded Danton to this open-air rug and ordered him to sit. Minutes later Catherine joined him.

Danton could see that despite Catherine's stamina, the journey was taking its toll on her. Fatigue softened her posture, and her breath came in shallow gasps. She refused to look at or acknowledge him. Her blond hair hung over her shoulders and blocked his view of her face. A face he still thought lovely beyond words, despite the streaks of dirt and fine scratches on her cheeks.

Rasid brought a pigskin flask and wordlessly handed it to Catherine. She drank greedily, the liquid trickling down her chin and spotting her bodice. When she was finished, Rasid gestured for her to give the water bag to Danton.

"Ayvaz," Rasid said to Danton.

Danton didn't like being called a man slave, but said nothing to the contrary. He waited for Catherine to give him the drinking pouch.

Licking her cracked lips, her eyes darted to his. He

chanced communicating to her with his gaze; to show her he loved her and he had not betrayed her. But she wouldn't read what she didn't believe possible.

His fingers brushed hers when he reached for the pigskin. He felt her spirit racing through his bloodstream and entwining with his soul. A sense of excitement sprung to life inside him, an instinctive response he couldn't quell in spite of his ruse. The tangible bond between them could not be shorn by words fleeced with lies.

The desire to caress her hand rioted in his fingertips and her name came to his lips. "Cath—"

"Pirate king." Sadi's beckon startled Catherine, and she pulled away from Danton, dropping the water flask into his empty palm. He damned the Turk.

"Sadi," Danton woodenly addressed his enemy.

"Tomorrow, Spaniard, I will be King of the Pirates." The Turk held a lime and a small paring knife in his hands. He cut into the peel, releasing the zesty juice to render a sweet-tart fragrance. "I will fight you and win."

"Fight me, yes. Win? No, Sadi," Danton said, taking a sip of water as if the drink were the finest wine from the finest of goblets. "I'm not defending a title, I'm gaining my honor. Remember that. The title means nothing to me. I was not the one to crown myself. Legend made me who I am."

"Legend?" Sadi's loose-fitting shirt rippled with his laughter. "A man who cannot live up to his *legend* is no man at all. Had you any intelligence, you would not be on your knees before me without the weight of a cutlass at your side."

Danton shot Sadi a penetrating look.

Sadi had fixed his gaze on a pulpy wedge of lime and was sucking the tart juice out with a loud smack. Grimacing, he pursed his mouth. *"Legend.* You make me laugh, Spaniard. The last duty of your epic reign will be drawing me the map. If it wasn't memorized in your head, I would . . . well"—he made a clicking noise with his teeth—"regardless, the outcome will be the same. When you see Ömer, tell him I never liked Uncle Yousef." Chuckling, he flicked the green rind at Danton and wandered off toward his tent.

"Mierda," Danton mumbled, but took hope in the fact that Sadi had not given Catherine a glance. The only

thought that kept him sane was knowing that after tonight the nightmare would be over. Catherine would be safe.

Appropriating the water bag from Danton's hand, Rasid affixed the stopper. Another man approached bearing two round plates dished with scant pilaf and handed one to Catherine and himself.

They ate their meals in silence, Rasid watching Danton's movements, affording him no margin to talk with Catherine. Afterward the pirate again bound both his and Catherine's wrists, then stayed several feet away as he ate his own supper.

The camp settled in for the night. The inches between himself and Catherine might have been miles, Danton thought. He felt the coolness radiating from the shell she'd locked herself in. She lay down on her side, her back to him. She had no blanket, and that fact irritated him. He would give anything to share his warmth with her.

Danton cast a wary eye to Rasid, plotting the possibilities of overpowering the man and taking his gun. He'd have to render him unconscious somehow and in a matter of seconds, get Catherine and escape into the forest. Frowning, he knew such a plan would be disastrous. If he were alone, he would risk heading off in the dark without a lantern and with his hands tied. But not with Catherine.

Rasid propped his back against a rosewood trunk and took out a beaded tobacco pouch. After rolling a *sigara,* he lit the paper and inhaled the pungent smoke. He rested the length of his long-barreled matchlock on his thighs and told Danton to stop looking at him and go to sleep or he'd hit him on the back of the head with a rock and make him go to sleep.

Danton cursed in a low voice, *"Hijo de la perra,"* and rolled onto his side a good foot away from Catherine.

The notes of a fiddle filled the air. Snapping coals died to glowing embers. The flutter of moths' wings whispered in the night.

And Rasid's quiet, unfaltering gaze.

"Danton . . ."

Childlike, her voice came to him, and he longed to answer her. He spared a glance at Rasid, who could not see

Catherine's face but could hear her talking. The guard's eyes grew suspicious.

"Just tell me that Madeleine is all right."

"Yes," was all he could say before Rasid aimed the tip of his gun at his head in a warning angle. He wanted to tell Catherine not to speak now, but she already was.

"Did you mean what you said, Danton?"

He opened his mouth to reply, damning Rasid's presence. But the Turk quietly cocked his gun and changed the direction of his aim—directly on Catherine.

"Danton . . . ?" she whispered, her voice worn and hollow. She did not move to face him.

And he did not answer her.

He could hear her start to cry, a hoarse and rasping sound in her throat that wrapped around his heart and squeezed.

Still, he did not answer her.

The shadowy caves frightened Catherine.

By midafternoon they'd reached the end of the forest and had come to a canyon with steep walls taller than three palm trees stacked one atop the other. Rowboats had lined the muddy banks, apparently from the Turkish pirates' ship and left behind when they could use them no further. She and Danton had been separated, he in the boat ahead of her.

She sat in a light wood rowboat, one of five filled to capacity with armed men. Unlike the caves fringing Danton's beach, these subterranean chambers were swollen with murky water too deep to wade. They navigated the stream that ran across Danton's isle, fed by the many rain pools in the *tsingy*. In places the river had grown so narrow the sluggish current could not have accommodated a paper boat much less a skiff; but in others, such as these caves, water fanned wide as the hull of Danton's square rigger.

The cavern echoed with dripping trickles of moisture and the dipping tips of oars as the pirates piloted the black river. Periodically, daylight streamed through small holes in the ceiling, mixing prisms of warmth with the cool air. Walls looking like frozen waterfalls of dusky red and brown breathed; a faint sucking sound that released the smell of minerals. The unearthly noises raised gooseflesh on Catherine's arms.

Anticipation and dread filled her. She feared the caves and wanted to flee them; but she also feared what the end would bring. Lately Danton and Sadi had spoken only Turkish and she hadn't been able to grasp what they were saying, even with Sadi's heated arm gestures.

A turn ahead allowed Catherine a quarter view of Danton. Like herself, he sat on a birch slat at the prow of the skiff, sharing company with men bogged down with pistols and swords. She caught a slice of his face as a shaft of sunlight spilled on him. Despite the gravity of their situation, a sharpness and confidence carved his profile. A stubbled growth of dark beard began just below his cheekbone and covered his set jaw. Subtle lines around his mouth and eyes muted the strength she knew him capable of unleashing. His ebony hair fell past his shoulder, and when he moved his head to watch the rippling water, she could see a flash of his earring.

She stared at him until the rowboat straightened and all she could see were the colorfully dressed men who sat behind him. But Danton's image remained in her head.

Sadly she relinquished her dreams of a life with him. She could no longer allow herself to picture his arms around her. Or his lips touching her mouth. She grieved for the loss, knowing she would never feel the shared intimacy that had once filled her completely.

The musings of making a home with Danton had disappeared in a mist of delusion when he had not answered her last night. His silence had said it all. It became hard to hold on to the possibility that they would be together had ever existed. She let her claims to happiness churn under with each stroke of pirates' oars. Her hope drowned, and with it her future became as uncertain as the monsoons. If it weren't for Madeleine, Catherine would have been exhausted and defeated. But the thought of her daughter kept her going.

For Madeleine, Catherine would weather her ordeal and return to Danton's house to reclaim her child. And then . . . then they would begin again. Just the two of them.

A ruby light glinted near the sheared banks, catching Catherine's attention. As the rowboats approached, the red glow became two tiny lights. They were the reflecting eyes of a crocodile as long as the skiff, floating in the water. Catherine's heartbeat sped, watching the animal glide toward them. Its sharp teeth were clamped together when it made a churring sound from the back of its narrow snout. Catherine drew her skirted legs in and away from the boat's sides and prayed the crocodile would leave them alone.

Coming from the first rowboat of the five, she heard Sadi's yell, then the flat smack of a paddle hitting the water. The loud splash caused cave-dwelling bats to spring from the ceiling in a whirl of wings. Catherine ducked. She feared the harmless bats as much as the jawed reptile. Keeping herself in the middle of her seat, she watched as the crocodile slapped its opaque tail and dove under the surface with a muffled splash.

Relief centered in her breast as her skiff passed the wavelets where the crocodile had been. Catherine craned her neck to see if it would emerge from the deep black. She saw nothing more and allowed herself to take small comfort.

Soon after, the caves grew brighter from a large opening ahead. The stream's current sped up to a fast rush that stumbled over sharp rocks. Catherine smelled the salty ocean and sand warmed by the sun. Her pulse surged and she braced herself for whatever tumult lay at the end. She would fight it with every fiber of her being.

The oarsmen quickly had trouble maneuvering the skiffs, and attempted to paddle backward to slow the boat. The bow and stern hit the outcrop of rocks, bumping and jarring them despite the Turks' frantic efforts. Catherine had no sure grip; her thoughts raced ahead to what she would do if they tipped over. She couldn't swim. In the back of her mind she dredged up what Danton had said about swimming. Hold her breath . . . hold her breath. She would hold her nose and let the current take her, praying all the way that the crocodile would not chase her.

The pirates shouted at one another and battled for control. They paddled in unison, bared arms straining with muscle against the flow of water. They made headway as they rowed into daylight, slowing the boat enough to aim for the sandy shore.

Catherine shielded her eyes with her tied wrists against the blaze of afternoon sun. When her eyesight adjusted to the light, she quickly scanned the beach. It was deserted. But anchored in the inlet was Sadi's colossal ship. The East Indiaman she'd seen in Zanzibar. Its standards of black with white skulls and pointed pennants in red waved a greeting in the breeze.

Sadi's skiff managed to plow into the rocky shore and the Turk disembarked, white foamy water curling around his calves and baggy pants. The other boats followed in rapid succession, the men pulling the crafts up to the bank and out of the stream before they were carried into the ocean.

Under duress, Danton left his boat before Catherine and stood on the uneven chunks of limestone that had once been a part of the *tsingy's* walls. Various fragments jutted to the sky like arrow points, half the cavern's height. To the south the beach swelled into oddly shaped trenches, apparently caused by weathering. The wind whipped the air, flapping Catherine's ruined skirt against her legs.

She was escorted out of her craft by Rasid, who then tugged her toward Danton. She met Danton's eyes and for a strange moment felt him touching her with a mere look. He commanded her with a single glint in his eyes. She read meaning into it: trust, hope, faith. *Love?*

She grew confused and suddenly weak. Grief tore at her heart and she felt as if her breath was cut off.

Sadi had pulled his flintlock from a belt beneath his yellow vest and was ranting while he walked to the pebbled sand. The sea churned over his boots as he stared up and down the beach, then to his ship.

Catherine knew something was wrong. The Turkish pirate seemed anxious and puzzled, incensed and thwarted all at once. Facing his East Indiaman, he cupped his left hand and yelled, "Ishak! Kamil! Pakize!"

No answer came from the East Indiaman. The snap of her lines, her sails tucked and tied, drifted to the shore.

Catherine glanced at Danton. His hardened face showed no surprise as he watched Sadi. *He knew.* Danton knew Sadi's crew wouldn't be here.

Sadi started up the beach to his waiting band of cohorts, his copper skin contrasting with the gritted white of his teeth.

"Catherine, listen to me," Danton said in calm English without loosing his gaze on Sadi, "and do as I say."

She glanced swiftly from Danton to Sadi.

"Catherine, come to me." Danton's voice had a low, silvery timbre. "Slowly."

Catherine questioned his objectives, hesitating and not moving.

"Catherine, come to me," he repeated.

She heard sounds all around her—muted and sharp at the same time. A war of emotions raged within her, and after a brief and troubled moment, she took a step toward Danton, only to hear Sadi's baritone bark barreling down on them.

"Spaniard!"

"Now!" Danton yelled, and suddenly Catherine was knocked to the ground.

*C*atherine felt the pain of the blow as a loud explosion rocked the earth. Unknown hands dragged her away. She could see nothing, not even the face of her rescuer. She heard Danton shouting in Spanish and French. The burning smell of gun smoke clogged her lungs. Gasping for air, she was leaned next to a high boulder and let go.

Turning her head, she looked into the shining eyes of an alligator on a braided hat band. Then she gazed at the wearer's face. It was Rainiaro.

"What is happening?" she asked in rapid French as he carefully sawed through the cords at her wrists with a narrow-bladed dirk.

"We've ambushed Sadi, woman." Another crescendo of flintlock fire set off a wave of frantic shouts. Rainiaro crouched lower and slammed his hand on Catherine's head to keep her out of harm's way. Then he resumed his task of cutting her free.

Catherine tried to find Danton, but her search was in vain. She could see nothing from her position behind the rock. "The gunshots . . ."

"Are ours," Rainiaro said with a final slice.

The cords raveled and split and Catherine attempted to stand, but Rainiaro held her still.

"Are you trying to get yourself killed, woman?" He

pushed her down and slid his dirk into its scabbard. "We're staying here." He freed his pistol and held the piece firmly in his hand.

"But Danton?"

"Can take care of himself."

Catherine couldn't control her trembling. She clasped her hands together, but only managed to press her nails into her palm. She took a deep breath and tried to calm her overwrought heartbeat; her efforts were useless. The deadly report of pistols and the metallic clang of engaged swords rang out, pumping turmoil through her. *Danton.*

He was risking his life for her.

His silence had been a lie. She'd been too tired, too discouraged to realize that.

"You've got to help him." Catherine's voice broke.

"Non, woman." Rainiaro kept his traveling pistol in his grasp, ready to charge if necessary. "He wants me here with you."

"But he needs you!"

"He needs you more."

Catherine bit her lip until it throbbed like her pulse. Needing to see if she could find Danton, she peered around the barrier that protected her.

"Don't do that, woman." Rainiaro's strong hand fit over her shoulder.

"I have to see if I can find him!"

"Antonio cut him free. He's all right."

Catherine refused to be put off. In a voice harsher than she'd wanted, she said, "I need to see if I can find him, Rainiaro. I have to know for myself."

The Malagasy's nostrils flared; in the end, he nodded.

The scene that met her gaze made her mouth go dry. Danton's men were everywhere. Death and destruction ravaged the beach.

Amid the hazy gray clouds of spent gunpowder, lengths of steel glinted and clashed. Sabers sliced through the air, the more primitive weapon replacing spent flintlocks. The lunge and thrust of high-booted opponents became a dance with no pattern or rhythm. Catherine saw in a flash why soldiers carried colors. Amid the upheaval, she found it hard to determine which side was winning.

She looked at the fighters but did not see the one man she sought, the man taller than all the rest. She did not find hair that gleamed like black satin and an ear bearing a cross that caught the sun. She did, however, find James Every, his thatch of red hair bright through the smoke. He passed out reloaded muskets after another pirate filled and packed them with powder. One of Danton's men took the ready gun from James and handed him an empty one as he sped off.

Catherine continued to scan the beach, looking for Danton. Her gaze skimmed over bodies lying lifeless on the sand. She had never seen a battle before. The scene being played out in front of her eyes awakened her to a pirate's life. To be a consort of a pirate meant bloodshed and death. Danger and adventure. She had long ago given up her desire for adventure; but from the moment Danton had come to her aid in Tamatave, she'd been in one big adventure, with this epic as the crowning glory.

When she'd thought of a life without Danton, he'd been alive and vigorous, living on his island. In all her dreams she'd never imagined him harmed. Danton Cristobal had been invincible.

"You've seen enough, woman." Rainiaro's light touch brought her to face him.

"I can't find him. . . ." She'd looked until her eyes stung. With a moan of distress, she held back her tears of horror and slumped against the rock. If she hadn't been on the desert beach that day . . . if Sadi hadn't taken her . . . none of this would be happening. And Danton . . . Danton would be safe.

As the agonizing screams of the maimed filled her ears, she felt her guilt working deeper and deeper inside her.

Danton climbed a natural rise in the rockbound coast, chasing Sadi. The Turk scrambled over the uneven steps, particles of rock sifting and collapsing underneath his feet as he struggled to keep from falling. Danton pursued him even though the climb was suicide.

His life flashed through his mind, past and present. He thought of the scant seconds when he'd shoved Catherine at his quartermaster. He'd relived the loss of his wife and his son. He could not bear bringing destruction to another woman he loved.

He allowed himself a little comfort knowing Rainiaro had sheltered her. And as the clang of sword blades and blasts of gunfire rose to him, he could only pray his men would do well in this, their last battle.

Danton scaled the sheer walls, grappling for a firm holding with his hands. The mineral blades sliced viciously at his fingers and palms, leaving him sticky with blood—an irony he couldn't ignore. The beginning of his exile had started with scars on his hands and feet. The ending would see him marked again.

Sadi was sustaining wounds as well, but attained his goal. The summit. He let out a triumphant laugh. Though his *shalwars* were torn and bloodied at the knees, his hands and the elbows of his wide-sleeve shirt stained red, he didn't show his pain. He turned and saw Danton, his unstable balance wavering. He quickly rectified his overstep by stretching out his arms and bracing his legs apart on the knifelike butte.

"Pirate king! You've played me for a fool, and you will die for your deception!" Sadi withdrew his blue iron flintlock.

Danton's reaction came without thought. He grasped his pistol, cocked the hammer, and took steady aim. The trigger was slick under his touch, and he fired before Sadi could kick off a shot. The range of distance between himself and the Turk lessened his accuracy by a few degrees, but he'd overcompensated and hit his mark: Sadi's weapon. The flintlock flew from Sadi's grasp and the crippled iron clattered over the side of the ledge.

Sadi cursed, tucking his powder-blackened hand under his arm and rocking forward. "Spaniard!" he screamed. "I will bring you down!" Then he bolted across the rows of spikes and disappeared from Danton's view.

"Mierda!" Danton's curse left his lips with an edge of urgency as he slipped his pistol into a leather pocket on his belt. He had no alternative but to go after Sadi. He couldn't let the man get away, never to know where he lurked and if he'd come after him and harm Catherine and Madeleine.

His cuts were beginning to sting mercilessly. Each new handhold brought fresh wounds. Fighting for stable ground,

Danton came to the narrow perch where Sadi had stood. He scanned the forest. To the end of the horizon all he could see were green bursts of treetops. The floret-looking clusters spired through gaps in the limestone pinnacles.

Sadi was gone.

Danton chose his steps carefully on the stone. There was hardly enough flat land to plant his feet. He slid a few inches and a razor-sharp shard of rock scored his boot's supple leather. He felt the slash go clean through to his ankle and nick him. He growled from the agony.

Jesu, if purgatory had barbs, this would be Hell.

Danton's pulse throbbed in his ears with a steady thrum. His only consolation was that he'd disarmed the Turk. Sadi could not kill him with a gun.

Rock falling to the right caused Danton to cock his head toward the trickling sound. He measured his surroundings and a primitive warning went off in his mind just as Sadi appeared from around a wall of rubble. The Turk came at him, sword in hand, bent on running him through.

Danton chose his steps with swift accuracy and moved aside. With deliberate calculation he clutched Sadi's arm and threw his opponent off balance. The Turk's eyes widened in alarm as he slipped on the loose pieces of limestone. Danton felt a wrenching jerk on his joints which shot through his elbow, and he let go before he could be pulled down by Sadi. The Turk tried to keep from falling over the cliff, but there was nothing to hold on to, nothing to break his descent. With a shriek, he was gone.

Sweat beaded on Danton's forehead and he stood still for a long moment.

A low moan echoed through the air. Like the wail of a wounded animal, the pitiful sound rode to Danton on the wind's humming current. He firmed up his footing and edged closer to the sheer drop-off. The first thing to fill his view was a large green lake on the forest bottom.

Then he saw Sadi, crumpled like Madeleine's rag doll, on a narrow shelf of the *tsingy*. His arms and legs were lacerated beyond repair; a shank of bone showed in his calf. Gashes bled on his cheeks and forehead; scarlet flowed out of his nostrils.

"Spaniard," Sadi rasped, loss of blood siphoning the color from his face.

Danton damned the man to Hades for cheating him out of the opportunity to fight him in an honorable way. To win back his old life. He'd wanted Sadi dead so he could bring Elena and Esteban back. But now he knew that was an illusion he'd conjured in his head to justify the end. There would be no going back, only forward.

Sadi choked and spasms raked his shoulders. "I will be see . . . seeing Allah this day."

"Damn you." Danton found no satisfaction in Sadi's slow torture, only pity.

Sadi mournfully chanted an Islamic proverb, his white mouth twisted with pain. *"Insan ancak kismetinde olani alir."* Then he fell into the jade pool, a splash of water swallowing him.

Man receives destiny's due alone.

His senses numb, Danton watched as Sadi's body began to sink into the dark lake. A stripe of alabaster drifted over the surface, then a narrow-snouted mouth became visible.

A crocodile.

Danton bowed his head and closed his eyes to the tail thrashing sounds below, feeling the tension ripple through him and escalate to a brain-pounding throb. He gasped, his lungs burning, then looked up to the sunset spilling golden light the color of Catherine's hair.

His pursuit of the past may have ended, but his quest for a future had just begun.

Danton began the grueling descent back to the beach. Once he reached the rise, he saw that Antonio had things in order. Sadi's crew had been disarmed and were kneeling on the sand. Rainiaro and James had enlisted twenty men and they'd begun to dig near a copse of baobab trees at the spot where the map indicated the treasure was buried. And Catherine . . . Catherine sat on the beach with her face in her hands.

"Sadi is dead," he said for all to hear.

Several of his crew shouted his name, and Catherine's chin shot up. He caught her teary gaze. She blinked and her eyes lightened. Smiling with a tentative and sad lift to her mouth, she stood. He walked directly to her and took her in his embrace, pressing his mouth on her hair, her cheeks, her lips, with quick, reassuring kisses.

"Rainiaro hit the box, Cap'n!" James's enthusiasm caught in his excited tone as he apparently overlooked the fact his captain was otherwise occupied. He cleared his throat, and Danton slipped his arm around Catherine's waist. "Men're bringin' it up. Rainiaro said to let you be the one to blast the lock open."

Danton looked deeply into Catherine's tear-filled eyes. He felt a pull in his heart so strong, the emotion gripped his chest and spread like fire throughout him. He wanted to kiss her forever, to explore her body and show her how much he loved her. But now was not the time or place to tell her how he felt about her—not with his crew as audience.

He jerked his stare away from her face, focusing instead on his group of loyal men. Some were wounded and bandaged; others had fared better and their mouths were set in grim lines. And there were those who had died. Danton mourned the loss in a moment of quiet reflection, then he gazed at those standing in a semicircle around a heavily banded trunk with a rusted lock. Many of these men had been with him that momentous day Sadi had plundered *La Estrella del Cabo*. This was as much their hour of reckoning as it was his.

Taking long strides, Danton neared his fate without a word. Rainiaro handed him a pistol. The weight of steel and ivory plate felt heavy in his hand, and he had a hard time grasping the grip with his cuts. Without preamble, he cocked the firing piece and pulled the trigger. The lock burst and fell to the sand. Tossing aside the pistol, he bent down on one knee, his heartbeat an even rhythm of certainty. He shoved the lid up and back, his crew coming in for a closer peek. They huddled around Danton as he looked inside.

On the top of the trunk were various flat folds of red silk and ivory satin. He dug around them to the lined bottom. He found a crushed velvet purse and lifted it to the sun. Even with his fingers cracked and bruised and still seeping blood, he could feel the shapes of stones and count them. There were twelve. Pulling the ribbon open, he poured the contents into his injured hand.

Glistening in his open palm were five diamonds with the

fire of a rose, four with a pale yellow brilliance, and three with a rainbow-glistening blue. Gazing at them was like going back in time.

A choke hold of emotions gripped him. When he'd set out to find Sadi four years ago, he'd never thought to regain what had been stolen from his ship's hold. All he'd wanted was revenge. But now he had Catherine and his needs had changed. Sweet Catherine . . .

Danton stood with a slow smile. "Rainiaro, let what remains of Sadi's crew sail. They're short of men and will be lucky to make it to Madagascar." He trickled the diamonds back into the pouch and handed them to Eduardo. "They'll most likely disband."

"Oui, Capitaine." Rainiaro was on his way.

"Antonio, take us to the ship."

"Sí, Capitán." The stalwart Spaniard nodded.

Fifteen minutes later Danton and Catherine walked the decks of his schooner. Rainiaro had kept the *Negro* moored in a cove just beyond the point where the battle had ensued. He led her down the steps of the companionway to his modest cabin. Once at the door, he turned the latch and stepped aside so she could enter.

As soon as they were inside, he bolted the door and took her in his arms again. He kissed her soundly on the mouth. Long and passionately.

"Catherine . . ." he murmured. "I love you."

He felt the wetness of her tears on his cheeks; he heard the shaky intake of her breath. "Forgive me for doubting you. I love you too. But maybe not enough. I should have believed you, Danton . . . I should have trusted you."

"Yes." He tilted her chin up with the tip of his finger. "Don't ever doubt my love for you, Catherine. Ever."

"No." She shook her head and reached for his hand. Seeing the wounds anew, she gasped. "Let me take care of you." She walked him to the pedestal washstand near the corner. He allowed her to tend to him. His hands were burning and he wanted to cool them in the water.

After pouring a liberal amount of water into the bowl, Catherine reached for the towel on the bar. "Put your hands in the water."

He complied, but the soothing relief he'd wanted was more of a tingling irritation. "Jesu . . ."

"I don't like to see you hurt," she whispered, swishing the water over his palms. "Promise me you won't get hurt again."

He could not predict what would happen to him when he returned the diamonds to Spain. He grimly smiled at her and withheld his thoughts.

The basin clouded with the dirt and the pink stain of his blood. Catherine took a small square of linen and began cleaning the pads of his hands, her hair falling over her shoulder. She quickly pushed the lengths away and set out to minister to him. Her gentle touch on his flesh made the pain bearable.

"You didn't promise," she said, squeezing water from the cloth.

"I can't." Danton grimaced as she cleansed a jagged line on his thumb.

She kept her gaze on his hands and nothing else. "What will we do now?"

He withdrew from her, wanting her to look at him. "Will you go to Spain with me? I intend to return the diamonds and clear my name." Danton took up the towel and blotted his hands dry. "I cannot promise you the king will be lenient. I have, after all, pillaged his ships under the title King of the Pirates."

"I'm not finished with your hands," she said with a hitch in her voice, not acknowledging what he'd told her. She was holding on to her tears, and he hated to see her so upset. Taking his hands in her own, she murmured, "You need these wrapped."

Danton pulled away from her, her heartache cutting him to the core. "Tear strips off the towel, then."

She made quick work out of dividing the soft cloth into sections and tying them around his hands. "You might need stitches." Catherine lowered her lashes, then lifted her gaze to his, and he saw a glimmer of moisture in her eyes. "I don't have a needle and thread. . . ."

"If need be, Tanala can stitch me when we go home."

She began to cry; silently, but with such a physical ache,

he saw her shoulders tremble. "I couldn't bear it if they put you in jail again."

"I have to take that chance," he said. "Without my honor, I have nothing to offer you and Madeleine. What kind of life would we live in seclusion? Always guarding our backs. I couldn't ask that of you."

"You've never fought for riches, have you?" she asked in a far-off voice. "It's always been for your honor. A man like Sadi fights for greed." Catherine turned and walked to the portal; the sun behind her cast her hair in gilt tones.

He came toward her and put his hands on her shoulders. She talked to the window. "Why were the diamonds here?"

"On Zanzibar," he explained, "I took a pouch from Sadi's neck."

"When you confronted him?" she asked.

"Yes. Inside was a map and a large diamond."

"One of the diamonds he'd taken from you—from your king?"

"Yes." He ran his exposed fingertips along her neck. Her skin felt soft and warm. Smudges of dirt and light abrasions from scratches marked her cheek. "Catherine, look at me." She did. Her eyes were remote and filled with tears again. "There was a treasure map in the pouch . . . to the diamonds Sadi had buried here, on Isle of the Lost Souls."

"Why would he do that?"

"Because he couldn't sell them without bringing attention to himself. Even a man like Sadi was not immune to the authorities. He buried them on my island not thinking I or my crew would ever reach the shore. When he found out I lived here, he came back and—"

"How?" She wet her lips. "How did he know where to find you?"

Danton softened his tone. "It's not important."

"Trevor Tate," she whispered. "You told me I'd done a horrible thing by lighting that fire, and I did. . . ." A tear splashed down her cheek.

"Catherine, listen to me." Danton braced her shoulders with his hands, ignoring the smart. "You did nothing to hurt me. You've done everything to save me. Catherine," he slid his hands to the curve of her neck, cupped her face, "I love you."

"And I love you," she whispered.

He felt her tremble beneath his touch. "I want to marry you. We'll live in Paris if that's what you want. I'll be a good father to Madeleine. God help me, I love her as if she were my own." Danton took her into his arms, feeling her warmth, her strength. "I want you both."

Catherine's voice was choked with tears. "Yes . . . I'll marry you. We'll go to Spain together and we'll get your honor, Danton."

He kissed her cheeks, her nose, and then her mouth. Her lips were warm and pliant under his, and he closed his eyes to drink in her sweetness. "We will be together," he whispered against her mouth, "and we will be happy. *Dios,* I pray the king will grant me immunities. If he doesn't . . ."

"Hush." She put her fingers on his lips. "Whatever awaits you, I'll be with you, Danton. Always."

He sealed her vow with a kiss. "You are mine, *mon petit maki sauvage.*" Catherine kissed him back, her gentle laughter surprising him and tickling his mouth. He raised his head, smiling and glad to see a promising happiness in her eyes.

"I've never understood why you call me your wild lemur," she said. Danton looked at her with amusement as she explained, "I'm not furry and I don't have a tail. Nor do I chatter and climb palms. I don't leap from trees for your attention." She gave his roughened chin a light kiss. "But you may keep calling me your wild lemur if you like." She sniffed and blinked away straggling tears. "Now that I think about it, it's a rather appropriate nickname."

"And why is that, *chérie?*" Danton asked, his voice heavy with emotion. The feel of her in his arms was heaven.

Catherine grazed his mouth with hers. "You make me feel like I can glide through the air without wings." She gazed lovingly into his eyes. "You make me fly, Danton."

Epilogue

September 1721
Cristobal Island

*D*anton, what have you done?" Her full cotton skirts
spread out around her in a peach cloud, Catherine sat on the
beach next to her husband. Together they watched
Madeleine dig a hole in the sand with a hand trowel.

"Nothing to work yourself into a fret over, *chérie.*"
Danton reclined on his side next to his wife. He indolently
crossed his long legs at his calves and leaned back on his
elbow. "Maddie, try a little more to the left."

"I never get myself into a 'fret,'" Catherine denied, her
voice lifting an agitated octave.

Keeping his gaze on Madeleine, Danton said with a
roguish smile, "You've been in a 'fret' off and on for the
past—"

"Here, *Papa?*" Madeleine asked, breaking into Danton's
grinning commentary. Catherine thought it just as well their
daughter had. Danton was right, but she wasn't in the mood
to admit it.

"*Oui,* puppet," Danton replied, and brought his knee up.
"Try right there."

Madeleine began to dig a new hole, adding to the half
dozen she'd already excavated. The tropical sun poured
over Madeleine's waist-length hair, highlighting the silken
waves to a shade of blond equaling Catherine's. Her daugh-

ter had grown nearly three inches in the past two years and had lost her cherubic face.

Catherine's eyes filled with nostalgic tears. Madeleine was no longer a baby, rather a blossoming young miss with her sixth birthday coming next week.

"What did you do, Danton?" Catherine clasped her hands together in her lap. "You didn't *really* plant something for her, did you? As much as I hate to admit it, she's getting too old to believe there's buried treasure on your beach."

"Our beach," Danton corrected. He caught and pushed a stray tendril behind her ear. His gentle touch made her feel cherished and lovely, even now when she was ambivalent about her appearance. He brushed the hollow of her cheek with his warm fingertip. "And if a trinket *is* buried in the sand, I have no knowledge of how it got there."

"Liar." But she couldn't help smiling.

While Madeleine busily scooped sand, Catherine saw Antonio approaching them, with Dokobe, Razana, and Pousse-Pousse running behind him.

As always, the Spaniard exuded vigilance, his face cast in a somber mold Catherine had given up trying to break. She'd come to accept Antonio was not a smiling man, but one filled with fierce loyalty and rare lapses of light in his eyes. She had grown comfortable with his presence. His addition to the household added a layer of tranquility beneath the boisterous sounds of Danton and Madeleine as they played silly games.

"Capitán." Antonio's skin had browned to a rich tan from his recent voyage for Cristobal Exports, from which he'd returned just an hour ago. Holding out a letter, he respectfully greeted in Spanish, *"Señora.* You look well today."

Antonio still used his words sparingly, but at least now Catherine could communicate with him. Danton had taught her and Madeleine Spanish. Though not very fluent, Catherine could hold her own in a conversation. *"Gracias,* Antonio. *Estoy bien."*

"Hola, Antonio!" Madeleine had bunched her calico dress over her knees and balanced on her haunches. She flicked a shovel full of sand from her hole and peered inside with a frown.

"Hola, pequenita," Antonio returned with a curt nod.

Danton sat up, tucked his legs in and took the parchment from Antonio. "I don't know why you insist on calling me *Capitán*. You sail *La Furia* now."

Antonio shook his head. "Always a *capitán*."

Catherine had heard this debate before and had to agree with Antonio. Though Danton had given up chasing galleons, he still looked like a captain of the sea. He'd made an attempt to subdue his appearance over the last two years, but not by much. He kept his hair a smidgen shorter; the blunt ends rested on the collar of his black shirt. The golden cross earring that had once dangled from his earlobe had been replaced by a tiny silver stud that was easily overlooked. Catherine kept the cross in her jewelry box as a memento of her husband's pirating days. Other than that, Danton Luis Cristobal was the image of the man who'd rescued her on Madagascar.

"Is the letter from James?" Catherine asked, leaning over to read the script in Danton's hand.

"Yes."

Catherine's disposition lifted to buoyant. "Open the seal and read the letter aloud." She absently fluffed the yards of material gathered for her skirt, poising herself for the words of James Every. It had been almost six months since they'd heard from the onetime British sailor, onetime young pirate. Danton had struck a bargain with the lad two years ago. He'd proposed James attend school in England with paid tuition and board. At the end of twelve months, if he still wanted to live on Cristobal Island, he could return.

The second year was rounding out and James Every remained in London.

Danton broke the blob of wax, unfolded the paper, and scanned the contents. "James says his reading and writing have improved to the point where he actually likes sitting down with stationery and quill to compose. He's written . . ." Danton fell silent a moment, then his face darkened. "He's written an epic tale of Indian Ocean pirates, shown the piece to his professor, who in turn purported James has a great talent as a writer and has arranged a meeting with a publisher."

"A publisher!" Catherine beamed. "Just think . . . our James is an author. What did he title his work?"

His head down, Danton grumbled, "He calls it, 'King of the Pirates,' and makes no bones about using my past exploits to illustrate his main character."

"Oh, Danton," Catherine laughed. "You're to be famous!"

"I don't want to be famous." Focusing on the letter once again, Danton read, " 'Say hello to everyone and tell them I will visit when the opportunity permits. I think of you all often. Especially Madeleine. Yours, James Every.' "

"Well, wasn't that nice?" Catherine enjoyed the disgruntled tone in Danton's voice. She thought it wonderful James had chosen his vocation—even if he rode on Danton's illicit escapades. "Since we haven't told James—and I am quite fine now, and we are certain of the outcome—we'll have to write him immediately and tell him about the—"

"Papa, I don't want to dig anymore." Madeleine plopped on her backside and impatiently tossed her shovel a short distance.

"Maddie, don't give up." Danton sat the letter down, rose to his feet and padded to Madeleine. He pointed his bare foot to a slight depression in the sand. "There. Dig right there." He helped get her started by using his toes as a trowel.

Catherine heard a soft laugh and leaned her head back to see Antonio. He'd cracked a slight smile. *So there was hope for him after all!* She sighed; a happy sigh. A reflective sigh.

A week after the incident on the beach with Sadi, she, Madeleine, Danton, and the entire crew of *La Furia* had been bound for Spain. Catherine met the king, who had sentenced Danton to prison. She'd worked herself into hating the man, but granted an audience with him, she'd felt something else entirely.

Danton resumed his spot next to Catherine and took her hand in his. He gently stroked her palm with his thumb. "You have a far-off look in your eyes, *linda.* What are you thinking?"

"I was remembering King Philip." She meet Danton's silver gaze. "I'd wanted to hate him for putting you through so much. But I found when I met him, I could not. I felt sorry for him. He wasn't in his right mind. Even when you returned his diamonds, it was his wife, Elizabeth, who gave you the pardon and your title back and said the events never should have happened at all."

"A wife can be a man's salvation," Danton said quietly, and Catherine recalled the words of Reniàla the day Danton had taken her to watch the ylang-ylang gathering. The old woman had said Catherine had come to the island to save Danton.

Instead, Catherine thought Danton had saved her. From a terrible mistake. After they'd left Spain, they'd gone to Paris to visit the gravesites of her father and brother and purchase headstones—just as they had done in Madrid for Elena and Esteban Cristobal. The place of her birth did not move her as it had in her youth. She'd felt crowded and constricted. The mass of people had been astounding and unbearable after the freedom of Danton's isle. But she and Danton had done one thing in France they could not have done on Cristobal Island—they'd gotten married. From there they'd gone on to England to settle James. And then home.

Home.

For so long that had meant Paris to Catherine. Now home was here. On Cristobal Island. The name Isle of the Lost Souls hadn't suited the island anymore. When Danton had taken up a new occupation, Catherine had pointed out that the letterhead need not be intimidating, lest they scare away potential clients. Danton had engaged in exporting ylang-ylang oil to places as distant as China, with Rainiaro overseeing the operation. The islanders gained most of the rewards—both monetary and improving their village by adding to its size, not only in buildings, but population. Nearly all of Danton's former crew had coupled off and were raising families of their own. Eduardo had married Mia, and they were expecting a second child by the end of the year.

Everything had changed for everyone, but the person who had changed the most was Danton. His walk was lighter, his head higher. He laughed. He smiled. He was a man at peace. Catherine had never seen him more handsome or alive. She loved him with all her heart. And soon there would be—

"I found something!" Madeleine's joyful cry interrupted Catherine's thought. "It's a box."

"Dig it up," Danton urged with a broad grin.

Catherine shook her head and chided her husband, "You *did* bury something."

Danton smiled.

Madeleine withdrew a small brass box and ran to show her papa. "Look!"

"Lift the lid, puppet."

Madeleine slowly raised the top and peered inside. She gave Danton a wide smile, her cheeks flushed. She held the trinket up to catch the sun. A ruby the size of a pea was suspended on a gold chain. "It's a ruby necklace!"

"Well, imagine that. I wonder what pirate left it there for his sweetheart?" Danton took the necklace from her and motioned for her to bend down so he could fasten the clasp.

She gave him a hug, then pulled back. "I'm not a little girl now, *Papa*. I don't suck my thumb anymore and I don't tell little girl secrets."

Danton's brows rose.

"I know *you* put the necklace there," she nodded, "but it's all right if you want to pretend that you didn't."

"I—" The denial fell short on Danton's lips. He mumbled under his breath, *"Mierda."*

"That's a Spanish cussing word," Madeleine was quick to suggest. "Antonio told me."

Danton looked over his shoulder and glared at Antonio, who shrugged with a helpless expression on his face.

"You can't say bad words in front of the baby." Madeleine ran her small hand down Catherine's round belly and patted the fullness.

Catherine shifted, trying to find a more comfortable position for the cumbersome girth of her middle. "You'd better listen to her, Danton. She's very smart for her age. The baby may be born and the first word it says will be the first word you ever said to me. And we all know what that word was."

"Even me," Madeleine added. "I was with *Maman* when you said it. You can't slip up anymore. Especially after next week."

"And what happens next week?" Danton asked.

Catherine shared a secret smile with Madeleine; then her daughter looked directly at Danton and said with all seriousness, "Because that's when *Maman* is going to have the baby. On my birthday. And you know what else?"

Catherine and Danton said "Hmm?" together.

"She's going to be a sister and we'll name her Nanette."

Author's Notes

I hope you've enjoyed reading *King of the Pirates* as much as I enjoyed writing the book. Working with small children underfoot is at times distracting and frustrating, but I couldn't have made Madeleine "real" without the help of my little girls. When you're old enough to read this book, you'll know what a daily impression you make on my life. Happy April 10 birthdays. I love you.

As for the other comments to be made about this book . . . Danton Cristobal's banishment was a key foundation in the plot, and I didn't want to "slander" a character in history just to make my story work. King Philip V of Spain could very well have sentenced Danton to life imprisonment, only to have that decree overruled by his wife, the queen. After the death of King Philip's first wife, Maria, in 1714, he suffered from severe melancholia. He remarried shortly thereafter to Elizabeth Farnese (Isabella). During the years 1716–17, his depression over losing his first wife and his political failures was so intense, the real government fell into the hands of Elizabeth. In 1724, Philip V abdicated his throne to his son Luis, but Luis died six weeks later and Philip had to take over again until his death. He lived out his life in a state of melancholy, secluded from the world in his sumptuous palace San Ildefonso de la Granja.

There are a few people I'd like to thank for their help. Scott Dorval, the meteorologist at Channel 2, KBCI Boise. Your time and expertise were of great value. A big thanks to a talented writer, Laurie Guhrke, for her extremely helpful comments. The same to Sue Rich and Barbara Ankrum. A long-distance hug to Judy Singer, whose knowledge of diamonds got me thinking. Thank you to my agent, Rob Cohen, for making it possible for me to continue my relationship with a terrific publisher, Pocket Books. Also a debt of gratitude to my editor, Caroline Tolley, who made me realize the value of smart dialogue. An "I love you, darling" to my husband Barry for giving the kids a bath every night when I was working. And lastly, a heartfelt thank-you to my writing friend and partner, my advisor, my inspiration when I'm down and thinking I can't write another word—Kathleen Sage. I would not have been able to do it without you.

I would enjoy hearing from my readers, and you can be assured I'll answer back. When writing, a self-addressed, stamped envelope would be helpful.

Stef Ann Holm
P.O. Box 121
Meridian, Idaho 83680–0121

The *New York Times* Bestselling
Author of <u>SWEET LIAR</u>

JUDE DEVERAUX

THE INVITATION

POCKET
STAR
BOOKS

Available
from Pocket Star Books

641-03